FIC CAT '96

2/95

Trust Me

Books by Jayne Ann Krentz

The Golden Chance
Silver Linings
Sweet Fortune
Perfect Partners
Family Man
Wildest Hearts
Hidden Talent
Grand Passion
Trust Me

Published by POCKET BOOKS

Trust Me

⟐

Jayne Ann Krentz

POCKET BOOKS

New York   London   Toronto   Sydney   Tokyo   Singapore

POCKET BOOKS, a division of Simon & Schuster Inc.
1230 Avenue of the Americas, New York, NY 10020

Krentz, Jayne Ann.
    Trust me / Jayne Ann Krentz.
        p.   cm.
    ISBN: 0-671-51691-4
    I. Title.
    PS3561.R44T78   1995
    813'.54—dc20   94-31755
                                                        CIP

First Pocket Books hardcover printing February 1995

10   9   8   7   6   5   4   3   2   1

For my husband, Frank,
the one I love and trust.

Trust Me

1

"*Y*ou're a woman, Miss Wainwright. Give me your honest opinion." Sam Stark paused briefly to drink from the glass of brandy in his hand. "Do you think it was the prenuptial agreement that spooked her?"

Desdemona Wainwright followed Stark's gaze. His attention was fixed on an object two floors below his study window. She had an uneasy feeling that he was brooding on the three large ice swans that were presently melting on the lawn of his austere garden.

By now her staff had probably finished clearing away most of the evidence of the abruptly cancelled wedding reception. Fifteen pounds of cold tortellini salad, two hundred miniature asparagus tarts, three platters of herbed goat cheese, and a hundred and fifty spring rolls had no doubt been loaded back into the Right Touch Catering van.

The cake, an elaborate five-tiered affair decorated with palest mauve and creamy white roses, would have been safely stowed in its special carrying crate.

But the ice swans were a problem. Not only were they extremely heavy, by now they would be getting quite slippery.

The swans would definitely be a write-off. Desdemona had taken an assessing glance at them as she had hurried to follow Stark into the concrete, steel, and glass fortress he called home. The swans' beaks had already begun to droop, and their tail feathers were blurred. Even if rushed immediately back to the Right Touch freezer, they couldn't be salvaged. Desdemona knew there was no way she could save them to use at the charity event her small business was scheduled to cater on Tuesday.

A dead loss, just like the Stark-Bedford wedding.

The easiest thing to do with the massive ice sculptures was to let them remain where they were until the late spring sun dissolved them. It wouldn't take long, a couple of days, perhaps. Seattle was enjoying a rare streak of sunny weather.

But Desdemona felt a pang of guilt at the thought of leaving the swans behind in Stark's coldly elegant garden. It seemed a bit callous to stick the abandoned groom with three such vivid reminders of the humiliating experience he had endured this afternoon. Especially since she was in the process of trying to stick him with the tab for the expensive debacle as well.

Desdemona set her jaw determinedly. She must not allow her natural empathy to weaken her resolve. She could not afford to be swayed by sympathy. There was too much cash at stake. She had gone way out on a financial limb to handle the Stark-Bedford reception.

She struggled to find a diplomatic response to Stark's question.

"I couldn't say whether or not Miss Bedford was concerned about a prenuptial agreement," Desdemona said gently. She leaned forward until she was sitting on the very edge of her chair.

She kept an eye on Stark's incredibly broad shoulders, making certain that he did not turn around as she reached across his glass and steel desk.

Quickly she edged Pamela Bedford's apologetic note aside. Then she carefully positioned the catering invoice so that Stark would be sure to see it when he came back to his chair.

"I just wondered," Stark said, his attention still on the swans. "I've always made it a practice to conduct a detailed failure analysis when things have gone wrong."

"Failure analysis?"

"It's standard procedure after a disaster."

"Oh. I see." Desdemona cleared her throat. "Well, it's not really any of my business, Mr. Stark. I'm just the caterer. Now, then, I believe my invoice is completely self-explanatory. If you'd care to look it over?"

"I made it clear right from the start that there would be one." Stark braced one big hand on the windowsill and continued to study the swans down below.

"A failure analysis?"

"A prenuptial agreement. Do you think she thought I'd change my mind at the last minute?"

"I have no idea, Mr. Stark." After a couple of seconds of further consideration, Desdemona reached across the desk again and flipped Pamela's short note facedown. "Unfortunately, I'm not going to be able to freeze the tortellini salad. And I don't have another menu featuring asparagus tarts scheduled for this week. I'm afraid I'm going to have to charge you for everything that Miss Bedford ordered."

"Damn it, what the hell was so unreasonable about asking her to sign a prenuptial agreement? What did she expect me to do? Did she actually think I'd trust her to stick around for the next fifty years?"

The bleak outrage in Stark's voice made Desdemona turn to stare, astonished, at his broad back. She realized he was genuinely baffled by his ex-fiancée's behavior. Amazing. The man was reputed to be brilliant. She had overheard one of the wedding guests refer to him as a human computer. But apparently he was quite dense when it came to the important things in life.

Even Desdemona, whose only association with Pamela Bedford had been the series of consultations regarding the reception arrangements, knew very well how Stark's fiancée had reacted to the notion of a prenuptial agreement. Last month Pamela had broken down and sobbed in Desdemona's office. They had been in the middle of choosing between the asparagus tarts and miniature mushroom quiches.

"A prenuptial agreement," Pamela had wailed into a tissue. "Can you believe it? He doesn't love me, I know he doesn't. Isn't that an awful thing for a bride to discover four weeks before the wedding? What on earth am I going to do?"

"Uh, the asparagus tarts are very popular—"

"No, don't answer that. It's not your problem, is it? I'm sorry to burden you with this, Desdemona. It's just that I've got to talk to someone, and I don't want to worry my parents. They're so happy about this wedding."

"Are you thinking of calling it off?" Desdemona had asked anxiously. "If so, please let me know now. I'll be ordering ingredients and supplies and hiring extra help soon."

"Of course I'm not going to call it off." Pamela had blown her nose one last time and then wadded up the tissue. She had straightened her shoulders and given Desdemona a brave look. Joan of Arc on her way to the stake. "I'll have to go through with the thing, of course. One doesn't cancel an affair of this magnitude at the last minute, does one? It isn't done. The family would be horrified."

"Perhaps you should go home and think about this," Desdemona had said. "Marriage is an awfully big step." *And it's impossible for me to return fresh asparagus and basil to my supplier.*

Pamela had heaved a small, tragic sigh. "He's a nerd, you know. Or maybe an android would be a more accurate description. He's got the brain of a computer and the body of a hunk. What a waste."

"Miss Bedford, I don't think we should be discussing this. Your fiancé's body doesn't have a whole lot to do with our menu decisions."

"He spent several years with a think tank in Colorado called the Rosetta Institute, you know. He specialized in applications of chaos theory. Some of his work was very hush-hush."

"I see." Desdemona did not know what she was supposed to say in response. Her definition of chaos was what happened at Right Touch when a member of her staff, many of whom were involved in the theater world, was unexpectedly called to an audition just before an important catering event.

"He has absolutely no sense of style. He wears running shoes, jeans, and an old corduroy jacket to work every day." Pamela blotted her eyes. "And little round nerdy glasses and, oh, God, a plastic pocket protector full of pens and pencils. It's so embarrassing."

"I guess it works for him."

"I've been doing my best to upgrade him, but it's very difficult. You have no idea of how hard it was for me to get him to buy a tux for the wedding. He wanted to rent one, can you believe it?"

"The mushroom quiches are nice, too, of course, but—"

"He's utterly bored by social events." Pamela gave Desdemona a mournful look. "He detests cocktail parties and charity affairs. He never goes to the opera or the theater. He even tries to avoid routine business entertaining."

4

"But I think the asparagus tarts would be more visually interesting," Desdemona said quickly.

"It's not as if I haven't tried. God knows, I've tried. After all, I'm the one who has to be seen in public with him." Pamela had sniffed back more tears. "But I'm not sure it's possible to change him. He simply isn't interested, you see, and you have to get Stark's full attention before you can do anything with him."

"On the other hand, we could go for an entirely different effect, here," Desdemona said. "Shrimp toasts, for example."

"I'm sorry, this isn't your problem, is it?" Pamela had said again, smiling bravely. "I have to remember that this marriage is not a life sentence. I can always get a divorce if things don't work out. Life goes on, doesn't it?"

"Right. Tomorrow is another day," Desdemona muttered.

"Let me see that menu again. Do you think we should go with the asparagus tarts or mushroom quiches?"

"The asparagus tarts," Desdemona said swiftly. "They're quite distinctive. A little more expensive, however."

"Cost is not a problem. As I told you, Stark will be picking up the tab for the reception. He insisted." Pamela's mouth had twisted bitterly for an instant. "I'd say that he offered to cover the costs of the wedding because he felt guilty about that damned prenuptial agreement, but the truth is, I don't think he felt at all guilty. A computer doesn't have emotions, does it?"

Looking back at that awkward scene in her office, Desdemona realized she should have heeded her intuition and declined to handle the reception. Stark was not an android, and he definitely possessed emotions. She could feel them swirling about somewhere deep inside him in the same way one could feel an approaching storm long before one got drenched.

In spite of her doubts, she had gone forward with the wedding plans. She was businesswoman enough to put intuition aside in favor of the practical benefits to be had from catering a major social event. The bride's impeccable family connections and the groom's swiftly evolving financial profile made the Stark-Bedford wedding *the* wedding of the season. As the caterer for the gala event Desdemona stood to reap a gold mine of publicity and contacts.

Business was business, after all.

But, Desdemona reminded herself, it was folly to ignore the Wainwright intuition. It was never wrong.

Stark took off his round, gold-framed glasses and polished them absently on the sleeve of his pleated shirt. "I'm trying to approach this problem in a logical, analytical manner, Miss Wainwright. I would appreciate your input."

Desdemona stifled a groan. "Perhaps the prenuptial agreement struck Miss Bedford as a little, shall we say, unromantic?"

That was putting it mildly. It didn't take a clairvoyant to realize that Pamela, blond, beautiful, and the apple of her parents' eyes, had grown up in a privileged world. It was a world that had always given her everything she desired. She had been crushed to learn that the man she was to marry had no intention of giving her his unqualified love and trust.

As the date of the wedding had neared, Pamela had grown increasingly tense. Desdemona had seen the mounting anxiety in her client each time they had met to go over the reception arrangements, but she had optimistically chosen to ignore it. The future happiness of the bride and groom was not her problem.

Desdemona had told herself that all she had to do was pull off a wildly successful reception, and that would be the end of her concern with the Stark-Bedford marriage.

Unfortunately, she had miscalculated. Pamela had panicked at the last minute, leaving not only Stark, but Right Touch, in the lurch.

"Unromantic? *Unromantic?*" Stark put on his glasses and swung around to confront Desdemona. His riveting green eyes glittered with an unsettling intensity. "What the hell kind of answer is that?"

"Well, I'm not sure," Desdemona admitted weakly.

"Probably because it's a useless, meaningless, illogical answer." Stark shrugged out of the black tux jacket and tossed it aside with a gesture of chilling disgust.

The movement made Desdemona grip the arms of her chair very tightly. The fact that Stark appeared to have his emotions under an ironclad self-control only served to make them seem all the more dangerous.

She was rapidly learning that Stark did not show his feelings the way the men in her family did. Wainwright men were volatile, exuberant, and flamboyant. So were the women, for that matter. Wainwrights were theater people, after all. They relished emotion.

But Stark was a different breed. His emotional depths were dark and murky. He was difficult to read.

For some inexplicable reason, she found him fascinating. She sensed that he was her exact opposite in many ways, and yet there was something oddly compelling about him. Part of her was drawn to him. She wondered rather wistfully what might have happened had they met in another place and another time.

She had become aware of him as a person only an hour ago when it had finally dawned on everyone that he had been abandoned at the altar. Until that point she had been too frenetically busy behind the scenes to pay any attention to the groom. She had not even caught sight of him until his best man, Dane McCallum, had made the dreadful announcement that had sent the guests home.

She could say one thing for certain about Stark, Desdemona decided. The man did look good in a tux.

He had the body of a medieval knight. Not overly tall, a shade under six feet, perhaps, but very hard and very solid. He was sleekly muscled, with no sign of flab anywhere.

He moved the way that a well-trained actor did, with grace and an instinctive sense of presence. When Stark entered a room, you would know he was there. Desdemona sensed that it was all unconscious on his part, however, not a carefully honed tactic to gain attention. He seemed completely unaware of the intensity that he projected. He simply was what he was, a self-contained force of nature.

The tails of his black bow tie hung down the front of his crisply pleated shirt. He had undone the tie a few minutes ago when he had stalked into his study. Now, as Desdemona watched apprehensively, he yanked open the collar of his shirt, exposing the strong column of his throat.

She stared in mute amazement as he impatiently ripped off his gold cuff links and tossed them onto the glass-topped desk. The twin spheres danced and skittered on the slick surface. Stark rolled up his sleeves, revealing sinewy forearms and a large, stainless steel digital watch that was adorned with a lot of miniature keys. It was the sort of watch that looked as though it could provide weather information, stock market reports, and breaking headlines in addition to the time of day. It was a high-tech gadget-lover's watch.

From what Desdemona had seen, everything in the fortress was a high-tech-lover's dream. Lights came on automatically when you walked into a room. The kitchen was state-of-the-art. A household computer regulated everything, from the inside air temperature and the blinds that opened and closed according to the angle of the sun, to the extremely sophisticated security system.

Even the art on the walls looked as though it had been generated by a computer. The pictures were brilliant explosions of light and color formed into complex, surreal designs.

Desdemona struggled to change the subject. "A prenuptial agreement does seem to make a business deal out of a marriage, doesn't it? But that's neither here nor there. You'll be glad to know that the champagne can be returned to the supplier. I've deducted the amount from the total, as you can see."

"What's wrong with treating marriage as a business deal? We're talking about a major financial commitment here, not some short-term affair. It's an investment, and it should be handled like one."

Desdemona wished she had kept her mouth shut. It was obvious that Stark had been looking for a target, and she had made the mistake of providing him with one. She hastily tried to backpedal.

"Right. A serious business," Desdemona said.

"Damn right. I thought Pamela understood that." Stark paced back to his desk and threw himself down into his chair. Amazingly enough, the chair did not so much as squeak beneath his not inconsiderable weight. Stark did not glance at the invoice. "I thought I'd made a good choice this time. She seemed so stable. So sensible. Not one of those temperamental, emotional types who drive a man crazy with one scene of psychodrama after another."

Desdemona arched a brow. "I don't know about that. I'd say Miss Bedford has a nice touch when it comes to dramatic scenes. Abandoning a man at the altar is definitely a colorful way to stage an exit."

Stark ignored the comment. "Her father and I got along well. Stark Security Systems did a job for his company last fall. That was how I met Pamela."

"I see." Desdemona knew that Stark's extremely successful computer security consulting firm was rapidly becoming the premier company of its type in the region.

Stark Security Systems advised many of the largest Northwest businesses on matters ranging from computer security issues to corporate espionage. Word had it that Stark, who had started with nothing three years ago, was now, at the age of thirty-four, as wealthy as many of his clients.

"I had every reason to assume that Pamela wasn't a silly, starry-eyed romantic. She was well educated. She came across as calm and rational." Stark drained the last of the brandy in a single swallow. His green eyes narrowed dangerously. "I'm beginning to believe that I was deliberately misled."

"I'm sure it was all a terrible misunderstanding."

"No, she misled me, all right. Made me think she was a reasonable, levelheaded female. She never said a word when we discussed the prenuptial agreement in my lawyer's office."

"Maybe it took her a while to get over the shock."

"What shock?" Stark glowered. "She knew all along that I planned to have a contract. Only reasonable thing to do under the circumstances."

"Sure. Right. Only reasonable thing." Desdemona eyed the empty glass that was positioned near Stark's big hand. Perhaps a little more brandy would get him past the surly stage.

"You're a businesswoman, Miss Wainwright. You understand why I wanted a prenuptial agreement, don't you?"

"To be perfectly honest, I haven't given the subject of prenuptial agreements a lot of thought."

"Never been married?"

"No. Now, I'll be able to donate some of the food to a homeless shelter, and my staff will eat some of the rest, but—"

"Neither have I. I didn't think I was asking for too much."

Desdemona got to her feet, seized the brandy bottle sitting on the corner of the desk, and leaned over to refill Stark's glass.

"Thanks," he muttered.

"You're welcome." Desdemona moved a pen a smidgen closer to his hand before she sat down. "I suppose prenuptial agreements do make sense. Sort of like having a catering contract for a wedding reception."

"Exactly." He looked morosely pleased by her perceptive response. "A business contract."

"Speaking of business contracts, Mr. Stark—"

"Logical, reasonable things, contracts. Lord knows, wedding vows don't amount to much these days. But a business agreement, now, that's something you can hold in your hand." Stark made a broad fist. "Something you can see. A business agreement has substance. It has teeth. A business agreement is binding."

"It certainly is. You'll notice that the business agreement in front of you was signed and dated by Miss Bedford, who made it very clear that you were going to cover the expenses for the reception."

Stark looked at her, really looked at her, for the first time. "What the hell are you talking about?"

"The expenses for the reception, Mr. Stark. The total is there at the bottom of the invoice. If you would just take a moment to make out the check, I'll be on my way. I'm sure you'd rather be alone at this unhappy time."

Stark scowled at the invoice. "What is this? Six thousand dollars? For a wedding reception that got canceled?"

"You only owe six thousand because I've already deducted the deposit that was paid at the time the contract was signed and the second payment which was made last month when the supplies were ordered."

"I don't remember giving you two previous payments."

"Miss Bedford said you gave instructions for her to collect whatever she needed from your accounting department. Someone at Stark Security Systems cut the first two checks. I've already cashed them."

"Damn. Things are out of control here. Give me one good reason why I should pay you another six grand."

It was clear to Desdemona that she finally had his full attention. The light of battle glinted in his eyes. It did not bode well.

"Because I've got a business contract that says you owe me another six thousand dollars," she said bluntly. "Look, Mr. Stark, I'm sincerely sorry about what happened this afternoon. I know what a traumatic event this must have been for you."

"Do you?"

"I can certainly imagine how upsetting it would be to be left at the altar."

"You get used to it."

She stared at him. "I beg your pardon?"

"I said you get used to it." Stark pulled the invoice closer and studied it with a gimlet gaze. "Second time it's happened to me. I'm a pro at being left at the altar."

Desdemona was horrified. "You've been through this before?"

"Two years ago. Her name was Lindsay Mills. Married a doctor instead."

"Good grief," Desdemona said faintly. "I hadn't realized."

"It's not something I bring up a lot in the course of casual conversation."

"I can understand that."

"She left a note, too. It said that I was emotionally frozen and obsessively fixated on the subject of trust and loyalty." Stark's teeth appeared briefly in a humorless smile. "She had a degree in psychology."

Desdemona shivered. Stark's eyes were colder than the walk-in freezer in the Right Touch kitchen. "You asked her to sign a prenuptial agreement, too?"

"Of course. She agreed to sign it on our wedding day. But she failed to show up at the altar. Sent a damned note instead. Said she had to marry for love."

"I see."

"A mutual acquaintance told me that she filed for divorce from the doctor six months ago."

"I see."

"Apparently she fell for a tennis pro."

"It happens."

"So much for a marriage based on love," Stark said with grim satisfaction.

"I don't think one should generalize," Desdemona said cautiously.

"The way I figure it, I got lucky," Stark said.

"Perhaps."

"At least I didn't get stuck with the tab for the reception that time." Stark picked up a pen and started going item by item down the invoice.

Desdemona breathed a small sigh of relief. He was at last examining the bill. That was at least one step closer to getting a check out of him.

Privately she thought she understood exactly why Pamela Bedford and Lindsay Mills had lost their nerve on the eve of marriage. It would take courage to marry Sam Stark.

His name suited him all too well. There was a hard, elemental quality about him that would give any intelligent woman pause.

The medieval knight image applied to his features as well as his build. His hair was nearly black, overlong, and brushed straight back from his high forehead. The broad, flat planes of his face and jaw looked as though they had been fashioned to wear a steel helm. His brilliant green eyes glowed with the power of very old gemstones. A prowling, predatory intelligence burned in those eyes.

All in all, there was a stern, unyielding, utterly relentless quality about Sam Stark. It was the sort of quality one might have valued in a knight a few hundred years earlier but that was unexpected and deeply disturbing in a modern-day male.

Desdemona told herself that she was profoundly grateful to know that as soon as she got her check from him, Stark would cease to be her problem.

On the other hand, she had never met anyone who had been abandoned at the altar, let alone abandoned twice.

"Two pounds of tapenade?" Stark glared at Desdemona. "What the hell is tapenade?"

"Basically it's an olive paste. You spread it on crackers."

"It costs a fortune. Wouldn't it have been cheaper to just serve a couple of bowls of olives?"

"Probably, but Miss Bedford wanted tapenade."

"And what about these cheese breadsticks? Who needs four hundred breadsticks?"

"Two hundred people were invited to the reception, Mr. Stark. Miss Bedford wanted to be able to serve two breadsticks apiece."

Stark continued down the list. "Stuffed mushroom caps? I don't even like stuffed mushroom caps."

"Apparently Miss Bedford was fond of them."

"More fond of them than she was of me, obviously. What are these swans at fifty bucks each? Nobody eats swans these days."

"They aren't real swans. They're ice sculptures. Rafael, one of my employees, did a beautiful job on them."

Stark glanced toward the window. "I'm paying fifty bucks apiece for those blocks of ice that are melting away in my garden?"

"Think of them as works of art, Mr. Stark. Rafael definitely considers himself an artist."

"They're made out of ice. I'm paying a total of one hundred and fifty dollars to water my garden with fancy ice sculptures?"

"I realize this is very difficult for you, Mr. Stark. I'll be glad to go over each item on the bill, but I can assure you that all the charges are quite reasonable."

"Your idea of reasonable and mine are two different things, Miss Wainwright." Stark went back to the invoice. "About this herbed goat cheese."

"Very popular these days."

"I don't see how it could be, at this price."

"It's very special goat cheese. Made by a local firm."

"What do they do? Raise the goats in their own private, waterfront condominiums?"

Desdemona opened her mouth to respond with a crack about the goats being worth it, but at the last instant she changed her mind. It dawned on her that Stark was using the line-by-line argument over the invoice as a means of venting some of the rage and pain he must surely be feeling.

She glanced at his very large fist, which was fiercely clamped around a slender gold pen. The muscles in his forearm were bunched and taut.

"I know the goat cheese is a little steep," she said gently. "But it's excellent, and it keeps well. Shall I leave it behind for you to eat?"

"Do that. I'll have it for dinner tonight. Leave some crackers and a couple of bottles of the champagne, too."

Desdemona frowned. "Look, I know this is none of my business, but are you going to be all right here on your own this evening?"

He glanced up swiftly, his gaze shuttered. "Don't worry, I'm not going to do something stupid like overdose on goat cheese and champagne."

"You've been through an emotionally exhausting experience. It's not always a good idea to be alone after that kind of thing. Do you have someone who can stay with you? A family member, perhaps?"

"I don't have any family here in Seattle."

Desdemona was startled. "None of them came out for the wedding?"

"I'm not close to my family, Miss Wainwright."

"Oh." She was unsure how to respond to that. The concept of being bereft of family sent a chill through her. Since she had become a member of the extended Wainwright clan at the age of five, family had been everything to Desdemona. The time before her mother had married Benedick Wainwright was a shadowed realm that Desdemona preferred not to revisit. "Well, is there a friend you could call?"

"I suppose I could send out for one of those inflatable, life-sized, anatomically correct dolls that are sold in adult entertainment stores," Stark said. "But with my luck, she'd probably deflate before I figured out the operating instructions."

Desdemona smiled faintly. "I'm glad your sense of humor is still intact. It's a good sign."

"Do you think so?"

"Definitely." Desdemona leaned forward and folded her arms on the desk. "Look, I'm serious here. I really don't think you ought to be alone tonight."

He gazed at her with unreadable eyes. "What would you suggest I do? I'm not exactly in the mood to throw a party."

Desdemona gave into impulse. "Tell you what. Let's finish going over this invoice. Then you can come back to the Right Touch kitchen with me and have dinner with my staff. Afterward you can go to the theater with us."

"Theater?"

"The Limelight down in Pioneer Square. It's a little fringe playhouse located underneath the viaduct. Know it?"

"No. I rarely go to the theater."

Desdemona had learned early in life that the world was divided into two groups, those who loved the theater and barbarians. She seldom socialized with the latter, but today for some reason she was inspired to make an exception.

"The Limelight is very small," Desdemona said. "It does a lot of experimental contemporary stuff. My cousin Juliet has a part in the current production."

Stark looked dubious. "Is it going to be one of those weird plays where there's no plot or scenery and the actors come on stage naked and throw things at the audience?"

Desdemona smiled blandly. "I see you're familiar with experimental theater."

"I've heard about stuff like that. I don't think it's the kind of thing I'd enjoy."

"Look at the positive side. To a man who is going to spend his wedding night alone, I would think that a live actress running around in the buff on stage would be a lot more interesting than an inflatable, anatomically correct doll."

Stark gave her a thoughtful look. "Point taken."

2

"It stunk. The audience hated it." Juliet Wainwright, clad in a skintight black leotard and a pair of jeans, collapsed into the booth next to Stark. "We're doomed."

Stark wrapped one hand around his small espresso cup and moved it out of range of Juliet's flying hair. Warily, he surveyed the newest Wainwright arrival. She looked a lot like the other members of Desdemona's seemingly endless family whom Stark had met this evening.

There was a distinctly feline quality to most of the Wainwrights. Tall, sleek, and graceful, they had sharp, striking faces, amber eyes, and tawny brown hair. As a group they were a handsome lot. Every move was poised, dramatic, or over-the-top.

Desdemona appeared to be the sole exception, so far as Stark could discern. Technically speaking, he had to admit that she was not as physically arresting as the rest of the family. She was a good deal shorter than the others, for starters. And she moved with energy and enthusiasm rather than languid, world-weary grace.

There was also something softer about her, he thought. Softer and infinitely more appealing. She had a full, gentle mouth, huge turquoise eyes, and a wild, frothy halo of unabashedly red curls. Surrounded by her more dramatic relatives, she stood out like a marmalade-colored tabby cat that had mistakenly been reared in a family of leopards.

It was late, and the cozy coffee house, aptly named Emote Espresso, was filled with Wainwrights and other theater people. Most of them were refugees from the shabby little Limelight, which was a block away. Members of the cast and crew mingled with the handful of stalwart theatergoers who had bravely endured the evening's performance all the way through the final act.

"They didn't hate it, Juliet," Desdemona said soothingly. "They just didn't get it."

"They despised it." Juliet closed her eyes in evident anguish. "You'd have thought the audience was sitting in a morgue watching an autopsy. The reviews will be lousy, and the show is going to close in a week. I can feel it."

Stark privately agreed with her, so he sipped his espresso and offered no comment. None was needed in any event. The Wainwrights were perfectly capable of carrying on a conversation without any help from him. In fact, it would have been hard to get a word in edgewise.

"Who cares about reviews?" Kirsten Wainwright demanded from the other side of the table. "This is fringe theater. Experimental stuff. Mainstream reviewers never get it. If they did get it, it wouldn't be fringe theater."

At least he wasn't the only one who hadn't understood *Fly on a Wall*, Stark thought. He looked at Kirsten. She was not a Wainwright by blood, but with her striking features, golden brown hair, and brown eyes, she fit right in with the rest of the pack. She had been introduced as the wife of Desdemona's cousin, Henry, who was also at the table.

The booth was crowded, but no one seemed to mind. With the exception of Desdemona, the Wainwrights lolled about in various arty poses, vying for space and attention. Desdemona sat in the center opposite Stark, squashed between Henry and Kirsten, who towered over her.

"Bad reviews mean people don't buy tickets and the show closes," Juliet wailed. "I'll be out of work again." She cradled her head in her arms. Her mane of hair flowed over her shoulders and cascaded down onto the table.

"So the show had a few problems. It was opening night, what do you expect?" Desdemona reached across the table to pat her cousin's heaving shoulders. "It wasn't your fault that the audience didn't get the significance of the flyswatter in the background."

"Hey, Juliet, cheer up." Henry Wainwright, handsome and tawny-haired like the others, gave the despairing actress a sympathetic look. "You couldn't help it if the theater was filled with a bunch of plebeians from the Eastside tonight."

"Henry's right," Kirsten said. "Everyone knows those folks from the 'burbs only want dinner theater stuff. It was the wrong audience."

Henry scowled. "It sure as hell was. What were they doing there, anyway? They should have been down at the Fifth Avenue Theater tapping their toes to the new road show production of *South Pacific*."

"The Limelight's in trouble financially," Juliet confided sadly.

"So what else is new?" Henry asked. "The Limelight has been in trouble since the day it opened. Most small theaters are."

"So Ian came up with what he thought was an incredibly clever way to fill the seats tonight," Juliet said. "He put together a package deal for Eastsiders. You know, dinner and a show in downtown Seattle. Transportation included."

Desdemona raised her brows. "Transportation?"

Juliet made a face. "He chartered a van to bring 'em across the lake."

Henry whistled softly. "Ian strikes again. A whole bus full of Eastsiders brought downtown to see fringe theater. It boggles the mind. He must have been desperate."

"Who's Ian?" Stark asked, mildly curious.

"Ian Ivers owns the Limelight," Desdemona explained. "Actually, he is the Limelight. Producer, manager, artistic director, you name it, he does it all."

"The Limelight is his baby," Henry said. "Ian's mission in life is to become known as the man on the cutting edge of Seattle's contemporary theater scene."

"Why?" Stark asked.

Every Wainwright at the table looked at him as if he weren't very bright. It was a novel experience for Stark. He was not accustomed to that expression on the faces of those around him.

Desdemona took pity on him. "So that he can go to New York and become really important, of course."

"I see," Stark said politely.

Desdemona bestowed a benign smile on him and then promptly turned back to the task of consoling Juliet. "Forget those people from the 'burbs. Your performance was brilliant. Absolutely brilliant. Wasn't it brilliant, Stark?"

Stark, never at his best in social situations, realized that he was expected to say something intelligent about Juliet's role in a play that had, to him, been more indecipherable than scrambled computer code. He groped for words.

"You were the most unusual flyswatter I've ever seen," he finally managed.

Juliet raised her head and looked at him with dawning hope in her golden eyes. "Do you really think so?"

"No question," Stark said.

Desdemona gave him an approving glance. "Especially at the end when she finally swatted the fly on the wall. Wasn't that a terrific scene?"

Stark cautiously edged his espresso cup out of the way of Juliet's billowing hair. "I could almost feel the sense of utter flatness that the fly must have experienced at the moment of impact."

Desdemona's look of approval changed to something resembling suspicion. Stark raised his shoulder a quarter of an inch. He was doing his best, but he could not deny that he was out of his league.

What surprised him was not that he hadn't understood a word of the crazy play, let alone the significance of the flyswatter, but that he had actually enjoyed himself, albeit in a perverse fashion.

It was because of Desdemona, and he knew it.

He was still not certain why he had allowed her to drag him back to the Right Touch Catering kitchens for dinner with her flamboyant staff, most of whom appeared to be unemployed actors. He was even more at a loss to explain why he had accompanied Desdemona and some of her relatives to the weird performance in a theater so small he could have fit the entire production, stage and audience, into his office.

On the other hand, it wasn't as though he'd had a lot of options this evening. If he were not sitting here in Emote Espresso in Pioneer Square with assorted members of the Wainwright clan, he would be sitting alone at home with a bottle of overpriced champagne, some goat cheese, and a too terse note from his bride. Which was exactly how he had spent his previous wedding night two years ago.

Stark was accustomed to being alone when things went wrong. For that matter, he was accustomed to being alone when things went right.

He had developed the habit of enduring defeat or celebrating triumph by himself long ago. It had become a way of life.

In that moment when he'd known with icy certainty that Pamela wasn't going to show, all he'd wanted was to be alone again. His immediate goal had been to get rid of the two hundred wedding guests, the catering staff, and all the trappings of the debacle as swiftly as possible.

Virtually everyone, including Dane McCallum, his friend, best man, and vice president of Stark Security Systems, had taken the hint and departed. The exception had been the caterer, one Desdemona Wainwright. Stark had been forced to pay attention to her for the first time when she had charged into the house, hard on his heels, waving her bill.

He had finally gotten a good look at her in his study. She had been dressed in a rakish little tuxedo not unlike his own, except that on her the style was a lot more interesting. Stark had been vaguely surprised to discover that even in the midst of his foul mood, he was capable of appreciating the sight.

Desdemona was not very tall, and her breasts were definitely on the discreetly pert side, but she was nicely rounded lower down. As far as Stark was concerned, that was where roundness mattered in a woman.

Her determination to get a check out of him had startled him initially. He had assumed that Pamela had taken care of the caterer's bill along with all of the other wedding details. Pamela was well aware that he knew nothing about handling such matters and that he had no interest in learning. He had little patience with the social side of business or life.

Unfortunately, his rapidly growing financial success had catapulted him into a whole new realm where social demands were inextricably entangled with business demands. He had concluded that he needed a wife, and he had set out to find one.

Stark had learned the hard way that he did best with cool, unemotional, undemanding women such as Pamela Bedford. Of course, judging by the day's events, that wasn't saying much. His best had obviously been a disaster.

Tall, willowy, golden-haired, and blue-eyed, Pamela defined the phrase "cool blonde." She had been endowed with the sort of aloof composure that was bred into the women of families whose money was old enough to have mold on it. She personified Stark's notion of a cultured, refined female.

She was just what he had been looking for in a wife, he had told himself three minutes after meeting her. With her background and family connections she was the perfect woman to deal efficiently with the increasing social obligations confronting him. She would know how to entertain his high-powered clients. She could handle the local politicos and the society ladies who were forever trying to get money out of him.

Making casual conversation at a cocktail party or a charity event was Stark's idea of a nightmare. Pamela, on the other hand, had grown up in a world where such skills were taught from birth. She knew the right thing to do and when to do it. Stark had looked forward to turning over to her all of the annoying details of his life outside of work.

Pamela had seemed so wonderfully predictable.

Abandoning her groom at the altar this afternoon was probably the first time in her life that she had ever done anything that would have offended Miss Manners or Emily Post.

Stark suspected that Desdemona Wainwright was, on the other hand, a perfect example of chaotic dynamics in action. Expressions flickered across her features with the speed and volatility of weather fronts moving across the Seattle skyline. Not a good sign. He had made it a lifelong practice to avoid volatile women. He knew that he was no good with the emotional type, and they found him equally frustrating.

The only sensible thing to do was steer clear of Desdemona, Stark told himself. He was intuitively impaired, and he knew it. Sure, he could second-guess computer thieves with uncanny ease, but he had no talent at all for understanding the dynamics of interpersonal relationships. As far as he was concerned, human relationships, not the new frontiers of math and physics, deserved the popular label of chaos theory.

Desdemona's catering firm was housed in an old, remodeled brick warehouse in Pioneer Square. There, seated at a table with the Right Touch staff, Stark had eaten a surprising quantity of the tortellini and asparagus tarts that had cost him so dearly.

In the process he had discovered that Desdemona's entire family, for three generations, had been theater people.

He'd always thought of theater people as high-strung, financially unstable, and temperamental. Nothing he had observed thus far this evening had altered his opinion.

But for some reason that didn't seem to matter tonight. He supposed he needed something to take his mind off his problems, and Desdemona and her relations had done a fair job.

He was even willing to concede that the production of *Fly on a Wall*, an ambiguous, obscure, totally incomprehensible bit of modern theater, had had its moments.

"The utter flatness of the fly." Henry nodded thoughtfully. "You know, that's a hell of an insight, Stark. I hadn't considered that element of Juliet's role. She really projected it, didn't she?"

Stark knew himself to be on dangerous ground. He hedged. "I was impressed by it."

Kirsten's eyes widened. "Absolutely. The *flatness*. It was perfect, Juliet."

"Do you really think so?" Juliet asked eagerly.

"Definitely," Desdemona said enthusiastically. She started to say something else but broke off as a shadow fell across the table. She looked up. "Oh, hi, Ian. Great show."

"Mona," the new arrival exclaimed. "Good to see you. Who's your friend?"

"This is Sam Stark. Everyone calls him Stark. Stark, this is Ian Ivers."

"Hello," Stark said.

Ian did a stagy double take. "Not *the* Sam Stark of Stark Security Systems."

Stark did not consider that the question warranted a response, so he took another swallow of espresso instead.

Henry stepped in to cover the awkward moment. "One and the same."

"How about that." Ian grinned and stuck out a hand toward Stark. "Glad to meet you. Didn't realize you were into theater."

"I'm not," Stark said. He had a feeling he was not going to like Ian Ivers.

Ian was in his mid-thirties. He was short, and as Stark discovered when he reluctantly shook hands, his palms were unpleasantly moist. Both his jawline and his waistline had already gone soft. Perhaps they had never been firm. He wore his shoulder-length hair, which was thinning on top, in a ponytail. There was a gold ring in one of his ears. His stylish, wide-legged, heavily pleated olive green trousers flowed over his shoes. His iridescent black and green shirt sparkled in the neon light.

"Couldn't help overhearing your comment, Stark," Ian said with an expression of deep admiration. "Henry's right. Great insight on Juliet's performance. Real flatness there. And don't overlook the cathartic sense of sexual release that occurred at the moment of impact."

Stark surreptitiously wiped his hand on a small napkin. "I'm not sure I picked up on that."

"It was very subtle," Ian assured him. "Listen, I gotta run. Got some money people waiting for me. Promised 'em I'd talk to 'em right after tonight's performance. But I'd really like to get together with you soon, Stark. Contemporary theater needs guys like you."

Stark stared at him. "I doubt it."

"Hey, I'm serious here," Ian said. "Not every man in your position appreciates the importance of fringe theater. I'll get back to you." He winked at Desdemona. "See you, Mona."

He lifted a hand in farewell and hurried off to a booth in the corner.

Desdemona wrinkled her nose at Juliet and leaned forward. She lowered her voice to a whisper. "Honestly, I can't believe you and Aunt Bess want me to go out with him. You know I never go out with men who call me Mona."

"Give him a chance," Juliet insisted in a low voice. "He's really a nice guy, and the two of you have a lot in common."

"Forget it." Desdemona rolled her eyes and gave Stark a wry look. "Juliet and my aunt are incurable matchmakers."

"I see," Stark said. He made a mental note never to call her Mona.

"You have to admit that Desdemona is a rather unusual name in this day and age."

"I chose it myself when I was five years old," Desdemona said proudly.

Stark nodded. "So, what's your real name?"

"Desdemona is my real name."

"I mean what were you called before you were called Desdemona?"

"Susan or something," Desdemona said carelessly. "I don't remember for certain."

Stark stared at her, amazed. No one at the table seemed interested in the topic. He reminded himself that actors frequently changed their names. Further evidence of their erratic natures, he supposed.

Juliet sighed glumly. "I wasn't trying for a cathartic sense of sexual release, you know."

Desdemona's eyes gleamed. "Are you sure?"

"Positive," Juliet said.

"I guess that explains why I didn't get it," Stark said.

"Maybe I should have gone for it," Juliet said. "Might have kept the Eastsiders interested."

"Don't worry," Henry said in a consoling tone. "It'll take at least a week to close the show."

"And you've always got your day job," Desdemona said cheerfully.

Henry laughed. "That's right." He put a comradely arm around Desdemona. "Thank God for the one member of the family who has achieved financial stability."

Juliet slumped gracefully against the back of the booth. "Sometimes I think I'm fated to stuff mushroom caps for the rest of my life."

"You can thank Stark for the fact that there are still mushrooms to be stuffed." Desdemona's eyes met his over the top of her cup. "Right Touch is going to make it through another tax quarter because he was chivalrous enough to pay the tab for his canceled reception this afternoon."

For some reason, Stark was embarrassed. "Forget it."

"Abandoned at the altar." Juliet was momentarily distracted from her own trials. "Incredible. I've never actually met anyone who was left standing at the altar. Sorry I had to miss it. I had rehearsal."

"I wish I'd missed it, myself," Stark muttered.

"Kirsten and I were handling the champagne," Henry told Juliet.

24

"We saw the whole thing. A very heavy scene. Audience of two hundred."

"No kidding?" Juliet's eyes widened as she gazed at Stark. "Two hundred people saw you get dumped?"

"A full house," Stark admitted.

Henry hunched over his espresso cup and peered intently at him. "Mind if I ask you a question?"

"Depends," Stark said.

"What was it like when you realized she'd ditched you? I mean, what was the first thing that went through your head?"

"The same thing that probably went through the fly's head a second before the swatter got him in *Fly on a Wall*," Stark said.

Kirsten grinned. "You mean you experienced a sense of being on the verge of a cathartic sexual release?"

"Not exactly." Stark glanced at Desdemona. "As I recall, it was more along the lines of 'What am I doing here when I could be having a nice day at the office.' "

Desdemona's soft mouth curved with wry sympathy. "That thought was no doubt soon followed by the realization that he was going to be stuck paying for a wedding even though he hadn't gotten married."

"The fiancée flamed out and left you with the whole tab, huh?" Henry shook his head. "Bummer."

"That's one way of putting it," Stark agreed.

"We're all very glad you paid the bill, though," Juliet said. "Desdemona had to buy a lot of the supplies on credit for that gig. If you hadn't come through with the cash, she'd have been left high and dry."

"Which would have been bad news for us Wainwrights," Henry added. "We depend on her to keep us employed when we're 'resting between engagements,' as my father likes to say."

"Desdemona's the first member of the family in three generations to have a steady job," Juliet said. "To tell you the truth, the older generation of Wainwrights finds it a little embarrassing."

Desdemona hoisted her cup in a mock salute. "A blot on the Wainwright family escutcheon."

"But a useful blot," Kirsten said. She looked at Stark. "Actually, I'm hoping to follow in her footsteps."

"You're going to get a steady job?" Stark asked.

"I'm going to start a small business, just like Desdemona did."

Stark sipped his espresso. "Catering?"

"Not exactly." Kirsten's eyes lit with the excitement of the incipient entrepreneur. "I'm going to open an upscale, very classy boutique right here in Pioneer Square."

Stark eyed the long, purple, tunic-length sweater that she wore over a pair of tight purple pants. "Let me guess. Designer clothing?"

"No way," Kirsten assured him. "There's a zillion clothing boutiques here in Seattle. I'm going to open a very special kind of shop. A place that will cater to women's sexual fantasies and consumer needs."

Stark wondered if he'd missed a conversational cue somewhere along the line. It happened all the time. "Sexual fantasies."

"You know, attractively colored condoms, for example. Women buy a lot of the condoms sold in this country, did you know that?"

"Uh, no. No, I didn't," Stark admitted.

"Some pretty lingerie. Maybe some light leather, vibrators, instructional videos, erotica written by women, for women, that kind of thing."

"I see," Stark said.

"But all sold in a tasteful atmosphere." Henry gave his wife a proud smile.

"Tasteful," Stark repeated cautiously.

"I'm going to call it Exotica Erotica," Kirsten said. "It will be a place owned and operated by a woman, catering specifically to female shoppers. Of course, men who are interested in buying sensual toys and such to give as gifts to the women in their lives will be welcome."

Stark looked at her. "Is that a fact?"

"Exotica Erotica will be the kind of place where professional women and suburbanites will feel comfortable."

"Even Eastsiders?" Stark asked.

"Especially Eastsiders," Kirsten said. "I envision a place that will remind them of their favorite mall stores. Very upscale, like I said."

"Not tacky," Juliet added in case Stark had not grasped the concept.

"Definitely not tacky," Henry agreed.

Kirsten leaned forward, her eyes filled with the zeal of a crusader.

"Do you realize that in this culture there are virtually no decent, pleasant places where a woman can shop for products that are geared toward her sensual needs?"

"Uh, I hadn't given the matter a lot of thought," Stark admitted.

"Who knows?" Henry said. "If the concept works, maybe Kirsten can franchise it."

Stark looked at Kirsten. "When do you plan to open your store?"

"Just as soon as I can convince Desdemona, here, to cosign the loan papers at the bank." Kirsten smiled at Desdemona.

Stark put down his cup with great precision. "So it's one of those situations."

Henry frowned. "What's that supposed to mean?"

Desdemona smiled a little too brightly. "Forget it, Henry. The man's had a bad day. It's getting late. Maybe we'd better break up this little party."

Henry checked the massive Mickey Mouse watch he wore on his wrist as he slid out of the booth. "It's only twelve-thirty."

"I've got a consultation for a new job in the morning." Desdemona scooted to the edge of the seat and stood. "Don't forget, I'll expect everyone who's scheduled to work tomorrow at Right Touch no later than ten. We've got a charity event in the afternoon."

"We'll be there," Juliet promised. "You really think I was good tonight?"

"You were terrific," Desdemona said.

"Excuse me," Stark said. "It's been a long day."

"Yeah, sure." Henry gave him a commiserating look. "We understand."

Juliet got out of his way. "Sorry about what happpened to you today."

"I'll live." Stark got to his feet and then paused, unsure of what to say to these strangers who had taken him under their collective wing for the evening. "Thanks for the show. And the coffee."

"No problem," Henry said. "The passes to *Fly on a Wall* were free, and you paid for the espresso."

"True," Stark agreed. "Nevertheless, I appreciate the company."

Henry shrugged. "For what it's worth, you played that scene this afternoon like a pro. Just the right combination of cynical disdain and arrogant pride. The crowd loved it."

"I've had practice." Stark took his corduroy jacket off the coat hook. He looked at Desdemona. "I'll see you home."

She smiled. "Thanks, but it's only three blocks, and I've got my car parked out front."

"I'll ride with you and catch a cab from your place," Stark said.

She gave him an odd look, but she didn't argue. Stark took her arm. It felt good. He guided her out of the crowded espresso bar and into the chilly spring night.

First Avenue, which ran through the heart of Pioneer Square, was crowded with people, as it usually was on a Saturday night.

Live jazz and heavy rock poured from the open doors of the packed taverns and bars that lined the street. Muscle-bound bouncers perched on stools at the entrances of the clubs. They flirted with wispy young women who wore heavy red lipstick on their mouths and rhinestones in their noses.

Desdemona's red Toyota was parked at the curb. She got behind the wheel and unlocked the door on the passenger side. Stark could not think of anything particularly witty or clever to say, so he stayed silent as she eased the little car into traffic.

After the first block he noticed that he did not feel the usual pressure to make conversation. It was a relief.

Two blocks later Desdemona turned a corner, drove partway down an alley behind an aging brick building, and used a remote control to open the steel gate of a parking garage. Inside, she slipped the Toyota into a parking stall.

Stark got out and walked her to the elevator.

"Do you want to come upstairs to my place to call a cab?" Desdemona asked as they waited for the elevator doors to open.

Stark suddenly realized that he wanted to go upstairs to her apartment more than he wanted anything else in the world. This was supposed to be his wedding night. "No, I'll get out at the lobby. I can find a cab on the street."

The elevator opened. Desdemona stepped inside. Stark followed. He thought she tensed as the doors closed again. He watched her out of the corner of his eye and could have sworn that she was doing some sort of deep-breathing exercise. Before he could figure out how to ask her politely if something was wrong, the elevator opened at the lobby level.

Desdemona leaned on the button that held the doors open as Stark got out. She searched his face. "Are you going to be all right?"

"Yes."

"I'm really sorry about what happened today."

"Forget it."

"It must have been hell for you."

"Like I said, you get used to it."

"I don't believe that for a minute." Desdemona fleetingly touched the sleeve of his corduroy jacket. "Take care of yourself."

"Okay." Stark paused. "Mind if I give you some advice?"

"On computer security matters?"

"No. Family matters."

The red highlights in her hair gleamed in the overhead light as she tilted her head to one side. "What advice?"

"Don't cosign those loan papers for your cousin's wife."

"I'm the only one in the family who has a decent credit rating," Desdemona said.

"It's too risky. It's virtually the same as loaning the money to her."

"So?"

"It's never smart to lend money to relatives," Stark said patiently.

Desdemona's expression turned oddly wistful. "Your family isn't very close, is it?"

"What's that got to do with anything?"

"Nothing. I'm sorry you couldn't meet my parents and my brother, Tony. Tony's in L.A. He's got a shot at a soap."

"He's in the laundry business?"

Desdemona laughed. "A soap opera. My folks are doing *My Fair Lady* at a dinner theater in Tucson."

"You seem to have a rather large family."

"Luckily for me."

Stark eyed her speculatively. "From the sound of it, I'd say they're the lucky ones. You're apparently the financial linchpin of the whole operation."

Her eyes widened in surprise. "You don't understand. We're a *family*. We all stick together. You know the old saying, the only thing a Wainwright can depend on is another Wainwright."

And they're all depending on you, Stark thought. "I've never heard that particular saying."

"It's a family motto. Say, before you go, let me give you this." Desdemona reached into the purse that was slung over her shoulder and took out a small business card. "I realize that the last thing you want to think about at the moment is the possibility of catering another major social event. But you never know."

Stark accepted the card. "Thanks."

Desdemona took her finger off the button. "Good night, Stark."

"Good night." Stark saw the curious tension return to her eyes as the elevator doors closed.

He hesitated a moment longer, and then finally he turned and walked out of the lobby.

He found a cab almost immediately. He got inside and leaned back against the seat. With one blunt finger he traced the words *Right Touch Catering* on the crisp white card Desdemona had given him. Then he put the card into the pocket of his jacket.

He felt weary and rather old.

He wondered where Pamela was and what she was doing tonight.

Maybe it was for the best. He knew in his bones that the marriage probably wouldn't have worked for more than a few years. Marriage was a fragile thing. Few people had the stamina for it. Most people opted out when the going got tough.

Stark knew a lot about the subject. His parents had been divorced when he was ten.

Stark had stayed with his mother, who had remarried and started a second family. For a while Stark's father had come around to see his son on weekends, but the visits had grown increasingly far apart. Eventually they had ceased altogether.

Looking back on that time, Stark was the first to admit that he had become difficult. He had turned sullen, rebellious, hostile, and uncooperative. His mother and stepfather, busy with their new baby, had lost patience.

He had been put into counseling, where he had retaliated by refusing to say a word. When the counselor threw in the towel, Stark's stepfather, a successful businessman who had been raised on the East Coast, had come up with an East Coast solution to the problem. Stark had been packed off to a boarding school some three thousand miles away.

West Coast born and raised, Stark had not fitted in well socially at the expensive school. He had kept to himself for the most part. But under the guidance of teachers who had seen past his anger to the keen intelligence that lay beyond, he had discovered mathematics, physics, and, eventually, computers.

He had soon learned that he fit perfectly into those calm, orderly realms where logic and reason held sway and where emotion did not intrude.

Stark's father had remarried twice in the years that followed his first divorce. Stark was vaguely aware that, in addition to his half sister and half brother on his mother's side, he had a pair of half brothers in Portland. He had never met them or their mother, Hudson Stark's third wife, and saw no compelling reason to make their acquaintance.

Boarding school had led to college, which had, in turn, led to the Rosetta Institute. The Institute had led to Stark Security Systems.

Life went on. What with one thing and another, Stark and his relatives had simply drifted out of each others' lives. No one had seemed to take much notice.

He had not lost touch entirely. He still called his parents on their birthdays. They, in turn, sent cards at Christmas.

He had sent wedding invitations to his mother and father, but neither had been free to attend. Stark was grateful. It had been humiliating enough to be abandoned at the altar without having to deal with his parents.

A thought struck him, slicing through his memories and bringing him back to the present. He reached inside his jacket and removed his personal digital assistant. He switched on the tiny computer and made a note to drop a line to his folks to inform them that he hadn't gotten married after all.

He hoped they hadn't bothered with gifts this time. Returning the crystal punch bowl his mother had sent two years ago had been a nuisance. He never had gotten around to sending back the silver candy dish he had received from his father's third wife.

3

A somber hush greeted Stark when he walked into the lobby of his headquarters in downtown Seattle on Monday morning, reminding him of the atmosphere found in the viewing room of a funeral parlor.

Rose Burns, the receptionist, smiled tremulously. It was a smile that held pity, horror, and a certain degree of sheer awe. It was the same smile she had reserved for him two years ago on the day after his last fiasco of a wedding.

"Good morning, Mr. Stark," she murmured. Her eyes were eloquent.

"Good morning, Miss Burns."

There was a grim pause during which Rose lowered her gaze the way mourners do when they stand at the edge of the grave. "Wonderful weather we're having today."

Stark looked at her. "Do you think so?"

Rose's face turned a brilliant shade of crimson. She hastily busied herself with an incoming call.

The hall that led to Stark's office was a gauntlet. Stark went down it with a sense of stoic resignation. The morbidly curious hovered in the open doorways on either side. He detected covert glances from the vicinity of the copy machine room. A few brave souls mumbled an awkward greeting before rushing off to the rest rooms, where they could compare notes with other eyewitnesses.

But the worst was yet to come. Stark set his teeth as he strode through the door of his office suite.

His secretary, Maud Pitchcott, peered at him over the rim of her reading glasses. Her pale blue eyes assessed him. Stark braced himself.

Maud was sixty-something. She had a round helmet of iron gray curls and favored gray suits to match. The suits were power suits. They were double-breasted, a style that, on Maud's sturdy figure, made her a force to be reckoned with at Stark Security Systems.

Her chief hobby, so far as Stark could discern, was hanging out in greeting card stores on her lunch hour. She was forever on a quest to find just the right inspirational verse for every occasion.

Her children, grandchildren, nephews, nieces, friends, and associates received cards from her on all major and minor holidays. Stark even got one on Boss's Day, an annual event of which he had been blissfully unaware until he had hired Maud. The constant stream of cards were a pain because he had the nagging feeling he should reciprocate in some fashion. He ignored the uneasy impulse and tolerated his secretary's eccentricity because Maud was incredibly well organized.

Unfortunately her greeting card hobby had influenced her view of reality.

"Good morning, Mr. Stark," Maud said. "I didn't think you would be in today. I was extremely sorry to learn about the unfortunate little incident on Saturday."

Only Maud would term it an unfortunate little incident, Stark thought. "Forget it, Maud."

"Remember, sir, as we travel along life's highway we are bound to stumble over the occasional stone. You must pick yourself up, dust yourself off, and start all over again."

"Saturday was not my best day, Maud. Nevertheless I'm pleased to say that I did at least manage not to trip and fall. Therefore, there is no need for me to pick myself up or to dust myself off."

"I wasn't speaking literally, sir," Maud chided gently.

"Weren't you?" Stark feigned surprise.

"Of course not. I was speaking metaphorically."

"I've never been good with metaphors."

"Onward, sir," Maud said briskly. "This is the first day of the rest of your life."

"I'll bear that in mind."

"You must turn your back on the cloudy days of the past and look toward the rainbow that promises a sunny future."

"Thank you for the advice." Stark went swiftly past her desk. Escape was at hand. He was almost at the door of his inner office.

"Tomorrow brings a new dawn and renewed hope, sir."

"Right." Stark breathed a sigh of relief as he shoved open the second door. "Send McCallum in, will you?"

"Yes, sir. And may I say, sir, that every obstacle that we successfully surmount helps us to blossom and grow."

"If you do say that, Maud, I will probably fire you on the spot." Stark went into his office and closed the door. Hard.

He tossed his briefcase down onto his desk, slung his jacket onto the brass coatrack in the corner, and stalked to the window. He stood there for a few minutes and brooded over the view from the fifteenth floor of the high-rise office building.

From where he was standing he could see the steel blue expanse of Elliott Bay and the snow-capped Olympic Mountains in the distance. There wasn't a cloud in sight, although, this being the Pacific Northwest, that was subject to change.

Ferries weighted down with tourists, as well as the usual compliment of commuters, moved busily back and forth across the cold, dark waters of the Bay. They reminded Stark of so many industrious spiders spinning invisible webs. They dodged giant container ships and picked their way through the flock of sailboats that had materialized with the good weather.

Stark thought briefly about how he ought to have been sitting on a beachfront lanai in Bora Bora. It had been Pamela's idea to go to the South Pacific for their honeymoon. Stark had raised no objections. He had left the matter to her, just as he had intended to leave his entire social calendar to her.

Pamela had arranged everything, hotel, airline tickets, and his schedule. He wondered if she had bothered to cancel the reservations or if he would be getting bills for an unused honeymoon.

The door opened. Stark turned as Dane McCallum strolled into the office.

Tall, lean, and aristocratically good-looking at thirty-five, Dane was Stark's fashion opposite. He had a taste for expensive tailoring and the ability to wear his beautifully cut suits with the stylish flair of a model. He got his blond hair styled in a salon instead of cut in a barbershop. He wore Italian leather on his feet, not scuffed running shoes, and he was never seen in jeans at the office.

He was Stark's opposite in other ways as well. He was at ease in the social situations that Stark detested, and he genuinely cared about the arts, fine wines, and even the opera.

He was also very good at managing people and money, qualities that made him invaluable to Stark.

The two men had met a few years earlier at the Rosetta Institute. Stark had worked on the technical side. Dane had been in management and finance.

When Stark had made the decision to go out on his own, he had approached Dane with an offer that amounted to little more than a gamble. He had not been able to hold out a fistful of money, because his first product, a computer encryption program, was still in his head. But he had promised Dane a vice presidency and stock in Stark Security Systems. To his surprise, Dane had jumped at the opportunity.

Dane had proved to be just as skillful at bringing new business in to Stark Security Systems as he had once been at bringing in funding for the Institute.

Stark was the first to acknowledge that he and Dane had little in common on the surface, yet somehow they had become friends. They were bound together by the mutual goal of making Stark Security Systems the leading company in its field. Hard work and success had welded them into a team.

"How bad was the hangover on Sunday?" Dane asked equably.

Stark shrugged. "I didn't have one."

"No?" Dane smiled faintly as he lowered himself into a chair and stretched out his long legs. "I realize you're not a heavy drinker, but I figured you'd make an exception Saturday night. If you didn't get drunk, what did you do? I called around eight, but there was no answer."

"I spent the evening at the theater."

Dane's brows rose. "Didn't know you went to the theater."

"I went Saturday night. Saw something called *Fly on the Wall* at the Limelight."

"I don't believe it. You went to see experimental theater? You must have been in worse shape than I thought. How the hell did you find your way to a fifth-rate playhouse like the Limelight?"

"My caterer and her staff asked me to join them. It wasn't as though I had anything better to do."

Dane blinked in surprise. "Your caterer?"

"Forget it. It's a long story."

"All right, you spent Saturday night at the theater. What did you do yesterday? I tried to get you on the phone a couple of times."

"I had the phone turned off," Stark said. "I was working on ARCANE."

Dane's eyes gleamed briefly. "To quote Maud, when life hands you lemons, you make lemonade, hmm?"

"This is not a good time to quote Maud," Stark warned.

ARCANE was his newest brainchild, a highly flexible computer security program based on principles he had developed from what the popular press called chaos theory. Stark preferred to term the new field that existed at the frontiers of math and physics "the science of complexity."

He did not like the word *chaos*. In his mind it did not conjure up what it did for most scientists, an image of seemingly random signals and movements awaiting the discovery of the patterns hidden in them. For Stark, true chaos was an empty universe shrouded in an endless night. It was a place where everything was meaningless. A place where he was utterly, completely alone. And it existed inside a sorcerer's cauldron that was buried somewhere deep inside him.

Dane laced his fingers together and eyed Stark with a thoughtful gaze. "I hate to inquire, but sheer, morbid curiosity compels me. Have you heard from Pamela?"

"No."

"Just as well, I suppose."

"I agree. Pamela and I don't have a lot to talk about at the moment."

"Look on the bright side," Dane said. "A cancelled wedding has got to be a hell of a lot cheaper than a divorce."

"You didn't see the bill from the caterer."

Dane chuckled. "That may be so, but I speak from experience. Don't forget, I'm still writing out checks to Alicia. I'll bet they're a lot bigger than your check to the caterer."

Stark didn't argue. Alicia was Dane's second ex-wife. The marriage had lasted less than a year. Dane had recently paid a fortune to her in the divorce settlement.

"I suggested that you have Alicia sign a prenuptial agreement," Stark said. "You should have learned your lesson after Elizabeth left you."

"Guess I'm just a romantic at heart." Dane's mouth twisted. "Unlike you."

Stark sat down behind his desk. "You saw where being logical and businesslike about marriage got me on Saturday."

"True. It was not a pretty sight. That makes two strikes. Think you'll ever go for a third?"

"Do me a favor," Stark muttered. "Don't even mention the possibility."

Dane twitched the crease in his slack. "What happens next?"

"Business as usual," Stark said. "I'm fine-tuning ARCANE. Now that I don't have to take ten days off to go sit on a beach in Bora Bora, I should finish ahead of schedule. I think I'll have the last of the bugs worked out of the program by August."

Dane pursed his lips. "That is ahead of schedule. Two months ahead."

"I'm not having much trouble with the usual program glitches," Stark said. "Things are going well. Have Lancaster start work on the sales projections."

"Right."

"And remember," Stark muttered, "I want conservative numbers, not blue sky figures."

"I'll tell Lancaster." Dane grinned. "But don't blame me if he comes back with rosy projections. I think he's sweet on Maud."

"God help us."

In the days that followed his cancelled wedding, Stark did what he always did when things went wrong in his life. He buried himself in work.

He did not surface until two weeks later when Maud stationed herself in the doorway of his office and cleared her throat in a manner that boded ill.

She had to clear her throat twice because Stark was concentrating on a spreadsheet that Dane, who was sitting in his favorite chair in front of Stark's desk, had just handed to him. He looked up reluctantly.

"What is it, Maud?"

"Your social schedule for the next three months, sir."

A chill of alarm went through Stark. "What social schedule?"

Maud held up a notebook. "The one Miss Bedford arranged for you before the wedding."

"Damn," Stark said. He thought quickly. "Cancel everything."

"I don't think that's such a good idea, sir." Maud glanced at Dane for backup.

"She's right," Dane said. "Pamela consulted with me a month ago regarding that schedule. Everything on it is business-related. You put that side of things in her hands, remember?"

"Hell, yes, I remember." Stark felt trapped. "But that was when I thought I was going to get married."

"I realize that," Dane said. "But business is business."

Stark eyed Maud warily. "What, exactly, is on that schedule?"

Maud glanced down at the list in her hand. "You're hosting cocktail parties and buffets following each of the seminars on computer security that we're putting on once a month. The first is in two weeks. There are three receptions for various clients and corporate officers scheduled, a couple of charity events—"

"*Charity events*." Stark glowered at her. "What do charity events have to do with business?"

Dane stirred in his chair. "Those are the kind of events where you mingle with the movers and shakers, Stark. It's where business contacts are made. Pamela knew that. It was why she put them on your schedule."

"Damn." Stark took off his glasses and rubbed the bridge of his nose. "Give me a minute to think."

Maud fell silent. Dane waited expectantly.

Inspiration struck. Stark slowly replaced his glasses. "What I need is a professional."

Maud tilted her head to one side. "A professional?"

"Yes." Stark opened a desk drawer and pulled out a folder full of business cards. He slipped Desdemona's out of the plastic envelope. "Give the owner of this firm a call. Tell her what we need. See if she'll commit to a contract to handle all of Stark Security Systems' social events for the next quarter. We'll need her to cater and act as hostess at the events."

Maud walked to the desk and squinted at the card. "Right Touch Catering Services. Got it."

Dane's brows rose. "That's the firm that handled your wedding, isn't it?"

"My nonwedding."

"A professional caterer under contract to us," Dane mused. "Not a bad idea."

"Thank you," Stark said. He was suddenly unaccountably pleased with himself. "I should have thought of this days ago."

Dane smiled. "You always were the brains of the outfit."

Maud beamed. "When life give you lemons . . ."

The door of Desdemona's glass-walled office slammed open shortly after ten on Monday morning. Rafael Crumpton, ice sculptor and part-time server, struck a dramatic pose.

He was dressed in the pristine white uniform and cap that all of Desdemona's employees were required to wear when on duty in the firm's kitchens.

"Desdemona, I don't know how to tell you this, but I must leave you. Please don't hate me."

Desdemona frowned. "Where are you going?"

"I must follow my destiny. I told you when I took this job that I was meant for bigger and better things. I know that it will be difficult for you to go on without me, but you will survive. You're strong, Desdemona."

"Rafael, close the door, sit down, and tell me what's going on."

Rafael straightened, shut the door, and dropped into the chair on the other side of Desdemona's desk. "I've got a new job."

Desdemona groaned. "Oh, damn."

"I'm going to the Fountains, the new hotel in Bellevue."

Desdemona was stunned. "You're going to leave me for a hotel job

39

on the Eastside? For crying out loud, Rafael, you'll be doing ice carvings for Sunday brunches. You call that destiny?"

Rafael gave her a mournful look. "I knew you would take this hard. It wasn't an easy decision, Desdemona. But I've been promised complete artistic freedom." He spread his hands. "How could I refuse?"

"This is all because I made you do those swans for the Stark-Bedford wedding, isn't it? You're still in a snit because I wouldn't let you sculpt your own designs."

"My designs were exquisite," Rafael retorted. "I took my inspiration from the *Kama Sutra*. They were perfectly suited to a wedding banquet."

"Rafael, be honest. Don't you think a series of ice sculptures featuring naked couples in various sexual positions would have been just a tad much for the buffet table of a formal wedding?"

"My designs were a superb realization of wedding-night ecstasy."

"What would you know about wedding-night ecstasy? You've never been married. In any event the Stark-Bedford reception was a very classy affair. Your sculptures would have shocked the guests."

Rafael gave her a reproachful look. "A true artist cannot allow himself to be chained by the mediocre tastes of the rabble. Nor can he allow his patron to dictate his creative vision."

"I'm not your patron, I'm your employer."

"Not anymore."

"You think you're actually going to be allowed to carve anything you want to carve at the Fountains?"

"That's what I have been promised."

Desdemona lost her temper. "All right, go ahead and take the job. See how long you get to enjoy your artistic freedom. When are you leaving?"

"Today."

Desdemona was outraged. "You can't leave today. I've got the Cosini luncheon on Thursday and the Lambeth-Horton wedding on Friday. I'd planned to have ice sculptures on the tables for both events."

"I'm sorry, Desdemona." Rafael got to his feet. "You must find someone else to do your silly swans and dolphins. I am no longer willing to compromise my integrity as an artist. I must seek my true path."

"Rafael, wait." Desdemona leaped out of her chair and started around the edge of the desk. "Let's talk about this."

"There is nothing more to discuss. I must be free of the shackles of commercial art." Rafael flung open the door.

"Damn it, you're going to regret this. If you think your new employer is going to let you do a bunch of sexy ice sculptures for the Eastside Sunday brunch crowd, you've got another thought coming."

The phone rang on Desdemona's desk. She snatched up the receiver. "Right Touch."

"Desdemona Wainwright, please."

Business first. Desdemona forced herself to speak calmly and pleasantly. "This is Desdemona Wainwright. How can I help you?"

"This is Maud Pitchcott. I'm calling on behalf of Mr. Stark of Stark Security Systems."

Desdemona's hand clenched around the phone. For some reason she was suddenly a little breathless. "What can I do for you?"

"Mr. Stark wants to know if you would be interested in a contract with this firm. He would like to hire you as a social event consultant."

"A social event consultant?" Desdemona waved Rafael out of the office. She sank slowly back down into her chair.

"You would assume the responsibility for handling all of Stark Security Systems' social commitments for the next three months. You would also act as his hostess when necessary. Are you interested in the contract, Miss Wainwright?"

"Are you kidding?" Desdemona grabbed a pen. "I mean, yes. Yes, I'm definitely interested."

"In that case, Mr. Stark would like to see you in his office this afternoon."

Anticipation and satisfaction surged through Stark as he watched Desdemona sign the catering contract. Absolutely perfect. He should have thought of this the day he'd found himself standing alone at the altar. He wondered what the hell had taken him so long to realize that Desdemona was the answer to all his problems.

She put down the pen at that moment and raised her eyes to meet his. She smiled. Stark stopped breathing. He felt something twist deep inside him.

Perfect.

He took a deep breath and pulled himself together. This was business, he reminded himself sternly. "You don't have any objection to acting as my hostess?"

"No, not at all. Most people in your position have someone around who can help them host a business affair. A wife or a husband or, a, uh, something. . . ." She broke off, blushing.

His recent debacle of a marriage hung in the air between them. Stark could see the sympathy in Desdemona's eyes, and it annoyed him. He didn't want sympathy. He wanted . . . something else.

He wanted her.

The realization poleaxed him.

"A something," he repeated carefully.

"Yes," she said hastily. "But once in a while a single person finds himself or herself in your shoes, and in those cases it's not uncommon to hire a professional hostess."

"Good. Excellent." He looked at her, unable to think of anything else to say. He badly wanted to delay her departure from his office, but he could not seem to find a clever way to do it. "Well, that's that."

"Right." She leaped to her feet as though the chair in which she had been sitting had been wired for electricity and someone had just flipped the switch. "I'll look forward to working with you. I'm sure you'll find Right Touch will suit all your catering needs."

"Needs." He had a lot of them, he though wistfully. So many needs. Odd that he hadn't realized how strong those needs were until this moment.

"I trust you'll be satisfied," she added earnestly.

"Satisfied. Yes. That would be nice."

"I will personally do my best to see that you don't regret this decision." She put out her hand.

He got to his feet and closed his fingers around hers. Tightly. "I'm sure I won't." He stared down into her eyes. After a moment he felt her fingers wriggle like so many trapped birds. He realized he'd been holding her hand for a long time.

She smiled very brightly as she tried to tug her fingers free. "Goodbye."

Reluctantly he let go of her hand. "Good-bye, Desdemona."

She bolted for the door, her copy of the contract clutched in her small fist.

Stark watched the door close behind her.

Perfect.

Juliet, Kirsten, and Henry were waiting for Desdemona two hours later when she sailed triumphantly back through the alley entrance of Right Touch.

"Did you get the contract?" Juliet demanded.

"I got it." Desdemona waved the contract in the air. "My friends, this is the beginning of a beautiful business relationship. Once the word gets out that we are the exclusive caterers for Stark Security Systems, we will be unstoppable. Companies all over town will be begging for our services."

Kirsten laughed. "Enough about the business side of this. I've got a more interesting question. Was Pamela Bedford right?"

"About what?" Desdemona regarded the contract in her hand with smug delight.

"Does Stark really wear jeans and running shoes to the office?"

"Yes, he does." Desdemona studied Stark's signature at the bottom of the precious contract. It was a big, bold, utterly masculine signature. "And a cute little plastic pocket protector."

Henry put a hand to his heart and groaned. "How can you work for someone who wears a nerd pack?"

Desdemona fixed everyone present with a steely glare. "I want to make something very clear here. There will be no nerd-bashing allowed. Stark is now a valued client. As such, unless he turns out to be a mass-murderer, he can do no wrong. Understood?"

Henry saluted smartly. "Understood, oh great, exalted leader."

Kirsten laughed. "Got it."

Juliet smiled, but her expression turned speculative. "Understood."

"Excellent." Desdemona swung around on her heel. "If anyone needs me, I'll be in my office admiring my new contract with Stark Security Systems." *And thinking about the deeply disturbing sensation she had experienced when she had seen him again that afternoon.*

Desdemona had a full measure of the Wainwright intuition. She could feel it humming inside herself at that very moment. This second encounter with Stark had been no accident. A Wainwright knew the hand of destiny when she saw it in action.

Two weeks ago when she had first met Stark she had wondered about what might have happened had they come together in another place and another time.

Now she would have a chance to find out.

4

wo weeks later Stark stood with Dane McCallum and surveyed
the lively crowd of people gathered in his living room. A sense of
relief flooded through him. No one looked bored or uncomfortable.
His guests appeared to be enjoying themselves. The food was terrific,
and the service was flawless.

This was the first event that Right Touch had orchestrated for
Stark Security Systems since Stark had signed the contract with Desdemona.

The cocktail party and buffet tonight followed a day-long seminar
on corporate security issues that Stark Security Systems had put on
for the benefit of potential clients. The seminar, so far as Stark was
concerned, had been the easy part. It was the socializing afterward
that he had dreaded. He always dreaded the social stuff.

No more. Desdemona had taken care of everything.

"You're going to have a hard time getting rid of this bunch," Dane
remarked. "They're all having a good time."

"I'm telling you, McCallum, the decision to hire a professional
caterer was the best idea I've had since I worked out the basic theory
behind ARCANE's programming."

"I'm not sure I'd go that far."

"I would." Stark was feeling almost euphoric with success. "Desdemona's operation runs like clockwork. There hasn't been a single glitch. And all I had to do was authorize the check. This is the way to do it, McCallum. Don't know why I didn't think of it earlier."

Dane's mouth curved. "Sort of like having a wife-in-name-only, would you say?"

Stark was pleased with the analogy. "Exactly. All the convenience, none of the hassle."

"And none of the fun?"

"I wouldn't know about that part." Stark took a swallow of wine from his glass. "I've never managed to get myself married."

"You don't know what you're missing." Dane cast a speculative glance at Desdemona, who was busy on the other side of the room. "Then again, maybe you aren't missing a damn thing. Maybe you've got it all."

"What's that supposed to mean?"

Dane shrugged. "You're a smart man. Everyone knows that. A smart man can get just about anything these days without having to pay full price."

Stark followed Dane's gaze to where Desdemona stood talking to an earnest-looking corporate manager who worked for an Eastside firm. Nervous about his own abysmal social skills, Stark had asked her to act as hostess and mingle with the guests when necessary. She had been subtle about it, but Stark had noticed that no one in the room had been left on his or her own for long.

He watched her as she guided the manager to a small group and introduced him. Then, with a vivacious smile, she moved across the room to round up another stray.

Her smile made Stark's insides twist with excitement. It was not the first time.

Desdemona was wearing a sleek little black dress that skimmed her body in interesting places but somehow managed to appear modest. Her red curls were restrained with a black velvet ribbon. Several fiery ringlets had escaped to dance around her small, nicely shaped ears. Her jewelry consisted solely of a pair of sparkling earrings. She managed to look simultaneously cool and hot. Touchable and yet untouched.

Stark recognized the tight, clenching sensation that seized his lower body. It was pure, unadulterated arousal. Along with it came a primitive possessiveness. The feeling hit him when he realized Dane was staring at Desdemona just as attentively as he was. Dane's blatant interest in Desdemona stirred the hair on the back of his neck.

"Go find your own caterer," Stark said.

Dane gave him a knowing grin. "Like that, is it?"

Stark did not reply. The question had been simmering inside him for the past two weeks. Longer than that, if he was truthful. He had not been able to put Desdemona completely out of his mind since the night of his botched wedding.

He had known things were serious when he had realized that thoughts of her were interfering with his concentration. Under normal circumstances, nothing ever interfered with his concentration.

Stark gazed thoughtfully at Desdemona, wondering if he had misread the warmth in her eyes. He knew he was not very good at interpreting the various subtle sexual cues that women used. Nevertheless, he could have sworn that she was as interested in him as he was in her.

"Not to change the subject," Dane murmured, "but have you heard from Pamela yet?"

"Who?"

Three hours later Desdemona saw her two assistants out Stark's kitchen door. Henry went first with a load of glassware.

Vernon Tate, the new ice sculptor and all-around gofer, paused on the back step. He gave Desdemona a diffident smile. Everything Vernon did was diffident and unassuming, she reflected. In temperament, he was the exact opposite of Rafael. Desdemona found him a pleasant change of pace.

"I think that's everything, Miss Wainwright," Vernon said. "I double-checked the kitchen. Henry took care of the living room. Will you be needing anything else tonight?"

"No, we're through for the evening," Desdemona said. "You and Henry take the van back to Right Touch and unload. I'll follow you in my own car."

"Okay." Vernon tightened his grip on the carton of plates that he was holding. "It went well, don't you think? I mean, everyone seemed to have a good time."

47

"Everything went beautifully." Desdemona gave him a grateful smile. "I don't know what we would have done without you, Vernon."

It was the truth. Vernon had been nothing less than a godsend. He had wandered into her office early last week and shyly asked for a job. When she had glanced at his employment application she had seen the magic words *ice sculptor*. She had hired him on the spot.

He had proven to be an industrious worker, eager to do whatever needed to be done. Best of all, he was not a prima donna when it came to his art. He was ready, willing, and able to sculpt to order. When Desdemona requested swans, she got swans. When she wanted dolphins, she got dolphins.

And he never got last-minute casting calls because he was not involved in the theater.

He was quiet, self-effacing, and a sober dresser. His features were regular, albeit rather nondescript. He appeared to be in his late thirties. Both his hairline and his chin were receding. He didn't smile much, but neither did he frown. He walked with a slight stoop to his shoulders, as though he had once spent a lot of time hunched over a desk.

Vernon gave a jerky nod, obviously embarrassed by her fulsome thanks. "I sure needed this job. I'm glad you took a chance on me, Miss Wainwright. I'll see you later, okay?"

"Okay."

Vernon went down one step and paused again. "By the way, I've got the ice carvings ready for tomorrow's luncheon. Dolphins, just like you wanted."

"If they're anything like the ones you did for the Sumner-Bench reception on Sunday, I'll love them," Desdemona assured him.

"Don't worry, I've been workin' real hard on 'em."

Unlike Rafael, who had created his masterpieces at Right Touch, Vernon preferred to work off-site. He had apologetically explained to Desdemona that he needed privacy in order to do his best sculpting.

"Great. See you later, Vernon." Desdemona raised a hand to wave to Henry, who had just started the van's engine.

Henry waved back as he waited for Vernon to climb into the van.

Stark came up to stand behind Desdemona in the doorway. "No

offense, but the new man doesn't quite fit in with the rest of your staff. He's a little too normal."

"I know. Makes a nice change." Desdemona closed the kitchen door and turned around to face her client.

Her first instinct was to step back because Stark was standing much too close. She still found him overwhelming in close quarters. There was no way to retreat, however, because the door was a solid barrier behind her.

She looked up at him and caught her breath. Behind the lenses of his gold-framed glasses, his green eyes were lit with the heat of a banked fire.

In that moment she knew for certain that he wanted her.

The sensual awareness that jangled her senses whenever she was near Stark made her edgy. The sensation had grown more intense each time she saw him. She was unsure of what to do about it because the feelings were new to her. Her Wainwright intuition urged her to throw caution to the winds, but she hesitated.

It wasn't that she was completely lacking in experience where men were concerned. She was twenty-eight years old, after all. True, her family had always been overly protective, especially her stepbrother, Tony, but her matchmaking cousin and aunt had sent her off on a number of carefully selected dates.

Her Wainwright intuition had never so much as stirred, let alone voiced a strong opinion, in the presence of any of those handpicked males, however. And none of the men Juliet and Bess had chosen had ever made Desdemona's insides turn to warm mush the way Stark did.

It was unnerving. Exciting, but definitely unnerving.

In addition to dealing with her own chaotic feelings and the powerful proddings of her Wainwright intuition, Desdemona had another problem on her hands.

She was very conscious of the fact that it was much too early to anticipate any sort of meaningful relationship with Stark. She reminded herself again that he was a deeply sensitive man. He needed time to recover from the traumatic experience of being abandoned at the altar.

She took a deep breath and smiled brilliantly to mask her uncertainty and the longing that lay beneath it. "All clear." She waved a hand at the neat kitchen. "I think it went well, don't you?"

"Perfect." He gazed at her mouth with a distinctly brooding expression. "Everything's just perfect. You're the best idea I've had in a long time."

"I'm glad you're pleased with the services," she said briskly. "Now, then, according to my schedule, our next event isn't for another ten days."

"I've got a party Thursday night. Will you come with me?"

Alarm shot through her. "Thursday night? I don't have it on my schedule."

"That's because I'm not the one giving the party," Stark explained. "Someone else is giving it. I need a date."

"A date?" Desdemona repeated breathlessly. *A real date.* She felt a rush of heady excitement. He was asking her out on a real date. The moment of decision was upon her. Too soon. Much too soon. But she did not think she could bring herself to refuse.

Stark's black brows formed a solid line across the bridge of his nose. "Sort of. I'd rather not go alone, but I don't feel like digging up a real date. I just need an escort for the evening."

"Oh." Desdemona was crushed. He wanted a stand-in.

"It's still a little awkward," Stark said, apparently oblivious to her reaction. "Everyone I know is aware of what happened between me and Pamela. I don't want to spend the evening fielding questions or listening to sympathetic advice."

"I see."

"Hell, I don't want to go out at all, if you want the truth. But McCallum and my secretary have both told me that I should attend this damn party on Thursday."

"Uh-huh. A business thing, probably."

"Yeah." Stark ran a big hand through his hair. "If I were married, my wife would accompany me."

"Naturally." Desdemona's mouth suddenly felt very dry.

"But I don't have a wife."

"I know."

"What I've got is you. On retainer." Stark turned away without any warning. He peeled off his jacket and slung it across one of the counter stools. "I'll pay you the usual hourly rate, of course."

Desdemona gasped in shock. An instant later she was consumed with fury. "Right Touch does not provide escort services. I'm a caterer."

He glanced back at her over his shoulder as he loosened his tie. His eyes were unreadable. "The idea of attending the party with me doesn't appeal?"

"The idea of being paid for it bothers me." She was damned if she would let him turn her into a stand-in wife.

He smiled humorlessly. "How about doing it for free?"

"I beg your pardon?"

"Come with me to the party. I won't pay you, but I think that I can make it worth your while."

She glowered at him. "I don't understand."

"You can use the evening to make new business contacts, just as I'm going to do. Who knows? Maybe you'll find some clients. That's how it works, doesn't it? Social connections lead to business connections." He smiled encouragingly. "We can troll for business together."

Desdemona forced herself to project an outward calm. She was a woman in control. She would not pick up the nearest object and hurl it across the room.

"I'll have to check my schedule," she said grimly.

"You do that." His shoulders stiffened. He swung around and paced back across the kitchen to stand in front of her. With his unknotted tie and unbuttoned collar, he looked a good deal less civilized than he had a moment earlier. "See if you can manage to fit me in."

She blinked and stepped back quickly, coming up against the door once more. "Good grief. Don't tell me you're angry just because I don't know whether or not I'm free to accompany you to a business affair."

"Why the hell would I be angry?" He leaned close, reached out, and planted his wide palms on the door behind her, effectively caging her. "I've got no right to be angry, do I?"

"No, you certainly do not." Out of the corner of her eye she could not help but notice the sinewy strength of his wrists. Stark was no doubt capable of being dangerous under the right circumstances. She was a little surprised to discover that he did not inspire any genuine fear in her, merely a thrilling feminine wariness. "If anyone has a right to be annoyed, it's me."

"You've got no call to be mad, either. I'm offering you a chance to do some business."

"Business is just fine for me these days."

"Getting better all the time, isn't it? Thanks to me."

"I've never asked you to do me any favors," Desdemona said.

"If you attend this thing on Thursday with me, we'll be doing each other a favor. Let's call it an even trade."

"A trade?"

"Yeah. How about it?" His mouth curved coldly. "If you're *free*, that is?"

Desdemona felt goaded beyond endurance. "All right." She lifted her chin. "If I'm free."

"Anybody ever tell you that you drive a hell of a bargain, lady?"

"As a matter of fact—"

His mouth came down on hers with the impact of lava on snow. She went utterly still for the space of three lilting heartbeats. The world stopped while her senses frantically struggled to cope with the overpowering sensation of being kissed by Stark.

He kissed her as though she were the only living woman on earth. It was a sensually devastating experience.

While the rational side of Desdemona's brain scrambled to formulate an appropriate response, Wainwright intuition took over. Somewhere inside her a switch was turned on. Her feminine emergency backup system kicked in.

She wrapped her arms around Stark's neck and kissed him back.

He groaned, folded his arms around her, and clamped her against his chest. Desdemona felt as though she were being swallowed alive.

Stark shoved his fingers into the coil of her hair and tugged the black velvet band free. Then he gripped the back of her head and held her still while he deepened the kiss.

Desdemona clung to him, her senses reeling. Kissing Stark was everything she had known that it would be, a searing, mind-altering, earthshaking experience.

It struck her in a flash of insight that this glorious, indescribable thrill was similar to what three generations of Wainwrights must have felt every time they went on stage. Being the only one in the family who could not act, she had never experienced it until this moment.

Stark's hands moved down her back to cup her buttocks. He lifted her up against him.

Desdemona could hardly breathe. He was hard, solid, strong. Deliciously masculine. She moaned softly and inhaled his indescribable scent. No after-shave or cologne. Just Stark and the soap he used. Everything that was female in her responded to it.

She was vaguely aware of the room shifting around her. She realized that Stark was carrying her somewhere. Perhaps to the couch in the living room.

Or perhaps to his bedroom, a dark, mysterious place she had not yet seen.

Too soon, she thought. *Too soon*. He was not ready for this. He needed time.

Desdemona knew she had to do something before they both got too carried away by the seething passion.

Stark came to an abrupt halt. Desdemona felt the jolt that went through both of them. She realized that he had backed into the wooden work island positioned in the center of the kitchen.

"Damn," Stark muttered.

The interruption was timely if not particularly welcome. Desdemona sighed and reluctantly lifted her lashes. She felt bemused and disoriented.

"Maybe it's just as well," she whispered.

"You're right. This'll do."

"What on earth?" Before she realized his intention, he turned around and sat her down on the edge of the work island.

He parted her legs and moved between them. With quick, deft movements he unzipped her dress. The bodice fell to her waist. An instant later his hand closed gently around one soft breast. Desdemona was shocked to the core by the desire that lanced through her.

"*Stark*." She clung to him as he kissed her throat. "This isn't what I meant."

"It's okay. It's clean. I saw that new guy on your staff wipe it off earlier."

"Yes, I know, but—" She broke off when he put his hands on her upper thighs. Her skin burned beneath the fine fabric of her dress. "Oh, my God."

He bit her ear with exquisite care. Desdemona shivered. Then his hand was under the edge of her dress, moving higher. He cupped her for a few seconds. She tightened her legs around him. His thighs were as hard as stone.

"I like that," he said. He seized a fistful of her hair and buried his face in it. "And I like this, too. You smell good."

The raw sensuality in his voice did strange and dangerous things to Desdemona. She heard something clatter on the kitchen floor. One of her black shoes had come off.

He pushed her backward until she was lying on top of the island, her legs dangling over the edge.

He leaned over her, pinning her to the wooden surface. His mouth sought the curve of her throat once more. His heavily aroused body was pressed against her. She could feel the hard, unyielding shape of his manhood. He stroked the crotch of her panties.

"You're soaking wet." He sounded dazed with wonder.

She was excruciatingly aware that he was right. For some reason the evidence of her own arousal brought back a measure of reality. "Stark, please. This has gone far enough."

He raised his head and looked down at her with glittering eyes. "What?"

"This is—" She levered herself up on one elbow and pushed hair out of her eyes. "This is all happening much too fast."

"Sorry," he said hoarsely. "I'll slow down if that's what you want. We've got all night."

"Wait." She braced one hand against his massive shoulder. "I mean we're really going too fast. For heaven's sake, Stark, one month ago you were on the verge of marrying another woman."

Confusion flared in his intent gaze. "But I didn't marry anyone else. There's nothing to stop me from making love to you tonight."

"Yes, I know, but that's not quite the point I'm trying to make. Let's look at the motivation for this, uh, incident."

"Incident?"

"We have to try to understand what's really happening here. Now, then, you were recently traumatized by the rejection you received at the hands of your fiancée."

"*Ex*-fiancée," he said grimly.

"Whatever. I suspect you were also very angry, too. Perfectly natural."

"You think so?" His voice turned unnaturally soft.

"Of course." Desdemona struggled to a sitting position. Stark did not move from between her splayed thighs. "That sort of thing is very hard on the ego."

"Are you going to turn this into a counseling session?" he demanded in disbelief.

"I told you, I think we should take a close look at your motivations here."

"Forget it. There is nothing complicated about my motivations."

She ignored that. "I'm afraid that what actually made you want to kiss me tonight was a need to prove that you can still make a woman respond to you."

He eyed her with a brooding stare. "You do want me, don't you? I didn't get that part wrong, did I?"

"That's got nothing to do with this," she assured him.

"My mistake," he said roughly. "I thought maybe the fact that your panties are soaking wet had something to do with this *incident.*"

She felt herself turn scarlet. "Stark, for goodness' sake."

"You think I'm making love to you on a countertop here in the kitchen because I'm trying to prove to myself that I'm not completely washed up as a man?"

"I never implied that you were washed up or that you had to prove anything. I'm just not sure that you're doing this for the right reasons."

"I don't believe this. You want me and I want you. We're mature, consenting adults. Neither of us is involved with anyone else. What better reasons could there be?"

Desdemona reached the end of her tether. "Never mind. If you can't figure that out for yourself, I'm not going to waste my time explaining it to you. Will you kindly let me off this table?"

"Damn it, I really hate that," Stark said.

"Hate what?"

"I hate it when a woman avoids a direct answer to a simple, straightforward question and then gets mad about the question."

"Tough. If you don't like the way I answer your questions, you can stop asking them. Move. It's very difficult trying to conduct a rational conversation with a man who is standing between my legs."

"What's rational about this conversation?" Stark asked.

"Nothing. I said *move*."

He looked down at her splayed thighs and then slowly, reluctantly stepped back a pace. Desdemona clamped her legs together smartly and jumped down off the island.

She promptly lost her balance when her shoeless foot touched the floor.

Her knees, still unsteady from the effects of Stark's lovemaking, gave way. She staggered and grabbed for the edge of the island.

Stark caught her easily. "I've got you." He steadied her. "Are you okay?"

Desdemona wanted to scream. She managed to hold onto her self-control with a great effort of will. "Of course, I'm okay. I just stumbled, that's all."

"Right." He released her as if she were too hot to hold.

Desdemona hurriedly fumbled with her zipper. Stark leaned back against the island, folded his arms, and watched her. He did not offer to assist her.

When she was finished, Desdemona looked up and met his eyes. "I'm sorry."

"So am I."

"I just don't think you're ready for another relationship yet."

"Thank you for sharing your views on the subject with me," Stark said in a dangerously even tone. "When and if you ever do consider me ready for another relationship, would you be amenable to having one with me?"

Longing welled up within her. "When you think about it logically, we're really not a very good match, you know."

"I know," he said quite casually. "I've already considered that problem."

She blinked. "You have?"

"Sure. You're from a theatrical family. That means you're inclined to be temperamental and emotional. Volatile, even. What happened just now proves it."

"I see," she said acidly. "A person such as myself would no doubt introduce an element of *chaos* into your life. We certainly wouldn't want that, would we? Chaos theory is all well and good when you're working with it on a computer, but who wants the real thing."

"My work is in the field of complex structures, not chaos." His gaze sharpened. "I usually don't get involved with women like you. They tend to be difficult."

"Is that so? Well, let me tell you something. I generally don't get involved with cold-blooded, cynical, overly logical males such as yourself. They tend to be boring."

"The fact that your panties are still damp doesn't impact your thinking on the matter?"

"Will you stop harping on the condition of my underwear?" she said through her teeth. "It's rude."

"Sorry. It's all I've got to cling to at the moment. So to speak."

"That's it. I've had it." Desdemona whirled around and started toward the door that led to the living room. "I quit. You can find yourself another caterer."

"You can't quit." Stark strode after her. "You're on retainer. We signed a contract."

"So what?" She opened the door of the hall closet and found her purse on one of the beautifully well-organized shelves. "You may put a lot of faith in contracts, Stark, but I've got news for you. Contracts were made to be broken."

"You sure as hell didn't take that attitude a month ago when you insisted that I pay you for my cancelled wedding reception."

A pang of guilt shot through her. "That's got nothing to do with this."

"A contract is a contract." He caught up with her at the front door. "Damn it, I swear I won't ever mention your panties again."

She glowered at him. "You are very possibly the most socially inept man that I have ever met."

"But I'm also one of the smartest men you've ever met. That means I'm educable. Give me a chance, Desdemona."

She groaned in sheer frustration. "This is insane."

"Look, I'll admit I'm not good at relationships," Stark said. "All of mine seem to end with me standing alone at an altar. Obviously I've been doing something wrong in the past. I've done some thinking about the problem, and I believe I know what I'm doing wrong."

"I don't think I want to hear this," Desdemona said.

He paid no attention. "I've been too results-oriented. It's only natural for me."

"What the heck does that mean?"

His eyes narrowed in a considering scowl. "It's true that my specialty is finding practical applications for theories derived from the science of complexity. I'm in that field because something in me wants to find patterns. I like to produce useful results. Do you understand?"

"I think so. You want to bring order out of chaos."

"I suppose that's one way of putting it. The point is, I tend to take the same approach in everything I do. I like to identify patterns. Establish goals. Produce results."

She eyed him uneasily. "This is the approach you've used in your past relationships?"

He shrugged. "I suppose so."

"Obviously it hasn't worked."

"No," he admitted. "But I'd like to try a different approach with you."

"What does that mean? That I'm going to be some sort of experiment?"

He looked pleased at her perception. "In a way. With you, I'm going to try to let myself go with the flow. For the first time in my life, I'm going to go into a relationship without being overly logical about it."

"Be still, my beating heart."

"Hell, this is coming out all wrong. I knew I shouldn't have started talking. I'm no good at talking."

"You noticed?"

"You've got a right to be annoyed," Stark said. "I'm really screwing this up, aren't I?"

"Uh-huh."

He braced one hand against the wall and regarded her with an expression of savage concentration. "Look, I've apologized. If I swear that I won't try to rush things between us again, that I'll give you plenty of space, that I won't pressure you, will you go to that party on Thursday night with me?"

Desdemona hesitated. Saying yes would probably be one of the dumbest things she had ever done in her life. On the other hand, her panties were still damp. She had never met a man who had such a lethal effect on her senses. And the siren's call of the Wainwright intuition was singing in her blood.

"All right," Desdemona said.

Relief flared in Stark's eyes. "You mean it?"

"Yes. Provided you stick to your promise."

"I will. And you're still my official caterer?"

"Business is business, isn't it?" Desdemona gave him a flippant smile that she hoped would hide her shaky nerves.

"Sure." Stark's expression was one of bone-deep satisfaction. "Business is business."

5

*I*t had been a near thing.

He'd come close to blowing it, Stark thought the following evening. He had a rare talent for screwing up his private life.

Stark sat in his darkened study and contemplated the elegant, colorful, seemingly random pattern he had created on the computer screen.

The apparent chaos was a thing of beauty to his eyes. It flowed endlessly from one fascinating shape into another. Impelled by a hidden mathematical imperative, it evolved, changed, and reformed itself until the original pattern disintegrated into nothingness.

But Stark knew how to retrieve the original pattern, and that was the secret that was going to make ARCANE the most sophisticated encryption and decryption software in the world. At least for a while.

Given the rapid pace of software design development, no single program could hope to remain state-of-the-art forever. ARCANE would need to be constantly improved and updated. But Stark was willing to bet that it would be a long time before anyone caught up with ARCANE.

Stark Security Systems stood to make a great deal of money off the security program. The biggest customer would be the U.S. Government, which wanted it to protect several of its most sensitive computer systems and those of its high-tech research labs.

Stark intended to plow the profits from ARCANE into the development of a variety of other security systems that would, in turn, be suited for the private sector.

It was all so beautifully complicated and yet so astoundingly simple. A perfect example of the dynamics of complex structures.

Stark wished he could employ the same mathematics on Desdemona.

She was entirely different from any other woman he had ever held in his arms. Not that there had been all that many. Long periods of celibacy punctuated by a few sputtering affairs had marked his adult love life thus far. He had not enjoyed the instability of the pattern. He wanted a predictable relationship, just as he wanted predictability in his software designs.

Marriage had, therefore, been the obvious solution. Except that he hadn't been able to implement it.

It was not as though he hadn't done his best to select a suitable mate. He had applied all of his powers of logic and rational thinking to the problem of obtaining one. But somehow, something always went wrong.

Desdemona had been right when she had guessed that she would be an experiment for him. She definitely did not fit his profile of a suitable wife. But he wanted her with a sense of deep, restless urgency that was startlingly new and excruciatingly intense.

Stark promised himself that he would not go into the relationship with the notion of making it permanent. That way lay disaster. For once in his life, he would allow the whims of fortune and fate to carry him where they wished.

It was a disturbing but strangely exciting thought.

Stark gazed at the glowing screen, aware that his whole body was already stirring in anticipation of Thursday night.

It occurred to him that his rationalization of an affair with Desdemona might simply be the by-product of another extended period of celibacy. The truth was, it had been a long time since he had gotten laid.

Pamela had been too busy for sex for at least two months before the wedding date. And things hadn't been what one would call lively between them before that.

Looking back on the string of excuses he'd heard during those last weeks before the wedding, Stark glumly acknowledged that he should have had a clue that something was amiss. But, as usual, he hadn't figured out that something had gone wrong in the relationship until he had found himself standing alone at the altar.

Thursday morning Desdemona was hunched over her computer when Henry and Kirsten swept through the doorway of her office.

"Be with you in a second." Desdemona nibbled anxiously on her lower lip as she hit the enter key to store the latest version of a luncheon menu featuring spinach and feta cheese in phyllo pastry. "Oh, damn."

"What's wrong?" Kirsten asked.

"I think I just lost the earlier version of this menu. I wanted to save it, too, in case I change my mind." Desdemona glared at the screen. "I wish Tony were here. He's the only one who actually understands this stupid machine."

"Forget the computer," Kirsten said cheerfully. "I've got a surprise for you."

Desdemona's attention was still on the menu. She was not overly fond of computers. The only reason she had one in her office was because Tony had talked her into it. Tony was fascinated by high-tech hardware. Whenever he was around, he was forever fiddling with her software. "My birthday isn't until next week."

"This isn't a birthday present," Henry informed her grandly. "It's a thank-you gift."

Desdemona glanced up from her work and saw that Kirsten held a large box in her arms.

Kirsten and Henry were both grinning from ear to ear. That was nothing new. They had been wearing similar expressions since Desdemona had agreed to cosign the loan papers for Exotica Erotica two weeks earlier.

"A gift? For me?" Distracted at last, Desdemona studied the box with interest. "That was very thoughtful of you. But you really shouldn't have. You ought to be putting all of your money into Exotica Erotica."

"This stuff didn't cost much," Kirsten assured her.

"Free samples, for the most part," Henry explained as he opened the box.

"Free samples of what?" Desdemona asked.

"The products I'm going to stock in Exotica Erotica." Kirsten reached into the box and lifted out a black leather garter belt trimmed with steel studs. "There's a matching brassiere in here somewhere. Also a darling mask and a red and black harness."

Desdemona stared at the garter belt. "Oh, dear."

"Two different sizes of battery-powered personal vibrators." Henry produced the small, anatomically correct implements with a flourish. "And a selection of massage balms and oils."

Desdemona felt herself turn very pink. "I don't know what to say."

"I threw in some feathers, some little velvet whips, and one of these things." Kirsten held up a device that consisted of two small balls linked by a string. A tag dangled from it. "Instructions are attached, as you can see. There's also a supply of condoms in assorted colors and some strawberry-flavored lubricant in here somewhere."

Desdemona was speechless. She gazed helplessly at the items in the box. "Uh . . ."

"Don't say a word," Kirsten said warmly. "I want you to have these things."

Desdemona cleared her throat and finally found her voice. "Won't you need this stuff as floor samples or something?"

"Kirsten wants you to have them." Henry fixed her with a determined expression. "And she's got the right idea. It's time you put some fun into your life, Desdemona. You live like a nun. You're practically married to Right Touch."

"I'm perfectly content the way I am," Desdemona said quickly. "Honestly I am."

"Impossible," Henry said. "You're a Wainwright. You were born for passion."

"Passion is dangerous these days."

He held up the box of condoms. "So you're going to be careful."

"It takes two to tango," Desdemona said weakly.

"Juliet and Aunt Bess have someone new for you to meet," Kirsten said. "An actor who's working on the Eastside in a dinner theater production of *Camelot*."

Desdemona dropped her head into her hands. "Not another blind date."

"Okay, so it's an ancient musical, and he's not exactly the lead," Henry said, not without sympathy. "You can't have everything."

"I know."

"Juliet says the guy's straight, single, and employed," Kirsten put in. "Bess knows his family. They're theater people, too. What more do you want?"

"This is getting embarrassing," Desdemona said. "Juliet's and Bess's blind dates never work out. Furthermore, I don't need any assistance with my love life."

Juliet came through the office door in typical Wainwright fashion, as though she were making an entrance onstage. "Once you get yourself a love life, we'll all bow out."

"For heaven's sake," Desdemona muttered.

Before anyone could pursue the argument, Desdemona's Aunt Bess swooped into the already crowded office. A tall, statuesque woman in her early sixties, she had flashing dark eyes and a wealth of silver hair.

Bess Wainwright had played everyone from Lady Macbeth to Guinevere in the course of her long career. She and her husband, Augustus, were officially retired, but they still found time for the occasional summer stock or dinner theater production, just as Desdemona's parents did.

There was an old Wainwright family saying: *You can take the Wainwright out of the theater, but you can't take the theater out of the Wainwright.*

"Desdemona, my dear," Bess said firmly, "you've simply got to get over this stage fright."

"Stage fright?" Desdemona stared at her aunt. "That's ridiculous. I don't have stage fright. I've never even been on stage except when I took acting lessons."

"I know stage fright when I see it," Bess said. "My dear, Augustus and I had a long talk. We concluded that your problem is that you put all your energy and Wainwright passion into Right Touch and none of it into your private life. There must be a reason for that."

Desdemona was exasperated. "The reason is that it takes a lot of energy and passion to run a business. At least I've got something to show for it."

"It's not normal," Bess insisted. "Not for a Wainwright."

"I haven't noticed anyone in the family complaining," Desdemona retorted.

Bess sighed. "We all admit that it's useful for someone in the family to have a steady day job, especially a business that can employ other members of the family. But that doesn't make it normal."

"For heaven's sake, Aunt Bess . . ."

"You're wasting the best years of your life on a business, for God's sake," Bess declared in ringing tones.

Juliet lounged on a corner of the desk. "Either you're just being too picky, or Aunt Bess is right when she says you have stage fright. You've got to come out of the wings and go out in front of the lights, Desdemona. You're a Wainwright."

Desdemona had had enough. She shot to her feet and confronted her well-intentioned relatives. "It may interest all of you to know that I have a date tonight."

Everyone stared at her in astonishment.

Juliet recovered first. "With who?"

Desdemona blushed. "Sam Stark."

Henry's mouth fell open. "Stark of Stark Security Systems?"

"Yes."

"The nerd?" Juliet's eyes widened in horror.

Desdemona rounded on her instantly. "I said there was to be no nerd-bashing around here."

"I beg your pardon," Juliet muttered. "Let me rephrase that. Are we talking about the Super Client?"

"We're talking about Stark," Desdemona snapped. "Just plain Sam Stark."

Henry groaned. "Stark, the human computer."

Desdemona turned on him. "He is not a computer."

Henry held up a hand. "Sorry."

"I'm sure he's a very nice man, dear," Bess said soothingly, "and a valued client. But you're a Wainwright. Wainwrights don't get involved with people who aren't in the theater. It isn't natural."

"I don't believe this," Juliet said. "What can you possibly see in him?"

Desdemona lifted her chin. "He's honest. He's sincere. He's trustworthy."

"How do you know that?" Bess shot back.

"Wainwright intuition," Desdemona said proudly.

There wasn't much anyone could say in response.

"Honest, sincere, and trustworthy." Henry made a face. "He sounds like a St. Bernard."

"He sounds dull," Juliet said. "But I suppose you've got to start somewhere. Just be careful, okay? Don't get too involved, because there can't possibly be any future for you with him."

"That's right," Bess said quickly. "He's not your type, dear."

Kirsten nudged the box full of samples. "Take this stuff home and keep it handy. Who knows? Maybe after you experiment a bit with the android, you'll want to move on to a real flesh-and-blood male."

Shortly before midnight, Desdemona sat in the front seat of Stark's car and watched as the locked gate of her apartment building rose. She was experiencing the same sense of anticipation that she always did when she watched the curtain go up on a new play.

But for the first time in her life she felt as though she were actually on stage, a real character in the drama, an *actor*, not part of the audience. This was the way a Wainwright was meant to feel, she decided.

A chill of exciting dread shot through her. Stage fright? she wondered.

She hoped that she had not made a mistake by inviting Stark in for coffee.

"You can park over there." Desdemona indicated an empty parking stall marked *visitor*.

"All right."

Silence descended as Stark eased the car into position. There had been a lot of silence on the way home from the cocktail party. They were like a couple of tongue-tied teenagers returning from a first date, Desdemona thought.

"Your car will be safe here," she assured him.

Stark nodded once and switched off the engine. He opened his door, got out, and walked around the rear fender to open her door.

Desdemona stood and smiled tentatively. "I thought the evening went well."

"Yes." Stark closed the door and took her arm. He walked her to the elevator.

More silence descended. The elevator arrived. The doors opened. Desdemona got in and automatically started to do her deep-breathing exercises. Stark followed her and stood quietly as she punched the button for the fifth floor.

The doors closed. Desdemona focused intently on the bank of indicator lights.

Stark frowned. "Are you all right?"

"Yes. I have a little trouble in elevators, that's all," Desdemona said tightly.

"Claustrophobic?"

"Yes."

"All your life?" Stark asked.

"Since I was five. I can just manage in an elevator because I can count the floors, and I know I'll only be confined for a few minutes. I have a totally irrational fear of getting trapped in one of these things."

Stark put an arm around her shoulders. Desdemona stiffened briefly and then found herself relaxing against him. The warmth of his body and the weight of his arm were oddly soothing.

Together they gazed at the indicator lights.

The doors opened on the fifth floor. Desdemona breathed her customary sigh of relief and fairly leaped out of the elevator.

Stark followed. "Which way?"

"To the left. Number 506."

He held out his hand for her key. Desdemona hesitated and then surrendered it to him. She was surprised by the intimacy of the small act.

He took the key and her arm, went down the hall to number 506 and opened the door.

Desdemona stepped into her darkened apartment and groped for the light switch. Before she could find it, something moved in the darkness.

She switched on the light and shrieked at the masked apparition that materialized out of the shadows.

"Welcome home, sweetheart," the creature hissed.

Desdemona instinctively flung herself backward and came up hard against Stark's unyielding frame.

The masked figure came toward her, arms outstretched. It was clad in a steel-studded red and black leather vestlike garment, black jeans, and boots. Eyes glinted behind the leather mask. Leather-gloved hands gripped a small whip.

"What the hell?" Stark did not even flinch as Desdemona crashed into him.

He shifted her aside with a swiftness that shocked the already stunned Desdemona. In one smooth movement, he shoved her out into the hall, then stepped into the path of the masked monstrosity.

He kicked out hard and fast, catching the creature in the ribcage.

"*Shit.*" The apparition crumpled, gasping for air. The whip bounced on the hardwood floor.

Desdemona gripped the edge of the doorway. "Stark, are you all right?"

"Yes." Stark didn't look at her. He walked toward his victim. "Call 911."

"For Christ's sake," the masked man managed hoarsely, "are you crazy? Desdemona, it's me. Do something before this idiot calls the cops."

"What on earth?" Desdemona stepped back into the hall and peered closely at the figure on the floor. "Tony, is that you?"

"Of course, it's me. Who the hell else would it be?" Tony glared up at Stark through the eyeholes of the black mask. "Call off your pit bull, here, will you?"

Stark looked at Desdemona. "You know this guy?"

"Yes, I do. That's my stepbrother. I hope you haven't hurt him."

"May have cracked a rib," Tony gasped.

"Oh, no." Desdemona started toward him. She halted when she heard a couple of doors open in the hallway behind her.

She glanced over her shoulder and saw two of her neighbors.

Miriam Eckerby, clutching the lapels of a faded housecoat, her gray hair in pink rollers, looked out through the crack in her door. She stared at Tony. "What's going on here? Want me to call the cops?"

"No, no, it's okay." Desdemona smiled apologetically. "Someone arranged a little surprise for me. I overreacted."

"No one ever bothers to surprise me, anymore," Miriam muttered. "Haven't had a real surprise since my husband, Clive, died. He didn't mind a bit of leather now and again, either." She banged her door shut.

Christopher Peters, owner of an art gallery located not far from

Desdemona's shop, appeared in the doorway of 508. His robe was fashioned of embossed black silk. The rings on his fingers glinted in the hall light. "Are you all right, darling," he demanded in his artificial British accent.

"I'm fine, really," Desdemona said quickly. "It's my brother. I wasn't expecting him. Sorry for the disturbance."

Desdemona slammed the door and whirled around to confront her visitor. "Tony, what on earth did you think you were doing?"

"It was just a little joke." Tony sat up cautiously. He winced and put a leather-clad hand to his ribs.

"Why are you wearing all that stuff?" she asked.

"Found it in your bedroom." Tony sucked in a breath and staggered to his feet. "Where did you get it, anyway? No offense, but it isn't you."

"Long story. Oh, Tony, it's so good to see you." She ran forward and threw her arms around him in welcome. "But you should have called. I wasn't expecting you."

"Ouch." Tony hugged her gingerly. "Take it easy. I'm still thinking of suing the pit bull."

"His name is Stark." Desdemona said. She stepped back and smiled. "Stark, this is my stepbrother, Anthony Wainwright."

Stark said nothing. Tony ignored the introduction. Neither man offered to shake hands.

Tony removed his mask, revealing his classic Wainwright features. He pointedly turned his back on Stark and looked at Desdemona. "I just got in from L.A."

"I thought you were busy with the production of that soap opera." She searched his face anxiously. "Oh, Tony, did something go wrong?"

"I'll tell you all about it later." Tony slanted Stark a speculative glance, as though sizing him up. Then he turned back to Desdemona with a familiar smile. "Mind if I bunk here for the night? I gave up my apartment when I left town, remember?"

Desdemona realized that Stark was watching her in stoic silence, waiting for her to decide which man would leave and which would stay. "Well . . ."

"Look, if it's a problem," Tony said sarcastically, "I'll find another place to sleep. Wouldn't want to interrupt anything here."

Desdemona flushed. "I'm sorry, Tony. Any chance you could go to Mom and Dad's apartment? They're still in Arizona."

He scowled, obviously startled by her decision. "You and the pit bull got something going, is that it? I'm surprised. He doesn't look like your type."

"Stark is a client of Right Touch," Desdemona said quickly.

"Since when do you bring your clients home with you?" Tony asked.

Stark folded his arms across his chest and propped one shoulder against the nearest wall. He regarded Tony with a cold, unblinking gaze. "Since she realized that a woman living alone can never be too careful."

"You think it's your job to protect her?" Tony jerked at the fastenings of the red and black studded vest. "Think again. I'm the one who saved her life when she was five years old, pal. I've been taking care of her ever since. She doesn't need a knight in shining armor. She's got me."

"Please, Tony, don't make a scene," Desdemona pleaded. "This is awkward enough as it is."

"Yeah, I can see that." Tony held up the leather vest, mask, and velvet whip. "Guess your big brother is in the way tonight, huh?"

"Tony . . ."

"You've changed during the past few months, kid," Tony tossed the leather gear aside in disgust. "Tell me, is the pit bull, here, the guy who introduced you to the fancy sex toys?"

"That's enough, Tony," Desdemona said sharply.

"Which one of you uses the whip?" Tony drawled.

"We like to take turns," Stark said.

6

*S*tark closed the door on the sullen-faced Tony. He took some satisfaction from the knowledge that the other man was temporarily out of the picture even though he suspected that the real battle had just begun. He watched as Desdemona hurried around the room, scooping up the leather accessories.

"This is so embarrassing," she said. "I don't know what to say."

Stark eyed the erotic gear piled high in her arms. "Say you'll get your locks changed as soon as possible."

She gave him a quick, surprised glance. "Because of Tony? There's no need. He's family."

"A stepbrother, you said?"

"That's right."

"Not a blood relation, then?" Stark asked carefully.

She scowled. "Well, I guess not, if you're speaking in the strictly technical sense of the word."

"I usually speak in the strictly technical sense."

"Tony is my brother in every way that counts," Desdemona said forcefully. "We grew up together."

Stark realized he had struck a nerve. "I didn't intend to start an argument about it. I just wondered, that's all."

Desdemona eyed him uncertainly for a moment and then appeared to relent. Her eyes softened. "My mother married his father when I was five. Tony was nine at the time. His mother had died when he was a baby."

"He said he saved your life when you were five years old."

Shadows swirled in Desdemona's turquoise eyes, the same dark shadows Stark had seen there a few minutes earlier when they had stood together in the close confines of the elevator.

"It's true." Desdemona turned away quickly. "But it's another long story. I'd really rather not go into it tonight. Excuse me while I put these things away."

Stark watched her hurry across the hardwood floor. When she disappeared behind the sliding panel of a shoji screen, he switched his attention to the rest of the loft.

The first thing he noticed was that there were no defined rooms. Raw brick walls formed the perimeter on three sides. Windows lined the entire front of the loft. Opaque shoji screens provided privacy for the bedroom area. A waist-high counter made of glass bricks marked off the kitchen. The bath was concealed behind more glass bricks and another shoji screen.

It was an open, airy, unconfined living space. A good place for a woman who did not like to spend too much time in small, close places such as elevators.

Stark walked around the corner of the low, glass brick counter and found the shiny black espresso machine. He located the dark-roasted coffee in a glass jar nearby.

Stark studied the machine for a moment. It was similar to the one he owned. He was good with high-tech gadgets.

He went to work.

"Whew. What a way to end an evening." Desdemona gave him an apologetic smile as she emerged from behind the shoji screen. "For a Wainwright, Tony sometimes exhibits lousy timing. Here, let me make the coffee. You're supposed to be my guest."

"I'm almost finished." Stark pulled a lever. The espresso machine hissed and steamed like a small, electronic dragon.

"So I see." Desdemona smiled uncertainly. "Okay, thanks." She sat down on one of the stools on the other side of the kitchen counter.

"Your stepbrother said something about having just returned from L.A."

"Yes. He went down there to work in a new soap. The fact that he's back after only three months means something probably went wrong. Launching a new soap opera is a very iffy project."

"I wouldn't know."

"Hollywood is a dreadful town for a true actor," Desdemona confided. "Definitely no place for a Wainwright. Wainwrights are theater people, not movie or television people."

"There's a difference?" Stark asked.

"Of course." Desdemona looked shocked. "For three generations Wainwrights have been on the legitimate stage. None of them has ever gone to Hollywood."

"Until Tony tried it?"

"The whole family hated to see him get involved in television, but he wanted to take a shot at it." Desdemona sighed. "And since nothing else has ever really worked for him, we all kept our fingers crossed that this time he'd find himself."

"In Hollywood?" Stark filled one tiny espresso cup. "That doesn't seem very likely. I've always thought of Hollywood as a place where people go to get lost."

Desdemona wrinkled her nose. "That's what Uncle Augustus said. Still, we had hopes. Tony has been growing increasingly frustrated for years. Nothing he has ever tried has succeeded. I worry about him. We all do."

Stark set the espresso cups down on the counter. "Did you ever take up acting as a profession?"

"I tried. Lord knows I tried. Took courses in fine arts. Took acting lessons. But eventually I had to face the fact that I was the only one in the family without any talent. It was hard for me to accept. More than anything else in the world, I wanted to hold up the Wainwright family tradition."

"But you're not exactly a true Wainwright, are you?" Stark pointed out softly.

Her eyes turned fierce. "I most certainly am a true Wainwright. I've been a true Wainwright since I was five years old."

"Take it easy. I didn't mean to upset you. I was just trying to get the facts straight. Were you adopted?"

"Yes." Desdemona's tone was frosty. "My name was legally changed to Wainwright."

"You said your mother married your stepfather when you were a little kid. Did your real father die?"

"Before I was born." Desdemona sipped espresso. "Car accident."

"So you and your mother were alone until you were five?"

"No. Not exactly." She looked down at the dark, rich coffee.

Stark got the distinct impression that she was sidestepping the explanation. That only made him all the more curious. "Your mother remarried twice, then?"

Desdemona hesitated. Then she shrugged. "A couple of years after my father died, she married his business partner, George Northstreet. He wasn't right in the head, but she didn't know that at first." A drop of espresso spilled over the edge of her cup. "Not until he began to have violent outbursts. He went into therapy. The doctor said he was making progress. But then he started to hurt Mom."

Stark went cold. "And you?"

Desdemona clutched the espresso cup so tightly that her fingertips blanched. "When he turned on me, Mom gave up on therapy. She packed me up, and we left in the middle of the night. I remember her telling me that we had to be very quiet. I was terrified."

"Sweet Jesus."

"I was so afraid of George Northstreet, afraid that I couldn't protect my mother from him, afraid of what he might do to me. My only clear memories of that time in my life have to do with being afraid. I don't like to think about it."

"Chaos," Stark said quietly.

"What?"

"The sense of fear must have seemed like a kind of chaos to a small child."

"I suppose you could say that."

"Where did you and your mother go when you left Northstreet?"

"California." The shadows retreated from Desdemona's eyes. She smiled. "Mom is a costume designer as well as an actress. She got work in a little theater down there that was doing a Shakespeare festival."

"Is that where you met the Wainwrights?"

"Yes. They took us under their wing. Made us part of their family. Mom and Benedick Wainwright fell in love."

"And you got a new name."

Desdemona nodded. "I wanted a whole new name to go with my new life. I wanted to be a real Wainwright. Everyone in the family has names from characters in Shakespearean plays, so I chose Desdemona."

"Any particular reason?" Stark asked.

"I just liked the sound of it."

"This isn't exactly my area, but wasn't Desdemona an innocent, faithful wife whose husband, Othello, didn't trust her?" Stark asked thoughtfully. "As I recall, she came to a bad end."

"I know." Desdemona made a face. "I told you, I was only five at the time, and I liked the sound of it. I admit that if I had it to do all over again, I might have chosen another name. Helena, maybe, from *All's Well That Ends Well*."

"So your mother and Northstreet eventually got divorced?"

"Mom started the paperwork, but Northstreet died before it was finished," Desdemona said quietly.

"How did he die?"

"He shot himself in the head." Desdemona shifted slightly, as though shaking off a dark, smothering cloak. "Look, if you don't mind, I'd like to change the subject."

"Sure." There was more to the story, Stark thought. But he sensed that he had pushed far enough for one evening.

He was vaguely surprised that he had probed at all. It wasn't like him to go digging into someone else's private life. He had always guarded his own privacy well and respected it in others. But for some reason he needed to know everything about Desdemona. Sooner or later, he promised himself, he would get all the answers.

Desdemona gave him a determined smile. "Enough about me. Where did you learn that neat trick you used on poor Tony? It looked like some kind of martial arts maneuver."

"It is."

Desdemona tilted her head to one side. "I don't think of you as the physical type."

Stark gazed at her without comment.

She blushed. "I mean, you look physically strong, but I don't think

75

of you as the kind of man who would study the martial arts. I see you as a brainy, scientific type. More intellectually oriented, if you know what I mean."

"I also lift a few weights," Stark said dryly.

Desdemona's eyes skimmed over his shoulders. Blatant feminine approval gleamed in the blue-green depths. "Now that I can believe."

Stark felt himself grow unaccountably warm. "I don't spend all of my time in front of a computer screen," he said gruffly.

"What, exactly, did you do before you came to Seattle? Your ex-fiancée said something about a high-tech think tank."

Stark raised his brows. "You and Pamela discussed me?"

"Well, yes. Sort of. Only casually, if you know what I mean."

"No," Stark said. "I don't know what you mean."

"Never mind." Desdemona gave him an overly bright smile. "It was nothing. Just something Miss Bedford mentioned in the course of a business discussion."

"A business discussion," Stark repeated in a deliberately neutral tone.

"Right."

"About me."

"No, not about you. About your wedding reception plans." Desdemona waved that aside. "Tell me about the think tank."

"It's called the Rosetta Institute."

Desdemona's eyes widened. "I get it. Named after the Rosetta stone? The artifact that gave the first clue to deciphering the Egyptian hieroglyphics?"

"Yes, that's right. The Rosetta Institute is a small, loosely knit group of people who work in the science of complex structures."

"You mean chaos theory? I've heard of that."

"It's a lousy catchphrase," Stark said, irritated. "I prefer the term 'complexity.' Chaos implies absolute meaninglessness. Complexity, on the other hand, exists at the edge of chaos, a frontier where there is still meaning. There are patterns in even the most complex systems. They're just hard to find and identify, that's all."

"What did you do at this Rosetta Institute?"

"My specialty was the study and development of encryption techniques. Most of the projects I worked on were tailored for intelligence and research applications."

"Wow. That's impressive. Were you a government agent of some kind? Did you help track down terrorists and hijackers?"

"Hell, no," Stark muttered. "At the most, I occasionally acted as a consultant on technical matters."

"Oh."

Stark smiled. "Disappointed?"

"No, just curious." Desdemona tilted her head to one side. "So why did you lift weights and learn the martial arts stuff?"

"The Institute is located in the Colorado foothills," Stark explained patiently. "It was a long drive to Denver or Boulder or anywhere else for that matter. There wasn't a whole heck of a lot to do except work. But sometimes a person needs a break. When I did, I worked out with weights and took the classes in martial arts."

She gave him an ingenuous look. "That's what you did for fun?"

"No," Stark said. "For fun, I worked."

"Right. You worked."

"I use the physical stuff to clear my mind."

"An antidote for stress," Desdemona said wisely.

"You could say that."

She gave him a mischievous look from beneath her lashes. "Were there a lot of female scientists and engineers at the Rosetta Institute?"

"Some. Not many. Why?"

"Would you say you lived a cloistered existence?"

"Cloistered?" Stark had the feeling that he was being teased, but he wasn't certain what to do about it. "I'm not tracking here."

"Okay, I'll spell it out." Desdemona braced her elbows on the counter and rested her chin on her folded hands. "Did you have any special female friends at the Institute?"

It dawned on him that she was asking about his past relationships. The not-so-subtle inquiry caught him off guard because he was not accustomed to discussions of this sort.

"Let me get this straight," Stark said cautiously. "You want to know if I had an affair with a research physicist or one of the engineers?"

Desdemona made an odd little gasping sound.

"What's wrong?" Stark demanded.

"Nothing," Desdemona got out in a choked voice. She grabbed a napkin and hurriedly covered her mouth. "Nothing at all." She shook her head wildly. Her eyes watered.

"Are you laughing at me?" He reached across the table to slap her lightly between the shoulders.

"Sorry." Desdemona flinched beneath the blow, and then she steadied herself. "It just struck me as funny."

"My past love life? It never seemed very amusing to me."

"Not your love life. Your response to my question. Do you always take personal questions so literally?"

"Literal is the only way I know how to be," he warned her.

"I suppose it comes with the territory, doesn't it?" She composed herself, but her eyes still danced. "I've heard that you scientific types are very literal-minded."

"Most of us are, I guess."

"I assume it's a product of all the emphasis on critical and analytical thinking that you get in the course of your education."

Stark considered the matter for a few seconds. "No, it comes naturally. People who think in literal ways gravitate toward engineering and the sciences because those disciplines suit the way they think."

"A sort of chicken-and-egg scenario?" Desdemona chuckled. "Maybe we Wainwrights tend toward the theater arts because we think in arty ways."

"You seem to be something of an exception in your family. The only one with a head for business, your cousin Henry said. The only one who can't act."

"Don't be fooled. I'm not a good actress, but I'm a first-class Wainwright." She grew thoughtful. "We really are different, you and I, Stark."

"I know."

"That should probably worry you."

"Yes." He got to his feet. "But for some reason it doesn't. Good night, Desdemona."

She studied him with a mysterious, unreadable gaze. "You're going?"

"It's late." He walked around the glass brick counter and came to a halt in front of her. Without a word he bent his head and brushed his mouth lightly across hers. "Be sure to throw the dead bolt on your door after I leave."

"I will."

"I'll call you tomorrow."

"All right." She hesitated. "I enjoyed this evening, even if it was just business."

"It wasn't just business."

Her eyes glowed. "I'm glad."

"My secretary tells me I'm on the hook for a charity ball next week. Apparently Pamela committed me and a couple of thousand dollars of my money to some kind of fund-raiser for the arts. I was going to skip it, but Maud and McCallum inform me that I ought to go. Want to come with me?"

She smiled. "So that we can fish for new business together?"

"I thought it worked out tonight," he said stiffly.

"It did," she assured him quickly. "And I'd love to attend the charity ball with you."

He relaxed. "Thanks. I'll get back to you on the details."

"You do that. Sorry about the scene with Tony."

"Forget it." It took an enormous effort of will to turn and walk toward the door but Stark managed to do it. He had made a plan before he left the house this evening, and he intended to stick to it come hell or high water.

One thing he possessed in abundance was willpower, he reflected. He was a past master at techniques of deferred gratification. Being alone a lot taught a man that much, if nothing else.

Desdemona slipped off the stool and trailed after him to the door. She waited until he had it open before she touched his arm lightly. "Good night, Stark."

He paused. "There was one thing I wanted to ask you before I go."

"What's that?"

"It's about that stuff Tony found in your bedroom."

Desdemona's cheeks turned pink. "Kirsten gave it to me. Samples from the product lines that Exotica Erotica will stock. It was a sort of thank-you gift."

"I thought that might be it," he said with grim resignation. "So you did cosign the loan?"

"Of course. Kirsten and Henry are family. The Wainwrights take care of each other. It's not a one-way street, you know. Kirsten and

Henry were there when I needed a lot of free labor at the beginning of Right Touch."

"Answer one more question for me," Stark said. "Can you handle it financially if you wind up having to pay off their loan?"

Her mouth tightened. "Kirsten will make Exotica Erotica work. She's a lot like me. She's not only a wonderful set designer, she's got a head for business."

"Sure." He kissed her lightly again, stepped out into the hall, and closed the door.

He waited until he heard Desdemona throw the dead bolt before he went along the corridor to the elevator.

While he waited, he considered the two new factors he had learned this evening that would likely impact his relationship with Desdemona. The first was the unmistakable possessiveness and resentment that he had seen in Tony Wainwright's eyes.

The second factor was the high probability that Exotica Erotica would succumb to the terrible fatality statistics that afflicted new businesses. Every business faced such grim statistics. Stark Security had faced them and survived, but many did not. He knew that if Kirsten's shop went under, it would threaten to drag Right Touch down with it.

But he also sensed now that nothing could have dissuaded Desdemona from cosigning the loan. He recalled the fierceness in her eyes when she had told him that she was a true Wainwright. It reminded him of the old saying about the danger of being more royalist than the king. Whatever had happened when she was five years old had made her more of a Wainwright than any real flesh-and-blood Wainwright.

He wondered what it was like to feel that kind of bond with the members of one's family, to know that whatever happened, you were never completely alone in the world.

The significance of the flashing red and blue lights on the two patrol cars parked in front of his steel, concrete, and glass house took a moment to register on Stark.

Then he realized that the police must have come in response to his silent alarm system.

"Damn." Stark pulled into the drive and switched off the engine. He contemplated the officer who walked toward him.

It was a bad ending to what had been a fairly decent evening, all things considered.

Stark opened the door and got out.

The officer came to a halt and took out a notebook. "This your house?"

"Yes. I'm Sam Stark."

"Afraid you just had an attempted break-in."

"The guy didn't get inside, did he?" Stark asked the question with cool confidence. The alarm system he had installed was unique. He had designed it himself.

"No. Just a couple of kids. Not pros. Tried to crack a window at the back. Never even got it open. They were still working on it when we got here."

"I see." His carefully engineered state-of-the-art security systems had all functioned properly. Stark took a moment's satisfaction in that knowledge. Well-thought-out design always paid off. "Kids, you said?"

"Yeah." The officer shook his head. "Seem to get younger all the time. These boys are only ten and twelve years old. Probably after stuff to sell for quick cash. VCRs, stereos, that kind of thing. Luckily they didn't just smash the window and climb inside the house, grab the goodies, and run."

"It would have taken them at least twenty minutes to get through the window even if they'd had a hammer," Stark said absently. "And by then you would have been on the scene. I've got a special clear coating on all the glass. Acts like a spider's web. If someone breaks the window, the coating holds the fragments in place."

The officer smiled. "I've got that stuff on my own windows at home."

"We live in uncertain times." Stark glanced at one of the patrol cars. He could see two small figures huddled together in the back seat. "What happens next?"

"A lot of paperwork, unfortunately."

The second officer walked toward Stark. "I just had an interesting conversation with the kids. They claim they're related to the owner of the house. Said when they discovered he wasn't home they tried to let themselves in to wait for him. They swear they weren't trying to steal anything."

"Damn," Stark got a sinking feeling in the pit of his stomach. "What did you say their names were?"

"I didn't say." The second officer glanced at his notes. "The twelve-year-old is Kyle Stark. The ten-year-old is named Jason Stark. They say they're from Portland. Know 'em?"

An odd sense of resignation settled on Stark. "I've never met them, but I know who they are. They're my half brothers."

The first officer cocked a brow. "Real close-knit family, huh?"

"You noticed?" Stark said politely.

An hour later Stark went into his study while Kyle and Jason dug into the tuna sandwiches he had made for them. He hadn't known what else to do except feed them while he tried to sort out the situation.

There were three messages on his answering machine, all from Alison Stark, his father's third wife. Soon to be ex, according to Kyle and Jason. Stark had never met her.

Alison's recorded voice was laced with tension and anger.

> Sam, this is Alison Stark. We've never met, but I'm your father's latest ex. Have you seen my sons, Kyle and Jason? They left a note saying they were going off to find you in Seattle. Please call.

In the next call, the urgent tone was even more pronounced.

> Sam, this is Alison Stark again. Call me as soon as you get this message.

In the last message, Stark knew he was listening to a woman at the end of her rope.

> Sam, it's Alison. I'm going to call your father. This is his fault. That bastard can damn well take some responsibility for once in his life. The boys have been acting out for the past six months, and their therapist says it's because of the divorce. I swear I've had all I can take. Kyle and Jason have been driving me up the wall, and now they've pulled this stupid stunt. It's too much, do you hear me? Call me, for God's sake.

Stark pressed the rewind button on the answering machine. This was the last thing he needed.

He contemplated his alternatives for a long moment. Then he picked up the phone and dialed.

A desperate-sounding Alison Stark answered midway through the first ring.

"It's about time you called me back, Hudson. I've been going out of my mind. Your sons took a bus to Seattle. Alone, for God's sake. They're only ten and twelve, in case you've forgotten, and they're all alone somewhere in Seattle. They'll never find their half brother. It's the middle of the night. They're probably on the streets right this minute, along with the drug dealers and the crazies. What are you going to do about it?"

"This is Sam Stark, Alison. Kyle and Jason are safe with me."

"*Sam*. I thought it was Hudson. My God, Sam, I've been so worried. If it hadn't been for Cliff, I would have gone out of my mind. He tells me I'm overreacting, but—"

"Who's Cliff?"

"Dr. Clifford Titus. A friend. The boy's therapist, actually. I was with him tonight when Kyle and Jason disappeared. I got home and found a stupid note saying they were taking the bus to Seattle. You're sure that they're okay?"

"A little hungry, but otherwise they're fine. They had my address. After they arrived at the main bus terminal, they managed to figure out the Metro system. Caught a bus that dropped them off a block from here. Not bad for a couple of out-of-town kids operating on their own."

"They're both smart enough when they want to be, although you'd never know it from their grades this past year," Alison said bitterly. "They used to get A's and B's. Since the divorce they've been bringing home nothing but D's and F's. They're failing, if you can believe it. And they're so bright. It has to be deliberate."

"Divorce can be rough on a kid."

"Well, I've got news for them, it's rough on everyone. Do they think they're the only ones who have suffered since their father walked out to go live with his thirty-six-C executive assistant? It hasn't exactly been easy for me, either, you know."

"No, I guess it probably hasn't."

"As if I haven't got enough on my hands. Kyle and Jason have gone out of their way to make my life a living hell. Cliff says they're acting out because of the anger and pain caused by the loss of their father. You'd think they were the only ones having emotional problems. They've shown absolutely no consideration for me."

"Uh-huh."

"I should have listened to Marlene."

"Dad's second wife?"

"She called me when she found out that Hudson was leaving her for me. Told me I'd be sorry. But like a fool, I didn't believe her. I thought I was the one who could change him."

"Look, Alison, I know you've got problems, but they're not my problems," Stark said calmly but very clearly. "What are you going to do about Kyle and Jason?"

"Now that I know they're safe with you, I'm not going to do a damn thing," Alison said resolutely. "God knows I can't handle them right now, anyway. I'm burned out. I have no emotional reserves left. I'll talk to my therapist in the morning."

"We're all supposed to sit around twiddling our thumbs here in Seattle while you wait to get guidance from a therapist?"

"The boys can stay with you for awhile, can't they? Summer vacation just started. They're not missing any school."

"Now hold on just one damn minute here. . . ."

"You're their brother, aren't you?"

"Half brother. I've never even met them until tonight."

"So what? For years Hudson has been impressing them with stories about how you're some kind of hotshot rocket scientist who does secret work for the government. They're into high-tech video games and computers, themselves. They think you're some kind of super-hero nerd."

"Alison, Kyle and Jason can stay the night, but that's all. You'll have to make arrangements to come and get them in the morning."

"I'm not driving all the way to Seattle tomorrow. I have an appointment with my therapist, and Lord knows I need it. Tell Kyle and Jason that I hope they realize what they've put me through this evening. Good night, Sam."

"Alison, wait—"

It was too late. The crash on the other end of the line told Stark in no uncertain terms that Alison had hung up the phone.

"Hell." Stark gazed blankly at the receiver.

A figure moved in the doorway of the study. "Was that Mom?"

Stark turned slowly. Jason stood there. He had half a sandwich in one hand.

"Yes. She's very worried about you."

"She'll feel better after she talks to her shrink." Jason took a bite out of his sandwich.

Kyle appeared behind his brother. "She always does."

"That's encouraging."

"Are you going to let us stay here tonight?" Jason asked.

Stark studied the eerily familiar features of his young half brothers. It was like looking into a mirror that reflected the past.

Both boys had near-black hair. Their intelligent green eyes were shielded by the lenses of their glasses. Both of them had Hudson Stark's high cheekbones and savagely blunt features, even at their young ages. Both looked thin, pallid, and hunched in on themselves.

The chief difference between himself and his half brothers, Stark thought, was that he hadn't had anyone to run to when his parents had divorced.

"You and Kyle will stay here tonight," Stark said. "We'll make plans to get you home in the morning."

"We don't want to go home."

"We'll discuss it in the morning," Stark said.

With any luck Kyle and Jason would be homesick by morning, he told himself.

7

$\mathcal{S}$tark hoped for inspiration by morning, but it did not arrive on schedule. When he walked into the kitchen shortly before seven, he discovered Kyle and Jason already there. They were dressed in the T-shirts, jeans, and sneakers they had worn last night. Both boys were seated at the black steel and glass breakfast table that overlooked the austere gardens.

They were eating again, Stark noticed. A box of cereal and a carton of milk sat on the table in front of them.

Kyle looked up from his cereal bowl. Neither his determinedly casual attitude nor the lenses of his glasses could conceal the anxious expression in his young eyes. "Morning, Sam."

"Good morning." Stark went to the counter and concentrated on making coffee. The task reminded him of the previous night when he had made espresso for himself and Desdemona.

"Morning," Jason mumbled very softly.

Stark nodded briefly and busied himself with the coffee machine. Maybe Alison had calmed down during the night. With any luck she was even now in her car, heading toward Seattle to retrieve her sons.

His half brothers.

The realization that he was actually related to these two young males hit him with an unexpected impact.

"Sorry about setting off the alarm last night," Kyle offered.

"Whenever we forget our keys to our house back in Portland, we get in through one of the windows," Jason said. "We thought the same trick would work on your window."

"It doesn't." Stark reached for a mug.

There was a short, taut silence from the table.

"You mad at us?" Kyle asked.

"No." Stark got a bowl out of the cupboard and poured cereal into it. "I just wasn't expecting you last night."

"I told Kyle you'd be mad." Jason took a large swallow of orange juice. "I told him you'd put us back on the bus this morning."

Stark thought about that possibility. It was definitely an option. Better yet, he could put them on a plane. The flight to Portland was very short. If he drove them to the airport right after breakfast, they'd be home by midmorning.

"How long did you intend to stay in Seattle?" he asked.

Kyle and Jason exchanged glances.

"Just for a while," Kyle said. He busied himself with his cereal.

"Kyle said we could stay with you for the summer," Jason blurted out.

"The *summer*." Stark glanced at his brothers. "You intended to stay for the entire summer?"

Kyle nodded wordlessly.

"Of all the—" Stark broke off abruptly. He added milk to his cereal and leaned back against the kitchen counter to eat.

Allowing the boys to stay with him for the summer was definitely out of the question. He supposed it wouldn't matter much if they stayed for a night or two, but they certainly could not stay for three months. He didn't even know these kids. They were strangers.

Strangers who happened to have the same father.

"Things have been different since Mom and Dad got divorced," Kyle said in a low voice.

"Dad says he and Mom have grown apart." Jason spoke in the sing song tone a child uses to repeat verbatim something an adult has said but that he does not comprehend. "He says they're different people than they were when they got married."

87

"Uh-huh." Stark munched cereal. He had heard the same explanations when he was ten.

"I don't think they're different," Jason said roughly. "They still look the same to me."

Kyle's mouth formed a thin line. "Mom says Dad's tired of us. She says he's got no sense of responsibility. She says he's screwing his bimbo secretary."

Jason looked up angrily. "So what? Mom's screwing our shrink."

Kyle shrugged one shoulder. "Dr. Titus says it's okay so long as he isn't her shrink. Which he isn't. She goes to Dr. Lachlan."

Jason glanced at Stark. "Dr. Titus says the divorce is Mom and Dad's problem, not ours, but that's stupid. How can it be just their problem? It's like me and Jason don't exist or something. But everything's changed for us, too, so it's not just Mom and Dad's problem."

Stark could not argue with the logic of that statement. He ate another spoonful of cereal.

"Dr. Titus says that divorce can be a positive move for the whole family," Kyle said. He sounded as if he had memorized the words. "He says it provides opportunities for all members of the family to grow and become more independent."

Jason scowled. "He says it's better for two people who fight all the time to split up. He says that way there isn't so much stress in the household."

"I don't see why Mom and Dad have to fight all the time in the first place," Kyle muttered. "If they just stopped fighting, we wouldn't have any more problems."

Stark chewed cereal. "A lot of kids have parents who get divorced."

"That's what Dad told us," Kyle said. "He says it's perfectly normal."

"Dr. Titus told me that over half the kids in my class have parents who have split up," Jason said. He studied his uneaten cereal. "I already knew that. I just didn't think Mom and Dad would do it, too."

"Yeah, well they did," Kyle said in a surprisingly harsh tone. "Dr. Titus said you've got to accept it. He says you're in denial or something."

" 'Scuse me." Jason jumped to his feet. "Gotta go to the bathroom."

Stark saw the gleam of moisture in Jason's eyes as the boy dashed past him out of the kitchen.

88

Kyle waited until Jason had disappeared down the hall. "Our shrink says Jason hasn't accepted Mom and Dad's divorce yet."

"Takes a while," Stark said.

"Yeah. I guess."

Stark set his empty cereal bowl down on the counter. "What made you decide to look me up?"

"I dunno. Been thinking about it ever since Dad came home to get the last of his stuff."

"When was that?"

"A couple of months ago." Kyle lowered his voice until his words were almost inaudible. "When he moved out he said that he'd come see me and Jason two or three times a week. He did for a while. But I guess he got busy."

Stark recalled hearing the same vague promise when he had been ten. Hudson had visited dutifully for a couple of months or so, and then the excuses had started. *Got an out of town trip, Sam. Got some business people coming in next week. Going to have to take a rain check on that fishing trip, son. You'll understand when you're older.*

Jason sauntered back into the kitchen. His cheeks were flushed. He did not look at Stark as he took his seat at the table.

Kyle made an obvious bid to change the subject. "Dad says you used to work for the government. He said you invented stuff that was supposed to keep terrorists and people like that from getting into computers."

"I don't work for the government now," Stark said. "I have my own business."

"Oh." Kyle looked momentarily disappointed. "Do you still do stuff with secret codes?"

"Yes."

Kyle brightened. "Jason and I have a computer at home."

"Do you?" Stark asked politely.

"Dad bought it for us a year ago," Jason said. "We learned how to use one in school, of course, but Dad taught us how to do some really great things on it. Stuff the other kids don't know."

Stark was not surprised by that news. A talent for things technical ran in the family. Hudson was an electrical engineer who had once done pioneering work on aircraft guidance systems. He was now a vice president of a successful engineering consulting firm.

"You're not going to let us stay, are you?" Kyle finally asked.

"I doubt that your mother would let you spend the whole summer here in Seattle," Stark temporized.

"Sure she would," Jason insisted eagerly. "She'd be glad to get rid of us for the summer. She says we're making everything a lot harder for her."

"I'll bet you could talk Mom into it with no trouble at all," Kyle said. "Dr. Titus says she's under terrible stress. Getting us out of the house for the summer would probably relieve a lot of it."

The phone on the wall rang. Stark glanced at the number illuminated on the screen of the incoming-call indicator. He didn't recognize the area code. He hoped it was Portland.

He picked up the receiver. "This is Stark."

"Sam, is that you? It's your old man. Haven't talked to you since you called me on my birthday." Hudson's vibrant, mellow voice boomed down the line. "Shit, that was what? Seven months ago? Time flies at my age. How's it hangin', son?"

The lid that concealed the cauldron simmering deep in Stark's guts lifted for a fraction of a second. Just long enough for him to glance inside and see the witch's brew of chaos that swirled in the bottomless vessel.

With a skill born of long practice, he slammed the lid back into place.

"Kyle and Jason are here," Stark said without inflection.

"Yeah, I know," Hudson said impatiently. "It's four o'clock in the morning here. We just got in. Alison's called the hotel three times. She's really ridin' me hard. Acts like it's all my fault that the boys took off for Seattle. She expects me to do something."

"Will you?" Stark saw that both Kyle and Jason had stopped eating. They sat very still, trying and failing to look unconcerned.

"Will I what?" Hudson asked blankly.

"Do something."

"Hell, not much I can do." Hudson heaved a deep sigh that was probably meant to convey regret. "I'm calling you from Maui. Jennifer and I just got in yesterday. We both needed a break."

"Sure."

"You know what it's like. Sixteen-hour days when the pressure's on. Nights and weekends, too."

"Nights and weekends with Jennifer."

"Don't know what I would have done without her," Hudson said. "She's fantastic. Helped me close the biggest deal of my life last week. I really owed her this trip to Hawaii."

"What about Kyle and Jason?"

"What about 'em? They're okay, aren't they?"

Stark wished he'd taken the call in his study. He was grimly aware that his brothers were hanging on every word. One more adult was making a decision that would affect their future. "Yeah. They're okay."

"Figured they would be. Alison says they got themselves all the way to Seattle on a bus and even found your place in the middle of the night. Those boys are sharp. They remind me of you when you were that age."

"Look, Hudson—"

"What's that?" Hudson sounded abruptly distracted. "Hold on a second, Sam. Jennifer's trying to tell me something."

Stark tightened his fingers around the receiver as he listened to the feminine voice in the background. Something about how late it was and that it was time for bed.

"You bet." Hudson's voice was muffled as he responded to the woman. "I'm almost through, honey. Be there in a minute. Damn, that little red thing looks good on you. Okay, Sam, I'm back. What were you saying?"

"We were talking about the fact that Kyle and Jason are here in Seattle."

"Oh, yeah. I don't know what to tell you, Sam. Alison stuck 'em both in therapy the minute I told her I wanted the divorce. Nothing like therapy to screw up a couple of kids." Hudson chuckled. "The fact that Alison's sleeping with their shrink probably doesn't help matters, either. But Jason and Kyle will be fine."

"You think so?"

"Trust me, they just need a little time. Hell, your mother and I got divorced when you were, what? Ten or eleven . . ."

"Ten."

"Whatever. My point is, you turned out okay, didn't you?"

"Sure." Stark thought about the years of being an outsider in his own family, boarding school, two failed engagements, and a lifetime of being alone. "I turned out okay."

"Right. The problems Alison claims Kyle and Jason are having aren't caused by the divorce, you know, in spite of what that shrink says."

"They're not?"

"Hell, no. Those boys are ten and twelve years old. Their problems are caused by the fact that they're young kids on the verge of turning into full-blown teenagers. They're going through a stage, that's all."

"You think so?"

"Damn right. It's the shrink who put all those fool notions in Alison's head. She ought to fire him. Hey, I've gotta run. Jennifer's waiting for me. Not the kind of lady a man keeps waiting. Say, tell Kyle and Jason I said hi, will you?"

"They're right here. Why don't you tell them yourself?"

"I would, but I don't have time. Like I said, Jennifer's waiting. So long, Sam. Good talkin' to you. Hold on, I almost forgot. Got your wedding invitation a couple of months ago. Didn't have time to get a gift off but congratulations anyway. Next time I'm in Seattle you can introduce me to your bride."

"There was no marriage. The bride didn't show."

"What the hell? Don't tell me this fiancée went south, too?"

"Yes," Stark said. "She did."

"Jesus, Sam. You need some tips on how to handle women. What did you do to spook this one?"

"Asked her to sign a prenuptial agreement."

"Well, look at it this way," Hudson said, not without sympathy. "Calling off a marriage is a lot cheaper than getting a divorce. Trust me, I speak from experience."

"Yes, I suppose you do."

"Take care of yourself. Maybe we can get together one of these days." Hudson hung up the phone.

The line was dead.

Stark replaced the receiver very slowly. He looked at Jason and Kyle. They watched him in stoic silence.

My point is, you turned out okay, didn't you?

Stark folded his arms across his chest. "If your mother will go for it," he said very cautiously, "you two can stay here with me for the summer."

Alison went for it.

An hour later Stark sat down at the desk in his study and dialed the number of the only person he could think of who might be able to help him.

"Right Touch Catering," Desdemona said when she answered the phone. Her warm, vibrant voice was laced with the enthusiasm of the optimistic entrepreneur anticipating fresh business.

"It's me, Stark."

"Good grief, it's eight o'clock in the morning. What in the world are you doing calling at this hour?"

"I've got a problem."

"What sort of problem?"

"My two half brothers arrived to stay with me for the summer."

"I didn't know you had any brothers."

"Yeah, well, I do. Their parents got divorced six months ago. Jason and Kyle are taking it kind of hard."

"Naturally." Desdemona made a soft, sympathetic sound. "What other way would they take it?"

"At any rate, Alison, that's their mother, is pretty stressed out trying to deal with them and her own problems, too. Hudson is in Hawaii with his new girlfriend."

"Hudson? That would be . . . ?

"My father."

"Oh. So you've got the boys for the whole summer?"

"Looks like it. I just got off the phone with Alison. She's more than willing to let them stay here in Seattle. She says the experience will be good for them. I think she's convinced herself that it's sort of like sending them off to summer camp."

"Camp Stark."

"Something like that. At least I've got a spare bedroom. Alison said she'd send some of their clothes to them."

"Fancy you as a camp counselor."

"I'm no counselor," Stark said grimly. "I don't know a damn thing about kids. Which brings me to the crux of my problem. Kyle's twelve and Jason's ten. They're new in town. They don't have any

93

friends or scheduled activities to keep them busy during the day while I'm at work."

"Welcome to the wonderful world of latchkey kids."

"That's just it. I don't think they should be left alone all day long. They're having some adjustment problems because of the divorce. They need companionship and supervision."

"And you want to know how to find what every working parent would sell his or her soul for—good, reliable day care," Desdemona concluded.

"They're not little children. They don't need day care. They just need someone to keep an eye on them when I'm not around. Someone who can take them places. Make sure they're occupied. That kind of thing." Stark gazed glumly out the window. "Hell, I don't what they need. I must have been crazy to get talked into this."

"Fear not, you came to the right place."

"I did?"

"You're in luck." The smile in Desdemona's voice warmed the phone in Stark's hand. "Cousin Macbeth just hit town. He's here for the summer, and he's looking for a day job. I was going to put him to work stuffing mushroom caps, but something tells me he'd rather babysit."

"Who is cousin Macbeth?"

"Whoever or whatever you want him to be," Desdemona said simply. "The man's a good actor. One of the best in the family, as a matter of fact, and that's saying something in this family."

"Now, look, Desdemona, no offense, but I don't want some flaky actor looking after Kyle and Jason. I need someone trustworthy. Someone who can ride herd on two young boys who're going through a rough patch."

"No problem. Macbeth is great with kids, and he's completely reliable. I'll send him over right away."

Stark frowned. "I don't know about this. Kyle and Jason aren't babies. They don't need a babysitter."

"Think of Macbeth as a mentor of young men."

"Listen, maybe we should discuss this a little more."

"Sorry, can't talk just now," Desdemona said. "Got to get ready for a fund-raiser luncheon today. Oh, I almost forgot. Want to come to my birthday party a week from Friday?"

Stark was starting to feel disoriented. "Your birthday party?"

"I'll be twenty-nine, not that I'm counting."

"I see. All right. Yes. I'll come to your birthday party."

"Terrific. Seven o'clock at the pasta joint around the corner from Right Touch." Desdemona rattled off the name of the restaurant. "Know it?"

"I'll find it. But, Desdemona, about this Macbeth . . ."

"Relax. Your problems are over."

Desdemona hung up the phone before Stark could think of anything else to say.

"But we don't need anyone to look after us during the day," Kyle complained. "We're used to being on our own when we get home from school. We're not little kids anymore."

"This is summer." Stark leaned back in his desk chair and regarded Kyle and Jason with determination. "You're not in school. You're going to have a lot of free time on your hands, and you don't know your way around Seattle. I can't be with you during the day. I've got a business to run."

"We can find our own way around town," Jason said quickly. "We're too old to have a babysitter."

Stark raised his brows. In the two hours since Alison had agreed to leave Kyle and Jason in Seattle, the boys had undergone a sea change. They had magically transformed themselves from anxious, grateful waifs seeking shelter from life's storms into blustering little would-be tyrants.

"As long as you live with me," Stark said softly, "you will live by my rules. And my rules say that you are not going to spend your days alone."

"Aw, come on, Sam, we're your brothers, not your kids." Kyle brightened. "We could go to your office with you."

"I can't work and entertain you two at the same time."

"But that's just it, we don't need to be entertained by anyone." Jason grinned. "I've been looking around. You've got a lot of neat stuff in this house. All kinds of computers, a stereo, TV, VCRs, a CD player."

"Yeah, this place is really well equipped," Kyle said. "All we need are some new video games and we'll be fine."

"And if you don't want to buy us some video games," Jason added helpfully, "We can look up the addresses of the nearest arcades in the phone book."

"Forget it," Stark said with sudden conviction. "You are not going to spend the summer lost in a video arcade."

"But video games teach reasoning and logic skills," Kyle assured him glibly. "They also develop eye-hand coordination."

Stark glanced at him. "Says who?"

"Dr. Titus, our shrink," Kyle informed him with relish. "He told Mom there's no harm in vids. He said they're better for us than TV because they're inter . . . inter . . ."

"Interactive?" Stark suggested.

"Yeah, right. Interactive." Kyle appeared pleased with Stark's perception. "And the virtual reality games are the best. It's like you go into a whole other world."

Another world where you're alone, Stark thought. "I know," he said quietly. "But I think that it would be best if you stayed in this world this summer."

The muted thunder of a heavy engine broke into the discussion. Stark heard a vehicle pull into the drive.

"What's that?" Kyle said, distracted from the argument about virtual reality. "Sounds like a monster truck or something."

The doorbell sounded. Stark got to his feet. "I'll see who that is."

Kyle and Jason trailed after him as he went down the hall. They all descended the freestanding concrete and steel staircase that formed the spine of the house.

Stark opened the door at the bottom of the two-story foyer.

A huge, unsmiling man stood on the front steps. He wore black, mirrored sunglasses, a biker's head scarf, and a faded denim shirt. He had a wide, stainless steel cuff on one thick wrist. A leather ammo belt slanted across his broad chest. There were no bullets in the belt, but that fact did not lessen the arresting impression it made. His boots were fashioned of pale gray snakeskin. A gleaming black Jeep trimmed with a lot of chrome stood in the drive.

"I think you've got the wrong address," Stark said.

"You Stark?"

"Yes."

"Desdemona sent me." The voice sounded like the jeep's engine. "I'm Macbeth."

"Is that a fact?" Stark smiled slowly. He glanced at his half brothers. "Jason, Kyle, meet your babysitter."

Kyle swallowed visibly. His eyes were very round behind his glasses. "Holy shit."

Jason just stared, awestruck.

Macbeth looked at Jason and Kyle. The boys' opened-mouthed expressions were reflected in his mirrored sunglasses.

"Understand we're supposed to have us some fun this summer," Macbeth said. "Get in the Jeep."

Desdemona stood in the doorway of the walk-in freezer and surveyed Vernon Tate's newest ice sculpture. She never went any farther into the freezer than was absolutely necessary, and she never remained within its cold steel confines any longer than was required to store or remove a container of food. The freezer was the same size as an elevator cab.

Vernon's latest masterpiece was a large ice bowl positioned between the wings of a frozen swan. The shape was graceful, even elegant. The ice glittered like rare crystal.

"It's perfect, Vernon," Desdemona enthused. "We'll heap the gelato in the bowl and place the whole thing in the center of the dessert section."

Vernon looked relieved and a little embarrassed as he always did when Desdemona praised his work. "Glad you like it. I'm still working on the dolphins you ordered for Mr. Stark's next big reception."

"Take your time. I'll look forward to seeing them. Are you certain that you don't want to store them here at Right Touch?"

Vernon flushed. "I'd rather keep them in my friend's warehouse freezer until they're perfect."

"I understand. Didn't mean to push you. Artists are like actors in some ways. They don't like people to see their work in progress."

"I guess that's true." Vernon smiled. "You know something, Miss Wainwright? I never really thought of myself as an artist until I came to work for you. It makes me feel kind of special or something."

"You are special. I'd be lost without you." Desdemona glanced at

97

her watch. "I'd better see if Juliet and Aunt Bess have finished those cheese straws yet. We've got to start loading the van."

"I'll handle the glassware," Vernon said as he followed her out of the freezer. He turned to slam the locker door shut.

"Thanks, Vernon." Desdemona crossed the white tiled floor, moving between two long, stainless steel counters. The lower portions of the counters consisted of twin rows of metal storage cabinets.

As always, Desdemona surveyed her small domain with a proud and possessive eye. Everything was sparkling clean and as neat as the galley of a ship. Right Touch was her stage, and she was the leading player. It was a good feeling.

Bess, her silver hair hidden beneath a white net, glanced up from her work on the cheese straws. "Almost finished, dear. Juliet just took the last tray out of the oven."

"Great. We're on schedule." Desdemona looked across the busy room to where Henry and Vernon were setting boxes of glassware on a hand truck. "Don't forget the small dessert dishes," she called.

"We won't," Henry called. "I've got the checklist."

"I'm going to change into my tux," Desdemona said. "I'll be right out."

She hurried into her office, shut the door, and closed the miniblinds on the windows that overlooked the work area. Then she reached for the black and white tuxedo she wore when she was on the job.

Her mother had designed and made the tux along with the other black and white uniforms that Desdemona's staff wore when they were at work. The elegant attire was one of the trademarks of Right Touch.

The office door opened without warning just as Desdemona started to unfasten the first button of her shirt.

She whirled around and smiled when she saw her stepbrother. "Tony. What are you doing here?"

"I've got to talk to you, kid." Tony glanced over his shoulder and then stepped all the way into the office. He closed the door.

"I can't talk now, Tony. I've got a luncheon scheduled for one o'clock. We're loading the truck. When I get back we can have coffee, and you can tell me all about Hollywood."

"Can you put me back on the payroll?"

Desdemona's heart sank. "Oh, Tony. What happened down in Hollywood?"

Tony leaned back against the door and watched her with troubled eyes. "The usual. Things went wrong. The money people never got their act together. The studio lost interest. The jerks who were handling the project dropped the ball. It's all over, Desdemona."

"I was afraid of that. I'm so sorry, Tony."

His mouth twisted into a bitter smile. "Yeah, well, it's sort of the story of my life, isn't it?"

"You're a fine actor. You just haven't had the right breaks."

"I know, I know. The right breaks." He ran a hand over his handsome face in a weary gesture. "Sometimes I don't think I'm ever going to get them, kid."

"You will, Tony."

"Nice to know you believe in me."

"The whole family believes in you, you know that," she said.

"Like Uncle Augustus always says, the only things Wainwrights can depend on are each other." Tony made a graceful, careless movement of his shoulders. "Look, I won't need a job forever. I finished a script while I was waiting for things to gel in L.A."

"A script?"

"It's called *Dissolving*. I'm going to talk to Ian about staging it at the Limelight."

"The Limelight is in trouble, Tony," Desdemona said dubiously.

"Okay, so we'll have to find an angel to back the production." Tony began to pace the small room. "We can do it. Ian needs a great script to save his theater, and I've got one for him. The thing is, I need a day job until I can get *Dissolving* staged. How about it?"

Desdemona smiled. "Okay. You're back on the payroll."

"Thanks." Tony stopped pacing and turned to look at her. "Sorry I embarrassed you in front of your date last night."

"Don't worry about it."

"How was I to know you'd be bringing a man home with you? Especially a guy like that. Is he the one who got you into the bondage and feathers stuff?"

"Don't be silly. Kirsten gave me that stuff a few days ago as a thank-you present. Sort of a joke, really. She's going to open Exotica Erotica soon."

"Oh, yeah. I forgot about her ladies' sex boutique." Tony eyed her closely. "So how serious are things between you and this techno-nerd?"

"Don't call him a nerd."

"Excuse me. How serious is this thing between you and Mr. Stark?" Tony said with elaborate sarcasm.

Desdemona blushed. "I don't know yet, but I have hopes. Tony, I've got to get dressed. If you want to get back on the payroll, go put on a uniform. You can help Henry and Vernon."

"He's not your type," Tony said softly. "He's not one of us."

"So they say," Desdemona said.

*Y*ou gave your stepbrother a job? Stark halted in the middle of the dance floor and stood glowering at Desdemona. "What is it with you, anyway? Do you have to find work for every single one of your unemployed relatives? Can't any of them hold down a real job?"

"Hush, you're causing a scene." Desdemona glanced uneasily around the crowded room. "The jobs at Right Touch are real jobs."

It was after ten on Wednesday night, and the Arts for the Future Guild ball was in full swing. The glittering downtown hotel ballroom was thronged with a curious mix of the elegant and the avant-garde as wealthy members of Seattle's social elite hobnobbed with a host of artists, actors, musicians, and writers. Tuxedoes and shimmering silk gowns mingled with tacky sequined jeans and studded leather bustiers.

Stark seemed unaware of the impropriety of halting in the center of a dance floor. His attention was focused completely on the subject of Tony. "I know the guy is your stepbrother, but that's no reason to give him a job."

"Oh, come on, Stark, he's family. Tony just needs a day job to tide him over until he and Ian can find a financial backer for Tony's new play."

JAYNE ANN KRENTZ

"I don't give a damn if he's family. What's that got to do with anything?"

"You ask me that? After you just agreed to take in your two half brothers for the entire summer?" Desdemona pushed forcefully against Stark's shoulder in an effort to get him moving again. It was like trying to restart a freight train.

"That's different."

"How is it different?" Desdemona wished she had resisted the impulse to mention that she had given Tony a job. The evening had been going rather well up until that point.

"Kyle and Jason didn't have anywhere else to go," Stark muttered.

"Neither does Tony."

"He's, what? Thirty-two? It's time he learned to fall back on his own resources."

"Wainwrights fall back on each other."

"They fall back on you."

"It works out for all of us," she said.

"You know what your problem is?"

"No, what is it?"

"You're a sucker when it comes to family. Face facts, Desdemona, there's nothing sacrosanct about family. Every con man, thief, and embezzler who ever lived was a member of someone's family."

A flash of uneasiness shot through her. She searched his face anxiously, telling herself that Stark could not possibly know about the unfortunate incident that had occurred ten years earlier when Tony had been falsely accused of embezzling funds from a small theater.

"Oh, now, that's a very shrewd observation," she retorted. "And utterly meaningless. You know what your problem is? You've worked with electronic encryption techniques and computer security problems for so long you've become permanently paranoid."

"I am not paranoid. I'm looking at this situation with the sort of logical, unemotional, analytical detachment that you don't seem to be able to manage."

She eyed him intently. "You really don't like my brother, do you?"

"He's your stepbrother, not your real brother. And you're right, I'm not overly fond of him."

"You don't even know him," she exclaimed, exasperated.

"Calm down, you're getting emotional."

"I'm a Wainwright. I was born emotional. It goes with the territory."

"You were not born a Wainwright," he reminded her grimly.

"How I became part of the family doesn't matter. The only thing that's important is that I *am* part of the family."

"Then you'd better find yourself a keeper before you lose your shirt trying to employ all of your shade-tree relatives."

"Is that so?" Desdemona no longer cared if anyone overheard the argument. "If you don't like the way I operate, maybe you'd better find yourself another caterer to put on retainer. Someone with a nice, logical, analytical way of doing things."

Stark's eyes became ice-cold emeralds. "Lower your voice before you cause a scene." He took her arm and marched her off the floor.

"I've got news for you, Stark," Desdemona said with great relish, "you've pushed me too far. I'm past the point of worrying about whether or not I make a scene."

"In that case, I'm taking you home."

"You wouldn't want to do that." She fixed him with a smile intended to outshine the chandeliers. "This isn't a real date. We came here to do some business, remember? We haven't turned up any new customers for Stark Security Systems or for Right Touch."

"You want to do business?" He came to a halt near the buffet table. "Then my advice is to start acting in a businesslike manner."

"You're a fine one to give advice. You started this."

"In that case, I hereby declare the subject closed for now." Stark picked up a tiny slice of toast topped with an herbed cheese spread.

"Who gave you the right to close the sub— *Umph*." Desdemona broke off as Stark gently stuffed the little round of toast between her lips. She glared mutely at him while she chewed.

She was so incensed that it took her a few seconds to realize that Stark was no longer looking at her. He was gazing at someone who had come up behind her.

"Hello, Pamela," Stark said very calmly. "I didn't realize you would be here tonight."

"Good evening, Stark," Pamela Bedford said quietly.

Desdemona nearly choked on the cheese toast.

"Desdemona." Pamela regarded her with an air of genuine surprise. "I hadn't realized that your firm had done the catering for this event."

"It didn't." Desdemona finally managed to get the last of the cheese toast down. She turned to face Stark's ex-fiancée. "I'm not here in an official capacity."

"Desdemona is with me tonight," Stark said.

"Oh, I see." Pamela smiled tremulously. There were fine lines around her mouth and an unmistakable anxiety in her blue eyes.

She was dressed in a discreetly cut sapphire blue gown that underscored the pale gold of her hair and left her fine shoulders bare. A diamond choker circled her long neck. It matched the earrings that dripped delicately from her ears. Pamela appeared to be fashioned of spun gold, moonbeams, and pearls.

Dressed in a narrow black gown with only a black velvet ribbon around her throat for ornament, Desdemona, still seething with irritation, felt like the bad-tempered witch of the west.

She was acutely aware of the tension in the atmosphere. It was impossible to tell from Stark's expression what was going through his mind.

Pamela gave Stark a wistfully apologetic look. "I thought we'd better get this first public meeting over. We can't go on avoiding each other forever now that we move in the same circles, can we?"

Stark picked up another slice of cheese toast. "Hadn't planned to avoid you forever." He bit strongly down on the toast. "Hadn't planned on avoiding you at all, as a matter of fact."

"I'm glad to hear that." Pamela slid a sidelong glance at Desdemona. "I know I left you in a very awkward situation at the wedding."

"What wedding?" Stark asked.

Pamela blushed. "I've been dreading this encounter. I knew it was going to be difficult." She turned to Desdemona. "Would you excuse us for a few minutes? I think Stark and I should finish this conversation in private."

"Desdemona and I were just about to leave," Stark said.

"Nonsense," Desdemona murmured. "You two go right ahead and chat. I believe I'll freshen up in the ladies' room."

"Desdemona," Stark began in a warning tone.

"I'll be right back." Desdemona waved cheerfully, whirled around, and plowed straight into the crowd. The throng of people closed behind her.

Desdemona headed for the nearest ballroom door. She was less than three yards from her goal when Dane McCallum stepped into her path.

"Fleeing the scene of the accident?" he asked. Wry amusement lit his eyes.

Desdemona grimaced. "I'm a coward at heart. Can't stand the sight of blood."

"I don't blame you." Dane glanced across the crowded room. "It was bound to happen sooner or later, though. They couldn't avoid running into each other forever."

"That's what Miss Bedford said." Desdemona followed his gaze, but she was not tall enough to see over the heads of the guests.

"It was Pamela's idea, I suspect."

"What? To force a meeting tonight? Yes, I think so," Desdemona agreed.

"Christ knows, Stark wouldn't have bothered. He sees things the same way a computer does. On or off. When something is finished, it's finished. Especially a relationship."

Desdemona studied Dane thoughtfully. She had seen him at the cancelled wedding and spoken to him briefly at the cocktail party Right Touch had staged for Stark, but she did not know him well. The only thing she really knew about him was that he was one of the few people Stark considered a friend.

He was taller than Stark, about the same height as Tony. He was built along the same lines as Tony and the Wainwright men in general, a lean, graceful man with long fingers and patrician features. By any traditional standard he was definitely better-looking than Stark, but Desdemona was unimpressed by that fact. She discovered to her surprise that she had developed an odd and totally unaccountable taste for men who were fashioned like sturdy medieval warriors.

"Running into each other tonight must be awkward for both of them," Desdemona said.

Dane smiled briefly. "I'm sure it is for Pamela, but I doubt that Stark's having much of a problem with it, at least no more of a problem than he generally has in social situations."

"I'm sure it's every bit as hard on him." Desdemona tried to peer through the crowd to see what was happening near the buffet table. "I just hope he doesn't cause a scene."

Dane chuckled. "Don't worry, he won't make a scene tonight. He's not the kind to explode in public. I've never even seen Stark explode in private, for that matter. He never gets very emotional about anything. Not his way."

Desdemona frowned. "She did stand him up at the altar."

"Trust me, from that moment on, he wrote her off as a mistake. As far as he was concerned, she became just another blip on his computer screen. A temporary glitch."

"You talk as though he's a computer or something."

"A lot of people think he is," Dane said simply.

"That's crazy. Stark has emotions just like everyone else. He hides them well, that's all."

"I've known him a lot longer than you have, Desdemona. His detachment is real enough. And I'll let you in on a little secret. I almost envy him at times."

"That's ridiculous. Please excuse me." Desdemona turned on her heel and marched toward the open doors.

It was a relief to escape the noisy, crowded ballroom. Desdemona hurried down the carpeted hall toward the rest rooms. She wondered how long she should give Stark and Pamela together before she returned to reclaim her client.

Then she wondered what she would do if Stark was not eager to be reclaimed.

Perhaps Pamela Bedford was having second thoughts about walking out on the relationship.

Desdemona pushed open the rest room door and stepped inside. A quick glance around told her that she had the place to herself. She heaved a sigh of relief and sat down on one of the velvet-covered stools in front of the mirror.

She contemplated her image for a long moment. The Wainwright intuition blazed in her wide, shadowed eyes.

"Damn, I've fallen in love with him."

The words were a soft whisper in the empty room.

Not nearly enough presence, considering the momentous nature of the occasion.

Desdemona leaped to her feet and slapped her hands down on the counter. She leaned very close to the mirror.

"I've fallen in love with him."

The words rang out loudly, bouncing off the walls and echoing down the row of empty stalls.

Much better. A bit more of Richard III defying all to seize his own fatal destiny.

"This is impossible," Desdemona said to the woman in the mirror. "Okay, I'm attracted to him. But I can't possibly be in love with him. He's my exact opposite. McCallum may be right. Stark may not be able to love anything except another logic circuit. The family is right, too. Stark's not even theater people, for God's sake. Wainwrights always marry theater people."

The door opened behind her. Pamela walked into the rest room. Desdemona met her eyes in the mirror.

"Am I interrupting anything?" Pamela asked gently.

"No. I was just talking to myself." Desdemona sank slowly back down onto the stool.

"I thought I might find you in here." Pamela came forward, her eyes never leaving Desdemona's in the mirror. "Stark is looking for you."

Desdemona drew a deep breath. "Did you two finish your conversation?"

"I don't know if you could call it a conversation." Pamela smiled wryly. "It was a little too one-sided for that. Rather like carrying on a dialogue with a computer."

"Don't say that," Desdemona whispered.

"Why not? It's the truth. I apologized, Stark said forget it. I told him that I felt we had never really learned to communicate, Stark said forget it. I explained that I wished things could have been different, Stark said forget it. I tried to tell him . . . well, you get the picture."

"Forget it."

"Exactly." The skirts of Pamela's sapphire gown rustled softly as she settled on the neighboring stool. "But at least it's over. I've been dreading this scene ever since I left that note the day of the wedding. We were bound to run into each other sooner or later."

"Yes."

"Tonight I realized almost immediately that I was the only one who had worked up a serious case of nerves over the encounter." Pamela grimaced. "I do believe Stark had trouble recalling my name, let alone the fact that we were once engaged."

"Of course he knew who you were."

"I'm not so certain of that. I think he'd already filed me away in some remote computer archive along with the rest of the obsolete and outdated programs. He's a strange man."

"He doesn't allow his emotions to show."

"I used to believe that was the case. But about one month before the wedding I finally decided that the reason he didn't show his emotions was that he didn't have any." Pamela hesitated. "I have no right to ask this, but do you mind telling me how you and he got together?"

"Business."

Pamela's fine brow furrowed slightly. "I don't understand."

"Business brought us together. You stuck him with the tab for the wedding reception, remember? I had to break the bad news to him that just because there was no wedding it didn't mean that the caterer didn't get paid."

"Yes, of course." Pamela flushed. "I'm sorry. I forgot all about the aspect of the thing."

"Everybody forgets the caterer. You probably had a lot on your mind."

"There's no need to be rude. I was very upset at the time. It was an extremely traumatic event for me. And then there were my parents to deal with. They were mortified, and I felt so guilty. You have no idea."

"Yes, well, life goes on, doesn't it?" Desdemona got to her feet. "Excuse me. I'd better go find Stark. He'll be wondering where I am."

"Probably. He said something about wanting to leave. He doesn't enjoy social affairs, you know."

"I know."

"I think that was one of the reasons he decided to marry me." Pamela's dainty jaw tightened. "He wanted a permanent social secretary and hostess."

"That's nonsense."

"No, it's not." Pamela reached for a tissue and sniffed delicately into it. "I can hardly complain. One of the reasons I got involved with him in the first place was because Daddy insisted that I be nice to him."

Desdemona stilled. "I don't understand."

Pamela burst into tears. "Daddy said that Stark is doing very well these days, but in a few years he'll be worth an absolute fortune. And

Daddy's had some financial difficulties lately. The blue chips aren't what they used to be, you know and, oh, God, I shouldn't be talking about any of this."

"No, probably not."

"It's a private family matter."

"Sounds like it."

Pamela raised a stricken face. "Promise me you'll never breathe a word about this to anyone. Mother and Daddy would just die."

"Trust me, I wouldn't dream of it." Desdemona had no intention of ever telling Stark that he had almost been married for his potential earning power.

Perhaps he had sensed that possibility right from the start, she reflected. There had been that business with the prenuptial agreement, after all.

"It wasn't just the money," Pamela went on quietly. "Daddy said the family needed new blood. He said it was time we restoked the gene pool with some fresh, raw talent. He said too many generations of Bedfords had married within their own social strata, and the result was a general weakening of the bloodline."

"Your father is a believer in the Darwinian approach to marriage, I take it?"

"You could say that." Pamela sighed. "Mother didn't agree with him, but she went along with the idea. Mother does believe in restoking the family fortunes from time to time. My point is, regardless of why we were introduced, I found Stark *interesting*."

"Interesting."

"In a physical sense," Pamela clarified.

"Right. A physical sense."

"You know what I mean." Pamela tossed the crumpled tissue into a waste can. "The man has abysmal social skills and absolutely no tact, but there is something sort of sexy about him."

"I think I'm getting the picture. You were physically attracted to him, so you thought you could tolerate marriage to him."

"I was wrong. The physical attraction soon faded. He made me nervous, if you must know."

"Nervous?"

"He was so . . ." Pamela groped for words. "*Intense*." She turned red. "I won't bore you with the details."

"Please, don't."

"Let's just say that he was a little too primitive for my taste." Pamela shuddered delicately. "At any rate, I finally realized that I couldn't go through with the wedding."

"Did you love him at all?" Desdemona asked before she could stop herself. "Even a little?"

Pamela frowned. "I've asked myself that same question any number of times. I'm still not certain of the answer. How do you define love?"

"I don't think you can. It's one of those things that you only recognize when you run smack into it. I'd better be on my way." Desdemona opened the door.

"Do you know," Pamela said, regarding her own lovely face in the mirror, "I think my apology tonight actually bored him."

Desdemona shot the princess in the mirror an impatient glance. "I doubt it. I think it's far more likely that he simply didn't know what to say."

Pamela considered that with a wistful expression. "I suppose I should have expected it. Stark never had a lot to say at the best of times, unless the conversation happened to be about computers."

"Yes, well, that is his field."

Pamela did not appear to hear her. "I think what bothered me the most was that he never had much to say after he finished making love. Doesn't it upset you that he just gets out of bed, says good night, and leaves?"

"Forget it," Desdemona said as she fled the rest room.

The short drive from the hotel to Desdemona's apartment was conducted in near silence. Stark apparently felt no obligation to make conversation, and Desdemona could not think of anything appropriate to say.

As annoyed with him as she was because of his nasty remarks concerning Tony, she still felt deep empathy for Stark. The man had to be suffering after his encounter with Pamela. No one could go through a scene like that without experiencing a lot of pain.

It was raining, a light, misty summer rain that dampened the streets and made the traffic lights shimmer. Stark drove through the city with a quiet competence that spoke volumes about his self-control.

"Are you okay?" Desdemona said as Stark eased the car into the garage.

"I'm fine." Stark scowled at the question. "Why?"

"I just wondered," Desdemona said.

"Do I look sick?"

"No, of course not. You look fine." More than fine, she thought. The man really did look good in a tux.

"Then why did you ask?" Stark slid the car into a slot and switched off the engine.

"Just making conversation. How do your brothers like Macbeth?"

Stark frowned at the change of topic. Then he shrugged. "They seem fascinated by him. I think they believe he stepped straight out of a virtual reality game. A real live video hero."

"Macbeth has that effect on kids of all ages. When he's in town he organizes plays for children who are living in shelters or institutions. They love him."

"He's got Kyle and Jason working as volunteer stagehands for some group called the Strolling Players."

"That's the company of actors and crew that puts on the children's plays," Desdemona explained. "It was Macbeth's idea. He started it a couple of years ago. Everyone's a volunteer, from the lighting director to the costume designer."

"I see."

"We Wainwrights are all very active in the Strolling Players. Even Right Touch gets involved. I cater the children's parties that are held before the plays are staged."

Stark nodded and made no comment. He opened the door, got out, and came around to open Desdemona's door. "I'm scheduled to see a matinee on Saturday. Something called *Monsters Under the Bed*, I believe."

"I'll be around before the show. I'm doing pizzas for the kids in the audience." Desdemona got out of the car. "Aunt Bess is in the play. She's one of the monsters. Uncle Augustus is running lights."

"Let's hope I understand this play better than I did *Fly on a Wall*." Stark took her arm and walked with her to the elevator.

When the doors slid open, Desdemona stepped inside and gazed straight ahead at the indicator panel. "Do you have time to come in for coffee?"

"Yes." Stark glanced at his watch. "Macbeth is with the boys. I told him I'd be home around one." He eyed her intently. Then, without a word he put his arm around her shoulders.

Some of Desdemona's claustrophobic tension ebbed away.

The doors slid open. Desdemona stepped quickly out of the elevator. She led the way down the hall to her apartment.

Stark took her key and inserted it into the lock as if he had been doing it for years. "There's something I've been meaning to ask."

"Yes?" Desdemona flipped on the light and walked into the loft apartment. She bent over to remove her high heels.

"Do you remember when I kissed you the first time? It was after the cocktail reception you put on for my seminar clients."

Desdemona, one shoe off, glanced up swiftly. "Of course I remember. What about it?"

Stark closed the door and turned to look at her. His eyes were brooding and intent. Very focused. "You said then that we needed time to get to know each other before we went to bed together."

Desdemona swallowed. "Yes, I know. You need time to recover from your experience with Pamela. That sort of rejection is very hard on a sensitive person."

"Let's leave the issue of my sensitive nature out of this. I was wondering if you could be more specific?"

"Specific?" Desdemona croaked. "About what?"

Stark glanced at the key in his hand. When he looked up, his eyes were fathomless pools of green. "About the length of time I'm supposed to wait."

"That's a difficult question to answer."

"Is it?"

"It's not exactly the kind of thing you can quantify." She stepped out of her other shoe. "I mean, there's no established waiting period."

"Just tell me how I'm supposed to know when it will be okay to ask you to go to bed with me," Stark said quietly.

Desdemona leaned back against the brick wall, closed her eyes, and took a deep breath. "We'll have to feel our way as we go along, I guess. I'm sure we'll both know when the time is right."

"I won't," Stark said.

"I beg your pardon?"

"I'm not good at feeling my way in a relationship. Especially in a situation like this where you're making all the rules."

Desdemona opened her eyes and glared at him. "You make it sound as though I'm inventing them as we go along."

"Aren't you?"

"Of course not. For heaven's sake, Stark, you just saw your ex-fiancée not more than an hour ago."

"What the hell does that have to do with anything?"

"I'm sure you're experiencing some very strong emotions." Desdemona straightened away from the wall and stalked toward the bank of windows on the other side of the room. "It must have been difficult for you."

"Is that why you asked me how I felt downstairs in the garage? You thought I was shaken by the meeting with Pamela?"

"Aren't you?"

"No." Stark followed her across the room. He came to a halt directly behind her and put his hands on her shoulders. "I don't give a damn about Pamela. I'm asking you for an estimate of how long I'm supposed to wait for you. It seems like a perfectly reasonable request to me."

"You think so?"

Stark touched the nape of her neck. "I can wait as long as necessary, you know."

Desdemona shivered. "Would you?"

"Yes. I'm a very patient man." He kissed the curve of her shoulder. "But right now I'd trade my soul for some idea of how long you're going to keep me dangling."

"Oh, Stark, you're impossible." Desdemona turned abruptly in his arms. She wrapped her arms around his waist and rested her hot face against his broad shoulder.

"Six weeks? Three months? Next summer?" he breathed into her hair. "Please, Desdemona. Give me a time frame. Any time frame. I can work with that."

She gave a choked laugh. "You'd wait until next summer?"

"I didn't say I wouldn't try to manipulate the time frame somewhat," he hedged. "But, yes, if necessary, I'll wait."

Desdemona took a deep breath and prepared to walk out on stage. "How about tonight?"

9

The unpredictability of complexity was nothing compared to the gloriously unpredictable nature of Desdemona, Stark decided.

He'd told her to give him a time frame, and she had done just that. She'd said here. Now.

Tonight.

She could hardly have chosen a more awkward moment if she had tried.

Stark surreptitiously glanced at his wristwatch and thought of Jason and Kyle waiting at home with Macbeth. His next thought concerned the small package of condoms he had tucked into the glove compartment of his car a few days ago. It was still there, right where he had put it, six floors below in the garage.

Desdemona had given him no warning that she was on the point of changing her mind about this aspect of the relationship. Hell, they'd had a blazing argument in the middle of a dance floor less than ninety minutes earlier. He'd had no way of guessing that she might be in a mood to make love by the time they got back here to her loft. She'd seemed downright distant, even cool, when she'd emerged from the rest room.

It was enough to drive a logical man a little crazy.

On the other hand, she'd just said yes.

Stark was not about to argue with a yes.

"Stark?" She raised her head from his shoulder. Her eyes were huge and mysterious, filled with questions, promises, and the mysteries that existed at the border between chaos and complexity.

"Did anyone ever tell you that you have lousy timing?"

She smiled. "No Wainwright has lousy timing."

Stark stared hungrily at her soft mouth and decided to ignore the awkward time frame. He was supposed to be very, very smart. He had a fistful of degrees in math and physics to prove it. He could work with any time frame.

"My God, Desdemona." He caught her face between his hands. "Do you have any idea how much I want you?"

"No, but I'm hoping that you want me as much as I want you."

He had never seen such sweet desire in a woman's eyes, at least not in the eyes of a woman who was looking right at him. He was lost.

He kissed her with all the pent-up need that had been simmering in him for the past few weeks.

Kissing Desdemona was akin to plunging headfirst into a spectacular piece of computer-generated fractal art. He was submerged in a universe of glowing colors and wildly intricate patterns.

Everything within him accelerated to the speed of light as he was swept into the dizzyingly complex design. He found himself in a dynamic creation that could have been produced by only the most exquisite of mathematical algorithms.

Desdemona's mouth was soft and damp and welcoming. The taste of her was indescribable. Stark wanted more. He wondered if he would ever be satisfied. Perhaps he was fated to search forever for the key to the shifting dynamics.

He tightened his hold on her, pulling her against him. He needed to feel every inch of her softness. The memory of how she had become wet and hot for him that night in his kitchen returned in a red-hot rush. It made his head spin.

Her arms slipped around his neck, and her head fell back beneath the onslaught of his kiss. He moved his mouth to her ear, her throat, her shoulder. She sighed and nestled closer.

Complex patterns shifted again, spreading outward to fill the void with light and energy.

Stark could feel Desdemona's breasts against his chest. Her dress and his shirt were in the way. He found the zipper of the black gown and tugged it downward. Desdemona lowered her arms, and the dress fell to her waist.

Her black slip and a small, lacy black bra were in the way now. Stark got rid of both in a few swift movements. All the clothing Desdemona wore except a tiny triangle of black lace and a pair of black thigh-high stockings pooled on the floor around her feet.

Stark looked down at her, riveted by the sight of her nearly nude body. He was so enthralled by her graceful breasts and the gentle flare of her thighs that he barely noticed when she went to work on the buttons of his shirt.

He ripped off his glasses and tossed them down on a nearby table.

Desdemona's fingertips brushed unsteadily across his chest and he realized that she was trembling. He caught her hand and brought it to his mouth.

"It's all right," he whispered. "Don't be frightened. I would never hurt you."

She smiled tremulously. "I know. I trust you."

He stared at her for a few seconds, spellbound. She stood on tiptoe and kissed his throat.

"This is going to sound stupid," he said hoarsely, "but I have to get something from the car."

She buried her face against his chest. "If you're talking about what I think you're talking about, you won't have to go downstairs. Kirsten gave me several packages. Assorted colors. They're in a box under the bed."

Stark groaned, torn between relief and wry amusement. "I take back everything I said about the inadvisability of making loans to relatives."

He scooped Desdemona up in his arms. Her soft gasp of excitement heated the blood in his veins.

"Am I as light as thistledown?" she asked demurely. "I've always wondered."

He considered the question carefully. "No. But you don't weigh nearly as much as a mainframe computer."

Her effervescent laughter cascaded over him like a crystal waterfall.

He carried her across the room to where the shoji screens concealed her bed. Stepping between the screens, he set Desdemona down on the white, down-filled comforter. She looked up at him, her eyes searching his face in the shadows.

He braced one knee on the bed and reached out to free her hair from the gold clips that secured it. The vibrant red curls tumbled across the fluffy pillows in a glorious froth. He wound his hands deep in the soft stuff and leaned down to inhale the fragrance of it.

Desdemona reached inside his open shirt and splayed her fingers across his chest. "I love the feel of you." She stroked upward to his shoulders. "So strong and beautiful."

Stark didn't think he could take much more. He had always considered himself a man of self-control, an expert in the art of deferred gratification, but tonight he was caught up in the flow of uncontrollable forces.

He fell on top of Desdemona.

She reached for him with an eagerness that dazed him. He covered one of her breasts with his hand and felt the taut nipple push against his palm. Hungrily he took the fruit into his mouth.

Desdemona made a soft, half-strangled sound.

"Did I hurt you?"

"No, *no.*" She gripped the back of his head and held him to her breast.

He filled his mouth with her once more and slid his hand across her soft belly. She arched her hips, straining against his fingers. He stroked her thigh. She bent her leg in response. The gesture conveyed passionate urgency. The silky feel of her stocking was incredibly erotic.

Stark touched the scrap of lace between her legs. It was already damp. The scent of her arousal was the most alluring perfume he had ever known. Satisfaction coursed through him as he realized that Desdemona was as wild for him as he was for her.

"Stark." Desdemona's nails dug into his back beneath his shirt.

He eased one finger past the narrow crotch of the panties.

Desdemona shuddered.

Stark raised his head and looked at her. He had never seen anything more beautiful in his life. She was lost in the moment. Her eyes were tightly closed. The mere sight of the elegant, utterly abandoned lines of her stocking-clad legs was almost enough to trigger his climax.

He fought for the last remnants of his control. He was sweating. He freed one hand to grope beneath the bed. He found the carton of Exotica Erotica products. His hand closed over a box.

He lifted the package and realized that it was sealed in plastic wrap. There was just enough light filtering through the windows to read the words *Big Boy Vibrator*.

"What is it?" Desdemona asked quickly.

"Wrong box." He reached under the bed again, and this time he found what he wanted.

His hands were shaking, but he managed to get his zipper down, managed to open a small foil packet, managed to do what needed to be done.

He did not manage to remove his pants or get his shoes off, however. He gave up on the attempt and fumbled briefly with Desdemona's lace panties.

"Please." Desdemona clutched at him. "I can't wait. I've never felt anything like this in my life. Please, Stark. Hurry."

Stark abandoned the effort to remove the black lace panties in the normal manner. He gripped the narrow strip of fabric and yanked it out of the way. The sheer lace tore in his hand.

Stark drove himself into Desdemona in a single, deep thrust.

She stiffened and sucked in her breath. "*Stark.*"

For an instant the flowing, shifting, impossibly intricate design stood still for Stark.

She was so small. Incredibly tight. He could feel himself stretching her. He knew that if she hadn't been so thoroughly damp with her own dew, it would never have worked.

"Are you okay?" he asked.

"Yes." She sounded breathless. "Just give me a second. You know, I hadn't realized that weight-lifting impacted so many different parts of a man's body."

"Christ, Desdemona, don't make me laugh. Not now."

She clung to him for a moment longer and then slowly, cautiously, lifted herself, inviting him even deeper inside.

He moved his hand downward, searching out the small, sensitive bud that was the source of her excitement. He could feel the electricity that shot through her. He wondered that it did not set him ablaze. She cried out, an enchanting, half-swallowed sound of stunned surprise.

Stark felt her clench even more tightly around him, saw her lips part, felt her legs close around his waist.

Her climax shimmered through him, sending him into the heart of a spectacular, exceedingly complex whirlpool of colors and shapes. He was in the middle of a fractal. For an instant Stark saw and understood all the patterns in their entirety.

For that brief moment in time he was no longer alone.

Rain struck the bank of the windows that formed one wall of Desdemona's loft. The wind had shifted.

Desdemona lay happily crushed beneath Stark's large, warm frame. His head rested on her breast. His legs firmly lodged between hers. The fabric of his formal black trousers scraped lightly against the inside of her bare thighs.

"You didn't even take off your pants, cowboy," she murmured.

"What?" Stark raised his head. He looked down at her with half-closed eyes. There was a distinct air of sleepy indulgence about him.

"I said, you didn't even take off your pants. Or your shoes." She stretched languidly beneath his weight. "I suppose I should be grateful that you don't wear boots, hmm?"

"Damn. I'm sorry."

"Forget it." She grinned. "I was just teasing you."

"Your sheets . . ."

"I can change them."

He groaned and glanced at his watch. Desdemona saw that the numbers on the dial were glowing softly.

"Do you know what time it is?" he asked.

"Howdy Doody time?"

"It's after midnight."

She gave him a dreamy smile. "No kidding."

"I've got to get out of here." Stark rolled off the bed and stood. "Macbeth will be wondering where the hell I am."

"He won't panic." It was cold without Stark to warm her.

"No, but Jason and Kyle might." Stark's gaze lingered wistfully on her black stockings and the scrap of torn black lace panties. His jaw tightened. He scooped his shirt off the floor and headed toward the bathroom. "I'll be right back."

"Take your time." Desdemona studied the high, shadowed ceiling of her loft and marveled at the interesting sensation between her legs. Not pain. Not quite an ache. More like the pleasantly used feeling that she experienced after brisk exercise. Her body had just done something it had been designed to do, and it felt good. It felt right. Satisfied with itself.

She got up and reached for the Kimono-style bathrobe that hung on the brick wall behind the bed.

Stark emerged from the bathroom, his big hands busy with the buttons on his white shirt. He had run his fingers through his dark hair. He crossed the room to retrieve his gold-framed glasses. His face was set in familiar lines of intent concentration.

"I don't suppose you have time for coffee?" Desdemona said as she tied the sash of her robe.

"No. Sorry." He grabbed his jacket off the back of the chair and slanted another quick glance at his watch. "I've got to get home. I'll call you in the morning."

"Promises, promises."

"What did you say?"

"Nothing. Just mumbling. A bit of postcoital disorientation, I guess. Or maybe I've been reading too many warnings in women's magazines."

He frowned. "Are you all right?"

She gave him a sugary smile. "Just peachy."

"You're acting weird."

"Nobody ever said that I was the best actress in the family." Desdemona realized that her knees were wobbly.

Stark hooked his jacket over his shoulder and walked to where she stood. "I wish I didn't have to leave like this."

"Me, too."

"You're sure you're okay?"

"Absolutely, positively okay."

"Good." He cradled her chin in his palm, bent his head, and brushed his mouth lightly across hers. "Like I said, I'll call you in the morning."

"Right."

He hesitated as though aware that he should do or say something else but was clearly baffled by what that something was. "Good night."

Desdemona recalled her recent conversation with Pamela Bedford in the ladies' room of the hotel.

I think what bothered me the most was that he never had much to say after he finished making love. Doesn't it upset you that he just gets out of bed, says good night, and leaves?

"Good night, Stark."

He nodded brusquely and started toward the door.

Desdemona trailed after him.

Stark let himself out into the hall. He quickly pulled the door almost closed and then turned to look at her through the narrow crack. "Be sure to lock up behind me."

"I will."

Stark hesitated. "Did I tell you that you remind me of a fractal design?"

"No, you didn't. Thank you." Desdemona paused. "What's a fractal?"

"I'll explain it later. I've got to run." Stark gently closed the door in her face.

Desdemona pressed her ear to the wood panel and listened to his footsteps recede down the hall.

She waited until she knew that he had reached the elevator before she yanked the door open again. She leaned out into the hall.

Stark was at the far end of the corridor, glancing impatiently at his watch.

"That's right, dash off into the night without bothering to ask if it was good for me, too." Desdemona called very loudly. "See if I care."

Stark turned, startled. "What the hell?"

"Who cares that I've just had my first orgasm? What does it matter to you? You've probably given tons of orgasms to zillions of women. No big deal for you, huh, Stark?"

The door across the hall snapped open. Miriam Eckerby, gray hair in pink curlers as usual, scowled at Desdemona. "What's going on out here?"

"Nothing." Desdemona smiled brightly at her neighbor. "I was just discussing a significant, life-altering event which recently occurred in my apartment. It was caused by that man standing down there at the end of the hall."

"Really?" Mrs. Eckerby leaned out to stare at Stark.

"It was a major turning point for me, Mrs. Eckerby," Desdemona confided in a clear, ringing voice that she knew carried the length of the corridor. Wainwrights knew how to project. "But I do not believe that the person responsible for it gives a damn. He just said good night and walked out."

Mrs. Eckerby sighed. "They're all the same, aren't they?"

"No, this one is actually quite different." Desdemona started to close her door. "Good night, Mrs. Eckerby."

"Good night, dear."

Desdemona slammed her door shut.

Stark's footsteps echoed in the hallway. A few seconds later he pounded on the door.

"Desdemona, open up."

"I wouldn't think of delaying you for another instant. Hurry on home, Stark."

"Damn it, open the door. I want to talk to you."

"Too late. You had your chance." Desdemona slid the dead bolt into place. She knew Stark must have heard the unmistakable sound. "Good night, sweet prince. Drive carefully."

"Desdemona, we've got an audience out here. Stop playing to it."

"Wainwrights always play to the crowd. Run along. Thanks for everything. And I do mean everything."

"Damn it to hell."

Desdemona sensed him hesitating a few seconds longer, and then she heard his footsteps heading back toward the elevator. This time she waited until she knew he was gone.

She opened the door again.

Mrs. Eckerby was not the only one peering out into the hall. Christopher Peters in 508 had also appeared.

"Everything all right out here?" Christopher inquired politely.

"Yes, thank you," Desdemona said.

Mrs. Eckerby clucked admonishingly. "Your very first orgasm, dear? You should have said something ages ago. I could have loaned you my vibrator."

*   *   *

Her first orgasm?

Stark could not believe it. She was so damned sexy. So responsive. So passionate. Surely she had experienced plenty of orgasms.

Then he recalled how tight she had been. He remembered her soft little gasps of surprise. In retrospect he realized that he had ignored a number of small signs, all of which indicated that Desdemona was a woman of extremely limited experience.

Damn. He never had been good at picking up subtle cues from the female of the species.

Stark had to call on all of his willpower in order to concentrate on the drive home. No woman had ever left him feeling so bemused after sex. Always in the past he had returned immediately to his normal, clearheaded state of mind after a sexual encounter.

For him, passion was a short-lived, very intense experience that temporarily clouded his brain in the same way a bad command scrambled a computer screen full of data.

Usually he simply rebooted and returned to full operating mode within minutes.

But tonight his brain was not responding to the customary prompts. Luckily it was late and the streets were nearly empty. Traffic was not a problem. Stark made it home in less than twenty minutes.

Macbeth was waiting for him. He surveyed Stark with cool interest as he collected his leather jacket and Jeep keys. "Have a good evening?"

"Yes," Stark said brusquely. He had a feeling that Tony was not the only member of Desdemona's family who felt protective toward her. "Jason and Kyle okay?"

"No problem. We sent out for pizza and played some video games. They went to bed around ten." Macbeth sauntered out onto the front steps. "See you in the morning."

"Right. Thanks."

Macbeth paused. "You coming to Desdemona's birthday party next week?"

"Yes."

Macbeth nodded. "Good. Bring Jason and Kyle."

"I will."

Stark closed the door and set the computerized security alarm system. He realized that he was not ready for bed. Memories of making love to Desdemona were going to make it hard to get to sleep tonight.

He decided to do what he usually did when he was feeling restless. He climbed the concrete and steel staircase to his study and switched on the computer.

The soothing patterns of ARCANE's intricate programming soon enveloped him. He did not look up from the screen until two small figures appeared in the shadowed doorway.

Jason and Kyle, garbed in pajamas, stood there.

"Thought you were asleep," Stark said.

"Jason woke up a few minutes ago," Kyle said off-handedly. "He wanted to see if you were home yet."

"It wasn't just me," Jason said quickly. "You wanted to see if he was here, too."

"I'm here," Stark said. "How did rehearsal go this afternoon?"

"It went great," Kyle grinned. "Everyone said we're going to bring down the house."

"Macbeth says we're headed for Broadway," Jason reported.

"Broadway in Seattle or Broadway in New York?" Stark asked.

"I dunno." Jason seemed unperturbed by the distinction. "Bess, that's Macbeth's mother—"

"She plays one of the monsters," Kyle explained.

"Bess said me and Kyle were the best stagehands the Strolling Players had had in ages. She said we're naturals."

"Yeah, she said they wouldn't be able to put on the show without us," Kyle added. "Augustus says that if we stick around long enough he'll teach me how to work the lights. That's what I want to do."

"I like setting up the scenery," Jason said. "I'm responsible for all the trees in the show."

Stark nodded. "Sounds important."

"It is. Real important. Macbeth says the trees are part of what sets the mood for the actors and the audience. He says without the right mood, nothing else works."

"Mood is important," Stark agreed.

"The lighting is important for atmosphere," Kyle said. "Macbeth says you use lighting to create whole worlds. He says you can do anything with the right lighting."

"I'll keep that in mind," Stark said.

"We're all set for our first performance on Saturday." A flicker of anxiety briefly darkened Jason's exuberant expression. "Are you still going to come see it like you said you would?"

"I wouldn't miss it," Stark promised.

"Something might come up," Kyle said with studied carelessness. "Business or something."

"I'll be there," Stark said.

Jason grinned triumphantly at Kyle. "See? I told you he wouldn't change his mind."

Tony was in Desdemona's office, fiddling with the computer when she walked in the next morning.

"Hi kid." He didn't look up. "I'm redoing the format of your inventory program so that it will highlight in color the stuff that's running low. Now you won't have to go through the supplies list item by item every day. Just look for anything formatted in purple."

Desdemona was instantly alarmed. "You didn't change any of the commands, did you?"

"Relax. I didn't alter the commands."

"You're sure? Every time you mess around with my computer I have to learn something new. You know how I hate that. Now that I've finally got the hang of the thing, I don't want to have to spend time relearning a new version of any of the programs."

"You gotta stay current to stay competitive. Regular software updates for specialized programs like this one are the wave of the future."

"In the catering business, staying current means that I know the difference between a vegetarian meal and a vegan meal. Tony, what's a fractal?"

"It's a computer-generated art. You must have seen some of it. Weird-looking, intricate designs in bright, intense colors. When you create fractal art on a computer screen it keeps evolving and changing. But you can freeze a single moment of it and frame it."

"Oh, right." Desdemona smiled, pleased. "I think I saw some

framed examples at Stark's house. The pictures looked like something from another planet."

"Yeah."

"I need my chair, Tony. I have to plan a vegan buffet menu for a luncheon next week."

"Sure." Tony hit a couple more keys and then got to his feet. He finally looked at her. "Something wrong?"

"No, of course not." Desdemona went around the edge of her desk and took her chair.

"You look kind of strange."

"Gosh, thanks. You're not looking too bad, yourself."

"I'm serious. You look . . . I don't know. A little different."

Juliet opened the office door and stuck her head around the corner. "Desdemona, if you've got anything on this weekend, cancel it. I've found Mr. Dream Machine for you."

"Forget it," Desdemona said. "I'm busy."

"No excuses. This guy is terrific," Juliet enthused. "He's the new artistic director at the Madison Street Theater. You're going to love him."

"No, I won't." Desdemona reached for her daily schedule book.

"Yes, you will," Juliet coaxed. "He's really a nice guy. Give him a chance."

"I said no." Desdemona gave her cousin a smug, complacent smile. "Thank you for the thought, but as it happens, I'm going to be busy."

"You mean you've got a catering job scheduled?"

"No, this is personal, not business."

Tony's face tightened. "What's up? You got a hot date this weekend?"

"Not yet," Desdemona said. "But I expect to have one."

"Really?" Juliet's eyes widened. "With Stark?"

"Yep."

"This is getting serious, isn't it?" Juliet murmured thoughtfully.

"Yes, it is."

"Hell," Tony muttered. "I still can't believe you've fallen for him."

Desdemona shrugged. "You know what they say about opposites attracting."

"Opposites?" Bess edged Juliet out of the doorway. "Did I hear someone say something about opposites attracting?"

"Yes, you did." Desdemona scanned a list of many items suited to a vegan meal. "Now, if you'll excuse me, I've got to get to work."

"Are we talking about Stark?" Bess demanded.

"Yes, we are." Desdemona glanced up. "Juliet, did you start the miniature spinach quiches we need for the baby shower today?"

"They're in the oven. And they're really cute. Why don't you do them for that luncheon you're planning? They'd look nice next to the buckwheat noodle salad."

"Forget it. This is a vegan menu, remember? No eggs or dairy products."

"That's right. I forgot." Juliet eyed her closely. "Are you serious about being serious about Stark?"

"Yes, I am."

"Shit." Tony slammed the flat of his hand against the office wall. "You're sleeping with him, aren't you?"

Desdemona blushed to the roots of her hair. "That's none of your business."

"The hell it isn't." Tony swung around to confront her. "You're my sister."

Desdemona sighed. "Tony, I'm twenty-eight, soon to be twenty-nine. I own my own business, I pay taxes, and I have an excellent credit rating. I think I'm old enough and stable enough to have a mature relationship."

"You *are* sleeping with him," Juliet breathed. "Desdemona, this is incredible."

"You're actually having an affair with a nerd?" Tony gritted.

Desdemona tossed aside her pen and leaped to her feet. "The next person who calls Stark a nerd gets fired, is that clear?"

"Calm down, calm down." Juliet waved her hands in a soothing motion. "No one's out to insult your client. We're just having a little trouble dealing with this, that's all."

"Wainwrights always marry their own kind," Bess announced in ominous tones.

Desdemona rolled her eyes. "Who said anything about marriage?"

A startled silence fell on the office. Three pairs of eyes regarded Desdemona with grave interest.

"When did this affair actually begin?" Juliet asked delicately. "I mean, in the technical sense."

"That is a private matter," Desdemona said.

Tony's eyes narrowed. "It was last night, wasn't it? You started sleeping with him last night. That's why you seemed different this morning."

"I said, it's a private matter," Desdemona snapped. "Now, if this inquisition is over, I really would like to get back to work."

Juliet put a hand to her brow. "My God. I see it all now. He seduced you after the ball. You were carried away by the glamorous setting, the tux, the music, the champagne. You lost your head."

"I did not lose my head," Desdemona said. "I knew exactly what I was doing."

"I hope you took precautions," Bess grumbled.

"It was probably just a one-night stand for him," Tony muttered.

Desdemona lost her temper. "It was not a one-night stand."

"How can you be sure of that?" Juliet asked.

"Because we're going to be seeing each other on a regular basis," Desdemona retorted.

"Are you certain?" Bess asked.

"Of course, I'm certain. He said he'd call today, in fact."

"Oh, Desdemona." Juliet shook her head in a pitying manner. "You're so naive sometimes. Don't you know they always say they'll call, and they never do?"

The phone rang.

Desdemona snatched the receiver out of the cradle, grateful for the interruption. "Right Touch Catering."

"Your first orgasm?" Stark asked without preamble.

Desdemona collapsed into her chair. She fought to conceal a silly grin. "Why, yes. Yes, it was, as a matter of fact."

"Interesting," Stark said.

"I certainly thought so."

"So, do you want to do it again sometime?" Stark asked.

Conscious of her audience, Desdemona twirled around in the swivel chair until she faced the back wall. She lowered her voice. "It's considered tacky to ask a lady out just to have sex."

"I knew that," Stark said. He cleared his throat. "Would you care to attend the theater with me?"

"That sounds lovely. When?"

"Tomorrow afternoon. The premiere of *Monsters Under the Bed*."

"I'd love to go with you," Desdemona said demurely. "As it happens, I'm very fond of the theater."

The crash of her office door being slammed shut made her glance over her shoulder. She saw Tony striding past the window.

He looked as if he was in a mood to do something violent.

"What was that sound?" Stark asked.

"Nothing important," Desdemona assured him.

*T*hundering applause greeted the final curtain as *Monsters Under the Bed* came to a close. Cheers and enthusiastic shouts filled the small auditorium. The actors took their bows.

From the last row of the tiny theater, a playhouse shared by several fringe theater companies and loaned to the Strolling Players for their performances, Desdemona surveyed the crowd of youthful theater patrons.

The too-adult expressions of wariness, cynicism, and uncertainty that had marked their young faces earlier, were gone, at least for the moment. The magic of the theater had enveloped them for a short while, giving the children a respite from the overwhelming stresses that plagued their lives.

"At least I understood this play better than I did the last one I saw," Stark said. "No flyswatters."

Desdemona laughed. "Congratulations. You're on your way to becoming a real theater buff."

"Want to go backstage? I've, uh, got passes."

"I'm impressed. You must have connections."

"I know a couple of people." Stark reached for her hand.

They waited until the herd of youngsters had raced up the center aisle to the small lobby. Desdemona took the opportunity to edge closer to Stark. She savored the strength in his grip. There was something very solid and sure about him, she thought. He might prove inflexible from time to time, perhaps even mulish under certain circumstances, but a woman could trust a man like this. If he made a commitment, he would stick to it.

Desdemona's fingers brushed the worn corduroy of Stark's slouchy jacket. She inhaled deeply. Stark's faint scent brought forth a warm rush of memory. She had not yet recovered from their lovemaking, she realized. She was still a little giddy.

"I understand you've met Jason and Kyle," Stark said as their path cleared. He drew her down the center aisle toward the stage.

"I certainly have. Macbeth brought them by Right Touch twice this week when we needed extra help to load the van. They were great."

"I'm afraid they've both been struck by stage fever."

"I know the symptoms well."

Jason popped out from behind the curtain. He waved wildly to get Stark's attention. "Over here, Sam. I have to put the trees away in the prop room. I'll be through in a minute. Hi, Desdemona."

"Hello, Jason. Great show. The trees were spectacular."

Jason beamed. "Thanks." He vanished behind the curtain again.

"Hi, Sam. Desdemona." Kyle hailed them from the wings. "How'd you like the way I handled the curtains?"

"I don't see how they could have opened or closed the show without you," Stark said.

"Yeah." Kyle grinned hugely. "The kids in the audience really liked the play, didn't they?"

"You were a hit," Stark said. "I was sitting in the back row, and I saw everyone in the audience applaud like crazy."

Macbeth loomed in the shadows. "Hello, Desdemona. Stark. Glad you could make it. Enjoy yourselves?"

"It was terrific." Desdemona released Stark's arm to give Macbeth a hug.

"Oh, there you are, Desdemona, dear." Bess sailed across the stage, the grotesque horns of her monster costume tucked under one arm. She had not yet removed her makeup. "Who's this with you?"

"Aunt Bess, I'd like you to meet Sam Stark. Stark, this is Bess Wainwright."

Stark inclined his head in his austere manner. "Mrs. Wainwright."

"Call me Bess." Bess came to a halt and surveyed him from head to toe. "So you're the one."

"Am I?"

"You're not quite what I expected," Bess informed him.

"Is that right?"

"You move well." Bess eyed him with a grudging approval. "You look like you've had some decent training."

"He has had some training," Desdemona said. "But not in acting. Aunt Bess, I absolutely forbid you to make any more personal remarks. At this rate it's only a matter of time before you embarrass me."

"Nonsense. No Wainwright was ever embarrassed by anything except a forgotten line or a missed cue."

"There's a first time for everything," Desdemona said.

Jason and Kyle reappeared. They were bubbling over with the glow of an acknowledged success.

"Want to see backstage?" Jason asked Stark.

"Yes, I would," Stark said.

"Wait'll you see the light booth," Kyle said. "They've got all kinds of neat gadgets up there."

Desdemona smiled at Stark. "I'll wait here."

He nodded once and then allowed himself to be led off, stage left.

Desdemona waited until the three of them had moved out of earshot before she turned to Macbeth. "Looks like the babysitting is going well."

"Yeah." Macbeth smiled slightly. "I was sure glad to see Stark in the audience today. Kyle and Jason had really counted on him being there. He'd told them he would come, but you never know."

"Corporate honchos like that have a way of turning up busy at the last minute, especially when it comes to little kids," Bess said grimly.

Desdemona shook her head. "If Stark says he'll do something, you can bet money on it."

"I think Jason and Kyle are starting to believe that," Macbeth observed quietly.

Twenty minutes later Stark reappeared. Kyle and Jason bounced around him like energetic puppies.

"We're going to get some pizza," Jason said when he spotted Desdemona. "Someplace where they have video games."

"You can come along if you want," Kyle said generously.

"Thank you." Desdemona smiled at Stark. "I'd like that."

Stark looked relieved, as though he'd been half afraid she would not want to join him and his brothers for pizza and video games.

Some of Jason's gleeful enthusiasm faded as they walked out of the theater. His expression turned thoughtful. "Sam, did you know that a lot of those kids in the audience don't have real homes? Macbeth says they have to live in shelters and cheap motels and places like that."

"Some even have to live in cars 'cause that's all their folks can afford," Kyle added.

"A home is a valuable thing," Stark said. "Not everyone has one."

Stark took aim at the hideous green monster and squeezed off the last shot. "Gotcha."

The creature collapsed and vanished in a puff of smoke.

"You did it," Kyle yelped in awestruck amazement. "You destroyed the Wyvern, and you found the treasure. You won the game. Hardly anybody ever wins this one."

Lights flashed, and a row of numbers appeared on the video screen.

Jason gazed at the numbers, entranced. "Wow. Look at that score."

Desdemona peered at the screen. "I didn't think adults were supposed to be any good at these games."

"I've got an edge on this one," Stark admitted as he stepped back from the machine.

"What kind of an edge?" Desdemona asked.

"I invented it."

Kyle and Jason stared at him in open-mouthed astonishment.

Kyle recovered first. "Is that the truth?"

"Yes." Stark fished quarters out of his pocket. "Want to give it a try?"

"Sure." Kyle moved into position. "What's the secret?"

"The secret is not to get greedy when you finally discover the location of the Wyvern's treasure. Leave the gold where it is until you clean the bad guys out of the caverns. Then go back for the treasure."

Kyle frowned. "Yeah?"

"The players who try to take the treasure and run for it always lose," Stark said. "I set it up that way."

Kyle grinned. "Got it." He seized the control sticks.

"It's designed to teach the concept of deferred gratification," Stark said dryly. He looked at Desdemona. "I'm something of an expert on the subject."

"Let me try, let me try," Jason said.

"I'm first." Kyle shoved coins into the slot.

Jason turned to Stark. "When did you invent Wyvern's Treasure?"

"About four years ago. I sold the software design to the company that manufactures it. Other designers update it periodically, but they haven't tampered with the basic structure of the game, so I can still win when I play."

"Cool," Jason breathed. "Way cool. Wait'll I tell my friend Kevin. He's good at this game. He always gets as far as Wyvern hunter status, but he's never gotten a score as high as yours."

Desdemona looked at Stark. "I thought your specialty was security and encryption programs based on chaos theory."

"Based on theories derived from the science of complex structures," Stark corrected patiently. "I told you, I don't like the word *chaos*. It's not a proper description of the field."

"Whatever. Did you invent Wyvern's Treasure just for fun?"

"No." Stark took her arm and guided her back to the red vinyl booth.

The aroma of fresh-cooked pizza filled the colorful restaurant. Stark had discovered that Kyle and Jason considered pizza to be nature's perfect food. He had eaten more pizza since their arrival than he had eaten in the past year.

Desdemona slid into the booth across from him and reached for her glass of sparkling water. "Why did you invent it, then?"

"I wrote the game program because I needed cash to start up Stark Security Systems." He studied her intently, marveling at how good it felt to have her sitting across from him.

The garish restaurant lighting turned her frothy red curls into coils of spun copper. Her turquoise eyes glowed with warmth and laughter. He thought about Wednesday night and burned.

"Thanks for inviting me along this afternoon," Desdemona said. "I love pizza."

"Do you? Personally, I think I'm in serious danger of overdosing on it." Stark glanced across the room to where Kyle and Jason were hovering over the video machine. "I want to thank you for sending Macbeth to me. Getting Jason and Kyle involved with the Strolling Players was a good idea."

"I'm glad they're enjoying it."

"It's taking them out of themselves or something." Stark was not certain how to put it into words. "Makes them feel a part of something important."

"It's always illuminating to discover that there are other people who are a lot worse off than you are," Desdemona said. "And that you can do something to help."

Stark switched his gaze back to her. "Maybe the next time we go out on a date, we can go alone."

"I'd enjoy that, too."

"And maybe we can go to bed together afterward," Stark suggested, feeling optimistic about life in general.

"You have a one-track mind."

"I realize that I tend to be somewhat linear in my thinking, but I'm trying very hard not to be tacky."

Desdemona sipped daintily from her glass of fizzing water. Her eyes sparkled. "Luckily for you, you're too sexy to be called tacky."

What with the responsibilities that came with being an older brother, as well as the demands of business and the ARCANE project, Stark found it extremely difficult to maintain political correctness in his thinking processes.

It was hard, for example, not to think tacky thoughts about Desdemona.

By Monday morning all he really wanted to focus on was how to be alone with her. It was a thorny problem, but he was more than willing to devote a great deal of energy to it. He was, after all, very goal-oriented.

Maud Pitchcott looked up as he walked through the door of his office.

"Good morning, Mr. Stark. A lovely day. Full of sunlight and fresh promise, isn't it?"

"It's raining."

"April showers bring May flowers."

"It's the middle of June."

"We wouldn't appreciate the sunshine if we didn't have to first experience the rain," Maud said with ill-concealed triumph.

"I give up. You win." Stark started past her desk toward the door of the inner office.

"Oh, Mr. Stark, I almost forgot. A package arrived for you." Maud reached for a large box wrapped in brown paper that sat on the table behind her desk. She handed it to him. "See? A surprise to brighten a rainy day."

Stark took the package. He glanced at the return address. "It's from my mother."

"How lovely."

"Probably a wedding gift. Looks like she didn't get my note telling her the bride ran off."

Maud's face fell for an instant, but she rallied quickly. "Never forget, Mr. Stark, nothing happens without a reason, even though in the darkest hours before the dawn that reason seems obscure. Every cloud has a silver lining. By the way, Mr. McCallum wants to see you as soon as you're available."

"Send him in."

Stark went into his inner sanctum, put the package down on his desk, hooked his jacket on a coat rack, and sat down. The intercom chimed gently.

"What is it, Maud?"

"There's a call for you on line two. A Mrs. Alison Stark." Maud's tone ended on a distinct question mark.

"Damn." Stark hesitated. He was not in a mood to talk to Alison, but he supposed there was no avoiding it. "I'll take it. Tell McCallum to wait." He punched line two. "This is Stark."

"Sam? This is Alison. I called to see how the boys are doing."

"They're doing fine." Stark studied the screen of his electronic calendar, mentally reviewing his schedule for the day. He wondered if Desdemona would be free for lunch.

"You're sure?"

The odd note in her voice got his full attention. "Of course, I'm sure. I just sent them off with their babysitter."

"You've got a babysitter for them?" Alison sounded flabbergasted.

"A friend of mine recommended him. He's got them involved in a children's theater project. They gave their first performance on Saturday, and it was a smash hit."

"Good grief. I had no idea Jason and Kyle were interested in theater."

"Is there a problem here, Alison? Because I've got a busy schedule today." Stark found a pair of scissors in his desk drawer. He went to work on the box his mother had sent.

"No, there's no problem here," Alison paused. "To be frank, I called because I thought that you'd be more than ready to pack Jason and Kyle up and ship them back to Portland by now."

"Like I said, they're doing fine."

"No offense, but I'm amazed to hear that. Maybe their therapist was right."

"About what?"

"Jason and Kyle may see you as a substitute for Hudson." Her voice dropped to a confidential tone. "You know, I was at my wit's end the night they ran off to Seattle."

"Forget it." Stark got the tape undone. He lifted the top of the box.

"I've been having intensive stress reduction sessions with my own therapist. I'm feeling much calmer now."

"That's nice." Stark picked up the card that was lying on top of the tissue paper. It read:

Dear Sam,

Sorry to miss your wedding. We'll be in Europe by the time you get this. Things have been hectic around here. Richard graduated from law school this spring. Fourth in his class. Katy just got engaged to a heart surgeon. We're thrilled. Excellent family. Brian and I are off to England tomorrow. We'll be gone two months. Business and pleasure trip. Will call when we get back. In the meantime, please give my regards to your bride.

Love,
Mother

Stark lifted several layers of tissue paper. A crystal punch bowl glittered inside the box. He was pretty sure he recognized it.

"Sam? Sam, are you listening to me?"

"I'm listening, Alison." Stark transferred the punch bowl to another table.

"I needed some space. I still do."

"Uh-huh." Stark switched on his computer.

"My therapist says that the stress I'm under has overwhelmed me, and the boys sense it. It makes them feel insecure."

"Right." Stark scanned his e-mail messages. He paused when he saw a familiar name and address.

sellinger@rosetta.edu

"It's been very difficult for all of us," Alison said defiantly.

"Right." Stark hadn't heard from Sellinger in months. He wondered why the director of the Rosetta Institute had contacted him today. The e-mail message was short and to the point.

Please call. Urgent.

"I appreciate your taking Jason and Kyle for a while. We all needed a break from each other."

"Right."

"At first the boys actually blamed me for the fact that Hudson walked out, you know. Their therapist says that's normal, and I've tried to be understanding, but their attitude has definitely added to my overall stress level."

"Right."

"Dr. Titus, that's the boys' therapist, has worked with them very extensively. He's tried to make them realize that the breakup of the marriage had nothing to do with them."

"Right."

"But they've been extremely uncooperative. Rude and sullen."

"Right."

"You're sure they're not a problem?"

"I'm sure." Stark hit a key to pull up his personal list of phone numbers that he kept stored in the computer.

"In that case," Alison said in a cautious tone, "the boys' therapist has recommended that I take a vacation."

"With him?"

There was a short, brittle silence. "Have the boys mentioned Dr. Titus to you?"

"They said you're having an affair with him."

"They know about my relationship with Cliff?" Alison asked in a strangled voice.

"Yeah." Stark found Sellinger's number.

"It's okay, you know," Alison said swiftly. "There's absolutely nothing wrong with my seeing Dr. Titus. He's their therapist, not mine."

"Right."

"I have my own therapist, Dr. Lachlan, and he says that it's good for me to have a relationship at this particular point in my life."

"Right."

"He says it's just what I need to rebuild my shattered self-esteem."

"Sure."

"He says I have to get past the sense of guilt and the anger."

"Uh-huh. Look, Alison, this kind of psychobabble always confuses me. Kyle and Jason are fine. I've told you that they can stay with me for the rest of the summer. Go ahead and take your vacation with your therapist."

"Dr. Titus is not my therapist. I told you that. He's the boys' therapist. Dr. Lachlan is mine."

"Hell, take them both on vacation if you like. I don't really give a damn."

"There's no need to be sarcastic," Alison said stiffly.

"I'm not trying to be sarcastic, I'm trying to get off the phone so that I can get some work done."

"I'll call the boys this evening and say good-bye."

Stark took off his glasses and rubbed the bridge of his nose. "Do you want some advice?"

"What advice?" she asked warily.

"Don't tell Jason and Kyle that you're going off on vacation with their therapist."

"There is nothing wrong with my relationship with Dr. Titus," Alison snapped.

"I didn't say there was. I just suggested that you don't make a big deal out of it with Jason and Kyle. It's hard enough for them to figure out who's sleeping with whom at the moment."

"They have to face reality," Alison said. "Damn it, I'm a mature adult. I refuse to pretend that I don't have adult needs. Jason and Kyle must understand that just because their father walked out, that doesn't mean that I don't have a right to a loving, caring relationship."

Stark wished he had kept his mouth shut. "Sure. Sorry I mentioned it."

"Their father is screwing his brains out with that bimbo assistant of his, you know."

"I know. Alison, all I'm suggesting is a little discretion."

"Discretion? You think that bastard, Hudson, is showing discretion? He and that blonde have gone off to Hawaii, for God's sake. I'm the one who got left with two children to raise. I'm the one who has to worry about keeping a roof over our heads. I'm the one who has to provide new shoes and put food on the table and pay for college."

"No."

"What the hell is that supposed to mean?"

"Whatever happens, you won't have to worry about keeping Jason and Kyle housed and fed, and you won't have to worry about their education," Stark said quietly.

"I've got news for you, Stark, Hudson convinced the judge that he only needs to pay minimum child support because I have a career. But I can assure you that I don't make nearly enough in my interior design business to maintain the standard of living that the boys and I had before the divorce. Hudson's support payments, assuming he even bothers to make them, won't make up the difference."

"I'll see that you and Jason and Kyle are taken care of."

There was a startled silence on the other end of the line. "Why would you do that?" Alison asked blankly.

"Because—" Stark broke off, unsure of what he wanted to say. "Forget it. Just don't worry about the money. You'll be all right. I really have to go now, Alison."

"All right," Alison said slowly. "Sam, I—"

"Good-bye, Alison."

"Good-bye."

As soon as the line went dead, Stark dialed Sellinger's number at the Rosetta Institute. He was put through at once.

"Stark, thanks for getting back to me."

Sellinger's plumy voice provoked memories. Stark experienced a brief pang of nostalgia for his days at the Institute. He had gone there immediately after graduating from college. It had been a somewhat cloistered existence, as Desdemona had guessed, but it had also been an important part of his life.

Stark had always respected Sellinger as a man of many talents. The old man was savvy, both in the ways of politics and in terms of sheer intellectual ability. The combination made him an ideal director for the Institute. He had held the post for fifteen years.

"Good to hear from you, sir," Stark said.

"I regret to say that this is a business matter, not a social one," Sellinger said apologetically. "Wanted to let you know that Kilburn has resurfaced. Somewhere in Europe, we believe. You asked me to keep you posted on new developments."

Stark leaned back in his chair and thought about Leonard Kilburn.

Kilburn had held the title of a department manager at the Rosetta Institute. He had worked on the management side, rather than the technical side.

He had vanished from the Institute two and a half years earlier. Sellinger had notified Stark that an extremely sensitive encryption program had vanished with him. The program had been designed by Stark during his days at the Institute.

As with most of the software that Stark had worked on while at the Rosetta Institute, the encryption software had been restricted by the U.S. Government for security reasons.

Kilburn had illegally sold Stark's high-tech programs to a foreign government. He had very likely made a fortune on the deal, because there were fortunes to be made in the murky world of restricted technology sales. The field was not as lucrative as international arms dealing, but it was catching up fast. In fact, the two businesses frequently overlapped. Most high-tech weaponry was linked, one way or another, to computer programming, and military intelligence depended heavily on it.

Fortunately, Stark had designed a hidden self-destruct feature into the encryption software Kilburn had stolen. It had triggered as soon as the foreign buyer had tried to install the program. No damage had been done, but everyone was aware that it had been a close call.

Kilburn, however, had vanished.

"Interesting," Stark said. "How did you find Kilburn?"

"Apparently he tried to broker a deal for some restricted software that was stolen from a weapons lab in Virginia. We got wind of it. Tried to track him through the computer link he used. Unfortunately, we scared him off before we could pin down his location. Have no idea what he's up to or what he'll do next, but I thought you ought to know he hasn't disappeared for good."

"I didn't think he would."

Sellinger chuckled, a rich, fruity sound. "I doubt he'll come anywhere close to Stark Security Systems. He's smart enough to realize that you took the theft of the encryption program two years ago rather personally."

"That was my design that he stole."

"Yes, I know. Luckily for us and our friends in Washington, you had it well protected. Well, I just wanted to bring you up to date."

"I appreciate the news."

"I realize you've wanted to get your hands on Kilburn ever since he made off with those programs," Sellinger said. "So have I. If you pick up any traces of him, let me know."

"I will."

"Good luck. Oh, by the way, sorry I couldn't make it to your wedding."

"You didn't miss a thing," Stark said.

"You don't mean—"

"Afraid so."

Sellinger sighed. "Sorry to hear that."

"When life gives you lemons, you make lemonade."

"What the devil does that mean?"

"Every cloud has a silver lining." Stark smiled to himself. "I'm now dating the caterer."

"Good lord."

The knock on the office door interrupted Stark before he could tell Sellinger the whole story. Dane walked into the office and raised his eyebrows in silent inquiry when he saw that Stark was on the phone. Stark waved him to a chair.

"Dane just came in," Stark said to Sellinger.

"Say hello to him for me," Sellinger said. "You two seem to be doing rather well out there on your own. Congratulations. Good-bye, Stark."

Stark hung up the phone. "That was Sellinger. He sends his regards."

Dane looked mildly surprised. "What did he want?"

"He was bringing me up to date on Kilburn. He says the bastard resurfaced again recently."

Dane whistled softly. "Any idea of where he is?"

"No. They weren't able to pinpoint him. He's gone to ground again."

Dane grinned. "Relax. He's not your problem anymore. Someone at the Institute will track him down one of these days."

"Sure." Stark shook off his annoyance. "Enough of old news. Tell me some good news."

"The Hammercomb job," Dane tossed a sheaf of papers onto the desk. "We got it. That's Hammercomb's signature on the contract. Stark Security Systems has just been hired to do a complete security analysis of their entire computer system and to recommend measures and strategies to protect it."

"Nice going." Stark pulled the papers toward him. "Very nice going. This was a big one."

"And it will lead to other big ones."

"Yes."

"We're hot," Dane said softly. "And once you finish working out the bugs in ARCANE, we are going to be even hotter."

Stark looked up from the contract. "I guess this means we won't have to beg for our old jobs back at the Institute."

"Are you kidding? The Institute will be coming to us one of these days. Wait and see." Dane sprawled in his chair and regarded Stark with a considering look. "Speaking of clients, all set for the reception at your place at the end of the week?"

"As far as I know. I'm leaving everything in Desdemona's hands."

Dane's mouth curved. "Everything?"

"Everything."

"This is serious, isn't it?"

143

"What? The reception? Of course it's serious. I hate these things, but it will be good for business."

"I'm not talking about the reception. I'm talking about you and your personal caterer. You're getting very close to her, aren't you?"

"So?"

"Watch out, pal. The last thing you need right now is another fiancée."

Stark scowled. "I'm not engaged to her. Hell, I'm not even thinking about marriage this time around."

"Are you sure?"

"Of course I'm sure." Stark felt a curious tension in his body. "This time I'm not looking any farther ahead than the next date."

"You're having an affair," Dane repeated neutrally.

"Right." Stark recalled Alison's words. "A mature, adult relationship."

"The last time you tried to have one of those, you wound up standing alone at the altar. Don't you think it's a little too soon for you?"

"What's that supposed to mean?"

"The thing is, I know you, Stark. You're a man who follows patterns. But this time you're not following your usual pattern."

"What is my usual pattern?"

"Generally speaking, you languish in celibacy for vast stretches of time between relationships."

"I've learned my lesson." Stark leveled his pen in Dane's direction. "I'm going to keep this simple and uncomplicated."

"Come off it. This is your old friend, Dane, remember? Let's have a little honesty here. Three years ago you set yourself the goal of getting married. You know how you are when you're working on a project. You just keep going until it's finished."

"Not this time. I have officially abandoned the goal."

Dane studied his manicured nails. "Just as well, since she's not exactly your type."

The comment irritated Stark. "I'm well aware of that. But I don't have to worry about it. I'm going to go with the flow in this relationship."

Dane smiled. "You? Submit to the chaotic forces of romance and unbridled passion? I'll believe that when I see it."

"I'm not submitting to anything. I'm having a simple uncompli-cated affair, and that's all there is to it."

"You always manage to complicate things," Dane said. "Trust me, it's your nature."

Alone in his shadowed study that evening, Stark sat at his computer and mulled over the effect Alison's evening phone call had had on Jason and Kyle.

On the surface things appeared to have gone fairly well. The boys had taken the news of their mother's vacation with Titus in stride, just as they had accepted their father's trip to Hawaii.

"Sam?"

Stark looked toward the door. Jason stood in the shadows. He was dressed in his pajamas.

"I thought you were in bed," Stark said.

"I was. But I couldn't sleep."

"Probably the pizza. I warned you not to order the Garbage Truck Special."

"It was good." Jason wandered farther into the room. "What are you doing?"

"I'm working on a program designed to protect computer systems."

Jason peered at the screen. "The stuff on the screen looks all scram-bled up."

"It is." Stark punched a couple of buttons. The random characters that cluttered the screen began to reform themselves. "But underneath the surface there's a pattern. I can retrieve it with the right code."

"Yeah?" Jason watched intently as the meaningless array of char-acters became two neat paragraphs. "I can read it now."

"That's the whole point."

"This is cool. Where did you learn how to do this stuff?"

Stark shrugged. "Most of it I taught myself."

"Can you teach it to me?"

"If we have enough time."

"Mom said we could stay here the whole summer. Is that enough time?"

"It's enough to get started."

A small sound in the doorway caught Stark's attention. He glanced around again and saw Kyle.

"What are you two doing?" Kyle asked.

"I was showing Jason how my new security program works," Stark said.

"The one you call ARCANE? I want to see, too."

"Okay." Stark hit a key. The screenful of data went back to its scrambled state. "ARCANE has several features. One of them is encryption. I can encode the information that I want to protect inside a lot of constantly shifting garbage."

"Is that what you call chaos?"

"Complexity. Now, then, the secret of complex structures is that they aren't truly chaotic. They just look that way at first glance. The variables that control them are very, very subtle. Once I discover them, however, I can use them to manipulate data."

"That stuff on the screen now looks just like the pizza we had for dinner," Jason said.

"Exactly. It conceals the data we want to protect behind a cloud of static." Stark pressed a few more keys. "By altering some more variables, I can retrieve the information that was hidden behind the static."

"This is great." Kyle looked at Stark. "Is this the kind of stuff you sell?"

"Yes."

"If I was as good as you are on a computer, I'd invent games," Kyle said. "Not business stuff."

Stark smiled. "Working with ARCANE is a lot like playing a very complex video game."

"Is it?" Jason asked.

"Sure." Stark hit a few more keys. "I told you, ARCANE has several features. In addition to encryption and decryption it can also act like an octopus."

"An octopus?" Jason looked intrigued.

"It has tentacles that can reach into other computers and probe network systems."

"Sam?" Kyle kept his attention on the screen.

"Yes?"

"Mind if I ask you a question?"

"Go ahead."

"Mom says you were about our age when Dad left you and your mother."

Stark kept his eyes fixed on the computer. "She's right."

"He never came back, did he? I mean, to stay."

"No," Stark said. "He never did come back to stay."

"He's not coming back to stay with me and Jason, either, is he?"

"No," Stark said. "He's not coming back. But things will be okay."

"Yeah?"

"Trust me," Stark said.

11

The card attached to the last birthday present read, "Happy Birthday to Desdemona from Stark."

Desdemona glanced up from the small, neatly wrapped package. A hush descended on the private dining room at the back of the restaurant. The colorful wrappings of a half-dozen recently opened gifts, including the turquoise and silver squash blossom necklace Desdemona's parents had sent from Tucson, littered the surface of the table. Only a few crumbs from the demolished birthday cake remained of the feast.

Everyone watched Desdemona as she went to work on the last package. The crowd of Wainwrights waited with piqued curiosity to see what Stark's idea of a birthday present was. Juliet and Kirsten looked curious. Macbeth and Henry were intrigued. Tony's eyes were narrowed.

Stark, himself, had a stoic expression on his face. He was clearly prepared for his present to be hailed as an unqualified disaster. Desdemona wondered how many gifts he had given in his life. Then she wondered how many he had received. She smiled at him.

"Hurry up and open it, Desdemona," Jason urged. "We went with Stark to buy it, and it's really neat."

Kyle grinned eagerly. "I bet you're gonna love it."

"I'm sure I will." Desdemona's fingers trembled as she carefully undid the elaborate red bow.

Her first gift from Stark, she thought with a sense of wonder. Whatever it was, she would cherish it forever.

"Well? Let's have a look at it." Augustus spoke from the far end of the table.

Desdemona gave her uncle a mocking scowl of disapproval. "I haven't even got the paper off yet."

"Don't rush her, dear," Bess said.

"She went through the others quick enough," Augustus retorted. "Same way she always does. How come this one's taking so long to open?"

"Hang on a second, Uncle Augustus." Desdemona carefully placed the bow on the table and peeled away the wrapping paper as though it were made of silk.

When she was finished she found herself holding a small box. The picture on the lid showed a flat, high-tech-looking metal object no larger than her hand. The label beneath the picture read *PDA X-1000*.

"It's beautiful," Desdemona breathed. "It's the most beautiful PDA X-1000 I've ever seen. Thank you, Stark."

She jumped to her feet and went around the table to give him an exuberant kiss. The stoic look vanished from his eyes.

"You like it?" he asked cautiously.

"It's gorgeous." Desdemona opened the box and removed the object inside. She touched it lovingly. "Just what I've always wanted."

"I knew she'd like it," Kyle said gleefully. "I was with him when he picked it out."

"Me, too," Jason said. "It's one of the new wireless models."

The majority of birthday party celebrants exchanged blank glances.

Augustus was frankly baffled. "What the devil is it?"

"It's a PDA X-1000," Desdemona said. Lovingly, she stroked the tiny little antennalike thing on the side of the strange machine.

"What's a PDA X-1000?" Bess demanded.

"What does it do?" Juliet asked.

Desdemona pretended not to hear the questions because she had absolutely no idea what a PDA X-1000 was, let alone what it did.

Tony unwittingly came to the rescue. "PDA stands for personal digital assistant." He leaned forward with grudging interest. "It's a very small computer that Desdemona can carry in her pocket or purse."

"A computer?" Henry frowned. "But it doesn't have any keys."

"You don't need keys," Tony explained. He took the gadget from Desdemona and examined it closely. "You write text directly on the screen with this little pen that's attached to it."

"Sam programmed it specially for Desdemona," Jason said proudly. "It will do all sorts of things just for her."

Desdemona removed the PDA from Tony's hand and looked at Stark. "You programmed it just for me?"

"Yes," Stark said.

"How thoughtful. What special things will it do?"

Stark took the small computer from her. "You can send and receive e-mail, for one thing. As Jason said, it's a wireless model. You don't need to hook up to a telephone jack or a computer."

"I've always wanted to be able to send e-mail," Desdemona said.

Tony glared at her. "I installed an e-mail package on your office computer. You've never used it."

"My office computer is too big to carry around with me," Desdemona pointed out.

Tony smoldered. Everyone ignored him. They were too busy watching Stark demonstrate the PDA.

"You can use a PDA to make notes when you're on a jobsite," Stark explained. "Or to do estimates and cost calculations. It's got a graphics package, too, so you can sketch a buffet layout."

"That's wonderful," Desdemona said.

"It translates your handwriting into typewritten characters on the display." Stark handed her the pen. "Here, try it."

Desdemona gingerly took the tiny computer from him and concentrated intently on learning how to use it. Jason, Kyle, and the Wainwrights gathered around her.

"Can I try it out?" Henry asked.

Macbeth inched his chair closer to Desdemona. "Let me give it a whirl."

"No one but Desdemona should use it," Stark said, his gaze on Desdemona as she bent intently over the PDA. "It's a very personal kind of computer. It will learn her handwriting and her work habits.

The more she uses it, the more efficient it will become. After a while it will be almost attuned to her."

"I've been wanting a pet of some kind," Desdemona said happily.

Several days later, Desdemona, garbed in a white apron and a hair net, stood at the center island in Stark's kitchen and issued orders in the manner of a general preparing for battle.

"Juliet, don't forget the chilled asparagus spears and the lemon sauce. Aunt Bess, have you got the cheese tray ready?"

"All set," Bess said. "Goat, sheep, and cow."

"Where're Henry and Vernon?" Desdemona glanced out the window into the drive that wound behind the garden. "They should be here with the van by now."

"Relax, dear," Aunt Bess said. "They'll be here by curtain time."

Juliet removed the tray of asparagus spears from the refrigerator. "Where do you want these, Desdemona?"

Desdemona took her PDA out of her apron pocket and checked the placement chart she had sketched on it. "The table behind the sofa in the living room."

"Got it." Juliet started toward the kitchen door.

Stark emerged from the hall and stepped straight into her path. He was dressed in an expensive dark suit, a brilliant white shirt, and a silk tie. "How is everything going in here?"

"Everything is just fine," Desdemona assured him. "We're on schedule, so don't get nervous. I don't have time to soothe a case of stage fright."

"I'm not nervous." He sounded disgusted.

"I'm delighted to hear that."

"But I'll be glad when this is over," Stark muttered. "I'd rather have gone to that science fiction film with Macbeth and Jason and Kyle. Does this tie look straight?"

Desdemona glanced over her shoulder. "Yes, it looks perfectly straight. Go on out to the living room and read a magazine or something. We've got another half hour before the guests start to arrive."

Stark frowned. "I'll wait upstairs in my study."

"Whatever. Just get out of here. Let us pros do our job."

"Are you sure there isn't something I should be doing?"

"I'm sure."

With a last, uncertain glance around the busy kitchen, Stark reluctantly withdrew.

Bess chuckled as he disappeared. "You'd think he was about to open on Broadway."

"In a lot of ways this reception is just as crucial to him. This is a major event. Some of his most important clients will be here." Desdemona heard a knock at the kitchen door. "That must be Henry and Vernon. Thank goodness."

She hurried over to the door and opened it. "I was beginning to wonder what had happened to you two." She broke off as she saw who was standing next to Vernon. "*Tony.* What are you doing here? I didn't schedule you for this evening."

Desdemona had prudently decided to avoid using Tony on any of the events that Right Touch handled for Stark Security Systems. It was clear that both men were unaccountably irritated by the mere sight of each other. There was tension in the air whenever Stark and Tony were in the same room. The night of her birthday party neither had spoken directly to the other, although both had been superficially polite.

"Sorry, kid." Tony smiled derisively over the top of a carton of wine glasses. "Henry got held up at rehearsal. Don't worry, I'll try to keep out of Stark's sight. Wouldn't want to upset Super Client."

Desdemona stifled a groan. "Try not to do that, will you? He's already nervous enough about this evening." There was no getting around the fact that Stark would not be pleased to see Tony here, but it couldn't be helped.

"Where do you want these glasses?" Tony asked.

"Put them on the counter and unpack them for me." Desdemona looked at Vernon. "Where are the ice sculptures?"

"In the van. Thought I'd find out where you want them placed before I unload them."

Desdemona consulted her computer sketch again and then slipped the PDA back into the pocket of her apron. "Follow me and I'll show you. Aunt Bess, did you find the toothpicks?"

"Got them right here." Bess held up a small carton. "Tony can help me insert them into the shrimp."

"Sure," Tony said.

Stark reappeared in the doorway. "Desdemona, what about the

sparkling water supply? Have we got enough?" He broke off abruptly when he caught sight of Tony. His gaze hardened. "What are you doing here?"

"I'm working for Desdemona, just like everyone else," Tony said in a voice laced with swaggering challenge. "Got a problem with that?"

"Maybe."

"Well, that's too damn bad, isn't it?"

Desdemona moved quickly to forestall trouble. "Stark, Henry's been delayed. Tony is filling in for him. Don't worry about the sparkling water. We've got enough to float a battleship."

Three hours later Stark had forgotten all about his earlier anxiety over the sparkling water. He had even managed to ignore Tony's presence in the kitchen. The reception was a flawless performance. Once again Desdemona had magically transformed him into a social success.

He had a house full of happy clients. Their spouses and companions seemed to be enjoying themselves. A pleasant hubbub of conversation rose above the Mozart concerto that played discreetly in the background.

People exclaimed over the food. The ice sculpture on the center buffet table sparkled. Augustus, aristocratic in black and white formal attire, was doing a fine job of entertaining everyone who stepped up to the bar for wine or seltzer. From the snippets of conversation Stark had overheard, he gathered that Desdemona's uncle was regaling people with tales of his past experiences in the theater.

Desdemona had saved his social hide once again, Stark thought. Knowing that gave him the confidence to move among his guests with some degree of ease. He recalled Desdemona's advice on how to answer questions. Few people wanted extended, in-depth answers, she had said.

The trick was to sound knowledgeable but not pedantic.

". . . Most of the concepts are derived from information theory," he said in response to an inquiry about the nature of complexity. He stopped himself before he could launch into a more detailed explanation. "But I won't bore you with a long discussion of it tonight. Tell you what, my staff has prepared some short papers on how the new concepts are being applied to computer security. I'll have some sent to your office. . . ."

". . . Encryption is one of the obvious applications of complexity, but there are others. Some of the most interesting will be in medicine and meteorology." Easy smile. Share the intellectual humor here. "You know how unpredictable the weather is. Talk about a complex structure. . . ."

To Stark's surprise, he actually got a chuckle from that one.

". . . The term *information highway* is just a catchphrase to describe the linking of a lot of the major computer networks which already exist." Pause to look thoughtfully concerned. "There are some serious implications for business as well as government, of course. Privacy and security issues involved, you know . . ."

Out of the corner of his eye, Stark caught Desdemona's approving smile. He turned his head as she brushed past him on her way back to the kitchen.

"How am I doing?" he asked softly.

"You're doing great. A natural. You should have gone on the stage. Break a leg." She hurried away.

Stark studied the way in which her sleek black dress skimmed her shapely hips. She was definitely the most interesting woman in the room. No, he thought, conscious of the pleasant throb in his lower body, make that the sexiest woman in the room.

It was good to have her here, he realized. Not only because she made this social stuff fly, but because he did not feel so alone in this crowd.

Alone. The word reverberated in his mind with stunning force. It was not a word that he used very often, because it made him think of true chaos.

He had often told himself that the word did not really apply to him. He was a solitary man, not a lonely man. There was a difference. A man of his nature functioned best in solitude.

He heard a droning sound nearby. He realized that he had just been asked a question by the spouse of one of his newest clients. He played back the last few seconds of his mental tape and caught the gist of it.

The woman had asked him a question about networks overseas.

"Yes, there are huge computer networks established in other countries," he said politely. "Users in the United States can access them just as easily as they do the networks here in our own country." He paused to assume what he hoped was a visionary executive expression. "When it comes to computers, there are no borders. Protecting proprietary or government-sensitive information is only going to become increasingly difficult in the years ahead. Good security is the key."

In other words, he added silently, your husband is going to need Stark Security Systems.

He was definitely getting the hang of this, Stark told himself as he joined another cluster of guests. Socializing was difficult, but it was not impossible.

A few minutes later, the tiny vibration from the pager attached to his belt jerked him out of his newfound complacency. He came to an abrupt halt in the middle of a discussion of encoding techniques.

"Excuse me," he said to the manager of a software company. "I'm being paged. I'll be right back."

She gave him a curious look. "Of course."

Stark started through the crowd. He caught a glimpse of Dane on the other side of the room and briefly considered letting him know what had happened.

But there was no time.

Desdemona gave him a quizzical smile as he went past. "Is something wrong?" she asked in a low voice.

"I'm just going to check on something in my study."

"Oh. I thought you might have been overwhelmed by your own success as a host. This thing turned into a real crush, didn't it?"

"Yes." Stark brushed past her.

He stepped out of the living room into the atrium foyer. There was no one around. He took the stairs two at a time to the second level of the house.

When he reached the upper landing he turned and went down the hall to the closed door to his study. He was relieved to see that it was still locked. Perhaps the pager had been triggered by an alarm malfunction. He punched in the security code that opened the door.

The lights came on as he stepped over the threshold. The study was empty.

For a few seconds Stark stood in the doorway, searching for some sign of an intruder. Then he walked across the room to where the computer was bolted to the steel frame of the desk.

At first he could see nothing wrong. But when he angled the halogen lamp so that the strong light fell directly on the back panel of the computer case, he saw the scratch marks around the key lock.

Someone had tried to use a metal tool to get inside the computer case.

"Damn."

Whoever it was must have realized that an alarm had been set off. He had fled, closing the door behind him, before Stark had made it to the top of the stairs.

Stark had passed no one on the stairs, which meant that the intruder might still be somewhere on the second floor.

He went out of the study and methodically checked his bedroom and the one Jason and Kyle used.

Empty. As were the baths and closets.

The door that opened onto the deck was closed. Stark opened it and stepped cautiously out into the balmy night. There was no one about.

The only explanation was that the intruder had waited in the shadows of the upper hall or inside a bedroom until Stark had gone into the study. He had then either slipped back down the stairs while Stark was occupied with investigating the scratches on the computer case or gone out onto the deck. From the deck, the intruder could have gone down the outside stairs and reentered the house through the kitchen door.

All of the door and window alarms were off for the evening because of the presence of so many people in the house.

Stark went back into the study and looked at the computer case again. Those shiny little scratches told their story all too clearly. Someone had tried to open the case and steal the hard disk that contained ARCANE.

Stark realized that he had a whole house full of suspects.

"Shit."

He took another, closer look around the study.

He was just about to leave when he spotted the tip of a toothpick sticking out from under the desk.

He went down on one knee and discovered a half dozen more toothpicks scattered about on the carpet. The intruder had obviously dropped them when he had fled the scene in panic.

A deep cold filled Stark's gut as he rose to his feet. He looked at the handful of toothpicks he held.

The list of suspects had suddenly been shortened.

Two hours later Desdemona watched uneasily as Stark tossed a handful of toothpicks down onto his desk. The little sticks bounced and skittered on the glass surface.

"It had to be one of your people, Desdemona. No one else here tonight would have had a reason to carry a bunch of toothpicks around in his or her pocket."

Desdemona stared at the toothpicks. "I don't understand." She was baffled, not only by the toothpicks but by the change that had come over Stark.

The last of his guests had departed a few minutes earlier. As soon as the car's taillights had disappeared down the drive, he had asked her to follow him upstairs. The icy cold emanating from him sent a frisson of alarm along all her nerve endings.

She realized that there had been only one other occasion when she had glimpsed him in this dark and dangerous mood. That had been the night Tony had greeted them at the door of her apartment dressed in the Exotica Erotica regalia.

Something was terribly wrong. Desdemona wiped her damp palms on her apron. Her stomach clenched.

"What don't you understand?" Stark watched her with a grim patience that was frightening in its intensity.

"Let me get this straight." She took a breath. "You think someone tried to steal your computer tonight?"

"Not the computer. That's not worth more than a couple thousand at most on the secondary market, and there would have been no way to get it out of the house undetected."

"Then what—?"

"The thief was after the hard disk inside. That's where the valuable stuff is stored. Any idiot knows that."

Desdemona swallowed. "You mean he was after your new project? The one you call ARCANE?"

"Yes, Desdemona. That's exactly what I mean. Whoever it was knew that there was no other way to get it except by stealing the entire hard disk. I keep this computer completely isolated. No modem is ever used with it. It's not linked to any network system. That means that no one can get into it through another computer."

"But why would anyone want to steal your special project? You told me it was locked in code."

"Given enough time, a very good hacker can break any code. Even one of mine."

She frowned. "But what would he do with ARCANE once he'd figured out how to break the code?"

"Sell it."

"To whom?"

"Any one of a number of foreign corporations or governments. It's called industrial espionage, Desdemona. Don't pretend you haven't heard of it."

"Well, of course I've heard of it, but it isn't something I worry about on a day-to-day basis," she retorted. "If someone really wants to steal my tapenade recipe, he's welcome to it."

"You may not worry about this kind of espionage, but I do."

She winced. "Yes, I suppose you do. You've made a career out of it, haven't you?"

"The theft of high-tech information is the new ball game. It's replaced a lot of the old-fashioned political espionage. Several of the old players are involved."

"What do you mean?"

"A lot of the pros who once stole and resold national security secrets have undergone career adjustments," Stark said evenly. "They're working in two new fields, arms dealing and the international market for technological secrets. Do you know what that means?"

"Uh, not exactly."

"It means," Stark said, "that the game of industrial espionage is a lot more dangerous than it once was because the players are not amateurs."

"Stark, if your aim is to scare me, you've succeeded. Please tell me what this is all about."

"Someone on your staff is playing the game."

"I don't believe it."

"You'd better believe it. The thief used you as a cover to get at my computer."

"That's crazy," Desdemona whispered. "All you've got are a few scratches on the computer case and a handful of toothpicks. Even if you're right about someone trying to steal your hard disk, why suspect a member of my staff?"

"Because someone on your staff had opportunity and motive."

"Now hold on just one minute here. There were a whole bunch of people in this house tonight. I'll bet a lot of them know more about computers than any of my employees."

"It had to be someone who knew the layout of this house," Stark said. "Most of my guests tonight had never been here before. They couldn't have known where my study is located, let alone anything about my security precautions."

"Wait a second, what about Mr. and Mrs. Ferguson? I know they were at the other party. And so were the Blaunts."

"Ferguson and Blaunt are old-style corporate types. Neither of them knows enough about computers to even contemplate stealing a hard disk."

"Well, what about your friend, Dane McCallum?"

"What about him? He's a marketing and finance man, not a technical man. Furthermore, I saw him downstairs at the same time that I got the page. He couldn't have been up here because he couldn't have been in two places at once."

"How about that guy with the little beard?" Desdemona was grasping at straws, and she knew it.

"Jessick?"

"Whatever. He's been here before. You said something about him being a software genius."

"I saw him downstairs at about the same time I saw McCallum. Got any other suspects you'd care to run by me before we take a close look at your staff?"

Desdemona frantically tried to think of another approach. "None of my people knows anything about computers. They're all theater people, for heavens' sake. Except Vernon Tate. And he's an ice sculptor and a waiter. He's no hacker."

"You're overlooking someone."

"Who?" she demanded furiously.

"Your stepbrother."

Desdemona stilled. She gazed wide-eyed at Stark. "No," she whispered. "Not Tony."

"Why not Tony?"

"He wouldn't do anything like that," Desdemona said. "He *wouldn't.*"

"He knows something about computers. You told me yourself he put your business on-line. I understand he's installed business software for Kirsten, too."

"Yes, but that doesn't make him a hacker or a thief."

"No?" Stark's eyes gleamed in the shadows above the halogen lamp. "He's got a history, doesn't he, Desdemona?"

Desdemona stopped breathing for a heartbeat. "What are you talking about?"

"I'm talking about the fact that he was once under suspicion for embezzlement."

"How do you know about that?"

Stark shrugged. "I did a quick background check on him the day after he turned up in your apartment."

"You did *what?*"

"You heard me."

She was stunned. "But you had no right to do that."

"I'm a security expert, remember?"

"A *computer* security expert. You're not a private investigator. All right, all right, it's true that Tony was in some trouble a few years ago, but it was all cleared up."

"You mean no one was able to prove anything so they dropped the embezzlement charges."

"No charges were ever filed," she hissed. "And no one actually accused him of embezzlement."

"I believe the phrase was 'mishandling of funds.' "

"He was young." Desdemona flung out a hand. "He took some chances on a plan to finance a new theatrical production, and it all fell apart. It was a case of bad judgment, not a criminal act."

"That depends on your point of view," Stark said bluntly. "In my business, the disappearance of several thousand dollars looks like embezzlement."

"Well, it would to you, wouldn't it? You take a suspicious view of everyone and everything. You don't even trust your own fiancées. You make them sign prenuptial agreements, for heaven's sake."

"Leave my ex-fiancées out of this. They've got nothing to do with it."

"Let's be logical about this." Desdemona ignored Stark's derisively raised brows. "Tell me, how would Tony know that there was anything of value stored in your computer?"

"Are you serious? It wouldn't be difficult for anyone to find out that I do my initial development work at home on an isolated system. Hell, Jason and Kyle know that much. They even know something about ARCANE. They could have mentioned it to Macbeth, who, in turn, could have told Tony."

"Good lord, now you're implicating my cousin and your own half brothers. Don't you trust anyone?"

"I'm not accusing any of them of criminal intent," Stark said evenly. "I'm just pointing out one possible route by which Tony could have learned about ARCANE. There are others. A lot of your people have been in and out of this house. They know the layout. Tony could have learned about it from any of your staff."

"But why would Tony want to steal your stupid project?" Desdemona raged.

"Two reasons," Stark said coldly. "The first is that it's worth a great deal of money to certain parties, and Kyle mentioned that your stepbrother just happens to be looking for a bundle of cash to finance his play."

"Every playwright who does a script wants money to finance his play. That doesn't mean he'd steal in order to get it staged. What's the second reason?"

"Revenge," Stark said simply.

Desdemona's mouth fell open. "Revenge? Against whom?"

"Me."

"But, why?"

"Because he wants you, and I've got you."

Desdemona was speechless. "Of all the—"

Stark leaned forward and planted his big hands on the desk. "Listen to me, Desdemona. Because Tony is your stepbrother and because I have no actual proof that he made an attempt to steal ARCANE, I'm going to let this die here tonight."

A tiny flicker of hope came to life in Desdemona. "You will?"

"Yes. But there will be no second chances. Tell Tony that, Desdemona. Tell him if I ever again have any reason to suspect that he's trying to steal from me, I'll nail him to the wall."

"Stark, listen to me—"

"I can do it, Desdemona."

She believed him. There was something very cold and hard and relentless in his face. This was not the man she thought she knew. This was not the man with whom she had fallen in love.

Desdemona took a step back. "I'm going to find Tony. I want to hear what he has to say."

She whirled around and ran for the door. She raced downstairs and nearly collided with Vernon on the floor of the atrium. He reached out to steady her.

"Whoa. Take it easy, Miss Wainwright." Vernon peered anxiously at her face. "Are you okay?"

"No. Where's Tony?"

"In the kitchen."

"Excuse me, Vernon." Desdemona freed herself and dashed into the kitchen.

Tony looked up from where he was repacking glassware when Desdemona burst into the kitchen. He frowned when he saw her expression. "What's wrong?"

She came to a halt in front of him. "Tony, tell me the truth. Were you in Stark's study earlier this evening?"

"Hell, no. Why would I go in there? It's locked, anyway, isn't it?"

"How did you know that?"

"Macbeth said one of Stark's brothers mentioned that it's got a special security code lock on the door."

Bess, Augustus, and Juliet stopped what they were doing and gathered anxiously around Tony and Desdemona. Vernon walked into the kitchen and stood to one side with a helpless expression.

"What's going on?" Bess demanded.

"Stark claims that someone tried to steal the hard disk in his computer this evening." Desdemona did not look away from Tony. "He thinks Tony is guilty."

"Son-of-a-bitch," Tony muttered. "And you believe him, don't you?"

"No, I think he's wrong," Desdemona said fiercely. "And I want you to confirm it. Tell me you didn't try to steal that damned hard disk tonight, Tony."

"I didn't try to steal anything from that bastard." Tony glanced past her. His expression hardened. "I swear it, kid. But I can't prove it."

"No, you can't," Stark said from the kitchen doorway. "Just as I can't prove that you did try to steal it. But that won't stop me if you try anything like this again, Wainwright. I'll find a way to deal with you. Trust me."

Tony stiffened. "Who are you going to believe, Desdemona? Your brother or this son-of-a-bitch?"

"I think Stark is mistaken," Desdemona said desperately.

"Mistaken?" Tony smiled humorlessly. "I think he's lying. I think he's concocted this whole damn story just to turn you against me."

"No," Desdemona whispered. "That's not true. Why would he do such a thing?"

"To get me out of the picture." Tony kept his gaze on Stark. "Don't you see? He knows that you and I have a special kind of relationship, and he can't stand knowing that. He's the possessive type."

"That's not true," Desdemona said.

"Sure it is," Tony insisted softly. "He wants you all to himself. For a while. When he's through with you, he'll chuck you out fast enough, but in the meantime he doesn't want any competition. Isn't that the real truth, Stark?"

"Desdemona's right," Stark said. "This isn't personal. It's business. Very big, very dangerous business. I'll give you some advice, Wainwright. If you're playing games with the international industrial espionage crowd, you're way out of your league."

"I'm not playing games of any kind." Tony switched his gaze back to Desdemona. "Is it going to work, Desdemona?"

"Is what going to work?"

"Is he going to succeed in turning you against me?"

"No one can do that, Tony. You're my brother."

"Your stepbrother," he corrected softly. He lifted a hand and touched the side of her face. "There's a difference, kid. And Stark knows it."

He turned and walked out of the kitchen. Desdemona felt the tears well up in her eyes.

Bess, Augustus, and Juliet watched in shock as Tony went out the door. Vernon stood in the center of the kitchen clutching his half-melted ice sculpture in gloved hands. He glanced nervously from face to face, clearly unhappy at being caught in the middle of a family scene.

"Tony certainly knows how to make an exit," Stark said laconically. "I'll give him that."

The cutting edge of Stark's voice jerked Desdemona out of her momentary paralysis. She whirled around to face him. "It's a family talent. If you'll excuse us, we'll finish cleaning up, and then we'll all get out of here. Right Touch has a policy of leaving the client's home in the same condition it was in when we arrived."

12

*H*e should have known that she would make a scene, Stark thought the following morning. Desdemona was a Wainwright. *Theater people.* Everything had to be done with a melodramatic flair.

His intention had been to deliver a simple warning, but she had turned it into a confrontation worthy of a soap opera. It was his own fault, he decided. He had virtually accused Tony Wainwright of attempted theft, and in Desdemona's mind, an attack against anyone in her precious family was an attack against her.

He had made a serious miscalculation. He had put Desdemona in a position where she felt forced to choose between his version of events and her stepbrother's. He should have thought it out more clearly ahead of time. He should have realized that he could not expect Desdemona to trust him rather than one of the Wainwright clan.

The kitchen was empty. Stark went through the routine of making coffee and pouring cereal into a bowl with a sense of weary fatalism. The day matched his mood, somber and gray.

He had gone over the scene with Desdemona a hundred times during the night in an effort to figure out how he could have handled it without alienating her.

He had not found an answer.

Another relationship down the tubes. Although he was not standing alone at the altar this time, for some reason the kicked-in-the-gut sensation was a lot worse than it had been the day Pamela had failed to show for the wedding.

What the hell was wrong with him? he wondered as he poured milk on his cereal. He had known from the beginning that it was not a serious, long-term relationship. He'd only been to bed with Desdemona once. It wasn't as if he'd asked her to marry him. He had told himself that he would go with the flow this time.

The flow had turned into Niagara Falls, however, and he had just discovered that he was going over in a barrel.

What was he supposed to have done? Pretend that her beloved Tony had never tried to steal the hard disk?

"Morning, Sam." Jason charged into the kitchen and grabbed the box of cereal that Stark had left on the counter. "You sure missed a good film last night."

"Is that right?" Stark carried his bowl to the table and sat down.

Kyle appeared. "It was all about this android that everyone thinks is human. Only he's not. He's really a super computer with all sorts of weapons."

"For some dippy reason he thinks he wants to be a real human being." Jason made a face as he upended the cereal box and proceeded to dump a large portion of the contents into his bowl. "That was the only dumb part. Who'd want to be human if you could be an android?"

"Good question." Stark munched cereal.

Kyle grabbed the cereal box from his brother. "The android's hand was actually a gun. And his eyes projected computerized heads-up displays of his targets the way computers do in the new fighter-bombers."

"There were a lot of really neat special effects," Jason said.

"Macbeth explained how some of 'em worked." Kyle went to the refrigerator to get a bottle of orange juice. "But he said you could probably explain how the special effects were produced better than he could because they're computer-generated and you know all about computers."

"He says theater people don't rely on gimmicks and computers the way the people who make movies do," Jason added.

Kyle poured juice into a glass. "Macbeth says creating an illusion in a theater is an art form, not a technological trick."

Stark raised his brows. "Are you sure Macbeth isn't slightly biased?"

"No, he's an expert," Kyle assured him.

"I see." Stark took another bite of cereal and finally noticed the unfamiliar taste. The stuff was as sweet as candy, but he was positive that he had not put any sugar on it.

"Macbeth says there's nothing like a live performance to capture the audience's emotions," Jason explained. "He says people get much more involved with a live performance than they do with a filmed one."

"He says live theater demands more from an audience," Kyle said.

Stark contemplated the bleak memories of the live performance in which he had acted the previous night. "He may be right." He cautiously tried another spoonful from his bowl. "Where did this cereal come from?"

"Macbeth took us to a store so that Jason and I could buy it and some other stuff," Kyle explained.

"What other stuff?"

Kyle shrugged. "Some soda and peanut butter and potato chips."

"A good assortment from the basic food groups?" Stark inquired.

"Yeah. Macbeth's taking us to the Limelight this morning. We're going to help him with some repairs on the stage."

Stark stopped chewing as a thought struck him. "Hell."

Jason looked up. "What's wrong?"

Stark wondered how to tell his brothers that Macbeth was unlikely to show up this morning. Desdemona would have gotten in touch with him by now and told him that the Wainwrights and the Starks were no longer on speaking terms.

Stark's next thought was that he would have to call his office and tell Maud that he wouldn't be in until he could arrange for a new sitter. The lid that covered the cauldron of chaos inside him had loosened sometime during the night. He was catching unpleasant glimpses of the contents.

"You okay, Sam?" Jason looked suddenly worried.

"Yeah, are you okay?" Kyle asked.

"I'm fine." This wasn't Kyle and Jason's problem, Stark reminded himself. He glanced at the clock. It was almost seven-thirty. Macbeth always arrived promptly at seven-thirty. "Listen. there may be a change in plans today."

"What kind of change?" Kyle asked.

"I'm not sure that Macbeth is going—" Stark broke off at the sound of Macbeth's Jeep in the drive.

"There he is now." Jason jumped off his chair. " 'Scuse me. I've gotta get my jacket."

"Me, too." Kyle made to follow his brother.

"Don't forget the dishes," Stark said automatically.

Jason and Kyle grumbled, but they both rushed back to the table, scooped up their bowls and glasses, and deposited them in the dishwasher.

"Bye, Sam," Jason yelled as he headed for the door.

"See you tonight," Kyle called. "Are we going to send out for pizza again?"

"We'll see." Stark got to his feet and followed his brothers to the door. He walked out onto the front steps.

Macbeth sat behind the wheel of the black Jeep. He was attired, as usual, in his black mirrored sunglasses, work shirt, and leather vest. He lifted a hand in greeting as the boys ran toward the vehicle.

"Mornin' Stark."

Stark went down the steps. He walked to the Jeep and braced one hand on the top of the cab. "I wasn't sure you'd show this morning."

Macbeth's teeth flashed briefly. "I heard about the fuss here last night." He lowered his voice as Kyle and Jason scrambled into the Jeep and reached for their seat belts. "Desdemona said you were pissed because someone tried to get inside your computer."

"Yes."

"She said you thought it was Tony."

"I have good reason to think that it was."

"Nah," Macbeth said easily. "Tony's no thief. He's a screwup, but that's different."

"Do you think so?"

"Hey, don't worry about it." Macbeth flashed a grin. "Desdemona's going to take care of everything."

"She is?"

"Yeah." Macbeth put the truck in gear. "She's going to hire some-one to look into the situation."

Stark stared at him. "She's going to do *what?*"

"Hire someone. You know, like a private eye."

"A *private eye*. Is she nuts?"

"It'll probably cost her an arm and a leg, and we both know Tony's the one who should pay for it, but he can't. No money. So Desde-mona is going to handle it. We'll all chip in whatever we can, of course." Macbeth smiled again. "Good thing I've got this great day job."

Stark stepped back when the Jeep's engine thundered. Kyle and Jason waved to him as Macbeth eased the vehicle back out of the drive.

Stark stood absolutely still for what seemed a very long time. Then he turned and went back up the steps. He strode into the kitchen and grabbed the phone.

"Desdemona, it's for you," Juliet yelled above the din of early-morning activity.

"I'll take it in my office." Desdemona put down a pan full of freshly shelled hard-boiled eggs and stripped off her plastic gloves. "Finish these stuffed eggs for me, will you, Aunt Bess?"

"Of course, dear." Bess took charge of the eggs. "Roasted red pep-per filling?"

"Right." Desdemona hurried into her office and closed the door. She picked up the phone. "This is Desdemona."

"What the hell do you think you're doing?" Stark asked without any preamble.

Desdemona caught her breath. *He had called.* She had been almost certain he would, but she had not been completely positive. There were too many things about Stark that were not yet predictable.

"At the moment, I'm stuffing hard-boiled eggs." She forced a de-termined lightness into her tone. "We're doing an eleven o'clock brunch for a sportswear company's clients. Do you have any idea of how long it takes to stuff a hundred eggs?"

"Forget the eggs," Stark growled. "I'm talking about your insane idea to hire a private investigator."

"Oh, that. Macbeth told you about my plan?"

"Have you gone completely nuts? It'll cost you a fortune, and it's a total waste of time."

"Not in my opinion," she said.

"Just what the hell do you think an investigator is going to find?" Stark demanded.

"The truth."

"He'll have to interview me first, and I'll tell him about the toothpicks, Tony's history of embezzlement, his working knowledge of computers, and his hostility toward me, and that will be the end of the damned investigation."

"I believe a good investigator will turn up some other suspects."

"Desdemona, I do not want a private investigator involved in my affairs."

"Why not? Have you got something to hide?"

"I do not intend to discuss Stark Security Systems' proprietary information with anyone," Stark said grimly.

"You can't expect us Wainwrights to take your accusations lying down. We have a right to defend ourselves."

"You act as if I'm accusing all Wainwrights of attempted theft. That's not the case."

"You've accused Tony of attempted theft, and you've as good as accused me of being a trusting, naive, gullible fool for believing in him. Do you deny it?"

"Desdemona, listen to me—"

"Do you deny it?"

"Damn it, I issued a warning to that fool stepbrother of yours, and yes, I do think you're gullible where he's concerned. You're a sucker for his hard-luck stories because he's family."

"So? As it happens, he's had a lot of hard luck."

"Desdemona, he's used you, and he's going to continue using you as long as you allow it."

"I don't care what you say, Stark, I'm going ahead with my plan."

"You'll be wasting your time. Your investigator won't get anywhere without my cooperation, and I don't intend to give it to him."

"Is that so?"

"What's more, I'll have a very long talk with your P.I. I will explain the facts of the situation to him. I will then explain the facts of business life to him. I'll inform him that if he interferes in my business affairs, I'll see to it that he never works for me or any of my clients."

"You'd issue threats to my investigator?"

"Yes."

"Well, it's going to be a little tricky issuing threats to yourself," Desdemona murmured. "I wonder if you'll back off or if you'll tell yourself to go to hell. I'm betting on the latter."

There was a distinct pause from Stark. "What are you talking about?"

"You're the investigator I intend to hire." Desdemona slammed down the phone.

Within seconds the instrument warbled like an irate bird. She picked up the receiver. "Right Touch Catering. May I help you?"

"I am a computer security expert." Stark sounded as though he were speaking between clenched teeth. "I don't do the kind of thrilling hard-boiled detective investigations that you read about in mystery novels."

"This is a computer security problem, isn't it? You're a computer security expert."

"The only kind of investigations I do are computer investigations." Stark's tone implied he was holding on to his temper through sheer will power. "I search computer files and follow computer trails through various kinds of networks and systems while seated at my desk. I do not interview suspects. I do not carry a gun in a shoulder holster. I do not conduct stakeouts."

"However you want to handle this is fine by me," Desdemona said easily. "Look, you don't tell me how to put on a buffet for two hundred, and I won't tell you how to do your job."

"This is crazy. Speaking hypothetically, because that is the only way in which we can even discuss this situation, just what do you expect me to discover?"

"I'm hiring you to find a suspect other than Tony who had both motive and opportunity to steal ARCANE. I want you to realize that my brother is not the only suspect or even a very likely suspect. I want you to stop focusing on Tony and look at the big picture."

"Damn it, Tony is the most likely suspect."

"You're reacting emotionally, not logically, Stark."

"If you mean I'm getting more than a little annoyed, you're right.

I am not, however, being illogical. You're the one who isn't being logical."

"I don't have any particular interest in logic, per se," Desdemona said. "Granted, it works for some people, but we Wainwrights rely more on intuition."

"Then apply your intuitive powers to the problem of paying my fee," Stark said in a thoroughly dangerous voice.

"What's that supposed to mean?"

"It means," Stark said very deliberately, "that you cannot afford me."

"Ah, now, that's where you're wrong," Desdemona said. "I have something you want, and you have something I want, and we're both business people. We should be able to negotiate a deal here."

There was a moment of acute silence. Stark's next words were coated in ice. "What, exactly are you offering?"

Desdemona tightened her grip on the phone. "In exchange for your services as a computer security investigator, I am willing to provide free catering to your company for one full year."

There was another long silence. "I see."

Desdemona scowled at the receiver in her hand. "What's the matter? You sound weird."

"I thought you were going to offer something else."

"My lush, lovely, nubile body?"

Stark cleared his throat. "That thought did cross my mind."

"Tacky, Stark, very, very tacky."

"Yes, I guess it was."

"Now, then, to get back to the terms of our deal."

"What deal?" he asked.

"Pay attention, Stark. You will have the services of Right Touch without charge for twelve months. We'll have to draw up a new contract, of course."

"Desdemona—"

"Keep in mind that the only thing you're getting for free is my services. You will still have to pay for the basic expenses: food, equipment, rentals, ice sculptures, that kind of thing. But I won't charge you for the planning, preparation, and cleanup."

"You're going to subtract your fee from the bills?"

"Right."

"Tell me," Stark said. "Do you have any idea of how little of my time you're going to be able to purchase with this arrangement?"

"I know you're expensive."

"Very expensive."

"But I figure that a hotshot security specialist such as yourself should be able to crack this case in short order. I have great faith in your talents, Stark."

"Let us suppose, just for the sake of argument, that I do turn up another possible suspect. That doesn't mean Tony isn't guilty."

"No, but it means that you can't dump all of your suspicions on him. You will be forced to acknowledge that there is a reasonable doubt. And," Desdemona concluded, "you will be forced to apologize to me."

"For what?" Stark asked blankly.

"For calling me a naive, gullible fool."

"Hell, if that's what's really bothering you, I'll apologize right now."

"No good. You don't mean it."

"Desdemona?"

"Yes?"

"What would it take for you to acknowledge that your stepbrother tried to rip me off last night?"

"Overwhelming proof, and you can't supply that, Stark, because it doesn't exist. I've known Tony since I was five years old, and he's not a thief."

"You can't get past the fact that he once saved your life, can you?" Stark asked quietly. "What did he do? Rescue you from a swimming pool?"

"No."

"Whatever it was, you've cast Tony in the role of hero, and you can't believe he might not still be one."

Desdemona glanced at her watch. "Look, I've got to run. Have we got a deal?"

"Desdemona, this is crazy."

"It's business. What's your answer?"

"I'll think about it and get back to you," Stark muttered.

"You do that. But don't take too long to make up your mind."

"Why not?"

"The trail will get cold. If you dawdle, I'll have to find another security expert."

"Is that a threat?"

"Yes, it is. You can call me here before ten with your decision. If you dither around until after ten—"

"I do not dither," he said ominously. "I think things through carefully before I act."

"Yes, well, if you think things through until after ten, you can reach me at Exotica Erotica later this afternoon. I'm catering the grand opening. Bye, Stark."

"Hell."

Desdemona hung up the phone. She perched on the corner of her desk and nervously swung one foot as she considered what she had just done. A shiver of dread went through her.

She reminded herself that she was a Wainwright. Wainwrights were *theater people*. Risk-takers by definition. Only a true gambler would stake everything on a career in front of the footlights.

The curtain had just been raised in a new drama that featured herself and Stark. She was stepping out on stage with an unseen script and an unpredictable leading man. There was no knowing how the play would end.

There were so many things that could go wrong. Stark might never call back. Or he might accept her offer to investigate and come to the same false conclusion that he had reached last night. He was, after all, a very stubborn man. A real linear thinker. A man who trusted only what he could see, hear, or touch.

The door of the office opened. Tony slouched into the room wearing an artificially beat-up leather jacket and black jeans. A young Marlon Brando, sullen and vengeful.

"I just talked to Aunt Bess and Juliet." Tony propped one shoulder against the wall. "They said you're trying to hire that bastard, Stark, to prove himself wrong."

"Yes, I am."

"That's stupid. Why the hell would he want to prove I'm innocent? He hates my guts."

Desdemona contemplated that. "I don't think so. But I will admit he's not exactly the trusting sort."

"Then why bother with him? Cut your losses, kid. The jerk isn't for you. He can't prove a damn thing against me, so he's not going to press charges. We've got nothing to worry about. Walk away from him."

"I can't," Desdemona said quietly. "I'm in love with him."

"Shit." Tony straightened away from the wall. "You're going to be sorry you ever got involved with him. Trust me, a guy like that will turn on you in a second."

"He won't turn on me."

"Are you kidding? If he ever decides that you're directly involved in what happened last night, not just my innocent, gullible victim, he'll tear you to pieces."

Desdemona stopped swinging her foot. She gazed at Tony, unable to think of anything to say. She had an uneasy feeling that he was right.

Dane closed the menu and set it aside. He glanced around the crowded downtown restaurant with a practiced eye. Stark knew that he was checking to see if there were any clients, past, present, or future, in sight. Dane always kept an eye on business.

When Dane had finished the automatic survey he regarded Stark with wry amusement. "I hate to be the one to bring this up, but has it escaped your attention that Miss Wainwright might be in this up to her cute little ears?"

Stark's fingers tightened around the menu. He had invited Dane to join him for lunch today because he wanted to discuss the bizarre situation in which he found himself. He was not very hungry, however. He wondered if the overly sweetened breakfast cereal he had ingested might have destroyed his entire digestive tract.

"You mean you think she's using Right Touch as a cover for her light-fingered relatives?" Stark asked with forced casualness. "That she's running a burglary ring?"

Dane cocked a brow. "I'd say it's a distinct possibility. I can't believe that you haven't already thought about it."

"Hmm." Something cooked without too much grease or sauce, Stark thought. That's what his stomach needed. Something mild. Something soothing.

"Maybe this is a regular routine for the Wainwright clan," Dane continued. "It wouldn't be the first time an entire, close-knit family has been involved in crime. You've got to admit there's a certain logic to it. Especially for a family that appears to have had no stable means of support for three generations."

"I know." Stark decided on the halibut and put down the menu. "A caterer is in a perfect position to rip off her clients. She sets them up through a legitimate business relationship. She and her staff have ample opportunity to case the premises and identify valuables."

"They make their move during a time when the house is full of people. There are literally dozens of suspects, assuming the victim even realizes when the theft occurred."

"Yes."

"So you've at least considered the possibility."

"Yes."

Dane raised his hands, palms out. "Then I will say no more." He grinned briefly. "Except to comment that you're beginning to sound like a genuine private eye. I'm impressed. You've even got an attractive female client, just like the fictional investigators always seem to get."

Stark ignored that. He was not at all sure if he still had Desdemona, and the uncertainty was eating at his insides. It was probably doing more damage than the cereal had done. He folded his hands on the white linen tablecloth. "I don't think we're dealing with a crime family."

"No?"

"No. The Wainwrights are theater people. They're romantic. Melodramatic. Emotional."

Dane looked thoughtful. "Meaning?"

"Meaning that if they were involved in criminal activities, they would be more likely to steal expensive necklaces or rare vases or paintings. Not hard disks and computer programs."

"I'll admit that stealing a hard disk isn't quite like stealing an expensive necklace or a rare vase," Dane said. "Special expertise is involved."

"Yes. And I think Tony Wainwright is the only member of the Wainwright clan who can tell a hard disk from a floppy disk."

"In all fairness, Miss Wainwright is correct about one thing," Dane said. "There may well have been some other people at the reception last night who possessed the skill and the will to dig a hard disk out of a computer."

"True," Stark said. "But none of them had the kind of motive or opportunity that good old, lovable Tony had. Or a past history of having been involved in an embezzlement case."

"So what are you going to do about Miss Wainwright's offer?"

Stark looked up, mildly surprised at the question. "I'm going to take it."

Stark had not called by four o'clock that afternoon.

Desdemona surveyed the buffet table she had arranged in the center of Exotica Erotica. The opening of Kirsten's shop was a gala affair. The sky was still overcast, but no rain had appeared. A good-sized crowd had materialized. The throng was composed of Wainwright family and friends, such as Ian Ivers, some neighboring shop owners, and curious passersby who drifted in off the streets of Pioneer Square. Everyone gathered beneath a colorful canopy of multicolored, helium-inflated condoms that decorated the ceiling.

Stark had not called.

The food was going fast. The guests munched on eggplant spread, mushroom pâté, marinated mussels, and a variety of dips and chips.

She had been so certain that he would call. Her intuition had told her that he would.

Kirsten's talents as a set designer had proved invaluable in the design of the new store. Exotica Erotica was a warm, stylish, upscale shop. She had hired a local artist to turn one wall into a colorful mural featuring a medieval maiden in a bower. Elegant glass display cases lined the walls. They housed a variety of paraphernalia, including vibrators, massage oils, condoms, and sexy garments.

The bookshelves of Exotica Erotica were stocked with sexual treatises that ran the gamut from the *Kama Sutra* to Masters and Johnson. There was also an extensive collection of cultural histories of sex and several authoritative guides to solving sexual problems such as frigidity.

Maybe she would never see him again.

Desdemona plucked a book titled *Secrets of the Female Orgasm* off the shelf. She thumbed through it dispiritedly.

"There you are, Desdemona." Kirsten appeared out of the crowd.

She was flushed and excited. The world always looked brightest to an entrepreneur on the first day of business. Taxes, economic downturns, and competition were all out of sight for the moment. "I've been looking for you. Everything's going fabulously, isn't it?"

Desdemona tried to summon up some genuine enthusiasm. The last thing she wanted to do today was rain on Kirsten's parade. "The shop is wonderful, Kirsten. It turned out just the way you said it would. Very tasteful. Very upscale."

"Tony programmed my computer for me. He's got a super inventory system on it. Low stock is highlighted in purple. Sales taxes are calculated in green. I've even got an e-mail capability."

Desdemona smiled wanly. "Now that I've finally learned how to use e-mail, we'll be able to send each other messages." The thought depressed her further. The only reason she had bothered to learn how to send and receive e-mail was because Stark had programmed her personal digital assistant to do so.

"I know Exotica Erotica is going to work." Kirsten glowed with excitement. "And I have you to thank for giving me this chance. Just think, the Wainwrights now have another stable business in the family. How can I ever thank you?"

"Forget it." Holding the book in one hand, Desdemona gave Kirsten a quick hug. "It was the least I could do. I haven't forgotten all the free labor you and Henry gave me when I opened Right Touch. I couldn't have made it without you. We're family, Kirsten. Wainwrights stick together."

"Yes." Kirsten froze in mid hug, her attention fixed on an object located somewhere behind Desdemona. "Well, well, well."

"What is it?" Desdemona stepped back. She frowned at the expression on Kirsten's face. Then she turned and followed her friend's gaze.

Stark stood in the doorway of Exotica Erotica. He was dressed in his customary uniform: worn corduroy jacket, jeans, and running shoes. The familiar plastic protector full of pens, pencils, and other assorted objects was in the pocket of his white shirt. Behind the lenses of his glasses, his brilliant green eyes were unfathomable.

He looked wonderful to Desdemona.

He was here.

"Stark."

He turned his head in her direction as if he had actually heard her over the din of voices. He saw her and resolutely started toward her.

Henry materialized at Desdemona's elbow. "I wouldn't have believed it if I hadn't seen it with my own eyes."

"I told you so," Desdemona said with great satisfaction. "Wainwright intuition is never wrong."

For the first time since last night she allowed herself to acknowledge just how anxious she had been. It was all very well to talk glibly about Wainwright intuition. The truth was, she had not really been sure that Stark would come through. She had a feeling that she had just rolled the dice in a desperate game.

Stark came to a halt directly in front of her. "I'll take the job."

"You won't regret it." Desdemona hugged him tightly.

He seemed briefly startled. But his arms closed around her with such force that Desdemona knew the contents of his pocket protector would leave imprints on her skin.

13

A great, surging wave of relief rolled through Stark. It left him feeling dazed. He crushed Desdemona closer. She still wanted him. He could feel it in the way she clung to him.

He could also feel something hard pressing against his lower back. He realized that the edge of the spine of the book she had been holding in her hand was digging into him. He ignored the discomfort.

"I was afraid you weren't going to show," she confided into his shirtfront.

"I can't make any promises," he warned, his voice rough with the need to make certain she understood.

"I know." She raised her head. "But the fact that you're here means you're willing to look for the truth. That's all I ask."

Stark gazed at her, so damned relieved by the welcome he had just received that he could not think of anything to say. She looked so good, so right, he thought with a sense of wonder. And he had come so close to losing her. The realization chilled him.

Tony appeared, stuffing a cracker loaded with dip into his mouth. He glared at Stark over Desdemona's head. "Just what do you think he'll find, kid? Even if he does decide that someone else had an equally good motive and opportunity, he won't give a damn. He'll still believe that I did it. Nothing is going to change his mind because he doesn't want to change it."

"That's not true." Desdemona straightened the black satin lapels of her tuxedo jacket as she stepped back from Stark. "Once he starts looking at other suspects, he'll find the real thief. I know he will."

"Bullshit. He'll pretend to do some sort of superficial investigation because he knows you won't let him sleep with you if he doesn't at least act like he's doing something."

"That's enough, Tony," Desdemona said very tightly. Red flags appeared in her cheeks, but her eyes were steady and her chin was firm.

Tony's mouth tightened. "What if, after his phony investigation, he tells you that I'm definitely the one who tried to get at his precious hard disk? What will you do then?"

"It'll never happen," she assured him.

"Don't be too sure of that. Tell me, kid, what will you do if your android lover decides that you're involved, too? That we're all involved?"

Desdemona's flush deepened. "Tony, stop it."

Stark eyed Tony with some interest for the first time. He recalled the conversation he'd had with Dane over lunch. The concept of the Wainwrights as a crime family was hard to swallow, but it was not at all difficult to envision young Tony as a member of what had once been termed the criminal class.

"I don't want to hear any more of this," Desdemona said brusquely. "You're spoiling my whole afternoon."

"My day isn't going so good, either." Tony smiled thinly. "Like they say in Hollywood, I've got a hot concept for you."

"What concept?" Desdemona asked.

"Try this, kid. There never was any attempted theft."

Desdemona frowned. "What are you saying?"

"That Stark faked the whole thing." Tony shrugged. "That no one tried to get inside his damned computer. That Stark invented the story."

"That's ridiculous." Desdemona's eyes widened in shock. "Why on earth would he do such a thing?"

"To get me out of the picture," Tony said softly. "He wants you all to himself, kid. He doesn't like the idea of sharing you. And he thinks he's found a way to get rid of the competition."

"Tony," Desdemona sounded desperate. "Shut up."

"Don't let him turn you against your family, Desdemona," Tony said. "Remember, you're a Wainwright. The only thing Wainwrights have ever been able to count on is each other."

He turned on his heel and walked out of the shop.

Stark watched him leave. "You know something? I'm getting real tired of his exit scenes."

"Never mind him. He's under a lot of stress." Desdemona grabbed Stark's hand and led him toward the buffet table. "Have some food. Doesn't the shop look terrific?"

Stark studied a display of condom packages artfully arranged amid a bed of artificial flowers. "It's different, I'll say that for it."

"And look at the size of the crowd."

"Desdemona, I'd like to talk to you for a few minutes."

"Okay." She picked up a small circle of toast layered with some sort of purple-gray spread. "Want some eggplant?"

"I don't have a lot of time." He glanced at his watch. "Kyle and Jason will be home soon. I have to fix an early dinner. I told them I'd take them to my gym later."

"The gym?"

"I'm going to see that they get some exercise this summer." He shrugged. "They're both a little scrawny."

"What are you planning to fix for dinner?"

"For dinner? Damned if I know. Maybe I'll send out for pizza again."

"I'm starting to worry about your diet, Stark."

"You and me both. Personally I've had enough pizza to last a lifetime, but Kyle and Jason are addicted to it. Desdemona, will you step outside for a few minutes? I want to talk to you in private."

She gave him a sidelong glance, as if trying to assess his intentions. "All right."

Stark took her arm and turned her toward the door. Before he could reach it, Ian Ivers bounced into his path.

Ian looked very much the same as he had the first time Stark had met him. He was wearing stylishly full taupe trousers and a silk shirt that was the same shade as Desdemona's eggplant dip. His thinning hair was in a neat ponytail, and the gold ring in his ear glittered.

"Hey, there, Stark. Good to see you again. Say, did you get a chance to look over that proposal for financing *Dissolving*? I hand-delivered it to your secretary a few days ago."

"I haven't looked at it."

"No problem." Ian was undaunted. "Tell you what, I'll schedule a meeting so that we can go over it together."

"Don't bother."

"Backing a play is a little different than making other kinds of investments. I'll explain some of the ins and outs. Trust me, this one's a winner. Tony's script is fabulous. It's gonna rip the guts right out of the audience."

"Sounds messy. I'm not interested."

Ian fluttered slightly, but he did not lose his smile. "Hey, I know this isn't a good place to talk. But I'll schedule something with your secretary."

Stark lost his patience. He walked straight past Ian and took Desdemona with him.

He finally got her outside. They came to a halt on the sidewalk in front of Exotica Erotica. Desdemona leaned back against the brick wall, one knee bent so that her small boot was braced. She looked up at him expectantly.

Stark tried to think of a subtle way to ask the question he needed to ask. "We've agreed that I'm going to look for another suitable suspect."

"Yes."

"In exchange, you're going to give me free catering services."

"Right." Her eyes gleamed.

Now what? Stark wondered. He shoved his hands into the pockets of his jacket and gazed moodily at the bag lady who was investigating the contents of a nearby garbage can. "What about us?"

"Us?"

"Our relationship," he said very carefully.

"Oh, that," Desdemona said.

He turned back to face her. "Well?"

She pursed her lips and looked down at the book in her hand. "I've been thinking about that."

"And?"

"And I'm wondering if we shouldn't put the personal side of our relationship on hold until we've settled our other problems."

Stark felt as if the wind had been knocked out of him. "I see."

"The thing is," she continued very earnestly. "We're in this pickle because we mixed the business and the personal. They're all tangled up together at the moment."

"Yes. They are." Chaos.

"It might be simpler if we untangled them for a while."

For some reason, perhaps because he did not know where else to look, Stark glanced at the title of the book she clutched. *Secrets of the Female Orgasm.* The memory of the way she had climaxed beneath him the other night crashed through him. He took a deep breath.

"You think it might be simpler to get your next one out of a book?" he asked. "Or to use one of those gadgets Kirsten gave you?"

She frowned. "My next what?"

"Orgasm."

She blinked. Then she turned a lovely shade of pink and glanced hastily down at the book she held. "Good heavens, Stark. What a thing to say in public."

"I seem to recall that you made a very public speech on the subject in the hallway of your own apartment building."

"Yes, well, I was not myself at the time. I was feeling a little giddy."

Something in her voice told him that she might be teasing him, but he could not be certain. He wished he could read her more clearly, but he had never been very good at reading women.

Stark took one hand out of his pocket and flattened it against the wall beside her head. The bricks felt warm and pleasantly rough beneath his palm. He could smell the faint fragrance of Desdemona's shampoo and the enticing scent of her body. He wanted her. God, how he wanted her. What was he going to do when he had to tell her that he could not find another suitable suspect?

"I know it's messy trying to combine the business and the personal," he said quietly. "But my specialty is complexity, remember?"

"This is not a mathematical problem."

"I have to know where I stand, Desdemona. Please don't play games with me."

She searched his eyes intently. "You're telling me that you want us to continue with the personal side of our relationship even though this other thing is going on?"

"Yes."

"Why?"

He stared at her, uncomprehending. "Why?"

She nodded and looked expectant again.

Stark had no idea what he was supposed to say next. "What kind of a question is that? I want you, and I think you want me. We're attracted to each other. We have been from the beginning. Isn't it obvious?"

She sighed. "Yes, I suppose it is."

He knew he had failed to give her the answer that she wanted, but he had no idea of what to do about it. He flicked an impatient glance at his wristwatch. Macbeth would be on his way home with Kyle and Jason.

"I have to go," he said. "Is this thing settled or not?"

"Gee, Stark. It's tough to know how to respond to such a romantic proposition."

A jolt of raw, primitive fear threatened to tear his insides to pieces. "I'm screwing this up, aren't I?"

"I wouldn't go that far, but I would have to say that you're not showing a great deal of finesse."

"Damn. I'm sorry." He fought to slam the lid back down on the boiling cauldron. "I wish I knew a better way to handle it. I don't know how else to ask the question except straight out. Do you want to go on with this affair? Yes or no."

Without any warning she gave him her most dazzling smile. "Yes."

He sucked in his breath, momentarily warmed by the laughter in her face. Cautiously he removed his palm from the wall. The lid was safely back in place. "Okay. Thanks. That's all I wanted to know." He glanced at his watch once more.

Desdemona opened her mouth to say something, but at that instant Henry came out of the shop. He held a black and gold box in one hand.

"Hi, Stark. How's it going?"

"Fine," Stark said.

"Glad you could make the opening." Henry came to a halt. "What do you think of Kirsten's shop?"

"Very interesting." Stark reflected briefly on Desdemona's position as cosigner on the loan papers. "Let's hope it works."

"It will. Kirsten will give it her all, and I'll help her. So will the other members of the family." Henry tossed the black and gold box into the air and caught it neatly. "Desdemona tells me you're working for her these days."

"Working for her?" Stark glanced at Desdemona, whose expression turned suspiciously demure. "I hadn't thought about it in quite those terms."

"You'll be glad to know she's a great boss. Here." Henry tossed the box in Stark's direction. "Compliments of the management."

Stark caught the box and saw that he held a package of multicolored condoms. "I don't know what to say."

"Don't say anything," Henry advised. "Just prove that Tony didn't try to filch your hard disk." He disappeared back into the crowded shop.

Stark dropped the package of condoms into his coat pocket. He looked at Desdemona again. "I'll call you."

"Okay."

"My evenings are a little tight these days. I don't like to leave Jason and Kyle at night any more than is absolutely necessary."

She smiled. "How about your mornings?"

"Mornings?"

"You can stop by my place after Macbeth picks up Jason and Kyle for the day. I'll fix you some blue-corn pancakes."

"Stop by your place?" His brain seemed to have short-circuited. "In the mornings?"

"Why not? You can go into the office a little later than usual occasionally, can't you?"

Stark smiled slowly as the anticipation unfurled within him. "Anything's better than the cereal I have to eat at home these days. I'll see you tomorrow morning."

"Good. Oh, wait, before you leave, take some of the eggplant spread home for dinner. I've got plenty, and it will add some vitamins to your menu."

"I don't know if Kyle and Jason will eat eggplant."

"Spread it on top of the pizza."

"Good idea. There's so much junk on the ones they order, they'll probably never even notice a little eggplant."

He was going to have to make some attempt at an honest investigation, Stark promised himself later that evening as he watched Jason and Kyle splash noisily in the end of the large gym pool.

He knew that a serious search for alternative suspects was clearly a waste of time. It was obvious to any logical, clear-thinking individual that Tony Wainwright was as guilty as sin. But he had promised Desdemona, Stark thought. He had to at least put forth some genuine effort. He'd made a bargain.

Tony's angry warnings to Desdemona flickered through his mind. *He'll only pretend to do some sort of superficial investigation because he knows you won't let him sleep with you if he doesn't at least act like he's doing something.*

"How was that, Sam?" Kyle clung to the edge of the pool and looked up for approval.

"Better. You're getting the hang of it. Try to do less splashing. Form is more important than speed," Stark said.

"Are you going to use the weight machines after we finish swimming?" Jason panted, hair dripping in his eyes.

"Yes."

"How long have you been working out?" Kyle asked eagerly.

"Since I was in college."

"Yeah? Then how come you don't look like that guy over there?"

Stark followed Kyle's gaze. He was staring through a glass window that divided the pool room from the weight training room. On the other side of the glass a massively bulked-up man with long blond hair strained mightily within the confines of one of the training machines. *Steroid city,* Stark thought.

"Because I'd rather have a real neck, and I like to be able to buy shirts that don't have to have the sleeves ripped out in order to fit," Stark said.

"Oh."

"If you get too bulked up," Stark continued, "you can't move the way you need to move in order to study karate."

"Karate?" Kyle's face lit with excitement. "Are we going to take karate lessons?"

"Might as well," Stark said. "We've got a whole summer ahead of us."

"Oh, boy, karate," Jason said. A wistful look appeared in his eyes. "I wish Dad could see me."

Stark tossed aside his towel and prepared to get into the water. "You don't do stuff like this for other people. You do it for yourself."

"Did Dad teach you how to work out and do karate when you were a kid, Sam?" Kyle asked.

"No," Stark said. "But I'm going to teach you how to do it."

"Oh, my God, oh, my God. *Stark.*" Desdemona dug her fingers into his thick black hair and lifted herself. This was outrageous. This was wild. Incredible. Astounding. It was going to drive her crazy.

Stark lay between her thighs, his mouth teasing the most intimate part of her body. The searing, shocking kiss was unlike anything she had ever experienced in her life.

The tension that had gathered within her released itself in an explosion of sensation. Desdemona rode the glittering whirlwind. The glorious release transfixed her. She shivered, gasped, and cried out softly.

Stark lifted his head. He watched her intently for a moment and then he moved up the length of her body. His weight crushed her against the kimono bathrobe that she had been wearing when she had answered the door a few minutes earlier.

The kimono was all that lay between Desdemona and the hardwood floor. They hadn't made it as far as the couch, let alone the bed on the far side of the loft. Stark's clothes formed a trail that started at the entrance of the apartment and continued halfway across the room.

"So good," he muttered as he drove himself into her still-quivering body. "So damned good."

He surged into her slowly, filling her carefully but completely. His mouth closed over hers. Desdemona tasted herself on his lips. She felt the passion in him. It converted the powerful muscles of his back and shoulders into steel beneath her hands.

He was so big. So heavy. So strong.

Without any warning, the cascading tremors of her climax started all over again.

Desdemona screamed in surprise, but the sound was lost in Stark's mouth. She felt him shudder, heard the groan that emanated from deep within him.

He went rigid, and then he collapsed slowly on top of her.

Desdemona lay sprawled in contentment beneath Stark and listened as his breathing returned to normal. She smiled up at the ceiling and toyed with his hair.

They were both damp. The scent of spent passion was unmistakable. It hovered in the air, creating a sense of stunning intimacy.

"I think I'm going to need another shower before I go in to the office," Stark said into the curve of her shoulder.

"So will I."

"Since time is of the essence here," Stark said deliberately, "what do you say we take one together?"

"You're assuming I can move."

"Only one of us has to move." Stark rolled off of her.

He got to one knee, scooped her up with effortless strength, rose, and padded barefoot toward the bathroom.

Desdemona rested her head against his sleek shoulder and splayed her fingers across his broad chest. She peered at the clock. "How much more time do we have?"

"About forty-five minutes. I didn't realize until I checked my PDA this morning that I've got an early meeting today."

"We'll make it a short shower and a very fast breakfast."

Fifteen minutes later, freshly showered and with her hair anchored in a twist at the back of her head, Desdemona poured blue-corn pancake batter into neat, round puddles on her griddle.

"Anything I can do?" Stark ran a hand through his damp hair as he sat down on a stool on the other side of the counter.

"Nope. I got everything ready before you arrived. I'm a pro, if you will recall."

"I have always had great respect for professional expertise," Stark said very seriously.

Desdemona glanced at him out of the corner of her eye as she reached for a spatula. She could not tell if he was trying to be funny or not. "How did your brothers like the eggplant spread?"

"They ate it. I put it on top of the pizza as you suggested, covered it with some extra parmesan, and reheated the whole thing."

"That was very creative of you."

"They didn't seem to notice anything different."

"Good." Desdemona piled the pancakes onto a plate. "Why don't you bring them over here for dinner one of these days?"

He gave her a look of surprise as she set the pancakes down in front of him. "You mean it?"

"Sure." She put the pitcher of maple syrup on the counter. "I won't promise to cook pizza, but I think I can come up with something that they'll eat."

"That would be nice," Stark said. "Thanks." He glanced at the clock as he picked up his fork.

"You've got plenty of time. You're only five minutes from your office."

"I know." He went to work on the pancakes. "This feels a little strange, that's all."

"Mind if I ask you a question?"

"Go ahead," he said around a mouthful of pancakes.

"Why did you take your brothers in for the summer?"

Stark stopped chewing for a few seconds. "Damned if I know." He forked up another bite of pancakes. "These are great."

"You must have thought about it."

"Blue-corn pancakes? Not really. I'm not sure I've ever had them."

"I'm talking about your decision to take the responsibility of your brothers for the summer. It was a big commitment. You didn't even know them."

"Yeah, well, you know how it is."

"Yes, I do," she agreed. "I have a lot of family, and I'm well aware of what that means. But it was a new concept for you."

"Do me a favor and don't use the word *concept*. It reminds me of Ian."

"You don't want to talk about why you took Jason and Kyle in, do you?"

Stark put down his fork and fixed her with a steady gaze. "What exactly do you want to know?"

"I want to know why you felt you had to take them for the summer."

"What's the big deal?" He raised one broad shoulder in a dismissing shrug and picked up his fork. "I just did, that's all. They didn't have anyplace else to go. Their father is gone for good. I know that, even if they're still hoping he'll return. Their mother is trying to get her own act together and doesn't have time for them right now. So, I let them stay."

"Because you're their brother."

"Because I didn't want them to feel—" He broke off, words having apparently failed him.

"To feel what?"

"That they didn't have a right to make some demands of their own. That they didn't have a claim on someone. That there wasn't a place for them." Stark scowled in obvious frustration. "Hell, I don't know."

"You didn't want them to feel what you felt when your parents got their divorce, is that it?"

"Maybe." Stark downed the last of his pancakes. "Not that I can do much about it. They'll have to learn to tough it out on their own. It's a rough world."

"I know. But sometimes some people are in a position to make it a little easier for others. The Wainwrights did for me and my mother what you're trying to do for Jason and Kyle."

"And you're still repaying the debt," Stark said grimly.

"I don't see it that way."

"I know. Forget I said that. Any more pancakes?"

"Yes." Desdemona went back to the stove. "You know something?"

"What?"

"I think Jason and Kyle are very fortunate to have you for an older brother."

"Uh-huh." Stark obviously wanted to change the subject. "You know I could get used to this."

"Having your brothers around?"

"No, stopping by here on my way to work in the mornings." Stark glanced speculatively toward the large, freestanding wardrobe in the corner. "Maybe I should keep some of my stuff here. Shirts, socks, a razor. What do you think? It would be more convenient."

Desdemona stilled. She stared at the blue-corn pancakes in the pan. The lacy edges were turning an interesting shade of blue-brown.

"Forget it," Stark said swiftly, casually, as if it were the most unimportant thing in the world. "Just a passing thought. This place isn't all that big, anyway. You don't have a lot of room to store someone else's clothes."

"It's not that." Desdemona carefully removed the second helping of pancakes and set them on Stark's plate. She wondered how to explain that no man's clothes had ever hung in her closet. "I just hadn't ever considered the idea."

"I don't blame you. A real invasion of privacy. Sorry I even mentioned it."

"All right."

He looked at her. "What?"

"I said all right." She carried the plate over to the counter and set it down. "You can leave a few things in my closet."

Desdemona was still contemplating the prospect of her clothes sharing space with some of Stark's staid white shirts when she walked down the alley to the rear door of Right Touch half an hour later.

There was nothing on the Right Touch schedule today, but Desdemona had decided to go into work early. She had left the apartment right after Stark had.

Thoughts of Stark filled her head. Her family was going to think that she had lost her mind when they found out that he was leaving personal belongings in her apartment.

No doubt about it, her mother was going to be seriously alarmed. Her father would be full of paternal misgivings. Bess and Juliet would issue dire warnings. Tony would have a fit.

But she was a Wainwright in love, Desdemona reminded herself as she dug her key out of her purse. Wainwrights took chances.

She did not notice anything wrong until she tried to insert her key into the lock.

The door was already open.

A jolt of fear went through her. Desdemona took a deep breath and squelched the unwarranted reaction. It was eight-thirty in the morning, not midnight. The door was unlocked because someone else had come in to work early. Several Wainwrights had keys.

Desdemona took a grip on her nerves, opened the door wider, and stepped into the vast kitchen. The miniblinds that covered the windows of her darkened office were closed, just as she had left them yesterday.

All of the overhead lights were off, but there was a faint glow coming from the walk-in freezer. Desdemona frowned when she saw that the freezer door was standing wide open. Someone had indeed come into work early. Whoever it was must have gotten mixed up about the morning events schedule for the week.

Desdemona started forward. "Juliet? Aunt Bess? What in the world are you doing here at this hour?"

A soft rasp of sound just off to her left brought Desdemona to a halt. Her office door had opened.

She whirled around.

A tall, shambling figure of a man loomed in the doorway. There was something terribly wrong with his face. It seemed contorted into an inhuman shape. A dirty cap was pulled down low over his eyes.

He had a gun in one hand.

Desdemona tried to scream and could not get the sound out of her throat. Terror paralyzed her. She saw the gun come up, point at her, saw the bizarre face twist.

Something glinted on the edge of Desdemona's horrified vision. It was light from the open alley door reflecting on a heavy steel soup kettle stored on a nearby shelf.

The bright steel broke Desdemona's trance. She grabbed the kettle with both hands and hurled it at the man with the gun.

He dodged instinctively and simultaneously pulled the trigger. The shot went wild. It struck the kettle, knocking it to the side.

Desdemona cast one helpless look at the alley door and abandoned any thought of escape in that direction. The gunman stood between her and the exit.

She turned and ran toward the walk-in freezer. The steel door was thick and well insulated. With any luck it would stop a bullet.

The gloom of the darkened kitchens provided her with some protection. She darted around the end of the long, stainless-steel work counter and rushed toward the freezer.

A second shot exploded behind her. It thudded into the old brick wall.

She heard footsteps, but she did not look back. She reached the freezer, hurtled into the small, icy chamber, whirled around, and pulled the thick door shut behind herself. It seemed to take forever to close.

Footsteps pounded on the tiles.

The door finally sealed itself with a soft sigh. Desdemona slammed the emergency exit handle downward, locking herself inside the freezer. Then she went down on her knees, facing the door, and hung on to the handle with both hands.

She could only pray that her weight pulling downward on the locking lever would be sufficient to prevent the intruder from unlocking the door on the opposite side. To open the door, he would have to shove the outside lever upward against her full body weight.

A chilling silence descended. A very chilling silence.

Desdemona squeezed her eyes shut and waited for a bullet to come through the thick steel door. She knew nothing about weapons. She had no idea of what kind of gun the intruder possessed, let alone whether it was powerful enough to shoot through a freezer door.

Nothing happened. No bullets tore through steel. There was no violent upward thrust on the door lever.

There was a muffled scraping sound and then a jolting crash of steel on the other side of the freezer door. The vibration of the impact reached into the cold room. It took Desdemona a few seconds to realize that the gunman had toppled a large, heavy object directly in front of the door.

Another silence descended.

Desdemona sensed that the kitchens were empty.

After what seemed forever she opened her eyes and got slowly to her feet. She was trembling from head to foot. Cautiously she stood on tiptoe and peered out the tiny thick-paned viewing window in the center of the heavy door.

From her vantage point she could see most of the interior of the Right Touch kitchens. The gunman was gone.

Desdemona leaned her head against the chilled door, breathing quickly. When she had caught her breath, she tried to open the freezer door.

It did not budge. Whatever it was that the gunman had dragged in front of the freezer now blocked the lever from opening. Desdemona was trapped inside the walk-in freezer.

Trapped inside a space that was smaller than a closed elevator.

Trapped in a room that seemed as small as the trunk of a car.

The old, choking fear welled up inside her. It blossomed into full-blown horror when she suddenly realized that she was not alone in the freezer.

With a dreadful sense of premonition, Desdemona turned slowly around to survey the small compartment. The blood in her veins became ice when she saw Vernon Tate's lifeless body propped in the corner.

There was a terrible red stain on the front of his shirt, and one of his beautifully sculpted ice swans lay at his feet.

14

$\mathcal{S}$he was trapped with a dead man in a room smaller than an elevator.

The claustrophobic fear nearly paralyzed Desdemona. For an instant she knew beyond a shadow of a doubt that she was going to go mad.

This was worse than any elevator. It was as bad as being locked in the trunk of George Northstreet's car when she was five years old.

The black bat-wings of her childhood terror assailed her, turning her into a shivering creature whose legs would no longer sustain her weight. The sense of doom was a crushing force.

Desdemona pressed her back against the icy steel door. Her knees gave way. Unable to take her eyes off Vernon Tate's body, she slid slowly downward.

Tony would not rescue her this time. It would be hours before anyone came in to work. Even if she survived the cold, Desdemona did not know if she could survive the awful claustrophobia and the presence of Tate's body. She wondered if it was possible to die of a panic attack.

Panic attack. That's all this was. The shallow breaths, the sense of terror, the rapid heartbeat. A panic attack. Desdemona hugged herself as she sank into a feral crouch.

She had survived being trapped in the car trunk all those years ago, and she could survive this. Poor Vernon was no threat to her. The only threat was the cold.

It was the *cold*, not the walls that seemed to be closing in on her.

The cold. Desdemona forced herself to focus on that element of the situation.

She was wearing jeans, a yellow pullover, and her red jacket. The jacket wasn't exactly a down parka; it was early summer, not mid-winter, after all. But the lightweight coat was lined with a cozy fleece. It would hold her for a while. She would not freeze to death immediately.

If necessary, she could borrow Vernon's clothes. He certainly did not need them.

The thought made Desdemona so ill she was afraid she might be sick to her stomach.

The nausea passed when she promised herself that she would not strip Vernon's body unless it became absolutely necessary. It wasn't necessary yet.

There was time to think. Time to act.

The most important thing to remember was that she was no longer five years old. She was not a helpless child trapped in the clutches of an insane man.

And she was no closer to Vernon Tate's body than she had been three minutes ago. The walls were *not* closing in on her.

She considered the possibility of hammering on the steel walls with one of the stainless steel freezer trays. She might be able to generate enough noise to attract someone's attention.

The flaw in that scheme was that it was highly unlikely that any of the neighboring shopkeepers had come in to work this early.

She needed another way to communicate.

She slid all the way down into a crouching position. Desdemona hugged her knees and tried to wrench her gaze away from Vernon Tate's body.

The slight movement caused the edge of her red jacket to shift. There was a small *clunk* as the object inside the right pocket brushed against the freezer wall.

Desdemona belatedly remembered her beautiful PDA X-1000. She had stuck it into her jacket this morning, just as she always did before she left for work.

Some men gave a woman flowers. Some gave perfume. But some, a rare few, no doubt, had an instinct for giving a woman the perfect gift.

Stark got Desdemona's e-mail message as soon as he switched on his computer.

> To: stark@sss.com
> From: desdemona@righttouch.com
> Trapped in freezer. Dead body. Please hurry.

Stark read the short message twice. It crossed his mind that Desdemona might be playing a joke on him. He picked up the telephone and dialed her apartment number.

There was no answer.

He dialed the Right Touch number. Again no response.

An unpleasant sensation gripped him. Desdemona was not comfortable enough yet with computers to play games on them.

He took a few seconds to type out a reply.

> To: desdemona@righttouch.com
> From: stark@sss.com
> I'm on my way.

He surged to his feet and headed for the door.

Maud looked up in alarm as he went past her desk. "Mr. Stark, is something wrong?"

"Something's come up. Tell Dane he'll have to handle the Connelly Manufacturing people by himself. If they don't like the fact that I'm not at the meeting, reschedule. You can reach me on my PDA."

"Yes, Mr. Stark." Maud straightened her shoulders. "Trust me, sir. I'll handle everything here. Flexibility is the hallmark of a successful secretary. We must learn to adapt to life's constantly changing winds. The branch that cannot bend will surely break."

Stark didn't have time to think of an adequate response.

He took the elevator to the street floor of the high-rise building and ran most of the six blocks to Pioneer Square. It was faster than getting the car out of the garage or trying to catch a cab.

He reached Right Touch a few minutes later. He went down the alley and found the rear door open. When he stepped inside, he immediately saw the heavy steel shelving that blocked the freezer door.

It did not take him long to move it.

He jerked open the freezer door.

"*Stark.*" Desdemona exploded out of the freezer and into his arms. She clutched her PDA X-1000 in one hand. She pushed her face into his chest and clung to him. "I got your message. I got it. I was going crazy, and then I got your message. I knew you'd come."

"What the hell happened here?" Stark hugged her fiercely.

Then he saw Vernon Tate's body in the corner of the freezer.

Hours later, after the police had finally left, Emote Espresso was overrun by Wainwrights.

They were everywhere, and they were all doing Shock and Horror. Stark decided that he had never really seen shock and horror done until now when he witnessed a whole family of theater people doing it.

Henry and Kirsten slumped elegantly on counter stools, espresso cups in hand. Bess and Augustus were draped languidly over a tiny table. They stirred their lattes with slow, desultory motions. Juliet, still somewhat ashen, sat at another table and toyed with a cup of cappuccino. Even Macbeth was there. He had Jason and Kyle with him.

Stark noted that Tony was the only one who was missing. Apparently he had not yet gotten the word.

Desdemona was center stage, seated at a small table. There was a cup of tea in front of her. Stark sat across from her.

"I still can't believe that poor Vernon is dead," Desdemona said for the hundredth time. "He was such a pleasant man. Such a quiet person. So reliable. An artist without an ego."

"A very rare individual," Augustus murmured. "Bland but rare."

"Tell me the whole story again," Stark ordered. "From the beginning."

"I've already gone over it a zillion times for the police."

"Do it one more time for me."

Desdemona sighed, wadded up a hankie, and stuffed it into the pocket of her jeans. "I went to Right Touch after you left this morning. The back door was open. I could see that the freezer door was open, too. I assumed someone had come to work early. Apparently that's just what happened. Poor Vernon must have got the morning schedule mixed up. He showed up early and surprised the burglar."

"Who shot him and stuffed his body in the freezer," Henry added in a strained voice. "And then the son-of-a-bitch tried to kill Desdemona."

"Oh, my God," Bess wailed. "I still can't believe it. Desdemona could have been killed."

"Now, now, my dear." Augustus patted her shoulder. "She's safe. It's all over."

Stark realized that he was gripping the edge of the small table so tightly the plastic threatened to crack beneath his fingers. He made himself loosen his grip.

Desdemona could have been killed.

Chaos filled his insides. He fought to cram the nightmarish feeling back into the cauldron where it belonged.

"You're sure you didn't recognize him?" he made himself ask.

She shook her head. "No. His features were all sort of twisted up. The police said it sounded as if he were wearing a nylon stocking over his face. He was tall and thin. His clothes were filthy."

"Some street person desperate for money to buy drugs," Kirsten whispered.

"That's what the cops think," Macbeth said.

"Why break into Right Touch?" Kirsten asked. "Desdemona doesn't keep cash on hand."

Desdemona dabbed at her eyes with a napkin. "The police said he was probably hoping to find something he could sell."

"He was in your office when you arrived?" Stark asked.

"Yes. He came out with the gun in his hand. I threw the soup kettle at him. He shot at it, but I think he must have been rattled. The shot went wild. So did the second one."

"Jesus," Henry said softly. "Two shots. Thank God you made it to the freezer."

"Vernon Tate wasn't so lucky," Desdemona said sadly. "The killer must have surprised him just as he was putting his ice swan into the freezer."

"The killer might have shot him and then put him in the freezer to complicate the investigation," Augustus said thoughtfully. "I recall a similar situation in a play I did a few years back. Dinner theater production down in California. A mystery called *Freeze Dried*. Had the lead. Remember, Bess?"

"I remember," Bess said. "You were brilliant, dear."

"Thank you. Role was that of the police investigator," Augustus continued. "Body was frozen in the snow. Had to deduce the actual time of death with some mighty clever sleuthing. Wasn't easy, I can tell you."

"I'm sure modern police techniques have come a long way since you did that play, Dad," Macbeth said.

"I've called my clients and cancelled everything through the weekend," Desdemona said. "Fortunately, all I had on the schedule was a small reunion brunch for a group of sorority sisters and a couple of luncheons. I transferred the business to another caterer."

"When can you get back into Right Touch?" Stark asked.

"The police told me they'd be finished in there sometime tomorrow," Desdemona said. "But it's going to take a couple of days to clean up."

Stark glanced around the room. "Where's Tony?"

Bess looked up from her latte. "Didn't you hear? Tony left a message on my answering machine sometime during the night. He said he was taking an early-morning flight back to Hollywood. Apparently he got a call from his friend down there. The soap is going into production after all."

"The Hollywood people bought him a ticket," Augustus explained. "Told him it would be waiting for him at the airport."

"Is that a fact," Stark said very softly.

"Wish that lad would stop pinning his dreams on a soap opera career," Augustus muttered. "Hollywood is no place for a Wainwright."

Shortly after noon the following day Desdemona sat down behind her office desk. She surveyed the chaos that surrounded her with a sense of dispirited gloom.

The police had finally finished their work. She knew from what one of the officers had said that they had found nothing that altered their original conclusion. Vernon had apparently been killed because he'd had the bad luck to interrupt an armed burglar at work.

It happened all the time.

Desdemona shuffled through the jumbled pile of papers that littered her desk, her mind on Stark.

Something she had seen in his eyes yesterday when Tony's name had been mentioned had alarmed her. She was not certain just what was brewing in Stark's razor-sharp mind, but it made her very uneasy.

The phone warbled. Desdemona was so wrapped up in her dismal thoughts that the sound made her jump. For no good reason her pulse started to pound. She took a deep breath to quiet it and reached for the receiver.

"Right Touch. This is Desdemona."

"You the lady who bought the ice sculptures from Vernon Tate?" The voice was that of a man. He sounded anxious.

Desdemona squeezed the receiver so tightly she wondered that it didn't crack. "Yes. Yes, I am. Who are you?"

"Heard on the news that he was dead. That true?"

"Yes, I'm afraid it is. Did you know him?"

"Hell, yes. I'm the one who did those ice carvings for him. He owes me fifty bucks for the swan."

"You did the carvings?"

"Yeah. And I really need to get paid, ma'am. He promised he'd give me the cash on Monday."

"I don't understand. I thought Vernon was an ice sculptor himself."

"Tate was no ice artist. He said he needed that job with your company real bad, so he lied. We made a deal. I supplied him with the carvings, and he paid me the extra that you paid him for them."

"I see." That explained why Vernon had always insisted on doing his work in private, Desdemona thought. "Who are you?"

"Larry Easenly. You going to make good on the fifty bucks?"

"Yes, of course. Give me your address, Mr. Easenly."

Larry rattled off a Capitol Hill address. "But I can come down there and pick up the check today."

"Things are in a mess down here, Mr. Easenly. I use my computer to write checks, and I haven't even had time to turn it on. You can come down Monday morning, if you like, or else I'll put the check in the mail to you so that you'll have it by Tuesday."

"I guess that'll be okay." Larry hesitated. "I appreciate this, ma'am. I know my deal was with Tate, not you."

"It's all right," Desdemona said wearily. "You did good work. The ice sculptures you sold to Vernon were lovely."

Larry cleared his throat. "You think maybe you'll need some more?"

"I may. I'll call you when I have everything sorted out here."

"Sure thing," Larry said eagerly. "See you then."

Desdemona hung up the phone and sat thinking about what she had just learned.

Vernon Tate had lied to get the job with Right Touch. She wondered what else he had lied about.

An hour later Desdemona drove slowly down a quiet residential street north of the University of Washington campus. She searched the addresses on the aging houses until she saw the one she wanted.

She eased the car against the curb and switched off the engine. For a few moments she sat behind the wheel and studied the scruffy-looking two-story home where Vernon had lived.

She had dug the address out of her files for the police yesterday. They had probably already been here in their search for Vernon's next-of-kin.

The overgrown yard was in no better shape than the house. It was choked with weeds, which had managed to snag and hold fast several stray candy wrappers and a couple of beer bottles. The front door had once been painted green, but it had faded and peeled to the point where there were only a few patches of color left. An old tire sat in the center of what had once been a lawn.

Desdemona did not know if Vernon had any relatives, a special friend, or even a roommate. He had mentioned his landlady once or twice, but that was all. He had not even provided a phone number to go with the address, so she had been unable to call ahead. It occurred to her once again that she really knew very little about Vernon Tate.

She was not sure what her next move would be in the event that no one answered the door of the rundown house.

She walked up the cracked concrete path and knocked on the once-green door. The sounds of afternoon television filtered through the thin wood panels. Desdemona knocked again, harder.

A scratching noise indicated that a lock was being undone somewhere inside. The door opened a crack. A woman of indeterminate years peered out suspiciously. She was dressed in a faded housecoat and a pair of fluffy slippers. Her frizzy gray hair stood out at odd angles around her head.

"What do you want?" The woman's voice had the scratchy hoarseness of a longtime smoker. The smell of alcohol was strong. "I already talked to enough people yesterday. You another cop or something?"

"I'm Desdemona Wainwright," Desdemona said. "I was Vernon's Tate's employer."

"Vernon's dead."

"Yes, I know."

"Spent an hour talkin' to cops yesterday. Then they spent an hour or two goin' through his things upstairs."

"You're his landlady?"

"Was. Name's Nadeen Hocks. Not that it's any of your business. I got better things to do than answer dumb questions."

"I don't want to ask you any questions, Ms. Hocks."

"Then what do you want?"

Desdemona lifted one hand in a vague gesture. "I just want to offer my condolences."

"To who? Vernon didn't have no relatives or friends. Leastways, none that I knowed of."

"None at all?"

"Nope." Nadeen scratched her wiry gray hair. "Spent all of his time with that blasted computer of his."

Desdemona stared at her. "He did?"

"Yep. As for me, I ain't gonna miss him much. Just the back rent he owed me." Nadeen gave her a sly wink. "But I took care of that problem."

"You did?"

"Damned right. I been rentin' out rooms for over thirty years. You learn a few things. And I stay informed. Got the television on all the time. Also got me a scanner radio. When I heard that some guy had been killed at a catering company early yesterday mornin', I didn't take no chances."

"What did you do?"

"Went right upstairs yesterday and helped myself to his computer. Good thing I did, too. 'Cause the next thing I know, the police was knockin' on the front door. They'd've probably taken it, even though there ain't no one for them to give it to. Can't trust anyone these days."

"I didn't know Vernon was into computers," Desdemona said carefully.

"You kiddin'? Computer stuff was all he cared about. No friends, no family, no girlfriend." Nadeen chuckled slyly. "And no boyfriend, either, if you take my meanin'. Figure I got a right to sell off his computer to make up for his back rent."

"You're going to sell it?"

"Yep. Lots of folks are into computers nowadays. Maybe I'll put an ad in the paper. Expect I could get a hundred and fifty, maybe even two hundred, for it."

Desdemona tried to think of what to do next. She needed some expert advice. "You know, I have a friend who's into computers. He might be interested in buying Vernon's stuff."

A distinct glint of greed appeared in Nadeen's eyes. "You think so?"

"I can call him right now, if you like. See what he says."

Nadeen looked doubtful. "He got enough money for a computer?"

"I think he can manage to come up with two hundred bucks."

"I ain't takin' no checks," Nadeen warned.

"I understand."

"You sure you ain't with the police?"

"Absolutely positive, Ms. Hocks."

"Well, all right, then." Nadeen stood back. "Come on in and call your friend."

"Thank you." Desdemona stepped into the dark, stale-smelling room.

The rank odors of old smoke and alcohol were overpowering. The smell clung to the faded drapes and seemed to waft upward from the threadbare carpet. Desdemona tried to take small, shallow breaths.

The shrill voices emanating from the television were annoying and much too loud, but Nadeen appeared oblivious to the noise. Desdemona glanced at the set. The afternoon talk show host was interviewing three men who were dressed in frilly maids' aprons. They were extolling the thrills of cleaning house for a dominatrix.

"Phone's over there on the wall." Nadeen pitched her voice above the drone of the talk show host. "Tell your friend I won't take a penny less than one-fifty. Cash."

"I'll tell him." Desdemona prayed that Stark would be in his office. She picked up the grimy phone and punched out the number.

"Stark Security Systems," Maud said in a sunny voice.

"This is Desdemona Wainwright. I need to speak to Stark."

"Certainly Miss Wainwright," Maud said cheerfully. "I'll put you through."

"Thank you."

"Quite all right. Have a nice day."

Stark came on the line. He sounded preoccupied. "Stark here."

"It's me, Desdemona. I need some advice."

"Advice? What's wrong? What's that noise in the background?"

"Don't ask unless you suddenly develop an overpowering urge to scrub a toilet." Desdemona waited until the television audience quieted briefly. "Listen, I'm out in the University District, at the house where Vernon lived. Stark, he was a computer buff. A hacker, maybe."

"Desdemona—"

"This is for real. His landlady says he spent all his money on computer equipment. She says he was always fussing with the stuff."

"Are you sure?"

Desdemona knew she had his full attention now. She could always tell when she had his attention. The focused energy coming through the phone line was enough to heat the plastic grip of the receiver. "Yes. When she heard about his death she worried that she wouldn't get her back month's rent, so she went up to his room and took his computer. She plans to sell it."

"Hmm."

"What do you think?"

"I think it raises some interesting questions."

"Well?" Desdemona asked tensely. "Should we buy it?"

"We?'"

Desdemona was exasperated. "You're supposed to be my hotshot computer security consultant, remember? I'm asking for a professional opinion. Do you think Vernon's computer might contain some useful information?"

"I don't now."

"Should we buy it and see?'"

"All right. Buy it."

Desdemona turned toward the wall and lowered her voice. "The landlady wants a hundred and fifty."

"What kind of computer is it?"

"I have no idea. That's a little beside the point, isn't it?"

"No. It could be worth anywhere between fifty or five hundred, depending on the brand, year, and what's inside."

"Stark, this is no time to be overly literal. We're not buying Vernon's computer as an investment. We're looking for clues."

"We are?"

She ignored that. "I've only got fifty dollars in my purse, and Ms. Hocks won't take a check. I'm afraid to leave here without the computer. She might find another buyer while I'm gone."

"Give me the address. I'll be there as soon as I can."

"Hurry. I have a hunch I'm going to have to watch some very strange television while I'm waiting."

Stark knocked on Nadeen's door thirty-five minutes later. Desdemona leaped out of her chair, galvanized by relief. "That'll be my friend, Nadeen."

"He'd better have the money with him." Nadeen padded across the tattered carpet and opened the door.

Stark loomed on the front step. "I'm Stark."

"We've been waitin' for you." Nadeen ushered him into the room. "Got the cash?"

"Yes. But I'll have to see the computer, first."

Nadeen appeared alarmed. "She said you'd buy it, no questions asked."

"I never buy anything unseen," Stark said.

Desdemona pointed to Vernon's computer, which sat in a box near the kitchen. "That's it over there."

Stark glanced at the television set as he walked across the room. He frowned briefly as the talk show host asked a man why he liked to videotape his wife in bed with another man. Then he looked down at the computer.

"Well?" Nadeen demanded. "What do you think?"

Stark studied the computer intently for a moment, and then he reached into his pocket for his wallet. "I'll take it."

Desdemona breathed a sigh of relief.

She waited until she had followed Stark outside and watched him stow Vernon's computer in the trunk of his car.

"What do you think?" she asked as he closed the lid of the trunk.

"I don't know what to think yet." Stark took her arm and walked her down the sidewalk to where her car was parked.

"I almost forgot," Desdemona said. "I learned something else about Vernon today. He wasn't a real ice sculptor. He lied about that on his résumé. He bought the carvings from a man named Larry Easenly."

"How did you discover that?"

"Easenly called today. He wants to be paid for the last swan. He said Vernon struck a deal with him for the ice work in order to get the job at Right Touch."

Stark paused in the middle of the sidewalk. He stared into the distance. "That would mean that Tate knew you needed an ice carver before he even walked through your door to ask for a job."

"Yes."

"How could he have known?"

Desdemona thought about it. "Well, it was no secret. Rafael had just left me for a job on the Eastside. He could have told any number of people that I was in the market for another ice sculptor. Everyone who worked for me also knew I needed one."

"A lot of people."

"Yes."

Stark started walking again. "I'll fire up Tate's computer tonight and see if there's anything interesting on it. But don't hold your breath, Desdemona. Odds are, Vernon was just an ordinary computer buff. It's very likely that the only things I'll find on his machine are a lot of games."

They came to another halt beside Desdemona's car. She opened the door and slid behind the wheel. She hesitated and then decided to take the bull by the horns.

"You haven't said anything about Tony, but I know what you're thinking," she announced.

"Do you?"

"Yes. But, Stark, trust me, there's no way he could be involved in this. I'm sure he really did get a call from the Hollywood people. That's why he left town yesterday morning."

"I don't know about the Hollywood call," Stark said, "but I did some checking. He was definitely booked on a flight to L.A. yesterday morning. But the flight didn't leave until nine-thirty. He checked in for it at the last minute. Almost missed it."

Desdemona was stunned. "You checked on his flight? How?"

Stark shrugged. "I used my computer to search the airline's records."

"Good grief. You can do stuff like that?"

Stark's mouth twisted wryly. "I'm a computer security expert, remember?"

"You actually checked the airline records," Desdemona repeated in amazement. "You don't take anything at face value, do you, Stark?"

"No."

"Is it legal to do that kind of thing?" she asked suspiciously.

"Let's not get into a discussion of technicalities. Checking airline records falls into the same gray area as buying Vernon's computer instead of telling the police about it. Drive carefully, Desdemona." Stark closed the car door.

Desdemona watched in the rearview mirror as he walked back to his car. He was as solid and unyielding as Mount Rainier. And somewhere inside he was still as cold as the glaciers on its summit.

*S*am. Sam, wake up."

"We brought you some breakfast."

Stark opened his eyes at the sound of Jason's and Kyle's voices. He took a few seconds to orient himself before he raised his head from his folded arms. He reached for his glasses, shoved them onto his nose, and automatically glanced at his watch.

It was nearly seven o'clock. *In the morning*.

"I must have fallen asleep in the middle of running the search program." Stark rubbed his jaw and absently noticed the rough stubble of an incipient beard. The last time he had checked the time, it had been three A.M.

He had learned one thing for certain last night. Whatever his deficiencies as an ice carver, Vernon Tate had definitely been qualified as computer literate.

Tate had employed an exotic operating system, not one of the common ones, and he had secured it and his files behind an invisible, highly sophisticated wall of high-tech wizardry.

It had not taken Stark long to realize that getting into Vernon's files was not going to be a piece of cake. He had made a preliminary survey with his newest password search program, but he hadn't expected it to work, and he had been right. Vernon Tate had been too savvy to use a real word or a name as a password. And as good as his password search program was, Stark knew it was unlikely to come up with a password that had been deliberately scrambled by an expert.

Sometime after midnight, Stark had opted for another approach to the problem.

Kyle set a bowl of cereal on the desk. "We already put the milk and sugar on the cereal for you."

"Here's a spoon." Jason handed one to Stark.

"Thanks." Stark picked up the spoon and started to eat the soggy, overly sweetened cereal.

Kyle came around the corner of the desk and peered at the glowing monitor that sat on top of Vernon's computer. "Did your special trapdoor search program work?"

"Yeah, did you find a way to break into the files?" Jason asked eagerly.

"I don't know." Stark stoically munched cereal. He was ravenous. "The trapdoor program was still running when I fell asleep."

"Hey, look, something just came up on the screen," Kyle said.

Jason crowded close. "Let me see."

Stark glanced at the monitor. He stopped chewing when he saw the prompt sign flickering gently against the dark screen. Cool satisfaction went through him.

"Gotcha," Stark said softly.

Jason looked at him. "Are you in?"

"I'm in."

Kyle grinned. "This is even better than Wyvern's Treasure."

Stark put down the cereal bowl and went to work at the keyboard. "Let's see what we can find."

"I'll bet Desdemona and the rest of the Wainwrights will be excited when they find out that Vernon Tate had a super secure system on his computer," Kyle said.

"Yeah," Jason said. "It means he might have been doing something really mysterious."

"It might simply mean that he liked his privacy," Stark said calmly.

"Mona, what the hell happened here?" Ian Ivers asked from the doorway of Desdemona's office. "Looks like a hurricane went through."

Desdemona put down the complicated insurance form that she had been working on all morning. "You must have heard that one of my employees was murdered Friday morning."

"Yeah. That's one of the reasons I came by." Ian dropped heavily into a chair. "Wanted to make sure everything was okay with you. Christ, I hadn't realized the killer had torn things up like this."

"The police think he was searching for a floor safe or something of value," Desdemona said wearily. She had been over the tale a dozen times since the murder. Her neighbors and the owners of the small businesses on the block had all wanted to hear the gory details.

"So the poor ice carver had the bad luck to walk in on him and got iced, himself, huh? And I hear you got locked in the freezer?"

"Yes."

Ian glanced at her, his eyes very intent. "You actually saw the guy?"

"I saw him, but I couldn't describe him. He was wearing a nylon stocking over his face. Was there something you wanted, Ian? I'm a little busy at the moment."

"What? Oh, yeah. I called Tony's number, but there was no answer, so I thought I'd see if you had heard anything from Stark. Think he's looked at the proposal for *Dissolving* yet?"

"I think it's safe to say that playing theatrical angel is not high on Stark's list of priorities at the moment."

"Mona, could you do me a favor here? You're close to Stark. Could you put in a good word for me? I have a hunch he'll listen to you."

Desdemona sighed and leaned back in her chair. "Look, why don't you give it up, Ian? Stark's not really into theater."

"Damn it, Stark needs this as much as we do."

Desdemona raised her brows. "He does?"

"Think what it will do for his corporate image. It's a fast way for him to become known as a patron of the arts."

"Maybe you shouldn't have told him that your goal was to put on a play that would rip the guts out of the audience," Desdemona said. "I think the concept had a negative impact on him."

"Yeah, yeah, maybe that's where I went wrong. His secretary says she's been instructed not to give me an appointment." Ian shot to his

feet and began to pace the office. "Maybe I need to rework the proposal."

"Good idea. Tell you what, you go rework your proposal, and I'll
finish cleaning up around here. Luckily the killer didn't bother to
mess up my computer." Desdemona swung around in the chair and
switched on the machine.

"Maybe the ice carver interrupted him before he got around to it,"
Ian suggested.

"I guess that's possible." Desdemona shivered as she punched in the
familiar commands that called up the weekly schedule. "I don't even
like to think about what happened in here."

"Say, do you know where Tony is? He and I were supposed to do
lunch today. We're gonna discuss possible casting for *Dissolving*."

"Tony's in L.A."

Ian abruptly stopped pacing. "L.A.? What the hell is he doing
down there?"

"He got a call from the soap people."

Ian was incensed. "Damn it, I thought he'd learned his lesson about
Hollywood. He knows that stupid soap is dead in the water. *Dissolving*
is at a critical point."

"You mean it might dissolve completely?"

"Very funny." Ian looked genuinely hurt.

"Sorry." Desdemona frowned as an unfamiliar message appeared
on her screen. "That's strange."

"What?"

"My computer is asking me if I want to recover some lost files."

Ian craned his head to see the screen. "That's a message you get
when there was a power failure in the middle of a work session or if
you accidentally turned off the computer without exiting the program
properly."

"What does it mean?"

Ian shrugged. "Just what it says. It means that the last work you did
was saved in a special emergency file. You'll have to call it up with
special commands to retrieve it."

"But, I didn't—" Desdemona broke off without finishing her sentence. For some reason she did not want to tell him that she was quite
certain that she had not accidentally shut down a program. Nor had
there been a power failure the last time she used the computer.

"Didn't what?" Ian glanced at her.

She cleared her throat. "I didn't know you were so familiar with computers."

"Who isn't these days? I use one to keep files of potential patrons and subscription lists and to handle the Limelight's financial records. Tony set up the programs for me."

"That's right. I'd forgotten."

"He's got a real knack for that kind of thing, doesn't he?"

"Yes." Desdemona did not want to pursue that. "Well, if you'll excuse me, I'd better get back to work."

"I can take a hint." Ian paused at the door. "Say, Mona?"

"Yes?"

"Do you think Stark would respond to a pitch that focused on how he would be hailed as a visionary patron of the arts if he were to back *Dissolving*? Corporate types like to grab on to the vision thing, you know. Good press."

"Gee, I'm not sure how Stark would respond to the concept of himself as a visionary corporate executive and patron of the arts." Desdemona smiled encouragingly. "Why don't you give it a shot?"

Ian slapped the doorframe in a gesture of renewed enthusiasm. "I'll do it. If you hear from Tony, tell him to get his ass back here to Seattle. That Hollywood crowd is all hype and no talent. We're *theater* people." He hurried off toward the front door, ponytail jiggling.

"I'll tell him," Desdemona said to herself. She waited until Ian was gone before she turned back to the computer.

She regarded the message about lost files for a long while. The only person who had ever used her computer other than herself was Tony. The possibility that he had been working on it shortly before Vernon's murder made her stomach churn.

Eventually she summoned the nerve to instruct the computer to recover the missing work. She punched a key. Nothing happened.

Desdemona groaned and reached for the manual. She hated having to resort to the manual. She never understood it.

The phone rang, slicing through her concentration. She picked up the receiver.

"Right Touch. This is Desdemona."

"Hey, kid, it's me, Tony."

Desdemona stilled. "Where are you?"

"L.A. Didn't Aunt Bess get my message?"

"Yes, but we were a little concerned. Did you hear that Vernon Tate was killed?"

"Killed? As in murdered?" Tony sounded incredulous.

"I walked in on it, Tony. The killer was still here. He took a couple of shots at me."

"*Jesus.*" Tony was appalled. "Are you okay? You weren't hurt?"

"No, I managed to get into the freezer and close the door. The killer left. But he dumped some shelving in front of the door and . . . oh, Tony, I was trapped in there."

"Shit, the *freezer?*"

"Yes."

"Were you . . . okay?"

"I nearly went crazy, as you'd expect. All I could think about was the trunk of Northstreet's car. And to make matters worse, Tate's body was in there with me."

"Oh, shit," Tony said again. Desdemona could hear the frustration and anger searing his words. "Oh, *shit.* Are you sure you're okay?"

"I'm okay, Tony. Remember the personal digital assistant Stark gave me? I used it to contact him. He got me out."

There was a short, pregnant pause. "Stark rescued you?"

"Yes. The place is a mess, but we should be ready to reopen on Monday. Tony, what's going on down there?"

"Nothing." Tony's voice dripped with disgust. "That's why I'm calling. The soap concept is still on the shelf. There are no plans to take it into production. And no one here wants to see my face."

"I don't understand. Why did they pay for your ticket if the project isn't going forward?"

"Damned if I know. No one down here knows anything about that, either. It's a little weird, to tell you the truth."

"Maybe it was just a clerical glitch."

"You mean somebody told a secretary to send a ticket to some other actor and it got sent to me by mistake?" Tony sighed. "Given my luck, that's a real possibility."

"What are you going to do now?"

"What can I do? I'm coming home." Tony paused. "Uh, there's just one small problem, kid."

"What's that?"

"I don't have the cash to buy a return ticket, and my credit cards have all been sort of temporarily cancelled. Can you buy a ticket for me? I'll repay you as soon as I can."

Desdemona groaned. "Take a bus."

"*A bus.*" Tony was scandalized. "All the way to Seattle? You wouldn't do that to me, would you?"

"I've got a question for you." Desdemona tapped the tip of her pen against the computer manual. "Did you do any work on my computer before you flew down to L.A.?"

"No. Why?"

"I'm getting a message on the screen that says there was a power failure in the middle of a work session and some files have been saved. I'm having trouble recovering them."

"No big deal. Pay attention. I'll walk you through the process."

A few minutes later Desdemona recovered the lost work. She gazed at it, frowning.

"What is it?" Tony asked.

"A string of gibberish. Just a bunch of keyboard characters run together."

"Sounds like someone tried to type up something personal on your computer and got interrupted before he could figure out how to save the document properly. I'll bet it was Kyle or Jason. They love to play with computers."

"That's true."

"About that airline ticket . . ."

"All right, all right. Take the plane. But you're going to owe me free labor here at Right Touch for a year."

"You got it." Tony paused. "How are things going with Super Nerd?"

"Call him that once more and you'll be taking the bus home from Hollywood."

"Message received."

Desdemona got into the Jeep and reached for the seat belt. "I appreciate the lift, Macbeth."

"No problem." Macbeth worked the gears and eased the big, black, four-wheel-drive vehicle out of the alley behind Right Touch. "I'm on my way to pick up Jason and Kyle, anyway. We've got a matinee this afternoon."

"I heard from Tony."

"Yeah?" Macbeth glanced at her. Light danced on the mirrored lenses on his sunglasses. "Anything come of that L.A. call?"

"No." Desdemona wrinkled her nose. "He talked me into buying him a return ticket."

"Damn. You know something? Maybe Stark's got a point. You let Tony take advantage a little too much."

"It's hard for me to say no to him. He's my brother."

"And he saved your life, I know, I know. But that was a long time ago. You've grown up, but I don't think he has."

Desdemona gazed unseeingly at the tourists who crowded the boutiques and shops along First Avenue. "I keep hoping that one of these days one of those dreams he's always chasing will finally come true."

"Not bloody likely. He's a Wainwright, but there's no getting around the fact that he's not the best actor in the family."

"Just as I'm not the best actress in the family."

They drove past the Seattle Art Museum. Desdemona glumly watched as the arm of the massive metal sculpture know as *Hammering Man* rose and fell. The figure, which stood in front of the museum, was doomed to an eternity of labor. *Hammering Man* might eventually rust, but he would never to able to rest. The sculpture reminded Desdemona of Tony. Futility in motion.

"Too bad Tony's got his heart set on acting," Macbeth mused. "He's actually fairly good with computers."

"I know."

"Be nice if Ian and Tony could get *Dissolving* off the ground."

"Not likely. Not if they're depending upon Stark to back it. Does it occur to you that when we talk about Tony we do a lot of wishful thinking?"

"Yeah."

Desdemona fell silent for the remainder of the drive to Stark's fortress.

When Macbeth pulled into the drive a short time later, Desdemona reached into the backseat for the picnic basket she had packed.

"Thanks again, Macbeth," she said as she got out of the Jeep.

"Right."

Desdemona walked up the steps. Kyle opened the front door just as she was about to knock.

"Hi, Desdemona. If you came to see Sam, he's busy. He worked on Vernon Tate's computer all night long. He only came out of his study once this morning, and that was to take a shower and change his clothes."

Desdemona brightened. "Has he found something interesting?"

"Don't know yet. He's inside the system though, and he's searching for some hidden files."

"Sounds hopeful." Desdemona held up the picnic basket. "I brought him some lunch."

"That's good. Jason and I made him breakfast, but we don't have time to make his lunch." Kyle glanced over his shoulder. "Hurry up, Jason. Macbeth's here."

"I'm coming." Jason dashed around the corner. "Hi, Desdemona." He raced past her down the steps. "Bye."

"See ya." Kyle followed his brother.

Desdemona waved to them as they got into the Jeep. She waited until the drive was empty before she went into the atrium foyer and closed the door.

It was easy to imagine that she was the only one in the house. A deep silence cloaked the two-story entrance hall.

Picnic basket on her arm, Desdemona went slowly up the steel staircase to the second level. There she turned and went down the corridor to the door of Stark's study. It was open.

The heavily shadowed interior was lit only by the cold glow of a computer screen.

Stark sat in front of the screen, his elbows propped on the arms of his chair. His fingers were steepled in front of him. The strong, blunt planes of his face were etched by the icy light. There was an alien remoteness about him, an eerie stillness that made Desdemona catch her breath.

He seemed so distant and so unreachable, a starship captain contemplating the vast reaches of interstellar space. A man without a home, doomed to wander the frozen reaches of the galaxy forever.

"Hello," she said softly.

"Hello." Stark glanced at her with a vaguely distracted air, his attention clearly on whatever occupied the computer screen. "What are you doing here?"

"I brought lunch." Desdemona smiled. "I'm your official caterer, remember?"

"Lunch? Stark looked baffled by the concept.

"You know. A meal that is traditionally eaten in the middle of the day."

"Right. Lunch." He removed his glasses and rubbed the bridge of his nose. "I forgot about it. Did Kyle and Jason leave yet?"

"A few minutes ago." Desdemona came farther into the room. She peered at the glowing screen. "What have you found?"

"Nothing yet." Stark put his glasses back on and followed her gaze back to the screen. "A whole lot of nothing. Too much of it, in fact."

"I don't understand."

"Vernon Tate knew his way around a computer. His files were locked up nice and tight. Very sophisticated system. I got in through a trapdoor."

"What's that?"

"It's impossible to make any operating system completely secure. There are always a few glitches, mistakes, oversights, you name it. With a lot of luck, patience, and good knowledge of the system, a determined intruder can get past the security."

"And you're a determined intruder?" Desdemona set the picnic basket down on the desk.

"I'm very determined. Tate has hidden some of his files. I'm going to find them."

The ironclad determination in his voice made Desdemona look at him. Stark's eyes glittered like emerald crystals in the chilled glow of the screen. He was one hundred percent *on*, she realized. Wholly focused.

The only other occasions on which she had observed this level of riveted awareness in him were when he made love to her.

"If the files are hidden, how did you discover that they even exist?" Desdemona asked.

"I instructed the computer to show me how much space has been filled up on the hard disk. The number it gave me doesn't match the figure I get when I add up all of the bytes used by the displayed files. Tate hid something. I've got ARCANE looking for it."

"Can you each lunch while you wait to see what ARCANE discovers?"

"Sure." But he did not look at the picnic basket. His attention was back on the screen.

Desdemona busied herself laying out the pita bread sandwiches she had made. She arranged one on a plate together with a cherry tomato and some celery stuffed with feta cheese.

She put the plate down on Stark's side of the desk. He picked up the sandwich without even glancing at it and bit into it.

Desdemona propped one hip on the corner of the desk and nibbled at the second sandwich.

"Tony called," she said after a bit.

Stark yanked his gaze away from the screen and pinned her with it. "When?"

"Earlier this morning." Desdemona did not like the predatory light in Stark's eyes. "He said the soap is off. He got the brush-off from the Hollywood crowd. He said no one down in L.A. can recall sending for him. He's on his way home."

"He claims he doesn't know who paid for his ticket?"

"Uh-huh." Desdemona finished her sandwich and brushed pita bread crumbs from her fingers. "Weird, isn't it?"

"Yes," Stark said softly. "Very."

"Want a chocolate-chip cookie?" Desdemona picked one up out of the picnic basket.

"Thanks." Stark took it from her fingers and downed it in two bites.

Desdemona got off the desk. "I'll clean up, and then I'll make some coffee."

"All right." Stark turned back to the computer.

Desdemona repacked the picnic basket, set it in the corner, and then went downstairs to make the coffee.

When she returned a few minutes later, Stark was on his feet behind his desk. His back was to the door of the study. He was stretching.

Desdemona came to a halt in the doorway, a mug of coffee in each hand. She watched, entranced, as Stark raised his arms over his head. He moved with the fluid power of a waterfall. His big hands clenched into large fists. His back and shoulder muscles shifted smoothly beneath his wrinkled white shirt. The motion jerked the tail of the garment free of the waistband of his trousers.

"I've got the coffee," she whispered.

Stark lowered his arms and slowly turned around to face her. His eyes locked with hers. He was still completely focused, but the direction of the focus had suddenly and without warning switched from the computer to her.

Desdemona stopped breathing. Ripples moved across the surface of the coffee. They were caused by her racing pulse. She knew that if she did not set the mugs down quickly she would spill the contents.

She managed to move her feet, but it took an effort. She walked across the room and carefully set down the mugs. "How's it going?"

"Nothing yet." Stark walked slowly around from behind the desk. He came to a halt in front of her. He took off his glasses and set them down on the desk. "I need a break."

"Stark?"

His hands closed over her shoulders. He pulled her against him. "What about you?"

Desdemona wrapped her arms around his neck. She smiled. "I guess I could use one, too."

"I'm glad to hear that." Stark covered her mouth with his own.

Desdemona was instantly enveloped by the storm. It rolled and crashed, sending shudders through her.

She wondered if she would ever grow accustomed to the impact of Stark's lovemaking. She knew that even if she were to become used to it, she would never, ever grow tired of it.

She felt his hands slide down her back, kneading her spine, pressing her closer. Stark groaned and wrenched his mouth from hers with obvious reluctance. And then he was kissing her throat, unfastening her blouse, undoing the front of her jeans.

He went down on one knee in front of her and tugged the denim down to her ankles and off her feet. Her panties went with the jeans.

The shadowy room whirled as Stark rose and lifted Desdemona. He settled her on the desk. The glass was cold beneath her bottom. Stark gripped her knees and eased her legs apart. She speared her fingers through his hair as he stepped between her thighs.

The urgent rasp of his zipper was very loud in the silence. Desdemona closed her eyes and reached down to cradle him in her fingers as he readied himself.

He touched her intimately.

Desdemona felt herself swell and soften.

He sucked in his breath when she tightened her hand around him.

"Wrap your legs around my waist," Stark said into her hair.

Desdemona obeyed. The position opened her further to his touch. He stroked her gently, slid a finger inside her and probed deeply.

Desdemona cried out.

He fitted himself to her. "I need this." His voice was jagged and torn, as though the words had been ripped from his soul. "I need you."

It was as close as he had ever come to telling her that he loved her. Perhaps it was as close as he would ever be able to come, Desdemona thought. From a man like Stark, the words were enough. They were real.

"I love you, Stark," Desdemona said against his shoulder. "*I love you.*"

Stark flinched as though he had been shot. He surged suddenly, uncontrollably, into her. His body convulsed. His hoarse shout could have been a cry of either anguish or triumph. It was impossible to tell.

Desdemona clung to his granite-hard shoulders. She did not know if he had even heard her soft confession of love. There was no time to wonder about it. She was already lost somewhere in a whirling vortex of sensation. Her only guide was the man who had taken her to the edge of chaos.

Stark returned to his senses slowly. He deliberately tried to make the process last as long as possible. The joyous pleasure of being inside Desdemona, of feeling as though he were a part of her, was too good to rush.

Her words rang in his mind. *I love you.*

Stark opened his eyes. His gaze rested on the glowing screen behind her. It took him a second to realize that a message had appeared.

He grabbed his glasses and shoved them onto his nose.

NAME OF HIDDEN FILE: Insurance.text

A second wave of satisfaction crashed through him. It was almost as intoxicating as the first.

ARCANE had worked.

Some days were definitely better than others.

"Gotcha," Stark said.

16

"$\mathcal{B}$ut what does it mean?" Desdemona demanded.

She was leaning so far over his shoulder that Stark was amazed that she did not fall into his lap. Not that he would mind if she did. His body still hummed with the aftereffects of passion.

He felt so good, so right. The way he did when he sensed himself on the verge of comprehending a vast, complex pattern. It was the kind of moment that pushed back the borders of chaos.

Desdemona had pulled on her jeans and rebuttoned her shirt, but she still smelled warm and moist and sexy. Her hair was a wild tangle of curls, and her mouth was still swollen from his kisses. The invisible bonds that bound them together when they made love still linked him to her.

Stark forced himself to concentrate on the screen. "*Insurance.txt* is the name of the hidden file. Look at the number of bytes in it. That's exactly the number that aren't accounted for when you add up the bytes used by the other files."

"Maybe it's just a private file he used to store insurance records," Desdemona said.

"Maybe. But I doubt we'll find the usual sort of insurance records. You saw his landlady and the place where he lived. I don't think that Tate was the kind of guy who bought a lot of insurance."

"So why name the hidden file *Insurance.txt*?"

"Let's find out." Stark gave the command to view the file.

The screen went dark for a few seconds, and then a short memo preceded by an e-mail address appeared. Stark saw that the address was that of an anonymous mail server. The message was short.

Order filled. Second half of payment must be received within five days of this date. Delivery of product will follow.

Desdemona scowled. "That string of characters at the top of the message is an e-mail address, isn't it?"

"It's an e-mail address, all right. To an anonymous server."

"What's an anonymous server?"

"It's an automatic computer mail service which receives and for-wards mail to and from people who want their identities kept secret."

"From each other?" She glanced at his face in astonishment. "But why would Vernon want to send a message to someone he didn't know?"

"There are all kinds of reasons why people want to remain anony-mous," Stark said quietly. "Let's see what else is in this file."

He hit a key, and another message appeared. It, too, was preceded by an e-mail address identified only as anonymous.

Price for chips is one thousand. Delivery by first of month.

The next message was one that Tate had received rather than sent.

Understand you can supply software for new hotwire program. Request info on price.

"I think I'm beginning to see a pattern here," Stark said.

"What on earth was Vernon doing?"

"It looks like he had set himself up in business as a sort of computer mercenary. A hacker who, for a price, would supply whatever the buyer wanted. He conducted business through the anonymous mail server."

Desdemona's fingers bit into Stark's shoulders. "You mean that he stole software and chips and things like that on demand?"

"Maybe."

"That line of work must not pay very well, judging by where he was living."

"Don't bet on it," Stark said. "Tate may have been stashing away some big bucks somewhere."

"Well, if he was making good money as a computer mercenary, why on earth did he want the job with me?"

"I'll give you one guess," Stark said.

"Oh, my God," Desdemona whispered. "He *used* me."

"Looks like it."

"You must have been one of his targets." Her voice rose in outrage. "And he used me to get to you."

"Someone probably hired him to go after ARCANE. With luck, maybe I can dig the messages covering that particular deal out of this file."

"Why, that slimy little weasel." Desdemona's eyes narrowed. "I liked him. He was so reliable. He was the only really dependable employee I ever had."

"Take it easy, Desdemona."

"You don't understand. I trusted him."

"So much for the famous Wainwright intuition," Stark muttered.

"Hah. That goes to show how much you know. I never got any kind of intuitive feelings one way or the other about Vernon. I just sort of liked him. He seemed like such a nice, quiet, inoffensive man."

"That's what they always say. Maybe next time you'll be a little more cautious about trusting someone just because he shows up for work on time."

"Oh, please." Desdemona crossed her arms beneath her breasts and gave him a scathing look. "This is no time for one of your pithy little lectures."

"Given the fact that I was Tate's intended victim on this occasion, I think I've got a vested interest in hoping that you've learned your lesson."

Desdemona threw up her hands. "Don't get any more paranoid on me than you already are. You must admit that this was an extremely unique situation."

Stark shrugged and said nothing. The facts spoke for themselves as far as he was concerned. He was not surprised that Desdemona refused to deal with them in a logical fashion. She was a Wainwright.

Desdemona brightened. "You know what this means, don't you?"

"What?" he asked warily. He knew that look on her face. It made him uneasy.

"It means you accomplished your mission, of course."

"My mission?"

"The job you were doing for me. Heck, you took it one step farther. You not only turned up another viable suspect besides Tony, you've as good as proved that Vernon was the would-be thief who went after ARCANE the night of your reception."

Stark could not argue the point. "The questions now are, why was Tate killed and who killed him?"

"What makes you think his murder is connected to his mercenary activities?" Desdemona asked in obvious surprise. "The police are probably right. He was in the wrong place at the wrong time. He walked into Right Touch the other morning and confronted a burglar. I did the exact same thing."

"I'm not a great believer in coincidences," Stark said. "You had an obvious reason to go to work early. But we still don't know why Tate was there."

"You don't think he simply got the schedule mixed up?" Desdemona's eyes widened. "Wait. My computer."

Stark shook his head. "Believe me, a guy like Tate would have no interest in your computer or in your business application programs. His own hardware and software were a hell of a lot more sophisticated."

"That's not what I meant," Desdemona said quickly. "I forgot to tell you that when I turned on my computer this morning I got a message informing me that a power failure had shut down some work in progress. The message asked if I wanted to recover the lost work. I did."

"So?"

"So as far as I know, there was no power failure during a work session. Tony called while I was fussing with the lost files. He helped me recover them. He speculated that someone had been fiddling around with my computer and had turned it off without quitting the program properly."

"Possible."

"But what if Vernon was the one who had been using my computer, and the burglar interrupted him in the middle of whatever he was doing?" Desdemona's eyes were alight with excitement.

"What time was the work saved?"

She frowned. "I don't know. I didn't make a note of the time."

Stark looked at her. "What was in the lost files?"

Desdemona bit her lip. "Garbage. Letters and numbers randomly strung together."

"Did you delete the file?"

Desdemona shook her head. "It's still on my computer."

"I think," Stark said as he got to his feet, "that I had better take a look at what you found."

Desdemona gestured at the screenful of anonymous messages. "What about Vernon's insurance file?"

"It's going to take a lot of time to work through it. I'll deal with it later." Stark shut down the computer. He realized his shirt was still unbuttoned. Automatically he started to refasten it. "Let's go back to your office. I want to see that garbage in the recovered files. I also want to check the time that it was saved."

Desdemona regarded him very soberly. "This is getting very messy, isn't it?"

"Yes, it is." Complex was the correct word, Stark thought. Dangerously so.

Stark managed to find a parking space on a Pioneer Square side street, got out, and followed Desdemona down the alley behind the building that housed Right Touch.

His mind was still focused almost entirely on the problem of Vernon Tate. When he walked through the back door of the large, gleaming kitchen, it took him a few seconds to adjust to the fact that, in addition to the familiar faces working to clean up the premises, a pair of strangers were present.

He very nearly ran into Desdemona, who had come to an abrupt halt at the sight of the newcomers.

Juliet hailed her from the far end of the kitchen. "Hey, Desdemona, look who just blew into town."

"Mom. Dad." Desdemona laughed with delight and dashed forward, arms outstretched. "What are you two doing here?"

Stark watched the reunion from the doorway. Juliet, Bess, and Augustus gathered around Desdemona and her parents. Everyone started to talk at once. The babble of excited voices swirled around Desdemona, enveloping her.

Once again, Stark was aware of feeling outside the pattern. The brief, temporary insights he had gained when he was connected to Desdemona seemed lost.

With the skill of long practice, Stark suppressed the dark loneliness and forced himself to study Desdemona's mother and her stepfather.

Celia Wainwright was a handsome woman who exuded a charm that was palpable from across the room. She wore a gauzy, ankle-length summer dress that looked vaguely southwestern in style. It was belted with a silver-and-turquoise-studded strip of leather.

Celia was shorter than the average Wainwright, about the same size, as Desdemona. Her graying red hair was bound into an elegant knot at the nape of her long neck. Her exotic eyes, similar in color to Desdemona's, dwelt on Stark with grave interest.

Benedick was a tall, silver-haired man whose strong features had only recently begun to blur a little with the years. He gazed as though he had consciously chosen to live the latter portion of his life immersed in the role of an aging old-world aristocrat. He looked at Stark as he released Desdemona. Regardless of the role he had elected to play, his eyes held unexpectedly keen perception.

When he spoke, his voice was so deep and resonant that Stark would not have been surprised to discover that he was secretly wired to a karaoke machine.

"Well, well, well," Benedick murmured. "So you're the man who has stolen my little girl's heart."

"Dad, really." Desdemona blushed furiously.

Benedick ignored her. He put out his hand in a gesture of calculated graciousness. "Benedick Wainwright."

Stark glanced at the proffered hand. He walked forward to take it. "I'm Stark."

"This is my wife, Celia." Benedick made a gallant motion to indicate Desdemona's mother.

Celia gave him a charming smile. "I'm told everyone calls you Stark."

"Yes. How do you do, Mrs. Wainwright." Stark inclined his head politely. "I didn't realize you and your husband were expected."

"They weren't." Desdemona stepped out of her mother's embrace. "What's up? Did the show close unexpectedly?"

Benedick shook his head sadly. "Folded three nights ago without any notice."

"What happened?" Desdemona asked.

"Apparently the Cactus Dinner Theater was operating on the edge of bankruptcy," Celia explained. "A fact which no one had seen fit to make known to the cast. The sheriff arrived one morning earlier this week and put everything under lock and key until the creditors can resolve the problems in court."

"That's terrible," Desdemona said.

Stark glanced at her. There was no real heat or surprise in her voice. He suspected she was accustomed to such tales of theatrical disaster.

"These things happen," Benedick said philosophically. "Celia and I drove back to Seattle with some of the rest of the cast. Been on the road for three days. Got into town an hour ago and came straight here. You can imagine how stunned we were to learn what had happened."

"Dreadful," Augustus murmured. "Absolutely dreadful."

"We're still in shock," Bess assured Benedick. "To think of poor Desdemona trapped in that freezer with a dead body."

"You might have been killed," Celia whispered, horrified. "Are you sure you're all right, dear?"

"I'm fine, Mom. Stark had given me this really neat little computer gadget that allows me to send messages. You know, e-mail. At any rate, I sent Stark a message. Told him I was locked in the freezer. He came down and got me out."

Augustus narrowed his eyes. "Reminds me of the time Tony saved her from—"

"Not now, dear," Bess murmured gently.

Celia turned to Stark. "We've been anxious to meet you, Stark. It's not every day that our Desdemona falls in—"

"*Mother.*" Desdemona's face turned a brilliant shade of pink. She slid a sidelong glance at Stark. "For heaven's sake, let's not get carried away here."

"Celia's right," Benedick said portentously. "About time I took a good look at the man you're thinking of marrying."

"Dad, Stark and I have a dating relationship." Desdemona sounded desperate. "We have absolutely no plans for marriage."

"That's not the way I heard it from Bess," Celia said gently.

"Well, Aunt Bess has it all wrong," Desdemona said.

Bess appeared mildly surprised. "I do?"

Juliet rolled her eyes. "Come on, Desdemona, we all know you and Stark are *involved.*"

"Is that a fact?" Benedick looked grim.

"We do not all know that," Desdemona said loudly. "What Stark and I do together is our personal business, and I would appreciate it if my family would stay out of it."

"Hold on here now." A troubled expression furrowed Benedick's regal brow. He glanced at Desdemona and then at Stark. "Did we misunderstand something here? I was told things were serious between you two."

"Well, they aren't." Desdemona turned toward Stark with a blindingly bright smile. "Are they? We're friends. And business associates. And we have a casual dating relationship. Isn't that right, Stark?"

Stark was stunned by the icy talons of pain that seized his insides. The words that Desdemona had whispered as she had shuddered in his arms earlier that afternoon had been quietly burrowing deeper and deeper inside him. He realized that he had been hoarding them like hot coals against a dark winter.

I love you.

Now he realized that she had probably not meant them, after all.

I love you.

Just words that had been spoken by a passionate woman in the heat of the moment.

I love you.

He was standing in the slipstream of chaos, buffeted and disoriented by the cold, random winds. Comprehension of the pattern was impossible.

"Whatever you say," Stark said politely.

"Whew. That was a close one." Desdemona hastily shut the door of her office, turned around, and sagged back against the glass panel. "I'm really sorry about that embarrassing scene with my folks."

"Forget it."

"They get a little excited sometimes. It's a family trait."

"I said, forget it." Stark watched as she went around behind her desk. What had he expected? he wondered. Desdemona was a Wainwright. She might have a casual dating relationship with a man like him, but that was probably as far as things would ever go.

"Stop saying forget it." She gave him a thoroughly exasperated glare. "I can't forget it. The last thing I wanted anyone to do was put you on the spot."

"What spot?"

She gave him an odd look. "You know. All that talk about us being seriously involved."

Stark looked at the blank screen of the computer. "I thought we were."

"Well, of course we are."

"We are?" This was the kind of conversation that always succeeded in baffling him, Stark thought. Still, he found himself seizing on the small flicker of hope her words had rekindled.

Desdemona flopped back in her chair, aimed her finger at him, and narrowed her eyes. "You know what your basic problem in life is, Stark?"

"No," he said. He switched his gaze back to her and waited, intent on the answer.

"You take everything a little too literally." Desdemona grinned. "For example, take a good look at yourself right now."

"I can hardly do that." He glanced around at the notes, clippings, and photos that covered the walls of the office. "There isn't a mirror in here."

"There. You did it again. You see what I mean? You're too literal minded. Very few people in this world say exactly what they mean."

Stark frowned. "I've noticed that."

"You have to look for the real meaning behind the words. Think of human communication as a problem in chaos theory."

"Complexity, not chaos. And communication applications are not my area of expertise."

She slapped a palm on the table. "There you go again. You interrupt a discussion of a very important topic just to correct me because I used a term you think is inaccurate. That's an overly precise way of thinking. It gets in the way of real communication."

He looked at her in surprise. "I would have thought that it facilitated it."

"Trust me, it doesn't." Desdemona drummed her fingers on the arms of her chair. "Now, to get back to my point about the similarities between human communication and the problems in chaos theory or complexity science or whatever you call it—"

"No offense, Desdemona, but you know nothing about the latter."

"That's what you think. What I was trying to say is, you should look for the pattern beneath the words. The real meaning, not the literal one."

"People should say what they mean."

"Maybe. But they often don't." She gave him an unsettlingly perceptive look. "Sometimes they can't."

"Of course they can." Stark told himself that he was on solid ground here. He could argue this point from a thoroughly rational perspective. The facts were obvious. "A failure to communicate clearly and accurately reflects sloppy thinking and muddled logic."

"Yeah, well, that's most of the human race for you. People get emotional, and when they do, they get sloppy and muddled."

That was undoubtedly why she had told him that she loved him a couple of hours earlier, Stark thought glumly. The passion had muddled her thinking processes for a time. "I see."

"The reason I told my parents that you and I have a business relationship combined with a casual dating relationship is because I know them. If I imply that you and I have anything more than a casual sort of relationship, if they think we're really serious, they'll think that we're on the brink of marriage."

"Marriage." The word seemed to lodge in his throat.

"Exactly." Desdemona swung the chair around to face the computer. She was suddenly very busy at the keyboard. "Wainwrights are a romantic lot. To them a serious affair implies commitment, and that implies marriage. The whole ball of wax.”

“I see.” Stark watched the computer screen come to life.

“Don’t worry, I think I managed to distract them from that notion.” Desdemona slanted him a quick, unreadable look. “Wainwrights are a little old-fashioned about some things. Family is very important to them. It comes from years of believing that they can only rely on each other.”

“I understand.”

“I know how you feel about marriage, Stark. Don’t worry, I’ll make sure no one brings up the subject again.”

“How do you feel about it?” Stark asked in a deliberately neutral tone.

“Marriage? Well, I *am* a Wainwright.” She gave him an apologetic smile. “Someday . . .” She raised one shoulder in a small shrug and let the word trail off into the mists.

“I see.”

“But, hey, someday is a long time off, isn’t it?” Desdemona gave him a mischievous smile. “And in the meantime I think what you and I have is pretty special, don’t you?”

“Yes. Special.” He wished to hell he knew what she was really saying.

He had the distinct impression that he was missing something in the conversation. It was as though Desdemona’s words were locked in code. He could see that there was a pattern, but he did not have the key to it.

Give him a nice, simple, straightforward problem in complex structures any day.

“Ah, there we go.” Desdemona studied the screen in front of her. “That gibberish you see there is what I found when I recovered the lost work. Just random characters. Tony’s right. A child could have typed them. What do you think?”

“Let’s see when this work was done.” Profoundly grateful for an excuse to move on to a topic that he could comprehend, Stark leaned over the keyboard and punched out a command with one hand.

The time that the gibberish had been entered into the computer appeared on the screen. Eight-fifteen.

Desdemona stared at the screen. "That was right around the time that Vernon was killed."

Stark pondered the gibberish. "The question is, who typed this nonsense? Vernon or the killer?"

"And why would either of them type it on my computer?"

"Good question." Stark studied the long string of characters for a moment. There was a pattern there. He could feel it. "I think it's more than garbage."

"What do you mean?"

"It may be an encrypted phrase."

Desdemona's eyes widened. "This is code?"

"Yes."

"But you have to have a special program to encrypt a message, don't you? I don't have one."

"It would have been simple for someone to load the encryption program from a floppy disk, code this message, and then remove the program from your computer's memory."

"But that would mean someone deliberately left this message for me." Desdemona shook her head. "It makes no sense. How could he be sure I'd get it?"

"It was a good bet that you'd check to see what was in the lost work file the first time you turned on the computer."

"I suppose so. But what made him think that I'd recognize an encrypted message if I saw it?"

Stark considered the obvious. "Maybe the message wasn't left for you."

"I'm the only one who uses this computer."

"Are you?"

"Of course." Desdemona looked up at him expectantly. "Can you decode this?"

He wished he could decode her as easily. "Probably. But first I have to get my magic decoder ring out of the cereal box."

Half an hour later Desdemona whisked into Exotica Erotica with two tall lattes that she had purchased at Emote Espresso.

She waited as a woman in a pin-striped, skirted business suit concluded her purchase of a long, fluffy feather boa, an erotic novel, and a pink and gold box of condoms. The woman smiled at Desdemona on the way out. Desdemona nodded.

"I'm going to have to stock more feathery things," Kirsten said as the door closed behind the shopper. "Anything with feathers on it seems to sell like hotcakes."

"I know what you mean. I go through a lot of swans in my business. Here, have a latte."

"A shot of caffeine. Just what I needed. I've been swamped all afternoon. This is the first break I've had, and I can't leave the shop. I'm the only one here."

"Where's Henry?" Desdemona set Kirsten's latte down on the counter. "I thought he was supposed to help out."

"Ian called and asked him to go down to the Limelight to meet with some potential money people."

"Hmm. I wonder if that means Ian has given up on trying to persuade Stark to became an angel?"

"Ian never gives up. You know that. He is tireless in his pursuit of financial stability for the Limelight." Kirsten removed the top from the latte cup and took a sip. "How are things going?"

"Mom and Dad just hit town. The Cactus Dinner Theater got shut down earlier this week. Financial problems."

Kirsten made a face. "So what else is new? Have they met Stark yet?"

"A little while ago. It was a near thing. Dad segued immediately into his Concerned Father role. I swear, if I hadn't stopped him, he would have demanded to know whether or not Stark's intentions were honorable."

Kirsten's brows rose. "How did you stop him?"

"I made it clear that Stark and I have only a casual dating relationship."

"Casual?" Kirsten choked on her latte. "I'd hardly call it that. You're sleeping with him. How long do you think you can keep Benedick in the dark about that? Everyone else in the family knows it."

"Is that so?" Desdemona was irate. "I'd like to know how everyone else can be so darn sure of my personal business. Stark has not spent so much as a single night at my apartment, and I have never spent a night at his house. What makes everyone think we're sleeping together?"

Kirsten grinned. "Gosh, I don't know. Call it Wainwright intuition."

Desdemona groaned. "What am I going to do, Kirsten? When Dad realizes that I'm in love with Stark, he's going to start making noises like an old-fashioned patriarch. I just know he will."

"So let him. He's good in that role."

"He'll expect Stark to either marry me or get out of my life and never darken my door again. He'll demand that Stark make a choice."

"Let Stark make his own decisions."

"I can't do that," Desdemona said. "I don't dare put any pressure on him at this stage. Stark doesn't know what he wants yet."

"I wouldn't be too sure of that."

17

*S*tark sat in the shadows of his study and brooded over the message on the screen in front of him. Decoding the encrypted words that had been left on Desdemona's computer had been child's play for AR-CANE. The message, itself, however, was anything but playful.

> Client: This is to let you know that I have id'd you. Did you think you could hide behind the anon address? As proof that I know who you are, I'm leaving this where I know you will be sure to find it. You're always fooling around with this computer. Price of my silence is fifty thousand. Same arrangements as last time.

Stark recalled Desdemona's euphoric relief when she believed that they had discovered evidence that Tony was definitely not the person who had attempted to steal ARCANE.

He wondered how she would react when he told her the bad news. The evidence was starting to indicate that her stepbrother was in this mess up to his ears. He might well have been the mysterious "client" who had hired Vernon Tate to steal the encryption program.

Desdemona had been mistaken earlier when she had assured Stark that she was the only person who ever used her computer. Good old

Tony had not only used it, he had installed the software and modified the original programs. The Wainwright family screwup knew his way around a computer. And the computer he liked to fool around with the most was Desdemona's.

It had no doubt been difficult for Tate to identify his client. To do it he would have had to backtrack through the anonymous server's files, a complex task, even for a skilled hacker. But once he knew Tony's true identity, things would have gotten much easier. It would have been no great trick to trace Tony to the Right Touch computer.

After a long while, Stark picked up the phone and dialed the Right Touch number.

"She's not here, Stark," Juliet sounded a little breathless, as if she had run into the office to answer the phone. "She went down the street to Exotica Erotica. By the way, as long as I've got you on the line, I want to invite you to dinner tonight."

"Dinner?"

"To celebrate Uncle Benedick and Aunt Celia being back in town. Everyone will be there. Bring Jason and Kyle."

"Where is this dinner being held?"

"Same restaurant we used for Desdemona's birthday. We'll be in a private room at the back. When you arrive, just tell the hostess that you're with the Wainwright party. See you."

Stark hung up the phone and dialed a second number.

Kirsten answered on the first ring, the energetic enthusiasm of a shopkeeper having a good business day vibrating in her voice. "Exotica Erotica."

"This is Stark. I'm looking for Desdemona."

"She's right here."

Desdemona came on the line. "Hi, Stark. What's up? Did you decode the message?"

"Yes." He gazed at the glowing screen and wondered how to tell her that her precious stepbrother was looking more guilty than ever. "It's a blackmail note."

"*Blackmail?*"

Stark read it to her. "My hunch is that the note was left by Vernon Tate for his client. He had learned the client's identity and wanted fifty thousand dollars to guarantee his silence. He was probably killed immediately after he'd typed and encrypted this note."

"But that doesn't make any sense. Why would Vernon have left the message on my machine?"

Stark let the silence grow heavy. But if he entertained any hope that Desdemona's famed Wainwright intuition would do his dirty work for him by providing the obvious conclusion, he was doomed to disappointment.

"Wait, wait, I've got it," Desdemona's voice was suddenly brimming with excitement. "Tate never intended the client to read the blackmail note on my computer."

"What makes you think that?" Stark asked gently.

"Don't you see? Vernon simply used my machine to type out the note and to encrypt it."

"On that, we agree."

"He probably intended to print out the encrypted message on my printer and mail it to his so-called client, whoever that is."

"Uh, Desdemona . . ."

"But he got interrupted by the killer before he could finish," she concluded triumphantly.

"You think he used your computer as a typewriter to produce a note he then intended to put into the mail?" Stark closed his eyes and leaned his head against the back of his chair. "The famed Wainwright intuition in action, I assume?"

"You've got to admit it makes perfect sense." Desdemona chuckled. "Even you can't argue with my logic on this, Stark."

Argue with it? He could crush her weak, absurd, faulty logic in two seconds flat.

All he had to do was point out to her that there had been no need for Tate to use the Right Touch computer and printer. Tate had his own hardware at home. And the blackmail note clearly stated that the message had been deliberately left where Tate knew his client would find it—on the Right Touch computer. Everyone, including Tate, knew that Tony was on Desdemona's computer all the time.

The correct conclusion was inescapable. At the very least, Tony was Vernon Tate's mysterious "client." If one concluded that the killed-in-the-course-of-a-burglary hypothesis was a little too convenient and too much of a coincidence under the circumstances, one could take it a step further. One could make a damned good case for casting Tony in the role of murderer.

240

Tony had a solid motive for killing Vernon Tate. Tate was trying to blackmail him. The casting of Tony as the bad guy would also explain why Desdemona had escaped with her life. Shooting his own stepsister had probably been a little too much for Wainwright.

Tony had probably had a bad case of nerves after the murder, had panicked, and jumped on the first plane out of Seattle. He had covered his tracks by leaving a message on Bess and Augustus's answering machine.

"We're making real progress here, Stark," Desdemona said. "We're going to solve this thing."

"You think so?"

"I feel certain of it. See you at dinner tonight. Tell Kyle and Jason that the restaurant does pizza."

Stark replaced the phone gently in its cradle. He sat quietly for a moment, contemplating the screen. After a while he rose and walked to the window. He stood looking out over the city and the sweep of Elliott Bay.

He was a fool to hope that Desdemona would someday come to feel the kind of bone-deep loyalty to him that she felt toward her stepbrother. How did a man even begin to compete with a woman's childhood hero? Stark wondered.

There would be no hope at all if he got Tony sent off to prison, Stark thought. Desdemona would never forgive him.

With a supreme effort of will, Stark forced himself to stay focused on the logic of the situation. This was no time to get dragged down into the chaos of emotion. There was too much at stake. At all costs, he had to make Desdemona see the truth about Tony. If Wainwright had become a killer, he was more than just an annoying screwup, he was genuinely dangerous. A man who had killed once could kill again.

Stark knew what had to be done, and he told himself that he would do it. But he also knew that Desdemona would not thank him for forcing the truth upon her.

No one ever thanked the messenger when the news was bad.

Desdemona finally got her key into the lock on the third attempt. She sighed with relief, pushed open the door, and let herself into the haven of her loft apartment.

She closed the door quickly, dropped her purse on the nearest table, and hurried across the room. She collapsed into the big red armchair in front of the high windows.

She was still shaking. She had been struggling to control the tremors ever since she had taken Stark's call at Exotica Erotica.

Stark believed that Tony was Vernon's client. He believed that Tony had killed Vernon.

True, Stark had not actually made the accusation aloud yet, but Desdemona knew that it was only a matter of time. She had heard it in his voice.

She had rushed to give him an alternative scenario, but she knew her logic had been flawed. There was great, gaping holes in it, and if she could see them, it was a cinch that Stark had seen them.

Desdemona took several deep breaths. She splayed her fingers wide across the plump arms of the red leather chair and willed herself to stop trembling. She had to stay calm. She had to think clearly and rationally. This was no time to give in to the natural Wainwright tendency to succumb to emotion.

She made herself think about the situation clearly. She had to rely on her intuition and her knowledge of her family.

The first and most important fact was that Tony was not a thief. He could not have been Vernon's client.

The second fact that she understood in her bones, even if she could not yet prove it, was that Tony was not a murderer. Desdemona told herself that she was realistic enough to acknowledge that anyone, Tony included, could kill under certain circumstances. But for Tony, or any other Wainwright for that matter, murder would have to be committed in the heat of intense fear or rage or in self-defense. It wasn't an act that could be cold-bloodedly plotted out beforehand.

And whatever else one could say about Vernon Tate, he was simply not the kind of man who inspired a great degree of passionate rage, not even if he was trying to blackmail you.

Her logic was faultless, Desdemona thought. It was backed up by her intuition. But she could not prove anything. In the meantime, she had a terrible conviction that Stark was moving remorselessly forward along his own trajectory.

She had to find a way to deflect him from his path and aim him in another direction before he managed to make Tony look guilty.

The phone rang, jarring her out of her morbid thoughts. Desdemona climbed slowly out of her chair and walked across the room to answer the summons. She picked up the receiver, hoping the caller was not Stark. She wasn't ready to deal with him.

"Kid, is that you?"

"*Tony.*" Desdemona clutched the phone. "Where are you?"

"I'm back in Seattle," Tony said in a strange voice. "But I'm not at my apartment."

"What's wrong? You sound very strange."

"Probably because I've just realized that something really weird is going on around here. Desdemona, don't freak, but I think someone is trying to set me up for the murder of Vernon Tate."

"Set you up?" Desdemona gazed blankly out the window. "What are you talking about?"

"I got home an hour ago. Someone was in my apartment while I was gone."

"How do you know?"

"I wasn't sure at first. I just had a feeling that something wasn't right. Know what I mean?"

"Yes." Desdemona did not question Tony's intuition. He was a Wainwright.

"I unpacked my suitcase and started to toss some dirty shirts into the hamper. But when I opened the hamper I realized that the green shirt I had left on top of the pile of clothes was no longer on top. I'm sure it was the last thing I threw into the hamper before I left for L.A."

"I don't understand. Where was it?"

"Farther down in the heap."

Desdemona frowned intently. "Someone went through your dirty clothes? Why on earth would anyone do that?"

"I don't know, but I got really nervous. I went through the entire apartment to see if anything had been stolen. Nothing had been taken, but something had been left behind."

"Tony, no offense, but this isn't the last act of a dinner theater mystery. Don't drag out the big revelation. What did you find?"

"A gun. A thirty-eight," Tony said. "It was in the bottom of the hamper."

"My God."

"Vernon Tate was killed with a thirty-eight, wasn't he?"

"That's what one of the cops said, yes." Desdemona's knees threatened to collapse.

"And the police didn't recover the murder weapon, did they?"

"No," Desdemona whispered. "At least, not that I heard."

"Guess where someone intended that gun to be found," Tony said bleakly.

"Oh, my God." Someone really was trying to make Tony appear guilty of murder, Desdemona thought. "But who was supposed to discover the gun? And when?"

"How the hell should I know? Maybe the police were supposed to find it later, after enough so-called evidence had accumulated to warrant a search of my apartment."

"Evidence?"

"Yeah. Evidence. *Planted* evidence. I'm sure the gun in my hamper was just the beginning."

Desdemona went cold. "That explains the message on my computer."

"I decided I'd better lay low. I got rid of the gun. I'm in a motel out on Aurora Avenue. I'm registered under another name, Stone Morgan."

"For heaven's sake, Tony, wasn't that the name of the character you were supposed to play in that soap you've been trying to get off the ground?"

"Yeah. It was all I could think of on the spur of the moment. Listen, kid, I'm a little spooked. Don't tell anyone, not even the family, that I'm back in town yet, okay? I need some time to figure out a way to deal with this mess."

"But Mom and Dad are in town, Tony. They arrived a few hours ago. They know you're expected. Surely I can tell them?"

"No. Don't tell anyone. Let everyone think I'm still down in L.A. You know how excited the family gets when there's a crisis."

"Yes, but—"

"I don't want to alarm everyone yet." Tony paused meaningfully. "And I definitely do not want someone accidentally telling the wrong person that I know I'm being set up to take the fall for a murder."

"The wrong person?" Desdemona was confused. "But who's the wrong person?"

"Can't you guess?" Tony's voice was bitter.

"Are you saying that you know who's behind this?"

"There's only one person who could be behind it. Your pal, Stark."

For an instant Desdemona could not breathe. "No."

"He's the only one with a motive. He hates my guts." Tony's voice gentled. "I'm sorry, kid. I know how this is hitting you."

"I don't believe Stark would do such a thing."

"It's the only explanation that fits the facts," Tony insisted. "Don't you see? He wants me out of the picture, and he'll do anything to get rid of me."

"You think he's jealous? Tony, that's ridiculous. Stark isn't the type to get insanely jealous."

"He's jealous all right, but that's only part of it. Don't forget that he also thinks I tried to rip off his damn security program. A guy like that doesn't forgive or forget. He's decided that he can kill two birds with one stone. He figures he can have his vengeance and turn you against me at the same time."

"For crying out loud, Tony, you're beginning to sound like a character in a play."

"You know what they say about real life and art imitating each other."

Desdemona closed her eyes and tried to think. "We've got to talk. We need to put everything down on paper and look at the facts in a clearheaded, rational manner. Frankly, Stark is very good at this kind of thing."

"For Christ's sake, Desdemona, whatever you do, don't tell Stark that I'm in town and that I found the gun. Stark wants to nail me, don't you understand? He's got his own agenda."

"Calm down, Tony. I promise you that I won't do anything without talking it over with you first." Desdemona reached for a pen and some paper. "Give me the address of your motel. I've got to do dinner with the family tonight. If I don't show up everyone will be wondering where I am. But as soon as I'm free I'll drive to your motel. We'll talk."

"Okay. But be careful, kid. Stark is dangerous."

"He speaks very highly of you, too."

"Hey, where's Tony?" Henry asked as he and Kirsten strolled into the restaurant's private dining room. "I thought he'd be back in time to join us."

Stark watched as Desdemona turned quickly and smiled very brightly.

"I was just telling everyone that he left a message on my machine. He said that he couldn't get a reasonably priced flight out of L.A. You know how expensive it is when you try to book at the last minute. He's going to see if he can get a better fare tomorrow or the next day."

Stark looked at her across the table. He knew beyond a shadow of a doubt that she was lying through her pretty little white teeth.

Desdemona gave him a fleeting smile. Her gaze slid away from his. She bent her head and immersed herself in a conversation with Kyle, who was seated next to her. Kyle launched into a detailed description of yet another critically acclaimed performance of *Monsters Under the Bed*.

Stark studied the graceful curve of Desdemona's neck.

She had definitely lied.

He contemplated that raw fact as he sat quietly at the table amid the flock of Wainwrights. He tuned out the cheerful din of voices that surrounded him and concentrated on the realization that Desdemona was lying not only to him, but to her family as well.

There was only one person on the face of the earth who could cause her to do that.

No one seemed to notice Stark's withdrawal from the conversation. The natural exuberance of a table full of Wainwrights together with Jason and Kyle was more than enough to mask his silence. It wasn't as though he was the world's greatest conversationalist in the first place.

Stark ate methodically, making his way through the grilled salmon he had ordered. The juicy fish had been excellently prepared with a crust of herbs and lemon, but it was sawdust in his mouth.

Stark knew for a fact that Tony was in town. He had checked the airline computers. Tony had arrived on a late-afternoon flight. And then he had vanished.

The question was why had Desdemona lied. Stark thought he knew the answer. She would do anything to protect her precious step-brother.

Bits and pieces of the lively Wainwright conversation floated past Stark's field of awareness. He registered them automatically with a portion of his brain.

. . . Ian still thinks that he's going to be able to get an angel to back one more production at the Limelight. He never gives up, does he? I swear, he'd do anything to save that theater. . . .

. . . Macbeth told me and Kyle that we can work on the next Strolling Players production. He says we're real pros now. . . .

. . . Our agent says that a small theater on the Eastside is planning to do an updated version of Taming of the Shrew. *He thinks Celia and I should audition as Kate and Petruchio. We're considering it. . . .*

. . . Glad to hear that you'll be able to get back on schedule at Right Touch, Desdemona. I still can't believe that you stumbled across a genuine murder victim. It's like something out of a play. When I think of you being trapped in that freezer, I get cold chills. . . .

. . . Exotica Erotica is a lovely store, dear. I'm so glad it's off to a flying start. Just imagine, we've got someone else with a stable income in the family. So useful. . . .

The dinner seemed to drag on forever. Stark was well aware that he was the only one who was not inside the magic, glistening bubble that enclosed everyone else at the table. He stood on the outside, the eternal observer, and watched what was happening. He realized that Jason and Kyle had been unofficially adopted into the Wainwright clan. They were a part of what was going on within the bubble.

They had a place in the complex pattern. He, on the other hand, was standing at the edge of chaos.

Desdemona glanced down the table in Stark's direction from time to time, but she did not make her usual effort to draw him into the conversation.

Stark was not particularly surprised when she announced that she had to leave.

"I've got to get up early in the morning," she said as she got to her feet with a show of reluctance. "The rest of you can talk the night away, but I've got a business to run."

Juliet looked surprised. "But we don't have an event scheduled tomorrow, Desdemona."

"No, but I've still got a lot of work to do putting everything back in order in my office." Desdemona collected a bronze-colored jacket from the coatrack. "Good night, everyone. See you tomorrow."

Stark pushed back his chair and got to his feet. Everyone looked at him expectantly.

"I'll see you home," he said quietly.

Desdemona's eyes widened. "That's not necessary. Really. I'll have the hostess call a cab."

"My car is parked out in front," Stark said.

"But I'm perfectly safe."

Benedick frowned with paternal concern. "Stark's quite right, my dear. There's no need for you to go back to your place alone. Let him see you to your door."

"Good night, dear," Celia said cheerfully.

Desdemona hesitated. Stark knew as clearly as though she had spoken the words aloud that she was searching for a way out of the dilemma. She did not find one.

"All right, Stark." Her smile did not reach her eyes. "If you insist."

"I do."

She waved to the others. "I'll send him right back."

Stark nodded to Jason and Kyle. "I'll see you in a few minutes."

"Okay, Sam," Kyle said.

"Can I order another dessert while you're gone?" Jason asked.

Stark paused. "How many have you had?"

"Just two."

"I think that's enough." Stark followed Desdemona through the door and out into the main dining room. He took her arm.

The tension in her was unmistakable. He could feel it vibrating through her whole body. She said nothing as he walked her out of the restaurant.

"It's a little cool tonight, isn't it?" she said in a chatty voice as he opened the car door for her.

"A little." He waited until she had settled into the seat and then he shut the door.

She slanted him an anxious glance as he got behind the wheel. "Jason and Kyle have certainly taken to the theater life, haven't they?"

"Yes." Stark eased the car away from the curb.

"Mom and Dad like you."

"Do they?"

"Definitely. I can always tell."

Stark said nothing. Beside him, Desdemona lapsed into a strained silence.

He wondered if Tony was actually hiding out in her loft. It would be just like the bastard to use her to shield himself.

Stark drove the short distance to Desdemona's apartment building and parked inside the garage. He put his arm around her during the short elevator ride, but she did not relax against him as she usually did. He waited to see if she would try to stop him from escorting her to her door.

He was surprised when she made no attempt to keep him out of the loft. She did, however, make a concerted effort to ensure that he did not linger.

She stepped hastily into the entrance area, turned, and gave him another artificial smile. "Thanks for the escort. Sorry you can't stay. I know you have to get Jason and Kyle home."

"Yes." Stark tightened his grip on his keys. He swept the loft with a single glance. It was possible that Tony was hiding in the bathroom or the wardrobe, but it was unlikely. Desdemona did not seem that nervous. She was just anxious to have him leave.

Her gaze softened, and her lips parted as though she wanted to say something else. Instead she stood on tiptoe and brushed her mouth softly against his.

"Good night, Stark," she whispered.

"Good night."

He could have sworn that he saw urgency in her expression, or perhaps it was anxiety. He was no good at interpreting such things.

He felt her fingertips glide along the side of his cheek. He did not take his eyes off her as she closed the door very gently in his face.

He stood in the hall for a moment, and then he turned and walked to the elevator. When the doors opened, he stepped inside and rode it down to the garage.

Once inside his car he reached for the phone. He dialed the number of the restaurant as he drove out onto the street.

"Would you please have Macbeth Wainwright come to the phone?" he said when the hostess answered. "He's with the party in the private dining room."

"Just a minute," the woman murmured. "I'll get him."

Macbeth came on the line. "Hello?"

"This is Stark. Any chance you could take Jason and Kyle home and stay with them for a few hours?"

Macbeth chuckled. "No problem. I had a hunch I'd hear from you. You and Desdemona can linger over your good-night kiss as long as you like. I'll take care of the boys."

"Thanks."

"Any time. Don't rush home. We'll see you when you get there."

"Right." Stark replaced the phone.

He parked the car on a side street in a position that allowed him to watch the steel grid door of the parking garage.

He did not have long to wait. Less than ten minutes later the garage door rose. Desdemona's red Toyota appeared. She drove out into the street and turned north.

Stark followed.

The question that had been gnawing at him for a long while had finally been answered. When push came to shove, Desdemona's loyalty to her stepbrother was stronger than whatever she felt for her lover.

Stark told himself he had no business being surprised. He had known all along where he ranked on Desdemona's list of priorities.

What amazed him was the dark emotion that had swirled to life within him. The lid that covered the cauldron of chaos had come off. The storm of loneliness that boiled out threatened to swallow him whole.

18

Desdemona parked between an aging Buick and a battle-scarred Ford and studied the seedy motel Tony had chosen as a hideout. The place had no doubt once been a respectable, modestly priced motor inn that had catered to young families and traveling businessmen. At some point in its murky past, however, it had fallen on hard times and had begun to attract a clientele to match.

The ill-lit motel looked precisely like the sort of place in which someone on the lam would hole up under an assumed name. Trust Tony to select an establishment with plenty of atmosphere, Desdemona thought as she opened her car door and got out. But that was a Wainwright for you. Ever conscious of the appropriate backdrop for the scene.

The parking lot was half empty. As she walked toward the door marked number six, a car pulled into the lot and parked at the far end. Desdemona instinctively clutched her purse more closely to her side.

A stout man dressed in light-colored slacks, white nubuck shoes, and a preppy-style pullover sweater got out from behind the wheel. He looked as though he had just stepped off a golf course or a yacht. The pale light gleamed on his balding skull. He glanced nervously around the seedy lot.

A painfully gaunt woman with a cloud of impossibly gold hair slid out behind him. She wore a tiny little slip of a dress that scarcely covered her breasts and barely reached the top of her thighs. Three-inch-high stiletto heels and black hose completed her ensemble. She had a cigarette in one hand. The expression on her thin face was a cross between stoic resignation and unutterable boredom.

"Number seven," she told the man in the world-weary, smoke-roughened voice. "You pay me up front, and you use a rubber. Understand?"

"Okay, okay. Keep your voice down, will you?" The balding man scowled at Desdemona and then hurriedly looked away.

"What's the matter?" the woman asked. "Afraid your wife is lurking in the bushes?"

"Just keep it down," the man muttered.

Desdemona walked briskly toward number six. When she reached it she knocked once.

"Who is it?" Tony asked from inside the room.

"It's me, Desdemona. Who else are you expecting?"

Tony opened the door a scant two inches and peered out. "You alone?"

"Of course I'm alone."

"Come on in." Tony opened the door wider. "Christ, am I glad to see you. Did you tell anyone where I am?"

Desdemona stepped into the motel room. She swept the tawdry little cubicle with a single glance and winced. "No. I told you that I wouldn't let anyone else know where you are. But, Tony, we have to talk. This is crazy. You can't hide out here forever."

"I haven't got enough money to leave town." Tony started to close the door. "That bastard boyfriend of yours has really run a number on me, kid. He's set me up for murder."

"Don't call him a bastard." Desdemona swung around to face him. "I refuse to believe that Stark would do such a thing."

"Well, he did." Tony turned toward her as he continued to push the door closed with one hand. His handsome face was twisted into an expression of seething fury. "It's the only explanation."

"Wrong," Stark said from the doorway. "There's another explanation. You're guilty."

"*Shit.*" Tony threw his full weight against the door.

He was too late. Desdemona glanced down and saw that Stark had the toe of one running shoe wedged securely in the narrow opening.

"Let him in, Tony."

"Are you crazy? The guy wants me dead." Tony gritted his teeth as he leaned against the door.

Stark planted his palm on the opposite side of the door and shoved hard.

"For heaven's sake, let him in, Tony." Desdemona was exasperated. "This is pointless. He obviously knows you're here."

Tony whirled and braced his back against the door. He was breathing heavily. The tendons of his neck bulged with effort. "The son-of-a-bitch is out to get me. Don't you understand? For God's sake, help me."

"This is ridiculous," Desdemona said. "Let him in."

"Whose side are you on here?" The heels of Tony's boots scraped along the threadbare carpet. He was losing ground.

A moment later the door slammed open. Tony lost his balance and reeled against the wall.

Stark walked into the room and closed the door.

With a snarl, Tony launched himself toward Stark. Stark side-stepped the lunge. He turned with an astonishingly casual movement, caught hold of Tony's arm, and sent him flying toward the opposite wall.

Tony landed with a thud.

"Stop it," Desdemona said fiercely. "Both of you. Stop it right now. I won't have this, do you hear me?"

Both men ignored her. Tony picked himself up and hurtled once more toward Stark, who watched him until the last possible instant. Than he moved to the side, turned, and went in low. Tony raised his hands to defend himself.

The two men collided, grappled, and fell to the floor.

Desdemona dropped her purse and ran to the bed. She grabbed the tattered chenille spread, yanked it free, and tossed it over the heaving fighters. It settled over their rolling, twisting bodies, muffling their blows and savage grunts.

"Stop it." Desdemona grabbed the stained sheets and the thin blanket and dropped those on top of the surging bedspread. "*Stop it*, I said." She was trembling.

The pile of bedding heaved one last time and then stilled.

As Desdemona watched, stunned by the violence, Stark's big hand appeared from underneath the tumbled bedclothes. He jerked the sheets aside and sat up. He gave Desdemona a single, unreadable glance. Then he got to his feet and looked down at Tony.

With a groan, Tony wrenched aside the confining bedclothes and levered himself to one knee. His jaw was rigid, and his eyes were mere slits.

"Son-of-a-bitch," he breathed. "You goddamned son-of-a-bitch. I know what you're trying to do."

"Do you?" Stark asked.

Desdemona realized she was still shaking. "Please," she whispered. "No more. We have to talk."

Tony turned on her. "Why did you bring him here, Desdemona? I told you that he was the one who's trying to set me up. How could you do this to me? I'm family. I trusted you."

"I didn't bring him here." Desdemona sank unsteadily into the nearest chair. She clasped her hands together to still the shivering in her fingers. "I have no idea how he—" She broke off as realization dawned. She looked at Stark. "You followed me, didn't you?"

"Yes." Stark met her eyes.

"I knew it," Tony howled. "You've probably had Desdemona under surveillance all along. You were just waiting for her to lead you to me. It's all part of your plot, isn't it?"

Desdemona threw up her hands in disgust. "For goodness' sake, Tony, calm down and listen to me. Stark is here because he was worried about me, aren't you, Stark?"

Stark stood like a chunk of granite in the middle of the tacky motel room. "You could say that."

Desdemona smiled wryly. "I knew you sensed that something was wrong earlier when we said good night."

"He sensed something was wrong?" Tony's voice rose in patent disbelief. "What are you talking about? He deliberately followed you tonight. He used you to get to me."

"No, no, no, you've got it all mixed up, Tony." Desdemona looked at him. "You asked me not to tell anyone where you were, so I didn't. But Stark and I have grown so close that one of us can tell when something is worrying the other. Isn't that right, Stark?"

"Sure," Stark said derisively. "Mental telepathy."

"In a way." Desdemona smiled.

Tony glowered at Stark. "Telepathy? Give me a break."

"It's true," Desdemona assured him. "I didn't have to say anything at all this evening. Stark immediately sensed that there was a problem, and that I couldn't talk about it. He was probably very worried, weren't you, Stark?"

"Let's just say that I knew I'd never get to sleep tonight until I found out what was going on," Stark muttered.

"There, you see, Tony?" Desdemona said. "It was perfectly natural for Stark to follow me here. I would have done the same if the situation had been reversed. You know how it is when you're in love."

Stark stared at her with unblinking eyes. He said nothing.

Tony erupted in frustration and outrage. "In love? Desdemona, are you nuts? The guy's not in love with you. He wants to use you. Hell, he's been using you right from the start."

"Tony, I know you're upset," Desdemona said soothingly. "But you don't have to become a full-blown paranoid."

"I'm pissed off, not upset." Tony clenched his hands into fists. "And, yeah, maybe I am a little paranoid. Do you blame me for being worried that my sister thinks she's in love with a cold-blooded computer who passes for human?"

Desdemona lost her patience. She leaped to her feet to confront Tony. "That's enough. Do you hear me? I know you're scared, and I know you're feeling trapped, but that is no excuse for insulting the man I love."

"He doesn't love you," Tony said tightly. "He's got his own agenda here, and he's decided he can use you to secure it."

"What agenda could he possibly have?" Desdemona retorted.

"Who knows?" Tony shot a furious glance at Stark. "This whole thing is beginning to feel like a conspiracy. Maybe Stark's involved in a high-tech deal with the wrong people. Maybe he's selling stuff he shouldn't be selling to foreign interests. And maybe he needs someone to take the fall."

"An interesting theory," Stark said. "I was working on a similar one, myself."

"Yeah?" Tony narrowed his eyes.

"With you as the lead."

"Stop it, both of you," Desdemona said loudly. "None of this is true."

Tony scowled at her. "How do you know? Look at the way he followed you here tonight. It was downright sneaky. A man who really loved you wouldn't have tailed you to see where you were going. It wouldn't have occurred to him that you would be going anywhere. He would have trusted you."

Desdemona raised her chin. "Stark does trust me. I told you, he followed me tonight because he was worried about me, not because he doesn't trust me. Now will you kindly shut up and sit down, Tony? We've got to talk this over rationally."

Tony threw himself into a chair. "All right. You want to talk? Go ahead and talk. Let's hear what your android lover has to say for himself."

Desdemona drew a deep breath and turned to Stark. "I'm sorry about this. Wainwright family arguments can get a little heated."

"I noticed," Stark said.

"And I'm sorry I couldn't tell you what was going on earlier this evening. Tony asked me not to tell a soul." Desdemona smiled tremulously. "It was very clever of you to figure out that I had a problem on my hands."

Stark looked at Tony. "What, exactly, is the nature of this problem?"

"Someone planted a gun in Tony's apartment while he was out of town," Desdemona said. "We have a hunch it may be the thirty-eight that killed Vernon Tate."

"You don't say," Stark murmured.

Tony's lips thinned in fury.

"What did you do with the gun?" Stark asked.

"I took a ferry ride to Bainbridge a couple of hours ago," Tony said in a low voice. "Halfway across Elliott Bay, I threw the gun overboard."

"Did you get rid of any other useful evidence while you were at it?" Stark asked politely.

"Bastard."

Desdemona ignored the byplay. "I think Tony's right about one thing. It's beginning to appear that someone may be trying to set him up for Vernon's murder. First, he's lured out of town so that it appears he's fled the scene of the crime. His absence also gave the killer a chance to hide the murder weapon in his apartment. Then that blackmail note appears on my computer."

Tony looked up. "What blackmail note?"

"Remember that lost work file you helped me retrieve?" Desdemona asked.

"Yeah. What about it?"

"I thought it was just gibberish. But it turned out to be an encrypted blackmail note."

"Says who?" Tony asked.

"Stark says so. He decoded it."

"Is that a fact?" Tony gave Stark a belligerent glare. "Maybe he just invented it to suit his own purposes. If the original message was gibberish, how would you know if he faked a blackmail note from it?"

Desdemona raised her eyes briefly toward heaven. "Let's not start up with the gratuitous insults again. We've got more important things to do here. Now, then, pay attention, both of you. Stark, I'm very glad you followed me tonight. It will save a lot of time."

Stark raised his brows. "Will it?"

"Of course." Desdemona sat down again. "I was going to explain everything to you just as soon as I had talked to Tony, anyway."

"Were you?" Stark asked in a dangerously even voice.

"Don't talk to her like that," Tony snarled.

Desdemona frowned. "I know you're both still overloaded with testosterone because of the recent physical violence, but I would appreciate it if you would control the hormones for a while. I'm trying to move this meeting forward."

"You call this a meeting?" Stark asked.

"For want of a better word." Desdemona crossed her legs and eyed the two men. "Let's recap. We've got a weird situation here. Someone apparently hired Vernon Tate to steal ARCANE from Stark. Vernon made the attempt the night of the reception. He failed. The next thing we know, poor Vernon is dead, and there is a blackmail note aimed at his so-called client left on my computer."

Tony's brows drew together. "Why was the note left on your computer?"

"That's obvious," Desdemona said. "Whoever left it wanted to make it appear that you were Vernon's client. The one who had paid him to steal ARCANE."

"Shit," Tony muttered. "And now the damned gun in my apartment. I knew it. A setup."

"There's a simpler explanation." Stark bestirred himself to walk the short distance to the nearest wall. He propped one shoulder against it. "It could be the truth."

"Bastard," Tony said.

Desdemona glowered at both of them. "I do not want to hear another unproductive word. Is that clear?"

Tony and Stark looked at her. Neither said anything.

"That's better." Desdemona composed her thoughts. "Now, then, as I was saying before I was so rudely interrupted, it's apparent that someone killed Vernon and then deliberately set out to make Tony look guilty. The killer was probably Vernon's mysterious client. Do we all agree so far?"

"It's a theory," Tony said grudgingly. "But if we buy that, we have to ask why the so-called client bothered to kill Tate."

Stark lifted one shoulder in a negligent movement. "It's possible that Tate actually had identified him and really was threatening to blackmail him."

"On my computer?" Desdemona asked quickly.

Stark seemed reluctant to continue with the line of reasoning he had begun. Desdemona got the distinct impression that he wished he'd kept his mouth shut.

"Maybe the real blackmail note wasn't sent on your computer," he said grudgingly. "It's possible that the client did get one from Vernon, but he probably received it the same way he got Tate's other communications. Via e-mail."

Desdemona widened her eyes as she realized what that implied. "That means that the blackmail note we found was a phony left by the client *after* the murder in order to make Tony look guilty," Desdemona concluded. "To provide a fake motive for him."

"I said it's a possibility." Stark shot Tony an irritated look. "A remote one."

"Yeah. Real remote," Tony agreed sarcastically. "If we rewrite the script so that you're the bad guy, the logic works even better."

"Neither of you is the bad guy," Desdemona said forcefully. "Now, let's continue. We have a real bad guy in this play. Someone we have not yet identified. We have to find him."

"We?" Stark's brow rose. "That's what the cops are paid to do."

Desdemona grimaced. "Don't be an idiot, Stark. We can't go to the cops at this juncture. They might jump to the wrong conclusions."

"You mean they might decide that Tony was guilty?" Stark nodded solemnly. "True. They might. I hadn't thought of that."

"The hell you hadn't," Tony said.

"As I was saying," Desdemona continued determinedly, "no one is going to the cops just yet. First we've got to try to find Vernon's real client." She looked expectantly at Stark.

He gazed steadily back at her.

"Well?" Desdemona prompted.

"Well, what?" Stark asked.

"How do you plan to go about finding Vernon's real client?" Desdemona asked patiently. "The person who killed him?"

"Why are you looking at me?" Stark asked.

"Because you're the security expert," Desdemona said patiently.

"Damn," Stark said.

Desdemona smiled with relief. "I knew you'd agree to help."

He was the security expert, all right. Stark was still berating himself for being an idiot as he followed Desdemona into the parking garage beneath her apartment building.

How the hell had he allowed Desdemona to manipulate him into helping that screwup brother of hers? he wondered for what must have been the thousandth time.

She had caused him to break his most cherished rule. He had stopped thinking and acting with the rational side of his brain. Instead, he had been sucked down into the chaos of emotion. Here in the sorcerer's cauldron, nothing was fixed in logic. Every move was treacherous and unpredictable.

His blood ran cold as he recalled Tony's attempt to persuade Desdemona that her lover was the real criminal mastermind behind a complex conspiracy.

It hadn't even struck Stark until now that, if one chose to shine a certain light on the subject, he could conceivably be made to look as guilty as Tony Wainwright.

Perhaps more so.

After all, Stark thought, chagrined, a disinterested observer could claim that he was the one who knew the major players involved in the world of illegal international technology deals.

He was also far more intimately acquainted with computers than Tony Wainwright was. Tony was good, but he was an amateur compared to Stark.

And there was another bit of damning evidence on hand, Stark reminded himself. He was the one who had hired Desdemona as a caterer and then seduced her, thereby setting the whole damned game in motion.

He was forced to acknowledge that Wainwright had a point. It was an inescapable fact that the attempted theft of ARCANE and the killing of Vernon Tate had taken place *after* Stark and Desdemona had formed a relationship. Viewed from that perspective, Stark thought, he was an excellent candidate for the role of the bad guy.

Jealousy was considered one of the classic motives for violence. Stark told himself that he wasn't the jealous type, but he wasn't certain anyone would believe it.

Thank God Desdemona had been no more interested in that scenario than she had been in the one that portrayed Tony as the villain.

Stark pulled into a slot, parked his car, and switched off the engine. He sat behind the wheel for a moment, watching Desdemona climb out of her Toyota. She waved at him over the roof of her car.

An eerie sensation washed over him as he gazed at her. His whole body tensed as though to do battle with some unseen threat.

Damn. He was perfectly capable of feeling jealousy.

The knowledge left him shaken. He finally opened the car door and got out.

"Do you have time for a cup of coffee?" Desdemona asked as he walked toward her through the silent garage.

Stark glanced at his watch. "I think so. Macbeth is with Kyle and Jason."

Desdemona stopped in front of the elevator. "I meant what I said earlier. I'm very glad you followed me tonight. It saved me having to talk Tony into asking for your help. He can be awfully stubborn."

Stark pressed the elevator call button. "He thinks I'm guilty. That I set him up because I'm jealous."

"Don't worry about that. He was just firing from the hip, as usual. He's a little emotional at the moment." The elevator doors opened. Desdemona stepped inside. "Can't blame him for being on edge. It does look as though someone is trying to set him up for murder, doesn't it?"

"Maybe."

"Thank goodness he found that gun before the police did. I'll bet whoever is behind this planned to give the cops an anonymous tip about it."

"Possible."

Desdemona froze. Fear flashed in her eyes. "The police might be looking for Tony at this very moment."

"You'll know if they're looking for him," Stark said. "The first thing they'll do is ask you or someone else in the family where he is."

"Good point. Well, since no one's been asked, we have to assume that Vernon's so-called client is lying low for a while."

Stark could not think of anything to say to that. He put his arm around Desdemona. This time she relaxed against him. He relaxed a little, too.

They rode the elevator to the fifth floor in silence.

Desdemona led the way down the hall and opened the door of her apartment. "I'll make the coffee."

Stark closed the door very deliberately. He had to tell her the truth, he thought. He had to get it out on the table. "Desdemona?"

She tossed him a smile over her shoulder. "Yes?"

"I didn't follow you tonight because I was worried about you or because I got some kind of telepathic communication. I followed you because I knew that you had lied when you said Tony was not back in town." Stark shoved his hands into the pockets of his jacket. "I figured you were trying to protect him."

"I was." She walked around the glass brick counter and went to work on the gleaming espresso machine. "And if you knew that I had lied, then you must have been on the same wavelength as me, because no one else in the family suspected it. It only goes to show how really close we are."

"Damn it, Desdemona, I'm trying to explain something here."

She glanced up with an inquiring expression. "What's that?"

261

He ran a hand through his hair, frustrated by his inability to make his point clear. "I don't know."

She grinned. "Poor Stark. You're overintellectualizing this, you know."

"I am?"

"Uh-huh. Relax. Things have been rather emotional for all of us lately. Try to stay focused on the problem of finding Vernon Tate's client."

He blinked. "*You're* telling *me* to stay focused?"

"Right." Steam hissed. "Here, have a nice hot cup of espresso. A jolt of caffeine should help settle your nerves."

"I do not have a case of nerves. I have never had a case of nerves in my life."

"Whatever." She set the cup down on the counter.

Stark sat down on a stool and wrapped his hands around the tiny cup. "What happens if it turns out that Tony really is the killer, Desdemona?"

"He isn't."

"Damn it, what if he is, and I'm the one who proves it?"

She stilled, her eyes suddenly troubled. "I don't know."

"Will you hate me for uncovering the truth?" he made himself ask.

"Hate you?" She frowned. "Why would I hate you? Our relationship isn't based on whether or not Tony's guilty."

"Isn't it?"

"Stark, you're not making any sense here. Tony is not guilty. But if, hypothetically speaking, he were guilty, it wouldn't change how I feel about you."

"It's called shooting the messenger," Stark said wearily. "Happens all the time."

She sipped her espresso. "You're going to have to trust me on this, Stark."

Stark's fingers tightened around the fragile cup. "Will you marry me?"

Several drops of coffee spilled from her cup. Desdemona did not seem to notice. She stared at him. "Why?"

"Why? What kind of thing is that to say?" Stark was suddenly angry. "This is a simple yes or no quiz, not an essay question. All I want is a straightforward answer."

"Okay."

"Okay, what? Yes or no? Will you marry me?"

"Calm down, I said okay, didn't I?"

He watched her from beneath half-lowered lashes. "You will?"

She gave him a strangely wistful smile. "If you're sure you want to marry me, I'll marry you."

Relief soared inside him. He fought the lightheaded sensation it created, afraid that if he abandoned himself to it he might do something stupid such as bounce off the walls and ceiling.

He had to keep himself focused.

Desdemona had just said that she would marry him, but she could easily change her mind. God knew he'd been through that scene often enough. The espresso cup in his hand rattled against its saucer. He let go of it quickly.

"I'm sure." Stark forced his voice to stay even. He seized the tiny cup again and swallowed the espresso in a single gulp. Then he glanced at his watch. "It's getting late. I'd better be on my way."

"Hold it right there." Desdemona narrowed her gaze into a severe glare. "Is that all you have to say?"

He gave her a blank look. "What?"

"I have just consented to marry you," she reminded him a little too sweetly. "Correct me if I'm wrong, but doesn't that warrant a few excited words? An exclamation of joy? Perhaps even a small sonnet?"

He felt himself turn a dark red. "I'm sorry," he said stiffly. "I don't do sonnets."

"I won't change my mind, you know."

He smiled humorlessly as he got off the stool. "No?"

"No. Look, I know you're an old hand at proposals and weddings and such, but this is all new to me. This is the first time I have ever accepted a marriage proposal. Now, I realize beginners always have a few stars in their eyes, but I really did expect something more than what I'm getting here."

"I see," Stark said cautiously. "What, exactly, did you expect?"

"Well, for starters, I had envisioned a more momentous scene." Desdemona waved a hand in the air. "Perhaps some roses and champagne. You're supposed to be on your knees, of course. There should be moonlight, I think, and maybe some small show of elated emotion from you."

"I may have had experience, but I'm not very good at this," Stark said.

"Hah. You're scared, aren't you? You're thinking about your past two spectacular failures, and you're as edgy as an actor on opening night. Admit it."

He rounded the edge of the counter and cradled her face in his hands. He looked down into her wonderful eyes. "I suppose I could ensure that you show up at the altar by hiring you to do the catering for our wedding reception."

"I am not going to cater my own wedding."

"I was afraid of that. I guess I'll have to take your word that you'll show, won't I?"

"Have a little faith, Stark. Trust me." She gave him a misty smile. "Just as I'm going to trust you."

He could not think of anything to say to that so he kissed her.

She put down her espresso cup and kissed him back. He felt her arms circle his waist. The scent of her body filled his head.

He relaxed when he heard her soft sigh. She melted against him, warm and sweet and welcoming. He might not always know what to say to Desdemona, he thought, but when he had her in his arms, he could communicate with her just fine.

$\mathcal{D}$ ane lounged back in his chair and contemplated Stark with an amused expression. "I can't believe you're going to try it a third time."

Stark looked up from the spreadsheet he had been studying. Reluctantly he switched mental gears. "What?"

"I said, I can't believe you've asked Desdemona to marry you. It's only been a couple of months since your last wedding. Are you sure you're ready to rent another tux?"

"I don't have to rent one," Stark said. "Pamela insisted I buy one for the last wedding, remember? I wore it to the charity ball. No reason I can't use it again."

"I know, I know." Dane grinned as he held up both hands. "I was just making a little joke."

"Very funny." Stark refocused his attention on the spreadsheet. "What the hell is this? It looks like Lancaster pulled these projections for the first year's sales of ARCANE right out of thin air."

"I was afraid of this," Dane murmured.

"Well, why didn't you stop him?" Stark picked up a red felt pen and drew a precise, straight line through a whole row of figures. "How many times have I told everyone that I want conservative cost and sales estimates."

"Lancaster is a glass-half-full kind of guy. A natural optimist."

"Optimistic financial officers are dangerous. I feel much more secure when I know I'm looking at worst case scenarios."

"I'll tell him to rework the numbers."

"Do that. Tell him if he needs help getting into a gloomy mood, I'm sure I can find a way to put him into one."

"As it happens, I wasn't talking about Lancaster when I said I was afraid of this," Dane said. "I was talking about your engagement."

"What about it?" Stark frowned at another row of numbers.

"I can't believe that you've asked a woman like Desdemona Wainwright to marry you."

Stark glanced up with a frown. "You're losing me here, McCallum. What, exactly, are you trying to say?"

A knowing smile flickered around the corners of Dane's mouth. "I'm just wondering if you've finally taken the big fall."

"The big fall?"

"Are you in love with Desdemona Wainwright?"

"McCallum, for a smart man, you occasionally ask some really stupid questions." Stark lined out another row of figures.

"I know. But, then, you were always the brains of the outfit, not me. I'm just along for the ride."

"What's that supposed to mean?"

"It means," Dane said, "that Stark Security Systems is your creation. You're the key to its success. Without you, this company is nothing."

"No business this size hinges entirely on one individual." Stark went back to the numbers.

"You're wrong. Everywhere you go, you're the star of the show," Dane said softly. "It was that way at the Institute, and it's that way here. How does it feel to always be number one?"

Stark ignored the question. He was too concerned about the next row of blue-sky numbers.

At eleven o'clock that evening Tony paced Stark's study with the restless, prowling stride of a caged cat. "I shouldn't have let you talk me into coming here. This is dumb. For all I know it's a trap."

"If I had wanted to trap you," Stark said, "I would have stood back and let nature take its course. The evidence against you has been mounting very nicely right from the start. It's only a matter of time before it comes to the attention of the cops."

Tony gave him a scathing glance. "With a little help from you?"

"That's the nifty part. I wouldn't even have to exert myself. You've got a natural talent for shooting yourself in the foot."

Tony's eyes narrowed. "Everyone says you're so damned smart, but you know what I think?"

"I haven't got a clue."

"I think you're a dangerous son-of-a-bitch who likes to use people."

"You're entitled to your opinion." Stark entered another command. ARCANE slithered through another layer of complexity, searching for patterns.

"Damn right I'm entitled." Tony walked over to stand behind him. "What, exactly, are you trying to do here?"

"I'm using ARCANE to study the anonymous server's files. I'm searching for the code that links the anonymous e-mail addresses with the users' real addresses."

Tony leaned closer to study the screen. "You think you can crack the code and find the real e-mail address of Tate's client?"

"Maybe. With a little help from ARCANE."

Tony frowned. "Where the hell is this anonymous server located anyway?"

"I don't know. Could be anywhere. Europe. Some island in the Caribbean. Southern California. Whoever set it up seems to be operating a clearinghouse service for hacker mercenaries like Vernon Tate. All the contacts between clients and mercenaries are made anonymously. Delivery of the stolen goods is probably handled through an equally anonymous shipping service."

"Are you going to blow the whistle on the operation after this is all over?"

"Yes."

Tony was silent for a moment. "Is this the kind of work your company does?"

"Yes."

"Sort of interesting."

"Yes, it is," Stark said. "Now will you shut up and sit down? You're making it hard to concentrate."

"All right, already." Tony went back across the room and threw himself into a chair. "Why did you ask me to come here tonight?"

"Because your neck is on the block, and Desdemona will be upset if someone swings the axe."

"It could just as easily be your neck."

"Yeah, but it's not, is it? Whoever is behind this planted the gun in your apartment and went out of his way to make you look guilty, not me."

"I still think there's a real good possibility that you're the one who's setting me up," Tony grumbled.

Stark glanced at him. "I'll make a deal with you," he said slowly. "If you'll leave off the melodrama for the next couple of hours and try some logical thinking instead of playacting, I'll stop taking every opportunity to point out just how guilty you look."

Tony scowled. "Why would you want to help me?"

"I told you, I'm doing this for Desdemona, not you."

Tony flexed his hands. "I don't know what the hell she sees in you."

"You know what they say, love is blind." Stark was ridiculously pleased by that thought.

"Yeah, well, she never had any trouble with her eyesight before you came along. In fact, she lived like a nun."

"A cloistered existence, would you say?"

"Yeah. Exactly. I can't figure it out." Tony slammed the arm of his chair with his palm. "You're all wrong for her. It's so damn obvious. Why can't she see that?"

Stark gave up trying to work. He swung around in his chair and studied Tony's sullen expression. "Why don't you try facing reality, Wainwright? She was bound to fall for someone, someday."

"Why did it have to be you?"

"You know what I think? I think you'd be acting like this regardless of whom she decided to marry. Did you really believe that you could keep her locked away in cold storage forever?"

"I'm not trying to keep her in cold storage." Tony propelled himself back out of the chair and stalked to the window. "I'm just trying to protect her."

"She's not a little girl anymore."

"I know that, but she's so damn sweet and kind, and I don't want anything to happen to her." Tony whirled around, his eyes glittering with violent emotion. "Don't you understand? I'm her brother. I've always taken care of her. I saved her life once."

"So I've been told," Stark said very quietly. "That's one of the reasons I'm trying to help you now. I owe you that much."

"You don't owe me a damn thing, you bastard. I don't want your gratitude. I want you to leave Desdemona alone."

"I can't do that."

"You're no good for her, don't you see? She needs someone from the Wainwright world. The theater world. Someone who understands her. Someone who can talk her language. Someone who will fit in with the family."

"Someone like you?"

Tony looked blank. "Me? And Desdemona? Are you crazy? I'm her brother."

"Stepbrother."

Tony shrugged. "I've always been her big brother as far as she and I are concerned. The guy who saved her life. But I can't stand by and watch her throw herself away on some jerk who won't appreciate her."

"What makes you think I don't appreciate her?"

"How could you?" Tony gave him a look of patent disgust. "There's no poetry in your soul, man."

"Maybe Desdemona sees a little deeper than you do."

"Bullshit. There's nothing more to see. Are you going to tell me that behind your nerd pack beats the heart of a creative, sensitive artist? That you're wired with emotions instead of microchips? Don't waste your breath."

Stark sat unmoving. "You're not trying to protect her, are you? Just the opposite. You need her to protect you from the truth."

Tony's mouth thinned. "What truth?"

"The truth of your own failures. Look at your track record, Wainwright. You're a failed actor, a failed theater financial manager—"

Tony looked as though he'd taken a body blow. "You know about that?"

"I know that you were implicated in an embezzlement case, yes."

"I didn't embezzle a damn cent."

Stark paid no attention to the hot defense. "Most recently you're a failed soap opera star. The only thing you ever did right was save Desdemona's life. And that's why you can't let her go, isn't it?"

Tony stared at him. "What the hell is that supposed to mean?"

"You need her, don't you? You need her around so that you can have some tangible proof that you're not a total and complete screwup. You did do something right once upon a time, and she's the only evidence you've got of that momentous occasion."

Tony froze. "I did save her life, damn you."

"Yes. You did. And she's been paying you back ever since, hasn't she?"

"You don't understand. How could you? You're not part of the family."

"Maybe that's why I do understand. The whole thing is very clear when you're on the outside looking in." Stark turned back to the computer.

Silence descended on the study. Stark was grateful.

After a while Tony spoke from the chair. "She made me a hero."

Stark ignored him. He eased ARCANE deeper into the anonymous server's secret passages.

"A real hero," Tony whispered. "I didn't just act the part, you know. I did the job. I saved her from that crazy bastard. He was going to kill her."

Stark hesitated. "What exactly did happen when Desdemona was five?"

"Celia's ex-husband, George Northstreet, came after her and Desdemona. Northstreet had been getting worse for some time, they said. He was completely over the edge by then. He must have stalked them for days before he made his move. He grabbed Desdemona first."

Stark did not move. "Where?"

"He took her right out of the parking lot in front of a small dinner theater." Tony gazed out the window, everything in him focused on the past. "I was there with her, teaching her to ride a bike. I was supposed to be keeping an eye on her while the family rehearsed a musical inside. I guess Northstreet thought that I wasn't much of a threat. He ignored me and stuffed Desdemona in the trunk of his car."

"The claustrophobia," Stark said to himself.

"Yeah, that's where it comes from. Northstreet drove off with Desdemona. I yelled for help, but no one heard me. I figured that by the time I went into the theater, got everyone's attention, and told them what was happening, Northstreet would be long gone."

"What did you do?"

"I knew the route Northstreet would have to take to get onto the main cross street. I jumped on my bike and cut across a couple of backyards and a playing field. I came out at a busy intersection just as Northstreet was slowing for the light."

"And?" Stark prompted when Tony fell silent.

"I rode my bike straight into his path and fell off right in front of his car." Tony smiled wryly. "I created a huge scene at the intersection. Gave the best performance of my life. Kid on bicycle struck by car. Traffic came to a standstill. Everyone got out to see what was happening. Someone went into a nearby store and called for an ambulance."

"Nice going," Stark said with grudging approval. "Quick thinking for a kid. For anyone, in fact."

"Once I had an audience, I miraculously recovered, ran around to the trunk of the car, and pounded on it. Desdemona screamed from inside. Everyone at the scene demanded that Northstreet open the trunk. Finally a cop arrived, and we got Desdemona out of the trunk. Ultimately Northstreet was arrested. He later shot himself."

"And you were a hero."

"Yeah," Tony said. "Desdemona made me a hero."

"Desdemona didn't make you a hero that day," Stark said. "No one can turn a man into a hero, just as no one can turn him into a coward. A man has to do either one all by himself."

Tony looked at him, frowning. "What does that mean?"

"The day you saved Desdemona's life," Stark said patiently, "you turned yourself into a hero."

There was another long silence.

"I never thought about it quite like that," Tony said eventually.

"That's your whole problem in life, Wainwright. You don't think much. You just emote. Come over here and take a look at this."

"What have you got?"

"ARCANE has identified the pattern beneath the encryption program."

Tony walked back across the study to stare down at the computer screen. "Are you serious?"

"Trust me, Wainwright, ninety-nine times out of a hundred you can bet the bank that I'm serious."

"What about the one time when you're not?"

"I'm asleep."

The following morning Celia fixed Desdemona with gentle, troubled eyes. "You're going to marry him? Oh, Desdemona, I was afraid of this. Are you absolutely certain he's the man for you?"

"Yes." Desdemona surveyed the gleaming interior of Right Touch. Everything was back to normal, and she had a busy week ahead. Among other things, there was an engagement party to plan. Her own. She intended to go first-class all the way.

The phone had been ringing all morning. For some reason that she was unable to fathom, the fact that there had been a murder on the premises had done nothing to hurt business. If anything, the publicity seemed to have helped.

"Don't misunderstand," Celia said quickly. "Benedick and I like Stark very much. It's just that he's so different from the kind of men you've always dated."

"All three of them?"

"I'm sure there must have been more than three, dear."

Desdemona chuckled. "Maybe so. But if Stark seems different than the others, it's probably because I managed to find him all by myself, without any assistance from Juliet and Bess."

"You know they were only trying to help."

Desdemona put her arm around her mother's shoulders and hugged her briefly. "Don't sweat it, Mom. Everything's going to be all right. I know what I'm doing."

"Are you sure? Tony doesn't think he's right for you," Celia said.

"You know how big brothers are. Tony doesn't think any man is good enough for me."

"Juliet and Bess happen to agree with him in this instance. Even Henry has a few doubts. They're worried that Stark isn't really your type. They think he's cold."

"Now that's just where they're wrong. Trust me, Stark is anything but cold." Desdemona picked up a stack of stainless steel bowls and carried them toward the sink. "He just isn't quite as demonstrative or as flamboyant as everyone else in the family. Don't forget, he lacks formal stage training."

"But Kirsten says he doesn't show his emotions at all."

"That's not true. He shows plenty of emotion. He's just very subtle about it." Desdemona set the bowls down with a clatter.

"Why have all those other women he's tried to marry left him standing at the altar?" Celia demanded. "There must be a reason, dear."

"There was." Desdemona reached up to take a cookbook down from a high shelf. "They didn't understand him. They chickened out when he asked them to sign a prenuptial agreement."

"A *prenuptial agreement*." Celia was aghast. "How awful. How unchivalrous. How dreadful. No wonder they backed out. They realized that he didn't love them."

"Mom . . ."

Celia was suddenly suspicious. "Has he asked you to sign one?"

"Not yet." Desdemona opened the cookbook. "I think he's a little nervous because of his previous experiences. This time around he'll probably wait until the very last minute."

"Why?"

"Because he'll tell himself that he has to be more crafty this time. He's already screwed up with two previous fiancées, remember. I expect that he'll spring the prenuptial agreement on me just as I'm ready to walk down the aisle. That way I won't have time to bolt. Or so he'll think."

Celia looked stricken. "Desdemona, you can't be serious about this. Why on earth would you marry someone so cold-blooded?"

"Because he's not cold-blooded at all," Desdemona said patiently.

"But you've just said that he'll want you to sign a prenuptial agreement."

"Yes, but he won't *mean* it, if you see what I mean."

Celia stared at her. "How on earth do you know that? Darling, I can't let you make the same kind of mistake I made with George Northstreet. Please, listen to me."

"Relax, Mom. Whatever else he is, I guarantee you that Stark is no George Northstreet waiting to go crazy."

"Tony says he's a computer inside a human body."

"Stark is no android. Look at the evidence."

"What evidence?" Celia demanded.

"Well, for starters, Stark took in two stepbrothers he'd never even met because he understood what their parents' divorce was doing to them."

"Yes, I know. Bess told me the whole tale. I admit that it was very kind of him to take Jason and Kyle for the summer."

"Stark wasn't being kind. That's the whole point," Desdemona said. "Stark doesn't think in those terms. He wasn't being consciously charitable. He just did it because it seemed like the right thing to do. That's the way he does things."

Celia looked thoughtful. "He took them in because Jason and Kyle were family, didn't he?"

"I don't think he analyzed it in those terms, either. He doesn't have a lot of experience interacting with relatives. Intellectually speaking, he's a little suspicious of family ties. He thinks family members are not above using and manipulating each other."

"Then why did he take Jason and Kyle?"

Desdemona grinned triumphantly. "Because his instincts are sound."

"You're going to marry him just because you think his instincts are good? What if you're wrong?"

Desdemona looked up from a recipe for olive- and cheese-topped focaccia. "Take it easy, Mom. Everything's under control here."

"Desdemona, I want you to be absolutely honest with me. Do you think Stark really loves you?"

"I think he will learn to love me," Desdemona said carefully.

"Good God. He hasn't even told you that he loves you?"

"He will. Eventually." Desdemona mentally crossed her fingers. "He's really quite bright. A very fast learner."

"Oh, darling," Celia sighed. "Why couldn't you have fallen in love with that nice Ian Ivers?"

"Coffee?" Tony set a mug down on the desk.

"Thanks." Stark didn't look up from the computer. The buried patterns were very clear now.

Jason, seated next to his brother, elbows propped on the desk, gave Tony a brief glance. "Stark says we're almost there. He says he can feel it."

"Shush," Kyle whispered. "He's trying to concentrate."

Tony dropped into a chair and sipped coffee. Together with Jason and Kyle, he watched intently as Stark punched in more commands.

A string of letters and symbols appeared.

"Hell, that's another e-mail address." Tony was on his feet. He leaned across the desk to get a better look.

"Let me see, let me see." Kyle crowded closer. Jason was right behind him.

"That's the anonymous client's real e-mail address?" Jason asked eagerly.

"ARCANE says it is." Stark contemplated the string of characters that had materialized.

anon@sss.com

"But it still has the word *anon* in it," Jason pointed out. "Doesn't that mean it's still just an anonymous address?"

"The client's name is still a secret," Tony explained. "But now we have a location, don't we, Stark?"

"Yes, we do."

"The *sss.com* part of the address is the place where the client's computer is located?" Jason asked.

"Yes." Stark said.

Kyle frowned intently. "How do we find out where *sss.com* is?"

"No problem," Stark said.

Tony glanced at him. "You know that address?"

"It's a Stark Security Systems e-mail address."

"Shit," Tony said.

"My sentiments exactly." Stark took off his glasses, closed his eyes, and rubbed the bridge of his nose.

At seven o'clock that night Desdemona's door bell rang. She punched the intercom button.

"Hello?"

"It's me," Stark said.

Relief rushed through her. "Thank goodness. I've been wondering what the heck was happening. Do you realize that I haven't heard from you since last night?"

"If you'll let—"

"And where's Tony? Is he with you?"

"No. At least not right now. Desdemona, open the—"

"Well, where is he?"

"If you'll let me into the building—"

"The least you could have done was call occasionally to let me know what was happening. When you get right down to it, we're supposed to be business associates, remember?"

"I remember," Stark said. "Desdemona, if you'll open the damned door I'll come upstairs and tell you everything. It's raining out here."

"Oh. Sorry." Desdemona pressed the button that unlatched the downstairs door.

When she heard the click that indicated Stark had entered the building she raced to her apartment door, opened it, and leaned out into the hall to watch for the elevator.

After what seemed like forever, it opened. Stark, looking weary, unshaven, and more rumpled than usual, got out. He walked toward her with a grimly intent look.

Desdemona forgot all about her annoyance at being left in the dark for ages. She rushed into his arms without a word.

He caught her close. One of the pens in his plastic pocket protector rammed into her cheek. She ignored it.

"What's wrong?" she mumbled into his corduroy jacket. "What did you learn?"

"ARCANE traced the anonymous address to Stark Security Systems."

"Oh, my God."

"Let's go inside." Stark draped a heavy arm around her shoulders. "I'll tell you what I know."

"Where's Tony?"

"He's at my place with Jason and Kyle. They've ordered take-out. I needed a break so I decided to take a couple of hours off to see you. I have to think, Desdemona."

"Have you had dinner?"

"No." Stark ran a hand over the rough stubble of his beard. "Tony, Jason, and Kyle ordered pizza. I just couldn't face it."

"I'll whip up some pasta primavera." Desdemona ducked out from under his arm and closed the door. "Have a seat."

He shrugged out of his jacket, tossed it aside, and settled on a counter stool. He folded his arms in front of him.

Desdemona opened the refrigerator. "I take it you have no way of knowing who Mr. Anonymous is at Stark Security?"

"No. It could be any one of my employees. Hell, even my secretary has her own computer. She knows how to send and receive e-mail just as well as I do. It could even be a janitor who's found a way to access one of the computers at night."

"Good grief."

"And the list of possible suspects doesn't end there," Stark said. "It could be someone outside the company. Someone who found a way into one of my computers through a modem hookup."

Desdemona stared at him in astonishment. "You mean it could be anyone who was smart enough to get through your security from some other computer outside the building?"

"Yes. There's enough money in this kind of thing to tempt anyone who was already leaning in the wrong direction," Stark said.

"How are you going to track down the villain of the piece?"

"An hour ago I set a trap."

Desdemona put a pan of water on the stove. "What kind of trap?"

"I sent a message to Mr. Anonymous at Stark Security."

Desdemona started to slice mushrooms. "What kind of message?"

"I posed as another mercenary who wanted to take over the contract that Tate failed to fulfill. I offered to do it at a discount rate. If I can get a response, I'll be able to nail him."

Desdemona stopped slicing mushrooms. "Stark, that sounds dangerous."

"I've got to lure Tate's client out into the open. To do that I need to make contact."

A shiver went through her. "I don't like this."

"Neither do I." Stark smiled wryly. "But look on the bright side. I'm finally convinced that good old Tony wasn't Tate's client."

Desdemona wrinkled her nose. "I told you so."

"Yes, you did, didn't you?" Stark glanced at his watch.

"In a hurry?"

"I was just wondering if I'd have time to seduce you after dinner."

"I can have this pasta on the table in ten minutes," Desdemona said demurely.

"Good." The weary look vanished from Stark's eyes. "I can eat it in eight."

It took determination and fortitude, but he got her all the way to the bed before he succumbed to the relentless tide of physical desire.

Forty-five minutes later, Stark savored the delicious ripples of Desdemona's impending release. Her whole body clutched at him, drawing him irresistibly, inevitably toward the glittering storm.

"Stark. *Stark.*"

Braced on his elbows above her, he looked down, captivated, as always, by the sight of her face in the moment of climax. Her eyes were closed, her lips parted. Her skin glowed with a damp sheen. Her nails bit deeply in his shoulder.

She was impossibly beautiful, impossibly sensual, a creature of magic. And she was going to marry him.

He groaned as he felt her tighten around him. He held himself back with an effort of will, wanting to delay his own release until he had experienced hers to the fullest.

At last it was over.

He began to move within her again.

"No." Desdemona kissed his throat. She opened her eyes and pushed against his shoulders. "My turn."

"What?"

"Hush. Let me do this." She pushed harder.

He hesitated. He was poised on the brink and the last thing he wanted to do was withdraw from her tight, moist body, even for a few seconds.

But he sensed her determination and found it deeply erotic. Reluctantly he allowed himself to be rolled onto his back. Desdemona came down on top of him. She fitted herself to him. Her eyes were brilliant in the shadows. Her body was still so hot that he wondered why it didn't set fire to his blood.

She rode him with a sweet, wild energy that took his breath.

He glimpsed the patterns at the border between chaos and complexity, and once more, just for an instant, he comprehended them.

"Stark?" Desdemona spoke from the other side of the shoji screen where she was dressing.

"Yes?" Stark picked up the shirt he had left midway between the kitchen and the bedroom area. He glanced toward the shoji screen. Desdemona's nude body was clearly silhouetted against the opaque white barrier.

"You said Vernon Tate's client received his e-mail communications through one of the computers at your company."

"Looks that way."

"And you said that theoretically it could be someone outside your company. Someone who's cracked your security system."

"Yes." He studied the lush curve of her hips as she bent over the bed.

"He'd have to be good to do that, wouldn't he?"

"Yes. But there's no such thing as a perfectly secure system once you're hooked up to a modem or involved in a computer network. All of Stark Security machines have vulnerable spots. That's why I do serious development and design work at home on a completely isolated computer."

"I was just wondering," Desdemona said, "do you have any enemies?"

Stark watched the sexy shadow of her figure as she moved about behind the opaque white screen. She raised her arms over her head for a moment. The action tilted her delicately curved breasts in a provocative manner. He was aware of a deep, satiated sensation thrumming through his body. And of the hunger that lay beneath it.

"I could probably name one or two if I tried." He buttoned his shirt. "Why?"

"I'm not sure. I just had a strange feeling." Desdemona appeared from behind the screen. She looked up from the task of tying the sash of her kimono robe. Her eyes were huge with concern.

"Is this another example of the famed Wainwright intuition?" Stark asked, amused.

"Maybe. There's something very intimate about this situation, if you know what I mean."

Wistfully he eyed her little bare toes. Damn, but he hated to leave here tonight. "I know what you mean."

She frowned. "I'm talking about the person behind the attempted theft of ARCANE. Stark, whoever hired Vernon Tate and then killed him knows a lot, not just about you, but about me. About us. Don't you see?"

Stark's fingers stilled on the last button of his shirt. "You think that whoever is behind this was the one who sent Vernon Tate to Right Touch to pose as an ice carver?"

"Yes. And that person also knew enough to realize that he could set Tony up to take the fall if things went sour. He had to know that Tony was into computers and that he was sort of a . . . well, you know."

"A screwup. Right. But that still leaves a lot of possibilities," Stark said quietly. "Down to and including my secretary."

"I suppose so."

"You're saying it's not my enemies I need to worry about. It's my friends."

"Maybe it's *my* friends we need to check out," Desdemona said softly. "Some of them know as much about computers as your secretary. All of them could have known about my relationship with you and also that I needed a new ice carver. And there's no getting around the fact that one or two are desperate for cash at the moment."

Stark buckled his belt. "You're thinking about Ian?"

Desdemona gave him an unhappy look. "Well, the thought did cross my mind."

"Forget it," Stark said. "It's not Ian Ivers."

"You're sure?"

"I'm sure. I've got my own kind of intuition."

280

20

Late the following afternoon Juliet stuck her head around the door of Desdemona's office. "Everyone else has gone for the day. Floors are mopped, counters are clean, and I'm off to rehearsal."

"Right. Thanks." Desdemona, immersed in the proposal for a wedding reception, did not look up. "Don't forget the charity luncheon tomorrow."

"I won't."

Desdemona studied the list of menu items she was considering. "You know, this reception literally cries out for ice sculptures. I wonder if that man, Larry Easenly, who did those carvings for Vernon Tate would be interested in a commission."

"Personally, I don't care if I never see another ice sculpture," Juliet said. "Every time I look at one I'm going to think of Vernon and this whole mess."

"So am I." Desdemona put down her pen and leaned back in her chair. "I'll be glad when it's over."

"All of us will be glad when—" Juliet broke off. "What's that sound?"

A tiny, muffled *beep-beep-beep* reverberated shrilly from some unseen location.

Desdemona glanced speculatively at her jacket, which was hanging on a hook. "I do believe that is the sound of my new, handy-dandy, state-of-the-art, personal digital assistant."

Juliet made a face. "It probably wants to give you the latest weather report."

"Or the final score of the Mariners' game." Desdemona reached into the jacket pocket and removed the PDA.

"Neither of which are of any great interest to you. Be honest with me, Desdemona, are you really sure you want to marry a man whose idea of a birthday present is a miniature computer?"

"It's the thought that counts. Don't forget, if it hadn't been for Stark's gift, I'd have been stuck in that freezer with poor Vernon for Lord knows how long."

"True." Juliet smiled. "Well, I'll let you deal with the fancy high-tech stuff by yourself. I've got an acting career to pursue. See you."

"Bye." Desdemona put the personal digital assistant on her desk.

Juliet waved farewell and disappeared. The front door of Right Touch closed behind her a moment later.

Silence filled the kitchen and Desdemona's office. It was broken only by the insistent *beep-beep-beep* of the PDA. Desdemona hoped she could figure out how to turn it off.

She read the message on the screen.

NEW MAIL

Someone had sent her a message via computer. Tony perhaps. Or maybe Stark had had a change of plans. Desdemona pressed the enter key. A tiny message addressed to her appeared on the screen.

Desdemona—Let's hope this thing works. Henry says he's got fabulous news. He and Ian have found a way to achieve financial stability for the Limelight. They want us to meet them there ASAP. Meet you in a few minutes, Kirsten.

Desdemona briefly considered sending an e-mail message back to Kirsten and then decided it was easier to pick up the telephone. She reached for the receiver and dialed the number of Exotica Erotica. There was no answer. Desdemona glanced at her watch. It was after five-thirty. Kirsten had already closed the shop and left for the Limelight.

Perhaps Henry and Ian actually had figured out a way to persuade an angel to back the Limelight for another season.

Desdemona replaced the PDA in her jacket pocket. She collected her purse, locked her office, and walked through Right Touch one last time to make certain everything was shipshape for the night.

As always, the sight of the gleaming counters and sparkling tiles filled her with a great sense of satisfaction. She stood in the center of the kitchen and turned slowly in a circle to examine her private, personal stage. Everything was back to normal, ready for the next performance.

Desdemona smiled to herself and went out the door. She paused to lock up carefully.

The balmy warmth of a long summer evening had settled over Pioneer Square. The last wave of shoppers was emerging from the boutiques and galleries that lined the streets. The taverns and clubs were still quiescent. They would not come to life until much later in the evening.

Desdemona walked down a side street toward the water, went around the corner underneath the viaduct, and down a row of dark, sullen, old warehouses until she came to the Limelight. There were no cars parked in front of the loading dock that served as an entrance. Henry and Kirsten had probably walked, just as she had. There was no one hanging around in front. The background roar of the traffic on the elevated highway was the only sign of life.

Desdemona knocked loudly on the black and white door. There was no response. Kirsten and Henry were probably already inside. It was too noisy to wait outside.

Desdemona opened the door and stepped into the gloom-filled lobby of the tiny theater. A single dimly glowing lamp lit the passageway that led into the seating area.

"Kirsten? Henry?"

She closed the door to cut off the roar of traffic. The soundproofing insulation that Ian had installed was surprisingly effective. Silence settled on the lobby.

"Ian?" A disturbing sense of uneasiness coursed along Desdemona's nerve endings. Wainwright intuition. She recalled the short conversation she'd had with Stark yesterday as he was leaving her apartment.

You're thinking about Ian?

Well, the thought did cross my mind.

Trust me. It's not Ian Ivers.

Stark knew about that sort of thing, Desdemona reminded herself. He would be the first one to harbor a suspicion of Ian if there were grounds. In any event, it wasn't Ian who had summoned her here. It was Kirsten who had sent the e-mail message.

Desdemona took a grip on her nerves and on the heavy black curtain that separated the lobby from the small auditorium. She lifted the curtain aside.

The weak glow of the dimmed footlights lit the tiny stage. The light illuminated the prone body of a man. He lay unmoving, his face turned toward the back of the stage. But Desdemona recognized the ponytail and the gold earring.

"Ian? My God, *Ian.*" Desdemona ran down the narrow center aisle. Dread rose within her. The thought of encountering another dead body was too much to bear.

She jumped up onto the stage, stepped over the footlights, and hurried to Ian's still body.

To her enormous relief, Ian groaned just as she reached him. He was alive.

"Don't move." Desdemona crouched beside him. "Let me see if you're bleeding. Then I'll call 911."

She leaned over him to check for a wound of some kind and nearly screamed when she saw that his eyes were open and filled with an urgent warning. It was a warning he could not verbalize because his mouth was sealed with duct tape.

"Oh, my God." Desdemona saw that his hands were bound. With trembling fingers she ripped the tape from his mouth.

Ian's chest heaved as he gasped for breath. "Get out of here, Mona. Now. The cops. Call the cops."

"I'll get them." Desdemona staggered to her feet.

A brilliant white spotlight struck the stage with the intensity of a star gone nova. Desdemona froze, trapped by the light.

"I'm afraid it's too late for heroics." The voice that boomed down toward the stage was disembodied and severely distorted by a deliberately abused microphone and sound system. It was the voice of a robot. Mechanical and completely unidentifiable. "We are gathered here this evening to perform a short play in one act. No one leaves until the final curtain."

"Shit," Ian muttered. His head fell back onto the stage in silent defeat. "I was afraid that he was still up there."

"Who?" Desdemona whispered.

"Don't know. Never saw him. Came up behind me."

Desdemona raised her hand in a futile attempt to shield her eyes from the blinding whiteness of the spotlight. She looked toward the control booth. The glare of the spot was so intense it hurt her eyes. It was impossible to see anything behind it.

"I don't know who you are," she said very loudly, "but you had better get out of here while you can. Other people are on their way."

"Your cousin Henry and his wife, Kirsten? Don't hold your breath, Miss Wainwright. I sent the e-mail message that brought you here. Your relatives know nothing about it."

Desdemona fought the fear that twisted her insides into a knot. "What do you want? If it's money, you picked the wrong people. Neither Ian nor I have very much cash. The Limelight is on the verge of bankruptcy, and everything I've got is invested in my business."

Ian stirred briefly. "Not bankrupt. The Limelight is going to make it," he muttered. "Got a new plan."

Desdemona ignored him.

The amplified voice thundered down from the lighting booth. "It's not your money I'm after, Miss Wainwright. And I do not give a damn about Ivers's impending bankruptcy, either. Unfortunately, he was in the way when I got here. It was you I needed. And now I have you."

"I don't understand," Desdemona said.

"I know you don't." The robotic voice seemed to grow even more metallic. "But Stark will."

"Stark?" Desdemona's heart thudded. "What has this got to do with him?"

"Everything."

"This is about ARCANE, isn't it?"

"Yes, Miss Wainwright," the distorted voice said. "It's about AR-CANE. It was always about ARCANE."

"What happens next?"

"We wait."

"For what?" Desdemona demanded.

"For Stark to bring ARCANE to me."

"Are you crazy?" Desdemona said. "He'll never do that."

"You're wrong, Miss Wainwright. He'll hand over ARCANE quite willingly in exchange for you."

Desdemona swallowed. "That's why I'm here? I'm a hostage?"

"You may as well sit down on the stage, Miss Wainwright. I just sent the e-mail message to Stark. It will take him a while to get here."

"He'll probably have the cops with him when he arrives," Desdemona warned.

"I don't think so," the mechanical voice said. "I told him what would happen to you if he brought the police. He likes to think that he's the star of the show, but this time I'm the director. This time I give the orders."

"And just what will happen to me?" she shot back recklessly.

"I will kill you, Miss Wainwright." The voice was chillingly hollow as it echoed off the walls. "Just as I killed Tate. I will also put a bullet through Ian Ivers while I'm at it. *Now sit.*"

The final words were a shattering blast of sound. Desdemona cringed and put her hands over her ears. She crouched down beside Ian.

Together they waited in the pool of hot, dazzling light.

Desdemona spent the time concocting a dozen different methods of escape. There were two basic problems with each scenario. They all depended on whether or not she could leap out of the spotlight and into the shadows before the man in the lighting control booth pulled the trigger. And they all required that she leave Ian behind to face the killer alone. She could not do that.

Desdemona drew her jeaned legs up and rested her forehead on her folded arms. It was the only way to gain some relief from the intense light.

She did not know that Stark had arrived until she heard his voice from the far end of the auditorium.

"Are you all right, Desdemona?"

"Stark." She scrambled to her feet and instinctively started toward the edge of the stage.

"Stop," the mechanical voice boomed. "Don't move, Miss Wainwright. Not another step."

Desdemona stumbled to a halt at the outer rim of the circle of light. She tried to see Stark, but it was impossible. "I'm okay."

"Good." Stark's voice was closer now. His large frame came into view. He walked down the center aisle.

"Get on the stage," the amplified voice ordered. "Move into the light. Hurry. I don't have a lot of time."

Stark stepped over the footlights and walked into the ring of light. His face was no longer in shadow. Desdemona smiled tremulously at him. He looked solid and reassuringly familiar in his rumpled corduroy jacket, jeans, and running shoes. He carried a briefcase-sized computer in one big hand. Desdemona suddenly felt much calmer than she had a few minutes ago.

"I'm sorry," Desdemona said quietly. "I got an e-mail message, and I walked right into this."

"I see." Stark swept her with an intent, searching gaze, as if making certain that she really was all right. Then he looked down at Ian. "What the hell are you doing here?"

Ian grimaced. "I walked into the mess a few minutes ahead of her. The bastard was waiting behind a curtain. Hit me on the head. Didn't knock me out, but I was dazed for a while. He tied me up, gagged me, and dragged me out here onto the stage."

"You two have been busy," Stark said mildly.

"Stark." The mechanical voice boomed once more from the lighting booth. "Did you bring ARCANE?"

Stark held up the small computer. "I loaded it onto this laptop."

"I have to be certain that this is not another one of your clever little tricks. Switch on the computer and punch up ARCANE. Turn the screen toward me."

"Whatever you say." Stark walked to the edge of the light and went down on one knee.

He set the laptop on the stage, opened it, and tapped out a series of commands.

Desdemona could not see the screen from where she was standing, but she heard the harsh sound of a quickly indrawn breath filtered through the speakers. The screen had obviously lit up.

There was movement at the back of the theater. Desdemona turned her head, startled. She realized that the man with the robot's voice had left the lighting booth. He was walking down the center aisle, microphone in hand. The white glare of the spot behind him made it impossible to see anything more than his dark, shadowed shape.

"Very good," the robot said with great satisfaction. "I didn't think that you would play games with me. Not when her life was at stake."

"You were right," Stark said.

"I've always understood what makes people tick. I know what motivates them. You were never any good at that kind of thing."

"No, I guess not."

"Slide the computer to the edge of the stage and then stand back." The voice still blared from the speakers even though the faceless gunman loomed in the aisle between the first two rows of seats.

Stark placed the laptop at the very edge of the stage, outside the ring of light. Then he moved back to join Desdemona and Ian.

"I appreciate your cooperation," the amplified voice said.

A black-gloved hand stretched out of the shadows to close the lid of the laptop.

The instant that the robot's fingers touched the metal case a scream of anguish screeched horribly through the loudspeakers.

Desdemona winced. Instinctively she covered her ears with her hands to deaden the metallic shriek that bounced off the walls.

"What the hell . . ." Ian whispered.

Out of the corner of her eye, Desdemona saw Stark move. He launched himself toward the faceless shadow as it recoiled from the laptop and fell back against the seats.

Stark dove off the stage and crashed into the reeling figure. Something clattered on the floor.

"The gun." Desdemona ran forward.

Once past the ring of fierce white light she was plunged into a swampy blackness. She stopped, blinking quickly in an attempt to adjust to the darkness.

The crashing sounds of the battle taking place in the front row made her whirl toward the right.

She could just make out the violently heaving shadows of Stark and the gunman. They reared up, toppled, and collapsed into the second row. She heard dull, sickening thuds and savage grunts.

Desdemona took another step and halted abruptly when her toe struck an object on the floor.

She bent down and groped around on the cold concrete. Her fingers closed over a gun. She picked it up carefully, startled by the weight of it.

She could see more clearly with each passing second. Stark's head and shoulders surged up above the first row of seats. She saw his fist raised.

He struck.

With a soundless sigh, the man with the voice of a robot collapsed between the first and second rows.

A sharp, piercing quiet settled on the theater.

"Stark, are you okay?"

"Get the lights." He stood upright and gazed down at the man on the floor. "Hurry."

Desdemona glanced at Ian. "Where's the control panel for the house lights?"

"In the light booth," Ian said quickly.

Desdemona put the gun down on a front-row seat and dashed up the short aisle. She found the flight of stairs to the lighting booth, went inside, and stared at the panel of switches arrayed in front of her.

She worked quickly, flipping switches at random until she had doused the bright spot and turned up the houselights. Then she peered through the opening of the booth.

Stark hoisted his victim up into an aisle seat. The man flopped there like a stunned fish. Desdemona could only see the back of his head and shoulders. She frowned. There was something familiar about him.

"Who is it?" she asked.

Stark looked up at the booth. His brows rose in surprise. "I thought you knew."

"No. Ian and I never saw his face."

"Probably because he didn't want you to be able to identify him," Stark said. He looked down at the man in the seat. "You were hoping you wouldn't have to kill again, weren't you, McCallum? It wasn't easy the first time, was it?"

"The bastard tried to blackmail me after he screwed up the job."

Dane's voice, no longer disguised by mechanical amplification, was barely audible. "He sent one last message through the anonymous server. Told me he knew who I was. He was lying, but I didn't realize it at the time."

"Tate tracked you as far as Stark Security Systems," Stark said. "The same way I did. Then he smoked you out with a bluff."

"I panicked. Told him I'd meet him at Right Touch to make the first payoff. I disguised myself in case I was seen."

"You killed Tate. Then you tried to cast Tony Wainwright in the role of murderer and would-be thief. You knew I was already suspicious of him."

"He was the obvious fall guy," Dane said wearily. "I needed him in case you got too close to the truth."

"You were on your way out of Right Touch when Desdemona arrived."

"I didn't want to kill her. Just scare her. I knew she couldn't recognize me. I figured I was safe if I just kept my head. But everything started to come apart after that. This afternoon when I saw the e-mail message waiting for me, I knew something else had gone wrong. I figured it was a trap."

"You were right," Stark said. "So why the second attempt to get hold of ARCANE tonight? Why didn't you just disappear? You could have been out of the country by now."

Dane lifted his head. "I couldn't leave without ARCANE. I made a deal with some people."

"Anyone I know?"

Dane was silent for a moment. "Kilburn."

"Kilburn? That traitor from the Rosetta Institute? You were a fool, McCallum. If you were dealing with Kilburn, you were in over your head from the start."

"Damn it, it was my idea, not his." Dane's voice was unexpectedly violent, almost anguished. "I'm the one who worked out the plan. I contacted Kilburn. Arranged to find Vernon Tate and get him on Desdemona's staff. I set everything up. It was brilliant."

"And now it's all in pieces," Stark said quietly.

Dane's head sagged in defeat. "You always were the brains of the outfit."

"That's where you're wrong," Stark said. "I can't be all that smart. After all, I trusted you, didn't I?"

Desdemona was worried about Stark.

Later that evening, ensconced in her favorite red leather chair, she surreptitiously kept an eye on his grim, unreadable face while he answered questions from the Wainwright clan, his brothers, and Ian Ivers.

A somber, melancholic mood had settled on him even before the authorities had arrived to handcuff Dane and take him away.

Stark had refused to discuss whatever if was that had settled like a cloud on his spirits, but he didn't need to spell it out. Desdemona knew that he was blaming himself for having put her in harm's way.

She did not know how to ease his mind. Stark was a man who would always be harder on himself than on anyone else.

"What the heck did you do to the laptop?" Henry asked. "Ian said it acted like some kind of stun gun."

"It did." Stark stretched out his legs, shoved his hands into his pockets, and regarded the small crowd of eager listeners. "I rigged it so that it would deliver an electrical jolt to whoever touched the case. I set the charge when I punched up ARCANE for him."

"Smart." Henry's grin held genuine admiration. "Like a scene out of a James Bond film."

"Except that Stark's hero was obviously Q, the guy who designed the high-tech toys, not Bond," Benedick remarked approvingly.

Tony turned a chair around and straddled it. He rested his arms on the back. "Stark rigged the case this afternoon just as soon as he realized that Dane McCallum was behind the attempt to steal AR-CANE."

"Jason and I helped him," Kyle said proudly. "Didn't we, Sam?"

"Couldn't have done it without you," Stark said.

Desdemona stirred. "Dane was jealous of Stark, you know. That's why he did it. He wanted to prove that he was smarter than Stark. That he could be the star of the show."

Stark glanced at her, frowning. "How do you know that?"

She shrugged. "The way he talked there at the end. It was obvious."

There was a small silence while everyone considered that. Then Tony spoke.

"Stark knew that sooner or later the thief would try again, and he wanted to be ready. It worked, didn't it?"

"Yes," Stark said. "It worked. But not quite as planned. I failed to consider the possibility that McCallum would use Desdemona as a hostage."

"How could you have known?" Desdemona said quickly. "Stark, you mustn't blame yourself for what happened."

He looked at her with expressionless eyes. Her heart sank.

Benedick frowned. "When did you conclude that it was McCallum who was behind all this nonsense?"

Stark took off his glasses and massaged the bridge of his nose. "Desdemona reminded me that whoever was responsible for Tate's death knew a hell of a lot about my personal life. And hers."

Desdemona blushed. "I was starting to get a little paranoid. I even had a few unkind thoughts about Ian."

"Me?" Ian looked pained.

"Good heavens." Kirsten's eyes widened. "Ian?"

"It wasn't such a far-out guess." Stark put on his glasses. "The list of people who could have figured out how to get into Stark Security Systems computers was unknowable. But the list of people who were at least passingly computer literate and who also knew a lot about my relationship with Desdemona, and about you Wainwrights in general, was a lot shorter."

"When he started going down the list this morning, he put McCallum's name at the top," Tony said. "That's when he worked out the trick with the laptop. He had already sent an e-mail message designed to lure the killer out into the open. The fish took the bait."

"But the fish had some bait of his own." Stark looked at Desdemona. "I want to emphasize that what happened next was not part of the plan."

"I'm glad to hear that," Ian muttered. He touched his head gingerly. "Not that it did me or Desdemona any good."

"No," Stark said heavily. "What happened to the two of you was my fault. I owe you, Ivers."

Ian brightened. He gave Stark a speculative look. "Well, now that you mention it . . ."

"And I owe Desdemona," Stark said.

"Forget it. I'll collect later." Desdemona reached out to touch his hand. His fingers did not close around hers as she hoped they would.

"You're a hero, Stark," Tony said wryly. "Why fight it?"

Desdemona saw Stark's jaw tighten. "The important thing is that we're all safe. The nightmare is over."

"Not quite," Stark said.

Everyone looked at him.

"I'd like to get my hands on Kilburn," Stark said softly. "According to McCallum, he'll be arriving at the airport late tonight to pick up ARCANE."

Tony's brows came together in a thoughtful frown. "He won't show when he learns that McCallum's been arrested."

"He doesn't know about that," Stark said. "The Feds took charge of the case this afternoon, and they've arranged to keep everything hushed up until tomorrow."

"They can do that?" Henry asked.

"Yes," Stark said. "The case is in their territory because it involves an attempt to steal restricted technology and take it out of the country."

"So what happens now?" Tony asked curiously.

"We're going to set another trap," Stark said.

Tony straightened in his chair. "Yeah?"

Jason bounced up and down. "What kind of trap?"

"The Feds would very much like to catch Kilburn in the act of buying ARCANE." Stark looked at Tony. "To do that they need an actor. Someone who can impersonate Dane McCallum long enough to trick Kilburn into going through with the deal."

Tony grinned slowly. "Well, what do you know. It just so happens that I'm between engagements at the moment."

Alarmed, Celia glanced from Tony to Stark. "Will it be dangerous?"

"Of course not," Tony said swiftly. "There's nothing to worry about, is there, Stark?"

"No guarantees," Stark said carefully, "but it should be as safe as these things get. According to McCallum, the exchange is scheduled to be made at SeaTac Airport tonight. Kilburn is supposed to arrive, pick up ARCANE, and leave within an hour on an international flight. The Feds will be there, ready to move in as soon as Kilburn accepts ARCANE."

"Piece of cake," Tony said.

Desdemona smiled. "You've always been very good in the role of hero, Tony."

Tony grinned. For the first time in a long while the bitterness was gone from his eyes.

21

Although he was prepared for the transformation, Stark did a double take when Tony walked into the international terminal shortly after midnight.

Outfitted in a blond wig, mustache, glasses, and a stylish silver-gray suit, Tony was a disturbingly familiar figure.

"I'll be damned," Stark said quietly to Benedick, who was seated next to him in the airport lounge. "He's a dead ringer for McCallum."

"Always said the boy had talent." Benedick beamed proudly from behind the newspaper he was ostensibly reading.

"He's even got the walk down right. He moves the way McCallum moves."

"A good actor does more with movement than he does with make-up." Benedick made a show of turning the page. "You said this Kilburn fellow has met McCallum face-to-face?"

"We all worked at the Rosetta Institute, but Kilburn hasn't seen McCallum in person for over three years, and they weren't exactly close then. They saw each other occasionally in the hall, but that was it. The deal for ARCANE was done through the computers. With any luck, the mustache and dark glasses will distract Kilburn long enough for the exchange to be made."

"No one expects someone to look exactly as he did after three years." Benedick shrugged. "Like Tony said, piece of cake."

Tony, laptop clutched in his hand, hovered near the newsstand. Stark thought that he displayed just the right degree of edginess for the occasion.

Ten minutes later, the gate opened to disgorge the passengers of an incoming flight. Kilburn, carrying a large briefcase, was among the first half-dozen people to get off the plane. Stark noted that he was apparently traveling first-class these days.

Kilburn had grown plumper over the years. Even the cut of his expensive suit could not contain his large belly. It strained the buttons of his shirt. His benign, cheerfully rounded face sagged around the jaw and spilled over his collar.

Kilburn swept the waiting area with a nervous, impatient glance. Then he paused to study the blond man in the silver-gray suit. Tony's back was deliberately turned toward the gate.

"He's spotted Tony," Benedick murmured. "Looks like the fish is going to take your bait."

Stark watched with satisfaction as Kilburn started toward the newsstand.

Tony did not turn around when Kilburn tapped him on the shoulder. He simply nodded and led the way toward a corner near the rest rooms. Kilburn followed, glancing uneasily over his shoulder.

There was no mistaking the exchange of the laptop computer for the briefcase. It was hurriedly done in the shadows. Kilburn opened the lid of the computer, bent over it, and tapped out some commands on the keyboard. Stark knew he was punching up ARCANE. Meanwhile, Tony opened the briefcase to display the contents. He glanced inside and nodded as if satisfied.

A done deal. Head still averted, Tony even shook Kilburn's hand.

The Federal agents, three men who had been posing as traveling businessmen, moved in.

At the last instant Kilburn realized what was happening. He stared wildly at the men closing in on him. Then he lashed out at Tony, who easily ducked the blow and stuck out a foot.

Kilburn stumbled over the obstacle and toppled heavily to the floor. A man in a nondescript suit crouched down to handcuff him.

It was over.

"Let's go." Stark got to his feet.

Benedick put down his newspaper and rose. Together they walked over to the corner near the rest rooms to watch the denouement.

A small crowd also gathered to watch the proceedings.

Kilburn looked up at the ring of onlookers surrounding him and spotted Stark. His face contorted with fury.

"You bloody son of a bitch," Kilburn said in a choked voice. "Everyone always said you were so damned smart. You goddamn *son of a bitch*."

"Gotcha," Stark said.

Twenty minutes later Stark leaned against the airport rest room wall, hooked a thumb in the waistband of his jeans, and watched as Tony removed the mustache, wig, and makeup.

"You handled that very well," Stark said.

Benedick beamed. "That's my boy."

Tony struggled to control a buoyant grin. He met Stark's eyes in the mirror. "Thanks."

"Want a job?"

Tony blanked. "Job?"

"I'm thinking of expanding Stark Security Systems services to include some investigative personnel. I'll need a few good people who are computer literate and who can also go undercover to gather evidence on-site. Interested?"

Benedick's brows twitched in surprise. He eyed Stark but said nothing. He waited calmly for his son's answer.

"Yeah." Tony spoke cautiously but his eyes were gleaming with excitement. "I might be interested."

"Okay," Stark said. "You're hired. Report to my secretary tomorrow morning. She'll arrange to get you on the payroll."

"Just like that?"

"Why not? It's my company."

Tony narrowed his eyes. "This wouldn't, by any chance, be a sneaky way of making certain that I no longer have an excuse to mooch off Desdemona while I'm between acting engagements, would it?"

"Do you want the job or not?"

"Yeah." Tony laughed as he ripped off the fake mustache. "I want the job."

The following morning Augustus put down his latte cup with an air of grave deliberation and surveyed his audience.

"I am not altogether certain," he intoned, "that I approve of this growing trend toward regular employment that has appeared among the younger generation of Wainwrights."

Desdemona, Celia, Bess, Juliet, and Kirsten, seated around two tables in the espresso bar, groaned in unison.

"For heaven's sake, dear." Bess patted Augustus's arm in a reassuring manner. "It's just a day job. Tony will still be free to pursue his acting career."

"But will he want to pursue it?" Augustus asked darkly. "That's what concerns me. All he can talk about is his new job as a computer spy."

"He's a Wainwright," Celia said calmly. "He'll never give up acting."

"Actually, the position at Stark Security Systems is a sort of acting job when you think about it," Kirsten pointed out. "Stark said he was very impressed by the way Tony performed last night at the airport."

"And just think of the added financial stability it will bring to the family," Celia said.

"There is that." But Augustus clearly remained unconvinced.

"Tony seems very enthusiastic," Bess said. "In fact, he seemed elated. Let's be honest here. We all know that for years he has been getting increasingly frustrated and unhappy. This morning when I talked to him he was a new man."

Celia nodded. "That's just what Benedick said."

"Can't deny that's important," Augustus admitted. "I suppose it will be all right. Stark is about to become a member of the family, after all. It's not as though Tony has gone to work for an outsider."

Desdemona couldn't stand it any longer. She grabbed a napkin and burst into tears.

Everyone turned toward her in astounded concern.

"What's wrong?" Celia asked anxiously.

"Bridal jitters," Bess declared.

"No, it's not that." Desdemona blotted her eyes. "Well, maybe it is in a way. I'm so worried about him, you see."

"About Stark?" Bess asked.

"Just when I thought he was learning to trust other people," Desdemona said, "this stupid mess with Dane McCallum had to happen."

Juliet frowned. "What in the world are you talking about?"

"Stark feels responsible for what occurred at the Limelight." Desdemona looked up from her tear-soaked napkin. "He thinks that he made a terrible mistake when he trusted McCallum. And he believes that I almost paid the price for his failure in judgment."

"Oh, dear," Bess said.

Desdemona wadded up the napkin. "This incident with McCallum has convinced Stark that he was right not to trust people, not to take chances. In the future, he's going to be more emotionally cautious than ever."

Kirsten's eyes widened. "Are you telling me that he doesn't even trust you now?"

"No, that's not it. The real problem is that he doesn't trust himself."

"What do you mean?" Bess said.

Desdemona gazed at the crumpled napkin. "Don't you see? He won't really be free to love and let himself be loved until he learns to accept the fact that he has real human emotions and needs and that he can make mistakes."

"Are you telling us that you've finally realized he may not make a proper Wainwright after all?" Henry demanded.

"I don't know." Desdemona gazed morosely down into her half-finished latte. "For years people have told Stark that he's a human computer. I think he's begun to believe it. Being a human computer is a nice, safe, invulnerable thing to be."

Kirsten looked thoughtful. "I think I see where you're going with this."

Desdemona gave her a shaky smile. "Poor Stark. He knows he's got a brain, and he knows that people respect him for it. But he doesn't want to admit that he's got emotions and feelings, too. Every time he's allowed those emotions and feelings to influence him, he's gotten burned."

Kirsten raised her latte. "I imagine that, to his way of thinking, the

McCallum incident is just one more example of the foolhardiness of allowing himself to trust."

"Exactly," Desdemona said. "He trusted McCallum, and look where it got him."

"You're afraid that the McCallum situation undid all the work you've done to get Stark to become more human, aren't you?" Kirsten asked gently.

"Yes," Desdemona gazed morosely out the window. "He's a work in progress. Sort of like an ice carving that's only partially completed. I can see the potential shape, but the outlines are still blurred and uneven."

"And cold?" Celia inquired softly.

Desdemona recalled the frozen expression in Stark's eyes. She shivered. "Yes."

Celia's eyes were shadowed with concern. "Be honest, dear. This is no time to make a mistake. Your future happiness is on the line. Are you having second thoughts about going through with the wedding?"

Bess scowled. "If you are, now is the time to get out."

Desdemona looked into the worried faces of her family and knew that Bess spoke the truth. Realization struck her with the force of a blinding spotlight.

"Oh, my God," Desdemona breathed in horror. "This must be what the other fiancées went through."

Stark contemplated his future father-in-law. Benedick was posed near the office window, the embodiment of old-fashioned paternal concern. It would have been amusing if Stark had not been in such a foul mood and if he had not had a strong suspicion that Benedick was not acting.

"I won't deny that I've had a few doubts about you right from the beginning, son," Benedick said deliberately. "Always felt that my daughter should marry someone who was more like her than you appeared to be."

"Let me guess. You wanted Desdemona to marry someone with artistic sensibilities?" Stark asked very politely.

"Not necessarily." Benedick gazed out over Elliott Bay. "My only concern was that she be happy. I thought she would be happiest with a man whose nature was more akin to her own. A man who would be at ease with a woman of strong emotions and warmth of feeling. A man who was capable of similar emotions and feelings."

"Someone with the soul of a poet?" Stark suggested.

"Well put." Benedick appeared pleased. "Well put indeed."

Stark drummed his fingers on the arm of his chair. "Someone who was from the theater world, perhaps?"

"I won't deny that I had assumed she would marry someone from our world. But I've decided that isn't necessary. I think you can make her happy."

That startled Stark. "Do you?"

Benedick turned his head. He regarded Stark with a considering look. "I think you'll do very well for my daughter."

Stark met his eyes. "I'm surprised to hear you say that after what happened at the Limelight."

"Let me rephrase that. I think you'll do very well for Desdemona once you've gotten past feeling guilty for that incident."

"Why shouldn't I feel responsible? I was responsible."

Benedick's bushy brows jiggled up and down. "Do you think you're the only man on the face of the earth who ever failed to protect someone he loved?"

Stark knotted his hand into a fist. "No."

"Then stop being so damned hard on yourself." Benedick walked to a chair and sat down. "You're only human. Let it go, Stark. I'm not saying you'll ever be able to forget it, but you have to let it go. Otherwise it will eat you alive. And if you allow it to do that, it will ruin your chance of happiness with Desdemona."

"This sounds personal."

"It is. I know what you're going through."

"Is that a fact?"

Benedick watched him from beneath half-lowered lids. "How do you think I felt when I failed to protect Desdemona from George Northstreet?"

Stark could not think of anything to say to that.

Benedick's mouth formed a grim line. "I had no excuses. I simply had not realized how dangerous Northstreet was. I didn't take sufficient precautions to protect my family. It was my fault that he got to Desdemona. He intended to kidnap her first and then return for Celia, you know."

"I looked up the old records of the case. Northstreet was crazy. You couldn't have known he'd try to kidnap Desdemona or her mother before he put that gun to his own head."

"No. I couldn't have known. But I told myself that I should have known. I couldn't forgive myself for a very long time afterward. Couldn't find any peace of mind for months. I kept thinking of how close I had come to losing my new daughter. I was afraid that Celia would never again trust me to take care of her and Desdemona."

Stark stared unseeingly at the screen of his electronic calendar. "How did you get past it?"

"Celia got me past it. She reminded me that I was a man, not a superman. That I couldn't take responsibility for everything that went wrong in life. She said that if I did, I'd be impossible to live with."

Stark looked up from the calendar. "What did she mean by that?"

"A man who holds himself accountable for everything that goes wrong in his world soon becomes what I believe is termed a control freak. He becomes rigid. Inflexible." Benedick paused delicately. "A computer, if you will."

Stark narrowed his eyes. "Did Desdemona send you here today?"

"No. Why do you ask?"

Stark reminded himself that the man was an actor. "Forget it. What's your point, Benedick?"

"My point is simple. A man who demands too much of himself makes other people uncomfortable. They figure if he can't live up to his own standards, they'll never be able to satisfy him, either. After a while they tend to drift away from him."

"So?"

"So, after a while he finds himself alone in the world."

"You're telling me that if I don't let myself off the hook for what happened to Desdemona, I'll drive her away?"

Benedick smiled faintly. "She's my daughter. She's loyal, but she's not stupid. She'll only bash her head against a stone wall for so long."

"I see." The deep cold of chaos swirled up out of the cauldron inside Stark.

"Listen up, son," Benedick said. "The world's a hard enough place as it is. Don't spend what time you've got in it alone."

Alone in chaos.

Stark looked down into the endless depth of the cauldron.

*   *   *

Two days later Desdemona set a platter of steaming tortillas onto the kitchen table in front of Stark, Jason, and Kyle. "Gentlemen, start your engines. Everyone at the table is responsible for creating his own taco."

"I don't want any hot peppers on mine," Jason announced.

"Then skip the hot peppers," Desdemona said. "I'll probably eat them all, anyway."

Kyle made a face. "You like hot peppers?"

"Love 'em."

Desdemona sat down and reached for a large flour tortilla. Stark reached for one at the same time. Their fingers collided lightly. The fleeting contact sent a tremor through Desdemona. She looked up quickly and managed an overly bright smile.

Stark did not return the smile. He met her eyes with an unblinking gaze. For an instant Desdemona could not look away. She saw the shadows brooding over his soul. The vision chilled her.

She knew then that somehow Stark had sensed her growing uncertainty about the wisdom of their marriage plans. He knew she was having second thoughts. *Just like the others.*

Desdemona loaded jalapeño peppers and hot sauce onto her taco, but when she took a bite it was all bland and tasteless.

At that moment something settled inside her. She could not leave Stark to his lonely fate. She loved him. No matter what the risks, she would not abandon her work in progress. She had begun the task, and she would finish it.

"Stark asked me and Kyle to be best men at your wedding," Jason said around a mouthful of taco.

"Really?" Desdemona asked. "Two best men? That will be unusual."

"He says we have to wear tuxes," Kyle said. "And we have to make certain he gets to the altar on time."

"A big responsibility." Desdemona concentrated on her taco.

"Who makes certain that the bride gets to the altar?" Jason asked.

Desdemona nearly strangled on another bite of taco.

Stark watched her. "The bride has to get herself there."

Desdemona swallowed the last of the taco and met Stark's eyes. "Don't worry about this bride," she said firmly. "She'll be there. You can count on a Wainwright. No one in our family would ever miss the opening of a show."

Stark searched her face for a moment, and then the fierce anguish seemed to fade in his eyes. He smiled slightly for the first time since Dane McCallum had been arrested. "So I'm told."

The doorbell rang.

"I'll see who it is." Stark got to his feet and walked out of the kitchen.

"Please pass the cheese," Kyle said to Desdemona.

The murmur of a woman's voice caught everyone's attention.

"Hey, that's Mom." Jason dropped his taco, shoved back his chair, and leaped to his feet.

"Mom's here?" Kyle let the spoonful of grated cheese fall back into the bowl. "I hope the shrink isn't with her."

Stark walked back into the kitchen before Jason and Kyle reached the door. He was accompanied by an attractive, dark-haired woman in her late thirties. She was stylishly dressed in a camel-colored pant-suit and a ruffled blouse.

There was no sign of a shrink.

"Hi, Mom," Jason said. "I thought you were on vacation."

"I decided to come home early," Alison said. "I wanted to see you two."

"This is our Mom," Kyle said to Desdemona. "Mom, this is Des-demona Wainwright. She's going to marry Sam in a few weeks."

Alison Stark smiled at Desdemona. "Is that so?"

"Yes," Desdemona said very firmly.

Stark looked at her. Some of the shadows disappeared from his eyes. He turned to Alison. "Want a taco?"

"Why not?" Alison said.

A couple hours later Desdemona, Stark, and Alison were alone in the kitchen. Jason and Kyle had finally wound down and had excused themselves to watch television.

Desdemona made coffee. She moved about quietly, sensing that Alison was preparing herself to say something important to Stark.

"Jason and Kyle seem to be doing well." Alison poured cream into her coffee.

Stark accepted his cup from Desdemona. "They're good kids."

"Yes." Alison stirred her coffee. "They've had a rough time of it for the past few months, and things aren't going to get any better in the future. Their father will never come back."

"No." Stark sipped his coffee.

"I suppose you know that better than anyone," Alison said.

Stark said nothing.

Alison looked down at her coffee. "Boys need a father figure."

Stark did not respond.

"Jason and Kyle appear happier than they have for months. I think Dr. Titus is right. You've become a substitute for Hudson in their eyes."

Stark made no comment.

"I think they need you," Alison said.

Stark sipped coffee.

Alison glanced at Desdemona as if seeking support.

Desdemona smiled encouragingly. "Stark is an excellent father figure. He has a real talent for the role."

Stark gave her a surprised look.

"I've been doing a lot of thinking lately," Alison said. "What would you say, Sam, if I told you that I'd like to move my interior design business here to Seattle?"

Stark shrugged. "It's your business."

"I've already got a handful of Seattle clients. I could build on that," Alison said.

Stark nodded.

Alison drew a deep breath. "It would mean that Jason and Kyle would have you in their lives on a regular basis. How would you feel about that?"

"Okay," Stark said.

Desdemona smiled to herself.

Alison appeared confused by the single-word answer. "I know they're not your responsibility, and God knows you probably don't want them hanging around all the time, but I can tell that their relationship with you has become very important to them and—"

Stark frowned. "I said okay."

Alison switched her gaze to Desdemona in a silent request for clarification.

Desdemona poured more coffee. "He said it was okay, Alison. That means it's okay with him if you move Jason and Kyle to Seattle so that they can have him in their lives. He understands the importance of family. You can trust Stark. He always means what he says."

"I see." Alison smiled tremulously. The tightness around her eyes and mouth eased. "That's good to know."

"Yes," Desdemona said. "It is."

How could she have had even a moment's doubt about marrying Stark, Desdemona wondered. Bridal jitters. That's all it had been. Now that they were over, she felt more confident than ever.

She smiled across the table at Stark. He reached out with one big hand. His strong fingers closed very tightly over hers.

Jason appeared in the doorway. "Hey, Mom, you want to come see our play tomorrow?"

Alison smiled at him. "I'd like that very much."

Jason grinned. "I told Kyle you would. What happened to the shrink?"

"Dr. Titus and I are no longer seeing each other," Alison said carefully.

"Maybe Bess and Juliet can find a husband for you," Jason said.

Desdemona laughed at Alison's blank expression. "That's not a bad idea, Jason. Bess and Juliet are going to need a new project now that I'm getting married."

"Yes," Stark said. "They are."

Desdemona charged into Stark's office the following afternoon. "Is he in, Mrs. Pitchcott?"

Mrs. Pitchcott smiled serenely. "Why, yes he is, Miss Wainwright. I'll tell him you're here."

"Thanks." Desdemona began to pace the outer office.

Mrs. Pitchcott kept an eye on her as she informed Stark that he had a visitor.

"Send her in, Maud." Stark's voice sounded preoccupied over the intercom.

"Go right in, Miss Wainwright." Mrs. Pitchcott beamed. "And may I say how happy I was to learn of your engagement to Mr. Stark. We're all just delighted here at Stark Security Systems. Third time's a charm, I always say."

"Thank you, Mrs. Pitchcott."

"The future glows brightest for those who face it with hearts full of love."

"I couldn't agree more." Desdemona opened the door of the inner office.

Stark did not look up from his computer screen. "Something wrong?"

"I just saw Ian." Desdemona planted both hands on his desk. "He says you've agreed to back *Dissolving*."

"Uh-huh." Stark scowled at the numbers on the screen. He hit a key.

"Are you certain you want to do this?"

"Consider it my contribution to the arts."

"That's ridiculous. You aren't particularly interested in the arts."

"I owe the guy. He got conked on the head because of me."

"You don't owe him this much," Desdemona said.

"Maybe not. But it's sort of a family thing." Stark issued a rapid series of commands to the computer.

Desdemona was dumbfounded. "A family thing?"

"Ian has promised to use as many Wainwrights as possible in the production. I figure that even if I'm not making an important contribution to the arts by playing theatrical angel, I'm at least making a contribution toward Wainwright family financial stability. Assuming *Dissolving* doesn't dissolve the first night."

Desdemona laughed. She went around the corner of the desk and dropped into Stark's lap.

No longer able to view the computer screen, Stark leaned back in his chair, put one hand on her thigh, and switched his gaze to her. "Was there something you wanted?" he asked politely.

"Yes." She fiddled with the top button of his shirt. "But I suppose I can wait until tonight. I know how big you are on deferred gratification."

Stark's eyes gleamed behind the lenses of his glasses. "My new policy is to defer certain kinds of gratification as seldom as possible."

He got to his feet with Desdemona in his arms, went around the desk, and locked the door.

"What will Mrs. Pitchcott say?" Desdemona asked as Stark carried her back to the desk and sat down.

307

"I don't know." Stark unbuckled his belt. "I'm not sure. Probably something about making lemonade."

"Lemonade?" Desdemona stared at him in amazement. "Why in the world would she—"

Her question was cut off in midsentence.

"I've always liked lemonade," Desdemona murmured a few minutes later.

"Me, too."

Six weeks later Stark closed the door of Desdemona's loft with a triumphant slam and reached for her. "Do you realize that from now on we'll be able to spend the whole night, every night, together?"

"That fact had not escaped my notice." Desdemona smiled as he lifted her high in his arms. The white satin skirts of her wedding gown billowed in gleaming waves over the black sleeves of Stark's tux. "Has it occurred to you that you won't need an inflatable, anatomically correct doll for your wedding night this time?"

"Yes, it did. I got a pretty good deal on the catering, too. This must be my lucky day."

"No doubt about it."

Stark laughed. Desdemona realized it was the first time she had ever heard him do so. It was a good sound, she thought. It boded well for the future.

Outside the windows, moonlight and neon illuminated the cityscape of Seattle. There were tickets for a trip to Hawaii in Stark's briefcase, but the plane did not leave until the following day.

The wedding night was to be spent in Desdemona's loft because Jason, Kyle, and Alison were staying at Stark's fortress. Alison planned to house-hunt in Seattle while Stark and Desdemona were on their honeymoon.

Stark carried Desdemona toward the shoji-screened bed. There was undisguised wonder in his eyes as he gazed down at her in his arms. "You're beautiful. Did I ever tell you that you remind me of a piece of fractal art?"

"Yes, you did, but you can tell me again." She kissed his throat and started to undo his black bow tie. "Did I ever tell you that you look terrific in a tux?"

"I don't believe that you've ever mentioned it." He settled her on the bed and leaned over her, caging her between his arms.

"Well, you do, and I love you," Desdemona said.

"Because I look good in a tux?"

"No. Just because you're you." Desdemona tugged on the ends of the black silk tie.

Stark did not fight the summons. He came down on top of her. His mouth covered hers in a kiss that echoed the promises they had made at the altar.

An hour later Desdemona raised herself on one elbow and looked down at Stark. His eyes gleamed in the shadows.

"I just thought of something," Desdemona said.

"What?" Stark traced the outline of her bare breast with the edge of his thumb.

"You forgot the prenuptial agreement."

"I didn't forget it."

"But I didn't sign anything," Desdemona reminded him.

"You gave me your word of honor," Stark said. "You promised to love, honor, and cherish me until death did us part."

Desdemona smiled. "And that's good enough?"

"With you it is." He framed her face with his strong hands. His eyes were intent and serious. "I love you, Desdemona."

"I know," she whispered. "You don't have to say the words."

He smiled slowly. "Trust me, you're going to hear them every day for the rest of our lives."